THE BEST MODERN CANADIAN SHORT STORIES

Margaret Atwood
Clark Blaise
Morley Callaghan
Jacques Ferron
Margaret Gibson
Dave Godfrey
Anne Hébert
Hugh Hood
Henry Kreisel
Robert Kroetsch
Margaret Laurence
Norman Levine
Gwendolyn MacEwen
Alistair MacLeod
Joyce Marshall
Alice Munro
Mordecai Richler
Sinclair Ross
Gabrielle Roy
Leo Simpson
Audrey Thomas
W. D. Valgardson
Rudy Wiebe
Ethel Wilson

THE BEST MODERN CANADIAN SHORT STORIES

Edited by
Ivon Owen & Morris Wolfe

Hurtig Publishers / Edmonton

Hurtig Publishers
10560 105 Street
Edmonton, Alberta

Canadian Cataloguing in Publication Data

Main entry under title:
The Best modern Canadian short stories

ISBN 0-88830-154-5

1. Short stories, English.   Wolfe,
Morris.   II. Owen, Ivon.
PS8321.B48   C813'.01   C78-002129-0
PR9197.32B4

Printed and bound in Canada

Contents

Introduction

Developments in the Canadian short story have been so rapid in recent years that it's become necessary to take stock every decade or so. *The Best Modern Canadian Short Stories* represents such a stocktaking.

Our basic aim in selecting the stories was to make the best book possible — a book that we ourselves liked and that we could reasonably expect our readers to like. We quickly abandoned the notion of attempting to make it historically representative. The Canadian short story, we believe, doesn't really begin until Morley Callaghan comes on the scene in the 1920s; apart from Leacock at his best, there is very little before that time that stands up for us as literature. It's remarkable how many of the stories included here have appeared in the last twenty years.

Our criteria for including a story were simple: the two of us had to agree that it was excellent in itself and would combine with the other stories to make a book that readers would find both stimulating and enjoyable. There is only one writer we would have liked to include who found us resistible — Mavis Gallant. Other notable writers of fiction are missing because we resolved to confine ourselves to works written as short stories, and to refrain from using excerpts from novels. This automatically excluded, for instance, Hugh MacLennan, Robertson Davies, and nearly all the distinguished novelists of French Canada, where the short story is not a major literary form. The story by Mordecai Richler that we have used was later expanded into a novel — to its detriment, we feel, and we are glad of the opportunity to present it in its original form. And Joyce Marshall's "So Many Have Died" will eventually be part of a novel, but in the meantime it stands as a particularly satisfying example of the short-story form.

Because we were assembling a book and not a cabinet, regional representation was not a major concern. Nevertheless, we were conscious that

Canadians and their literature are highly regional. Hence it was interesting, once the selection was made, to see the regional pattern that had emerged, a pattern that we have chosen to stress by arranging the stories in a roughly west-to-east order. Robert Weaver's *Canadian Short Stories,* edited in 1958 and published in the World's Classics series in 1960, makes an interesting comparison for a number of reasons: because of the twenty-year interval, because it was the first anthology to include stories translated from French, and perhaps because one of the editors of the present book had a share in the shaping of the earlier one, so that the points of view are not utterly different.

The Weaver volume, which included stories published from 1895 to 1957, reflects a marked regionality. There is only one story in it (P.K. Page's "The Green Bird") whose geographical background is not specific and essential. The rest are readily classifiable: two from the West Coast, three from the Prairie Provinces, nine from Ontario, ten from Quebec, two from the Atlantic Provinces. And in every case the author was a native or at the time of writing a resident of the region described.

Twenty years later, regionality is still strong. Again there is only one story (Leo Simpson's "The Lady and the Travelling Salesman") that might occur in any city. But there are significant differences. Ontario and Quebec, taken together, still bulk large, but now they account for less than half the collection. There are six stories set in the Prairie Provinces — a quarter of the total, which is substantially more than their share of the population. The Atlantic region with two stories and the West Coast with three are represented, as it happens, roughly in proportion to population; it might have been expected that communities that have been settled so much longer than the prairies would have a bigger part to play.

The really striking change, though, is that settings can no longer be matched so neatly to authors. Canadian writers have broken out of their regional compartments and taken possession of the country as a whole. Thus we have Alice Munro, who made her name with her convincing realizations of small-town Western Ontario, contributing "Material," one of the three Vancouver stories. Margaret Atwood writes of Edmonton and its region in "Polarities" — though admittedly she sees them with a Central Canadian eye: "the clenched landscape,... tightlipped, ungiving, good for nothing and nothing." Of the two stories set in the Atlantic region one, "The Boat," is by a true Nova Scotian of Hebridean descent (now an exile in Western Ontario), the other, "Bloodflowers," by a Manitoban whose Icelandic ancestors of a thousand years ago might have sailed past the Labrador island he describes.

Life outside North America, whether in Europe or in the so-called Third World, has become a much commoner experience for Canadians in the last twenty-odd years, and appropriately one story, Margaret Laurence's "A

Gourdful of Glory," is set in West Africa and another, Norman Levine's "A Canadian Upbringing," in England.

In the Weaver anthology ten stories out of twenty-seven take place in cities; the rest have small-town, rural, or wilderness settings. In this book, of the twenty-two stories that take place in Canada thirteen are wholly or predominantly urban, ten have small-town or rural settings, and the wilderness has vanished.

As one travels across the country through these stories one is struck over and over again by the extent to which geography shapes and influences people's lives. The sea and mountains Ethel Wilson's Mr. Willy sees through his window are a constant reminder of the life he left behind him and of the new life he's now too old to experience fully. Living on the prairies reinforces Mr. Solchuk's view in "The Broken Globe" that the world is flat. Margaret Atwood's characterless Edmonton in "Polarities" provides a perfect backdrop for Louise, a woman with no clear sense of identity. Gabrielle Roy's tramp offers his newfound "cousins" in Manitoba the most moving geography lesson of their lives as he talks about the St. Lawrence River as if it were a living creature. In Hugh Hood's story "Three Halves of a House" the St. Lawrence actually *becomes* a living creature—"the ships are swimming over me and the river through me and the horns are inside my head." (This story is a kind of prologue to Hood's recent novel *A New Athens,* where the whole region of Ontario bordering the upper St. Lawrence is the protagonist, dominating and directing the human figures it contains.) Alistair MacLeod's "The Boat" eloquently evokes the constant presence of the sea in the life of the family of an east-coast fisherman.

The stories in this book set outside the cities tend to take on a cosmic quality that one doesn't find in the urban stories; the lives of city people seem too cramped, too fragmented for larger questions about man's place in the universe to arise. In Robert Kroetsch's "That Yellow Prairie Sky," Tom's response to the elements is to pick up a handful of hailstones and hurl them at the heavens from which they've fallen on his crops. In W.D. Valgardson's "Bloodflowers," a city-trained teacher finds that a myth he has learned in the academy can turn into menacing reality on a remote island in the Atlantic. The central character in Dave Godfrey's "The River" has to leave the city and step again into a river he frequently visited as a youth before he can truly understand that life is a process.

These stories reflect the increasingly cosmopolitan character of Canadian life. Indeed, it's surprising how few of the stories in this book involve people who are "old" Canadians. Mr. Willy in "The Window," like his creator, Ethel Wilson, comes from South Africa via England. Henry Kreisel and Rudy Wiebe write about Ukrainian and Mennonite farm families in

Alberta. We meet Jewish survivors of the holocaust in Dave Godfrey's Toronto. Clark Blaise, himself a cosmopolite *par excellence,* writes of Norman Dyer, "a semi-permanent, semi-political exile" from the United States, who teaches a class of new Canadians at McGill; his class is made up of South Americans, Greeks, Germans, and Spaniards, many of whom want to learn English in order to move to the U.S.

Education is revealed here as a mixed blessing. In Henry Kreisel's "The Broken Globe" Nick Solchuk's career as a geophysicist forever separates him from his father. In "The Boat," the son's decision to go to school and *not* follow in his father's footsteps drives a wedge between him and his mother. Mrs. Poorwilly tells Danny Thorson in "Bloodflowers" that "wives with too much education" cause a lot of trouble. "They're never satisfied. The young fellows around here and on the coast have enough trouble without that." Louise's madness in Atwood's "Polarities" becomes a wild parody of her academic profession as she imposes a completely irrelevant pattern on things.

It's not surprising that one of the themes in these stories is the situation of French Canadians. In "A Tramp at the Door" Gabrielle Roy offers a view of French-Canadian Manitobans, cut off from their roots in Quebec, and terribly susceptible to the beautiful lies of someone like Gustave. Nick's father in "The Broken Globe" assumes that his son is learning French so that he can spite him by marrying a French woman. Clark Blaise's teacher in "A Class of New Canadians" has a patronizing view of his French-Canadian students; they're "like children" when it comes to learning English. Augustin in Anne Hébert's "A Grand Marriage" has enormous admiration for the Pelletiers who "since the time of the Conquest. . . had been able to maintain and expand their business and even deal with the English as equals."

There are no Indian or Inuit authors represented here, and the Indian characters who appear are figures of despair. In "Polarities", an Indian woman lies outside a cheap hotel with her legs apart drunkenly chanting, "Come on, boys, what're you waiting for." In Gwendolyn MacEwen's "House of the Whale" a Haida from the Pacific coast is swallowed, Jonah-like, by Toronto; he is fated "to become neither Indian nor white but a kind of grey nothing, floating between two worlds." That's what has become of the Métis Délia in "A Grand Marriage." Délia is a better Christian than Augustin or Canon Painchaud, but her inability to be a hypocrite destroys her. At the end of the story we find her refusing to take communion for fear of offending the God who has abandoned her.

"I am terrified only of the mediocre," says Erica in Audrey Thomas's "Aquarius." And many of the stories in this collection deal with men and women who share that terror. Mr. Willy, who has tried to structure a life that protects him from everyday experience, admires a bird that dashes its brains out against his window, "killed by the rapture of its flight." Margaret Gibson's Jenny rages against life in a mental institution; it's only after she's had thirty shock treatments and something goes "ping in her head" that she accepts her confinement. Hugo in Alice Munro's "Material" is uninterested in the commonplace life of the "harlot-in-residence"; but later he transforms the experience of living in the same rooming-house with her into a work of art. In Morley Callaghan's "A Wedding-Dress", Miss Schwartz's desire to keep alive a certain "tempestuous feeling" leads her to steal a dress she can't afford. Old Man Tudor in Rudy Wiebe's story is a loner convinced he's descended "from them same Tudors that was Kings of England" and that *he* ought to be King of England. The imagination of the boy in Sinclair Ross's "One's a Heifer" turns the lonely bachelor who puts him up for the night into a crazed cattle-thief.

Though a strong comic sense is implicit in many of these stories, only three of them are primarily meant to be funny — Mordecai Richler's "Mortimer Griffin, Shalinsky, and How They Settled the Jewish Question," Leo Simpson's "The Lady and the Travelling Salesman," and Jacques Ferron's "Mélie and the Bull." Richler's satire is familiar. Leo Simpson's reminds one of Shaw. He speaks of the new emancipated woman as someone who "talks like a longshoreman, and is as touchy as a nun." "Dullness," he says, "is a punishment you receive for doing the right things. I don't so much mind the bad reputation you get — people saying you're too good to be true, or you must be hiding something, or atoning for something. It's the filthy monotony I can't stand." Simpson's satire, dealing as satire must with a serious issue, takes wing and soars into pure high-spirited comedy. Jacques Ferron's fantasy, a kind of story rarely found in English-language writers, is pure and glorious fiction of the absurd. Or is there after all a satirical purpose in the tale of a bullcalf who becomes a barrister? Dr. Ferron, one recalls, was the founder of that significant political movement, the Rhinoceros Party.

It will be noticed that apart from "Mélie and the Bull" all the stories in this book are traditional in form; there is nothing that can be called experimental. We didn't plan it that way, but whether it reflects a fact of contemporary Canadian writing or the conservatism of the editors' taste we cannot say. Others will have to decide.

Ivon Owen
Morris Wolfe
Toronto
May 1978

THE BEST
MODERN
CANADIAN
SHORT STORIES

Audrey Thomas
Aquarius

They had been warned what to expect; yet the explosion—what else could you call it?—and the quantities of water which leapt at them—for as the whale descended the water did, indeed, seem to leap, as though it had almost taken on the shape, or at least the strength, of the great beast which had violated its calm—there was a collective "aaahh" from the little group of spectators, and a band of elementary-school children drew in closer to their teacher and shrieked in fearful delight.

"Brian, Daniel," called out the honeyed, public voice of the teacher. "Settle down now; come away from the side."

The man started, as if he had heard a voice calling to him from a dream. He felt disoriented, his glasses spattered with water—as though he were looking out from the lower portholes of the whale pool, not in and down from outside— and his head still echoed to the sound of the whale's re-entry into the pool. And disoriented in another way as well, for something had happened to him as the whale leapt up toward the sound of the keeper's whistle: like the water, he, too, had felt the shape and thrust of all that energy and had been strangely thrilled by it and strangely envious. Standing there now, still only vaguely aware of the school teacher, the children, the other spectators, blinking as he rubbed his glasses clean, terribly conscious of his thin body and his pale scholar's hands, he felt abandoned, cast down from some unimaginable height of strength and brute beauty and thrust. Wished, for a moment, to be one of the children who could close up, like delicate petals, around the tight bud of their teacher's serenity. He felt his separation from the whale. "O Ile leape up to my God," he remembered, "who pulles me downe?"

As if in answer he heard his wife give a low laugh and murmur something to her neighbour, an American who was worriedly examining the water-splashed lens of his camera and paying no attention to the whale who was now circling the pool, faster and faster, just below the surface of the water. Occasionally a brief island of dark, rubbery back would rise up above the surface and then disappear again, as the whale plunged deeper and deeper into the heaving water. The attendant, perched on his little platform like a circus artist, explained through a hand mike that the whale could reach speeds of up to thirty miles an hour. Mentally he went round and round with the rushing whale, faster and faster, five, ten, fifteen, twenty—he riding the slippery back as though it was the easiest thing in the world, waving his hand to Erica as he passed, casually, as one might wave to an old, almost forgotten friend seen suddenly from a taxi window; then up and up with the whale, out away from the blue water of the pool, which burned upward after them like transparent, ice-blue fire. A triumph against gravity, captivity, everything. "O Ile leape up to my God."

Erica laughed again. Before the performance began she had moved around to the other side of the pool, almost directly under the platform so that she could be in front of the whale as it leapt. He took off his glasses once more, nervously, for he did not need his eyes to see her: long hair tied back artful carelessly with a bright silk scarf, the top button of her cardigan undone, a mannerism he had observed in her for almost twenty years. He knew the shape of her neck as it rose from the cardigan, and the texture of that neck, with its tiny orange mole, like a rust spot, and the texture of her pale, coarse hair. She would be smiling up at the attendant, of whom she had already asked one or two extremely intelligent questions, amused no doubt by the boy's look of amazement and respect. How could *he* know the way her mind worked, or the extraordinary talent she had for seeming to know more than she really did. He had watched her leaf quickly through the paperback on whales which had been on display in the souvenir shop as they came in. But the boy was not to know this, or to know that years before she had typed for him an article on the reality factor in *Moby Dick*. She would look up at him, leaning back a little, and ask her questions with an air of polite apology, as though only too aware that *everyone* knew the answer except her; and the attendant (or museum guide or gallery official) would regard her with a kind of wonder—as if he had heard a flower speak. Yet sex was not really her game—not in these casual encounters at any rate; she simply wanted, had to be, always, on the side of the professionals.

And that, he thought (his mind reflecting, ruminating, while his body still unconsciously swayed slightly in a circle, in time to the rhythm of the whale), was precisely where he had failed her. A serious poet—a new Eliot if not a wild, new, apocalyptic bard—was one thing; a scholar who wrote poetry for a hobby was quite another. What was this fellow's name? Perry or Percy—something like that. The little mini-skirted girl had announced him at the beginning of the show. Something Frenchified and out of keeping with his T-shirt and sneakers and buckets of raw herring. What had his mother been thinking of when she gave her son that name? Perhaps she hoped he'd grow up to be a poet. His name should have been Harry or Dan or even just Red.

"Now I'll get Skana to give me a kiss," the boy said, descending from his perch and standing next to Erica, but in front of the low glass breakwater. He blew his whistle twice.

The whale stopped circling immediately and sped over toward her master, lifting her great blunt head up toward his inclining cheek. They touched and the spectators "aaahhed" again. Then the young man held up a fish directly over the whale's head, so that her mouth gaped open and her 44 teeth, blunt and sawdust-coloured ("George Washington must have looked like that when he smiled," he thought irreverently) were exposed. The boy patted her on the head and gave her the herring. She thrust her head up again and the audience duly chuckled. He gave her another fish and another friendly pat.

Again the watching man felt a strange thrill of identification and envy. There was nothing patronizing in the boy's attitude: he and the whale were a team — they complemented one another. The boy explained that the teeth were used only for holding and grasping. The man felt his tongue move almost involuntarily in his mouth, trying to imagine the tactile sensation of a mouth full of those quaint, wooden-looking molars, trying to imagine the stress of those molars against something they had chosen to grasp and hold. And suddenly he remembered the feel of Erica's teeth that first time, and how something had willed him, just for a moment, to set his teeth against her determined seeking, a something that had been almost immediately forgotten in the great conflagration of his desire.

Tipping the rest of the bucket into the water, the attendant thanked them all for coming, switched off the mike and prepared to walk away. The older man, on the other side of the pool, watched his wife touch the boy lightly on the arm (just one more intelligent question for the road). The man moved back toward the door where he stood idly, used to waiting, rubbing his index finger against his thumb and still feeling that terrible sense of loss. He decided he would have to come again, without her, and try to define more explicitly what it was he really wanted from the whale. For he wanted something, that much he was sure of: maybe a new poem; maybe only reassurance; maybe something more. As his wife turned he noticed that her sweater and the front of her slacks were wet. He was annoyed — not because she would insist upon going home, but rather because she would stay, moving unconcernedly and triumphantly amongst the curious. And she would have a story to tell the children or her friends.

"My dears, I was nearly *swallowed up*, like a female Jonah or Pinocchio or someone!" and still later he would watch her bury her face in the wrinkled clothes, inhaling the faint aroma of her triumphal morning, before she

17

tossed them in the hamper. Suddenly he was thoroughly disgusted and decided to ignore her smile and wave (was he mistaken, or was the red-headed young man beginning to look just a trifle bored?), moved out with the last of the stragglers, back into the aquarium proper. Now just Erica and the boy were out there by the pool. Erica and the boy, and somewhere below them, Skana, the killer whale. The children, pulled along by their teacher's authority, as though by an earnest tug, had long since disappeared to look at other things.

Had Erica experienced a genuine thrill when the whale leapt? She might have, once. And the creature was powerful and female, sleek and strangely beautiful—like the woman herself. He had always associated her, too, with the sea—because of her name and her pale blond hair and cold blue eyes. When he first loved her he even saw himself as something Scandinavian, a Siegfried, and exulted in her restrained, voluptuous power and her ice-blue eyes. ("Except for that one moment," he thought, "when I set my teeth against her thrusting tongue. Strange I had forgotten that.") Later, because the Siegfried role was not his true self-idealization, he allowed himself to be mothered by her. She had been lonely when he met her and he sensed she needed to be needed. She had taught him all he ever knew of sex (he never asked her where she got her knowledge), and cooked for him thick homemade soups in a huge copper kettle she had discovered at the Salvation Army shop. And she it was, too, who willed him to be a poet, encouraged him, made do with bare floors and tipsy, mismatched chairs. She was afraid of nothing, neither accidents nor poverty nor death. "I am terrified only of the mediocre," she told him once, and he had thrilled to hear her say it, wrapped in his old dressing gown, drying her long, pale hair by firelight. It had all been heaven then: the thick soups, the crazy chairs, the bottles of cheap wine, the crusty bread, the basement flat which—with her incredible luck—had contained a fireplace and a priceless, abandoned, Hudson Bay "button blanket" on the wall.

She had seemed the ultimate in womanhood, the very essence of female with her full, Northern figure and her incredible self-assurance and practicality, so different from the flat-bosomed, delicate foolishness of his own well-bred female relatives. And what excited him most, although he would never have admitted it, and indeed felt actually ashamed, at first, even to himself, was a certain sluttishness about her—the top button of her inevitable cardigan always left undone or missing, her legs crossed thigh over thigh, quite casually—his mother and sisters had always crossed only at the ankles. Her strange desire to make love when she had her period. But even more than this, the things she said. Once, in the very early days, she had run her hands along his thin flanks and kissed him there and laughed with delight at his thinness.

"I will fatten you with kisses," she had cried. And indeed, he could feel his body firmer, fuller, where she had traced her fingers and her lips. Then suddenly she had grabbed his head between her hands, kneading his scalp in her beautiful capable fingers and licking his face with her warm tongue—as though he were her kitten. He had already grown a beard, even then, and she had whispered, rubbing her cheek against him, "Your beard is all soft and springy—like pubic hair." So that his face flamed up at her bold words and for days he found it difficult to go outside, to expose his face to others, so deep was his sensual delight, so wanton his happiness.

He walked slowly along the illuminated displays and admired the care that had been taken with the lighting and accessories of each exhibit. Shells, sand, gravel, anemones, and kelp: like with like or near-like. Everything conspired to give the illusion of a real beach or cove or lake or ocean home. It was spacious, tasteful, and most effective. Yet he felt cold and claustrophobic in the aquarium, as though it were he who was shut in, not the fish and other specimens. An iguana observed him wipe his forehead with a cynical, prehistoric eye; the octopus flattened his disgusting suckers against the harsh reality of glass; the alligators slept with tourists' pennies clinging to their heads and backs. The wolf-eel, however, looked as if a mere quarter-inch of glass would not stop *him*. "Fishermen will sometimes cut the line," he read, "rather than handle this fish." He believed it. The thick, sensuous lips, the small eyes, the conical front teeth convinced one that here was evil incarnate, a creature who would not hesitate to attack. Erica, he thought, would have laughed loudly and squatted down with her nose against the glass, grinning, daring the eel to pit his aggression against hers.

He read that they had been captured up to a length of eight feet. Taller than a man. Imagine finding *that* on the end of your line! Where was Erica?

Had it all been a trick, her violent lovemaking which somehow was in keeping with her Nordic looks—a love like waterfalls and mountain torrents, a love that suggested terrible deeds to be done for love or hate or kinship, quite in contrast to his own soft, dreamlike attitude. But in those early days she could rouse him up until he forgot that he was thin and lank and weak of vision; and he would take into himself her passion and her fury until the little flat rang with their cries, like the harsh, triumphant cries of eagles or giant sea-birds, and he thought his heart would burst from excitement and exertion. He was transformed, transfigured, under her incredible shaping hands. He entered her as Siegfried leaping through a wall of fire. He lived.

But she had never been able to rouse him to the heights of poetry. All his best work was done before he met her. He felt, now, that this was as much a failure in her as it was in him. Vampire-like she had renewed herself with his passion; and then, having won him and worn him out, she had begun to cast him off as worthless—to shed him as a snake might shed its winter skin. On

19

the strength of the acceptance of his first book they had married. When his second group of poems had been repeatedly rejected she initiated her first affair. Her children, tall and blond like her, came to take the place of the poems she had urged him to create, just as her anonymous lovers (sometimes he could even smell them on her skin—what a bitch she was!) had taken his place in her body. It was as if, after the first wild, dream-like years when he made poetry all day and love all night (she blond and buxom, like a seventeenth-century genre painting then in her spotless kitchenette, with the first child, round and rosy-cheeked, hugging the backs of her knees; and at night a rich dim honey-coloured nude), it was as if she had peered down into a well, assessed the amount of liquid remaining there, and then, with a practical shrug of her shoulders, had shut up the cover and gone elsewhere for her water.

And the water in the well became stagnant, scum-covered, undrinkable. Noises from outside filtered down, as distant as summer thunder— and as deceptive. When he tried to write about his anguish he found that he was no longer interested in the old preoccupations with beauty and order and truth. He could only dryly mock himself, forsaken merman, and mocking, failed again. The money from his mother's estate, the small advance from his first book: these vanished even more quickly than his dreams. He had always taught part-time, to guarantee they wouldn't starve. Now Erica suggested coldly that he apply for a full-time job; and he, with a sinking heart, accepted his defeat. He began to see himself as a man walking slowly toward the exact centre of a low-walled bridge. He had not yet reached the centre but it would draw him on and on and someday—over. He taught reasonably well, but he was always tired; and the mountains just beyond the city, mountains which had always thrilled him, began to oppress and even frighten him. They seemed to be growing larger, hemming him in against the sea. A worrisome phrase kept running through his mind: "with one stride came the dark." Often, lately, he had had to leave his class for a few minutes and light a cigarette in order not to weep. Sometimes he wished that Erica were dead.

"Open water fishes," he read, "are darker above than below." To fool the enemy. Not the wolf-eel though. But is an eel a fish? And where was Erica?

But the paleness might be a camouflage, not a symptom. Like Erica's pale hair and honeyed skin. "The good heroines of the Western world are always blond and fair," he thought, "like Erica." But the Vikings were blond too, or red-haired and fair. The "Rus." And destructive. Ravenous in appetite if not appearance. "The fish's pallor is a mask," he said to no one in particular. Where was Erica? Not making love to the young attendant, even if he had turned out to be a novice marine biologist. Oh, no. Her taste ran now to higher things: historians, art critics, young writers (especially poets) on fellowships. A boy in a T-shirt, whose hands smelled of herring, would no longer physically excite her. And he remembered again, "The only thing I'm afraid of is the mediocre."

He hesitated in front of the Mozambique Mouth-Breeder, attracted by its name. Were the young fry snug or struggling — which? — behind the closed gate of their mother's teeth, coming awake in the slimy warmth of their mother's mouth? How did she eat without swallowing them? How catch her food? Or did she not eat at all while she carefully manoeuvred the African waters, aware of her incredible mouthful. He had always felt the aloneness of his own infant children, had carried the first strapped to his back in a harness of his own devising — his unique example of mechanical inventiveness. He had told her it was to save money — for he had been slightly afraid of her, even then — and she had been very proud of him. They had been, he reflected now, naïvely picturesque as they padded along the busy streets on Friday mornings. Friday had always been a day of reorganization for them, of doing the weekly shopping and changing the bed and answering any letters. Later she would wash her long blond hair while he worked on the latest poem, the child asleep on his lap. They were poetic about their poverty too, acting out the romantic role of the artist and his barefoot wife, for she had given up shoes (at least indoors) long before it was fashionable to do so. And had named their first child Darius. It was all so transient: money and fame were not beneath them but just ahead of them; and they accepted their poverty with style and good grace because they knew it was only temporary, accepted it the way the wise accept the bitter winter, knowing of the spring.

But it was not to be. Wherever he sent his work it came back rejected: first (on the strength of his book) accompanied by a kind and sometimes helpful letter, later by the now-familiar oblong of paper or card, clipped to the upper left-hand corner. Thank you for your submission. Thank you for giving us the opportunity to read... Thank you but no thank you. He couldn't believe it. Eventually he had to. Once he had received his manuscript back with a letter, quite a long one, only to discover it was from a fellow-struggler who had received the two manuscripts clipped together under a single message of dismissal. The writer of the letter was ironic and amused; but he was furious, and felt publicly exposed in front of this stranger from Brickchurch, New Jersey, USA, who had also offered inadequate libations to the gods. He even thought of writing to the editors. Surely there was an ethical principle involved? But in the end he didn't — it was too humiliating.

And so, finally, she took a lover and he a full-time job. That night he had shaved off his beard in a fury of bitterness — a mask for the wrong dance. Why had he ever let it grow again?

He looked at his watch. Where the hell was she? Surely she couldn't be *still* talking to that boy. And he was bored with all these strange, slippery

21

creatures that surrounded him, lost in their own dream-like, antiseptic coffins. The vague bubbling noise and shifting light had given him a headache. And it was nearly lunchtime. She would want to go to Chinatown and have a meal, knowing he hated the kind of restaurant she always chose—the dirtiest, tackiest one she had not yet tried, with peeling, musty oilcloth-covered tables and slimed menus, where the lukewarm soup was served in heavy, cracked white bowls and the smells from the kitchen made him gag. "Ahh," she would exclaim, giving him a wicked smile, "Now this isn't one of your bloody tourist traps, my darling; this is the real thing!" She would enjoy watching his discomfort, would eat quickly and with great show of appetite, scooping the liquid up toward her bent, blond head, almost lapping it up like a cat, in her haste to get on to the next course (which was usually a revolting and expensive something that was not on the regular menu), afterward licking the film of grease from her upper lip with one sweep of her tongue. He couldn't bear it, not today. He'd have to find some excuse.

She always laughed when he told her such places disgusted him—"You weren't always so discriminating!" And it was so. He felt a physical revulsion now for anything that smacked of foreignness or dirt or unclean, hidden things. Three nights before she had unexpectedly thrown her heavy, blue-veined thigh over his as she was getting into bed, and had cried out in triumph, "Look how thin you are getting! I could crush you!" And his sudden leap of desire had been quenched by a smudge of lipstick on her teeth. He couldn't bear it if someone forgot to flush the toilet.

He was beginning to feel a little giddy, and turned back toward the fish, as if seeking some answer or relief. Perhaps she had simply gone home without him? She liked to mock him, now, in front of their nearly-grown children, and she had to work out the story of her wet clothes. "Darlings, I was nearly drowned! This morning—at the aquarium—you nearly lost me!" She was afraid of nothing and she despised him. The Pacific prawns, delicate as Venetian glass or transparent drinking straws, moved gently just ahead of him. How beautiful. He wondered at their strange reversal of sex and envied them their beauty and, for a long moment, their eternally ordered environment. He and Erica had had a reversal too—but ugly, unnatural. She had dominated him always, more and more, had emasculated his body and his soul and having done so, cast him aside, an empty shell. Even this trip to the aquarium was her suggestion. He had wanted to cross the bridge and drive out to Horseshoe Bay, have a quiet lunch beside the water. It appeared to him now that even the exhibits he had seemed to choose at random had been chosen first by her, as living illustrations of her strength and his incredible, female, weakness.

He remembered how she had told him, captive, everything about her labour during the birth of their third child. Had described it in such detail he had sickened and begged her to desist—this in the semi-private room at the hospital, while the women in the other bed remained an implied smile behind the plastic curtains. She had raped him — truly — as the Vikings raped their conquered women. And she had desecrated him and everything he dreamed of. That night, while he sat wretchedly with his head between his knees, she talked of herself and the young doctor who assisted her as if they had been lovers who created the child between them. And he had visualized the gloved hands of the doctor reaching forward between her bloody thighs to draw out the thing that was *his*, and had fallen from the chair and onto the coolness of the hospital floor. That story was one of her best ones.

He decided to go home. Let her walk or take the bus. Let her disappear forever. Let her get knocked down by a taxi cab or knocked up by the chairman of the Symphony Committee: it was a matter of indifference to him. But out in the corridor he saw the door to the pool was standing open and felt irresistibly drawn to the dark shadow of the whale, floating down there somewhere below the surface of the water. No one was about. A bucket of fish and the big pink plastic ball stood ready beneath the empty platform. The red-haired boy was nowhere to be seen. He was vaguely aware, through the glass, of the back of Erica's cardigan and her bright scarf near the counter where they sold the shells.

At the water's edge he hesitated, peering down uncertainly, then stuck his fingers in his mouth and whistled twice, a high, thin sound that came back to him out of his childhood, a sound that would reach down and pierce the heavy blanket of the water and draw the big whale up to him. He inclined his cheek, waiting. "Skana," he whispered, "Skana." But the surface of the pool remained a calm, indifferent blue. The whale did not hear or did not choose to answer.

He got up, slowly, awkwardly, and went to join his wife.

Audrey Thomas (1935-) was born in Binghamton, New York, and settled in British Columbia in 1959. In addition to novels such as *Mrs. Blood*, and the novellas *Munchmeyer & Prospero on the Island*, she has published several collections of stories including *Ten Green Bottles* and, most recently, *Ladies & Escorts*.

Alice Munro
Material

I don't keep up with Hugo's writing. Sometimes I see his name, in the library, on the cover of some literary journal that I don't open—I haven't opened a literary journal in a dozen years, praise God. Or I read in the paper or see on a poster—this would be in the library, too, or in a book-store—an announcement of a panel discussion at the University, with Hugo flown in to discuss the state of the novel today, or the contemporary short story, or the new nationalism in our literature. Then I think, will people really go, will people who could be swimming or drinking or going for a walk really take themselves out to the campus to find the room and sit in rows listening to those vain quarrelsome men? Bloated, opinionated, untidy men, that is how I see them, cosseted by the academic life, the literary life, by women. People will go to hear them say that such and such a writer is not worth reading any more, and that some writer must be read; to hear them dismiss and glorify and argue and chuckle and shock. People, I say, but I mean women, middle-aged women like me, alert and trembling, hoping to ask intelligent questions and not be ridiculous; soft-haired young girls awash in adoration, hoping to lock eyes with one of the men on the plat-form. Girls, and women too, fall in love with such men, they imagine there is power in them.

The wives of the men on the platform are not in that audience. They are buying groceries or cleaning up messes or having a drink. Their lives are concerned with food and mess and houses and cars and money. They have to remember to get the snow tires on and go to the bank and take back the beer bottles, because their husbands are such brilliant, such talented incapable men, who must be looked after for the sake of the words that will come from them. The women in the audience are married to engineers or doctors or businessmen. I know them, they are my friends. Some of them have turned to literature frivolously, it is true, but most come shyly, and with enormous transitory hope. They absorb the contempt of the men on the platform as if they deserved it; they half-believe they do deserve it, because of their houses and expensive shoes, and their husbands who read Arthur Hailey.

I am married to an engineer myself. His name is Gabriel, but he prefers the name Gabe. In this country he prefers the name Gabe. He was born in Romania, he lived there until the end of the war, when he was sixteen. He has forgotten how to speak Romanian. How can you forget, how can you forget the language of your childhood? I used to think he was pretending to forget, because the things he had seen and lived through when he spoke that language were too terrible to remember. He told me this was not so. He told me his experience of the war was not so bad. He described the holiday uproar at school when the air raid sirens sounded. I did not quite believe him. I required him to be an ambassador from bad times as well as distant countries. Then I thought he might not be Romanian at all, but an impostor.

This was before we were married, when he used to come and see me in the apartment on Clark Road where I lived with my little daughter, Clea. Hugo's daughter too, of course, but he had to let go of her. Hugo had grants, he travelled, he married again and his wife had three children; he divorced and married again, and his next wife, who had been his student, had three more children, the first born to her while he was still living with his second wife. In such circumstances a man can't hang onto everything. Gabriel used to stay all night sometimes on the pull-out couch I had for a bed in this tiny, shabby apartment; and I would look at him sleeping and think that for all I knew he might be a German or a Russian or even of all things a Canadian faking a past and an accent to make himself interesting. He was mysterious to me. Long after he became my lover and after he became my husband he remained, remains, mysterious to me. In spite of all the things I know about him, daily and physical things. His face curves out smoothly and his eyes, set shallowly in his head, curve out too under the smooth pink lids. The wrinkles he has are traced on top of this smoothness, this impenetrable surface; they are of no consequence. His body is substantial, calm. He used to be a fine, rather lazy-looking, skater. I cannot describe him without a familiar sense of capitulation. I cannot describe him. I could describe Hugo, if anybody asked me, in great detail—Hugo as he was eighteen, twenty years ago, crew-cut and skinny, with the bones of his body and even of his skull casually, precariously, joined and knitted together, so that there was something unco-ordinated, unexpected about the shifting planes of his face as well as the movements, often dangerous, of his limbs. He's held together by nerves, a friend of mine at college said when I first brought him around, and it was true; after that I could almost see the fiery strings.

Gabriel told me when I first knew him that he enjoyed life. He did not say that he believed in enjoying it; he said that he did. I was embarrassed for

25

him. I never believed people who said such things and anyway, I associated this statement with gross, self-advertising, secretly unpleasantly restless men. But it seems to be the truth. He is not curious. He is able to take pleasure and give off smiles and caresses and say softly, "Why do you worry about that? It is not a problem of yours." He has forgotten the language of his childhood. His lovemaking was strange to me at first, because it was lacking in desperation. He made love without emphasis, so to speak, with no memory of sin or hope of depravity. He does not watch himself. He will never write a poem about it, never, and indeed may have forgotten it in half an hour. Such men are commonplace, perhaps. It was only that I had not known any. I used to wonder if I would have fallen in love with him if his accent and his forgotten, nearly forgotten, past had been taken away; if he had been, say, an engineering student in my own year at college. I don't know, I can't tell. What holds anybody in a man or a woman may be something as flimsy as a Romanian accent or the calm curve of an eyelid, some half-fraudulent mystery.

No mystery of this sort about Hugo. I did not miss it, did not know about it, maybe would not have believed in it. I believed in something else, then. Not that I knew him, all the way through, but the part I knew was in my blood and from time to time would give me a poison rash. None of that with Gabriel, he does not disturb me, any more than he is disturbed himself.

It was Gabriel who found me Hugo's story. We were in a bookstore, and he came to me with a large, expensive paperback, a collection of short stories. There was Hugo's name on the cover. I wondered how Gabriel had found it, what he had been doing in the fiction section of the store anyway, he never reads fiction. I wondered if he sometimes went and looked for things by Hugo. He is interested in Hugo's career as he would be interested in the career of a magician or popular singer or politician with whom he had, through me, a plausible connection, a proof of reality. I think it is because he does such anonymous work himself, work intelligible only to his own kind. He is fascinated by people who work daringly out in the public eye, without the protection of any special discipline—it must seem so, to an engineer—just trying to trust themselves, and elaborating their bag of tricks, and hoping to catch on.

"Buy it for Clea," he said.

"Isn't it a lot of money for a paperback?"

He smiled.

"There's your father's picture, your real father, and he has written this story you might like to read," I said to Clea, who was in the kitchen making toast. She is seventeen. Some days she eats toast and honey and peanut butter and Oreos and creamed cheese and chicken sandwiches and fried potatoes. If anybody comments on what she is eating or not eating, she may run upstairs and slam the door of her room.

"He looks overweight," said Clea and put the book down. "You always said he was skinny." Her interest in her father is all from the point of view of heredity, and what genes he might have passed on to herself. Did he have a bad complexion, did he have a high I.Q., did the women in his family have big breasts?

"He was when I knew him," I said. "How was I to know what had happened to him since?"

He looked, however, very much as I would have thought he would look by now. When I saw his name in the newspaper or on a poster I had pictured somebody much like this; I had foreseen the ways in which time and his life would have changed him. It did not surprise me that he had got fat but not bald, that he had let his hair grow wild and had grown a full, curly beard. Pouches under his eyes, a dragged-down look to the cheeks even when he is laughing. He is laughing, into the camera. His teeth have gone from bad to worse. He hated dentists, said his father died of a heart attack in the dentist's chair. A lie, like so much else, or at least an exaggeration. He used to smile crookedly for photographs to hide the right top incisor, dead since somebody at high school pushed him into a drinking fountain. Now he doesn't care, he laughs, he bares those rotting stumps. He looks, at the same time, woebegone and cheerful. A Rabelaisian writer. Checked wool shirt open at the top to show his undershirt, he didn't use to wear one. Do you wash, Hugo? Do you have bad breath, with those teeth? Do you call your girl students fond exasperated dirty names, are there phone calls from insulted parents, does the Dean or somebody have to explain that no harm is meant, that writers are not as other men are? Probably not, probably no one minds. Outrageous writers may bounce from one blessing to another nowadays, bewildered, as permissively reared children are said to be, by excess of approval.

I have no proof. I construct somebody from this one smudgy picture, I am content with such clichés. I have not the imagination or good will to proceed differently; and I have noticed anyway, everybody must have noticed as we go further into middle age, how shopworn and simple, really, are the disguises, the identities if you like, that people take up. In fiction, in Hugo's business, such disguises would not do, but in life they are all we seem to want, all anybody can manage. Look at Hugo's picture, look at the undershirt, listen to what it says about him.

Hugo Johnson was born and semi-educated in the bush, and in the mining and lumbering towns of Northern Ontario. He has worked as a lumberjack, beer-slinger, counterman, telephone lineman and sawmill foreman, and has been sporadically affiliated with various academic communities. He lives now most of the time on the side of a mountain above Vancouver, with his wife and six children.

27

The student wife, it seems, got stuck with all the children. What happened to Mary Frances, did she die, is she liberated, did he drive her crazy? But listen to the lies, the half-lies, the absurdities. *He lives on the side of a mountain above Vancouver.* It sounds as if he lives in a wilderness cabin, and all it means, I'm willing to bet, is that he lives in an ordinary comfortable house in North or West Vancouver, which now stretch far up the mountain. He has been *sporadically affiliated with various academic communities.* What does that mean? If it means he has taught for years, most of his adult life, at universities, that teaching at universities has been the only steady well-paid job he has ever had, why doesn't it say so? You would think he came out of the bush now and then to fling them scraps of wisdom, to give them a demonstration of what a real male *writer*, a creative *artist*, is like: you would never think he was a practising *academic*. I don't know if he was a lumberjack or a beer-slinger or a counterman, but I do know that he was not a telephone lineman. He had a job painting telephone poles. He quit that job in the middle of the second week because the heat and the climbing made him sick. It was a broiling June, just after we had both graduated. Fair enough. The sun really did make him sick, twice he came home and vomited. I have quit jobs myself that I could not stand. The same summer I quit my job folding bandages at Victoria Hospital, because I was going mad with boredom. But if I was a writer, and was listing all my varied and colourful occupations, I don't think I would put down *bandage folder*, I don't think I would find that entirely honest.

After he quit, Hugo found a job marking Grade Twelve examination papers. Why didn't he put that down? Examination marker. He liked marking examination papers better than he liked climbing telephone poles, and probably better than he liked lumberjacking or beer-slinging or any of those other things if he ever did them; why couldn't he put it down? *Examination marker.*

Nor has he, to my knowledge, ever been the foreman in a sawmill. He worked in his uncle's mill the summer before I met him. What he did all day was load lumber and get sworn at by the real foreman, who didn't like him because of his uncle being the boss. In the evenings, if he was not too tired, he used to walk half a mile to a little creek and play his recorder. Blackflies bothered him, but he did it anyway. He could play "Morning," from *Peer Gynt*, and some Elizabethan airs whose names I have forgotten. Except for one: "Wolsey's Wilde." I learned to play it on the piano so we could play a duet. Was that meant for Cardinal Wolsey, and what was a *wilde*, a dance? Put that down, Hugo. *Recorder player.* That would be quite all right, quite in fashion now; as I understand things, recorder playing and such fey activities are not out of favour now, quite the contrary. Indeed, they may be more acceptable than all that lumberjacking and beer-slinging. Look at you, Hugo, your image is not only fake but out-of-date. You should have said you'd meditated for a year in the mountains of Uttar Pradesh; you should have said you'd taught Creative Drama to autistic children; you should have shaved your head, shaved your beard, put on a monk's cowl; you should have shut up, Hugo.

When I was pregnant with Clea we lived in a house on Argyle Street in Vancouver. It was such a sad grey stucco house on the outside, in the rainy winter, that we painted the inside, all the rooms, vivid ill-chosen colours. three walls of the bedrooms were Wedgwood blue, one was magenta. We said it was an experiment to see if colour could drive anybody mad. The bathroom was a deep orange-yellow. "It's like being inside a cheese," Hugo said when we finished it. "That's right, it is," I said. "That's very good, phrase-maker." He was pleased but not as pleased as if he'd written it. After that he said every time he showed anybody the bathroom, "See the colour? It's like being inside a cheese." Or, "It's like peeing inside a cheese." Not that I didn't do the same thing, save things up and say them over and over. Maybe I said that about peeing inside a cheese. We had many phrases in common. We both called the landlady the Green Hornet, because she had worn, the only time we had seen her, a poison-green outfit with bits of rat fur and a clutch of violets, and had given off a venomous sort of buzz. She was over seventy and she ran a downtown boardinghouse for men. Her daughter Dotty we called the harlot-in-residence. I wonder why we chose to say *harlot*; that was not, is not, a word in general use. I suppose it had a classy sound, a classy depraved sound, contrasting ironically—we were strong on irony—with Dotty herself.

She lived in a two-room apartment in the basement of the house. She was supposed to pay her mother forty-five dollars monthly rent and she told me she meant to try to make the money baby-sitting.

"I can't go out to work," she said, "on account of my nerves. My last husband, I had him six months dying down at Mother's, dying with his kidney disease, and I owe her three hundred dollars board still on that. She made me make him his eggnog with skim milk. I'm broke every day of my life. They say it's all right not having wealth if you got health, but what if you never had either one? Bronchial pneumonia from the time I was three years old. Rheumatic fever at twelve. Sixteen I married my first husband, he was killed in a logging accident. Three miscarriages. My womb is in shreds. I use up three packs of Kotex every month. I married a dairy farmer out in the Valley and his herd got the fever. Wiped us out. That was the one who died with his kidneys. No wonder. No wonder my nerves are shot."

I am condensing. This came out at greater length and by no means dolefully, indeed with some amazement and pride, at Dotty's table. She asked me down for cups of tea, then for beer. This is life, I thought, fresh from books, classes, essays, discussions. Unlike her mother, Dotty was flat-faced, soft, doughy, fashioned for defeat, the kind of colourless puzzled woman you see carrying a shopping bag, waiting for the bus. In fact, I had seen her once on a bus downtown, and not recognized her at first in her dull blue winter coat. Her rooms were full of heavy furniture salvaged from her marriage— an upright piano, overstuffed chesterfield and chairs, walnut veneer china cabinet and dining room table, where we sat. In the middle of the table was a tremendous lamp, with a painted china base and a pleated, dark red silk shade, held out at an extravagant angle, like a hoop skirt.

I described it to Hugo. "That is a whorehouse lamp," I said. Afterwards I wanted to be congratulated on the accuracy of this description. I told Hugo he ought to pay more attention to Dotty if he wanted to be a writer. I told him about her husbands and her womb and her collection of souvenir spoons, and he said I was welcome to look at them all by myself. He was writing a verse play.

Once when I went down to put coal on the furnace, I found Dotty in her pink chenille dressing gown saying goodbye to a man in a uniform, some sort of delivery man or gas station attendant. It was the middle of the afternoon. She and this man were not parting in any way that suggested either lechery or affection and I would not have understood anything about it, I would probably have thought he was some relative, if she had not begun at once a long complicated slightly drunk story about how she had got wet in the rain and had to leave her clothes at her mother's house and worn home her mother's dress which was too tight and that was why she was now in her dressing gown. She said that first Larry had caught her in it delivering some sewing he wanted her to do for his wife, and now me, and she didn't know what we would think of her. This was strange, as I had seen her in her dressing gown many times before. In the middle of her laughing and explaining, the man, who had not looked at me, not smiled or said a word or in any way backed up her story, simply ducked out the door.

"Dotty has a lover," I said to Hugo.

"You don't get out enough. You're trying to make life interesting."

The next week I watched to see if this man came back. He did not. But three other men came, and one of them came twice. They walked with their heads down, quickly, and did not have to wait at the basement door. Hugo couldn't deny it. He said it was life imitating art again, it was bound to happen, after all the fat varicose-veined whores he'd met in books. It was then we named her the harlot-in-residence and began to brag about her to our friends. They stood behind the curtains to catch a glimpse of her going in or out.

"That's not her!" they said. "Is that her? Isn't she disappointing? Doesn't she have any professional clothes?"

"Don't be so naïve," we said. "Did you think they all wore spangles and boas?"

Everybody hushed to hear her play the piano. She sang or hummed

along with her playing, not steadily, but loudly, in the rather defiant, self-parodying voice people use when they are alone, or think they are alone. She sang "Yellow Rose of Texas," and "You Can't Be True, Dear."

"Whores should sing hymns."

"We'll get her to learn some."

"You're all such voyeurs. You're all so mean," said a girl named Mary Frances Shrecker, a big-boned, calm-faced girl with black braids down her back. She was married to a former mathematical prodigy, Elsworth Shrecker, who had had a breakdown. She worked as a dietician. Hugo said he could not look at her without thinking of the word *lumpen*, but he supposed she might be nourishing, like oatmeal porridge. She became his second wife. I thought she was the right wife for him, I thought she would stay forever, nourishing him, but the student evicted her.

The piano-playing was an entertainment for our friends, but disastrous on the days when Hugo was home trying to work. He was supposed to be working on his thesis but he really was writing his play. He worked in our bedroom, at a card table in front of the window, facing a board fence. When Dotty had been playing for a bit, he might come out to the kitchen and stick his face into mine and say in low, even tones of self-consciously controlled rage, "You go down and tell her to cut that out."

"You go."

"Bloody hell. She's your friend. You cultivate her. You encourage her."

"I never told her to play the piano."

"I arranged so that I could have this afternoon free. That did not just happen. I arranged it. I am at a crucial point. I am at the point where this play *lives or dies*. If I go down there I'm afraid I might strangle her."

"Well don't look at *me*. Don't strangle *me*. Excuse my breathing and everything."

I always did go down to the basement, of course, and knock on Dotty's door and ask her if she would mind not playing the piano now, because my husband was at home and was trying to work. I never said the word *write*, Hugo had trained me not to, that word was like a bare wire to us. Dotty apologized every time, she was scared of Hugo and respectful of his work and his intelligence. She left off playing but the trouble was she might forget, she might start again in an hour, half an hour. The possibility made me nervous and miserable. Because I was pregnant I always wanted to eat, and I would sit at the kitchen table greedily, unhappily, eating something like a warmed-up plateful of Spanish rice. Hugo felt the world was hostile to his writing, he felt not only all its human inhabitants but its noises and diversions and ordinary clutter were linked against him, maliciously, purposefully, diabolically thwarting and maiming him and keeping him from his work. And I, whose business it was to throw myself between him and the world, was failing to do so, by choice perhaps as much as ineptitude for the

job. I did not believe in him. I had not understood how it would be necessary to believe in him. I believed that he was clever and talented, whatever that might mean, but I was not sure he would turn out to be a writer. He did not have the authority I thought a writer should have. He was too nervous, too touchy with everybody, too much of a showoff. I believed that writers were calm, sad people, knowing too much. I believed that there was a difference about them, some hard and shining, rare intimidating quality they had from the beginning, and Hugo didn't have it. I thought that some day he would recognize this. Meanwhile, he lived in a world whose rewards and punishments were as strange, as hidden from me, as if he had been a lunatic. He would sit at supper, pale and disgusted; he would clench himself over the typewriter in furious paralysis when I had to get something from the bedroom, or he would leap around the living room asking me what he was (a rhinoceros who thinks he is a gazelle, Chairman Mao dancing a war dance in a dream dreamt by John Foster Dulles) and then kiss me all over the neck and throat with hungry gobbling noises. I was cut off from the source of these glad or bad moods, I did not affect them. I teased him sourly:

"Suppose after we have the baby the house is on fire and the baby and the play are both in there, which would you save?"

"Both."

"But supposing you can just save one? Never mind the baby, suppose *I* am in there, no, suppose I am drowning *here* and you are *here* and cannot possibly reach us both—"

"You're making it tough for me."

"I know I am. I know I am. Don't you hate me?"

"Of course I hate you." After this we might go to bed, playful, squealing, mock-fighting, excited. All our life together, the successful part of our life together, was games. We made up conversations to startle people on the bus. Once we sat in a beer parlour and he berated me for going out with other men and leaving the children alone while he was off in the bush working to support us. He pleaded with me to remember my duty as a wife and as a mother. I blew smoke in his face. People around us were looking stern and gratified. When we got outside we laughed till we had to hold each other up, against the wall. We played in bed that I was Lady Chatterley and he was Mellors.

"Where be that little rascal John Thomas?" he asked thickly. "I canna find John Thomas!"

"Frightfully sorry, I think I must have swallowed him," I said, ladylike.

There was a water pump in the basement. It made a steady, thumping noise. The house was on fairly low-lying ground not far from the Fraser River, and during the rainy weather the pump had to work most of the time to keep the basement from being flooded. We had a dark rainy January, as

is usual in Vancouver, and this was followed by a dark rainy February. Hugo and I felt gloomy. I slept a lot of the time. Hugo couldn't sleep. He claimed it was the pump that kept him awake. He couldn't work because of it in the daytime and he couldn't sleep because of it at night. The pump had replaced Dotty's piano-playing as the thing that most enraged and depressed him in our house. Not only because of its noise, but because of the money it was costing us. Its entire cost went onto our electricity bill, though it was Dotty who lived in the basement and reaped the benefits of not being flooded. He said I should speak to Dotty and I said Dotty could not pay the expenses she already had. He said she could turn more tricks. I told him to shut up. As I became more pregnant, slower and heavier and more confined to the house, I got fonder of Dotty, used to her, less likely to store up and repeat what she said. I felt more at home with her than I did sometimes with Hugo and our friends.

All right, Hugo said, I ought to phone the landlady. I said he ought. He said he had far too much to do. The truth was we both shrank from a confrontation with the landlady, knowing in advance how she would confuse and defeat us with shrill evasive prattle.

In the middle of the night in the middle of a rainy week I woke up and wondered what had wakened me. It was the silence.

"Hugo, wake up. The pump's broken. I can't hear the pump."

"I am awake," Hugo said.

"It's still raining and the pump isn't going. It must be broken."

"No, it isn't. It's shut off. I shut it off."

I sat up and turned on the light. He was lying on his back, squinting and trying to give me a hard look at the same time.

"You didn't turn it off."

"All right, I didn't."

"You did."

"I could not stand the goddamn expense any more. I could not stand thinking about it. I could not stand the noise either. I haven't had any sleep in a week."

"The basement will flood."

"I'll turn it on in the morning. A few hours' peace is all I want."

"That'll be too late, it's raining torrents."

"It is not."

"You go to the window."

"It's raining. It's not raining torrents."

I turned out the light and lay down and said in a calm stern voice, "Listen to me, Hugo, you have to go and turn it on, Dotty will be flooded out."

"In the morning."

"You have to go and turn it on *now*."

"Well I'm not."

"If you're not, I am."

"No, you're not."

"I am."

But I didn't move.

"Don't be such an alarmist."

"*Hugo*."

"Don't *cry*."

"Her stuff will be ruined."

"Best thing could happen to it. Anyway it won't." He lay beside me stiff and wary, waiting, I suppose, for me to get out of bed, go down to the basement and figure out how to turn the pump on. Then what would he have done? He could not have hit me, I was too pregnant. He never did hit me, unless I hit him first. He could have gone and turned it off again, and I could have turned it on, and so on, how long could that last? He could have held me down, but if I struggled he would have been afraid of hurting me. He could have sworn at me and left the house, but we had no car, and it was raining too hard for him to stay out very long. He would probably just have raged and sulked, alternately, and I could have taken a blanket and gone to sleep on the living room couch for the rest of the night. I think that is what a woman of firm character would have done. I think that is what a woman who wanted that marriage to last would have done. But I did not do it. Instead, I said to myself that I did not know how the pump worked, I did not know where to turn it on. I said to myself that I was afraid of Hugo. I entertained the possibility that Hugo might be right, nothing would happen. But I wanted something to happen, I wanted Hugo to crash.

When I woke up, Hugo was gone and the pump was thumping as usual. Dotty was pounding on the door at the top of the basement stairs.

"You won't believe your eyes what's down here. I'm up to my knees in water. I just put my feet out of bed and up to my knees in water. What happened? You hear the pump go off?"

"No," I said.

"I don't know what could've gone wrong. I guess it could've got overworked. I had a couple of beers before I went to bed elst I would've known there was something wrong. I usually sleep light. But I was sleeping like the dead and I put my feet out of bed and Jesus, it's a good thing I didn't pull on the light switch at the same time, I would have been electrocuted. Everything's floating."

Nothing was floating and the water would not have come to any grown person's knees. It was about five inches deep in some places, only one or two in others, the floor being so uneven. It had soaked and stained the bottom of her chesterfield and chairs and got into the bottom drawers and cupboards

and warped the bottom of her piano. The floor tiles were loosened, the rugs soggy, the edges of her bedspread dripping, her floor heater ruined.

I got dressed and put on a pair of Hugo's boots and took a broom downstairs. I started sweeping the water towards the drain outside the door. Dotty made herself a cup of coffee in my kitchen and sat for a while on the top step watching me, going over the same monologue about having a couple of beers and sleeping more soundly than usual, not hearing the pump go off, not understanding why it should go off, if it had gone off, not knowing how she was going to explain to her mother who would certainly make it out to be her fault and charge her. We were in luck, I saw. (*We* were?) Dotty's expectation and thrifty relish of misfortune made her less likely than almost anyone else would have been to investigate just what had gone wrong. After the water level went down a bit, she went into her bedroom, put on some clothes and some boots which she had to drain first, got her broom and helped me.

"The things that don't happen to me, eh? I never get my fortune told. I've got these girl friends that are always getting their fortune told and I say, never mind me, there's one thing I know and I know it ain't good."

I went upstairs and phoned the University, trying to get Hugo. I told them it was an emergency and they found him in the library.

"It did flood."

"What?"

"It did flood. Dotty's place is under water."

"I turned the pump on."

"Like hell you did. This morning you turned it on."

"This morning there was a downpour and the pump couldn't handle it. That was after I turned it on."

"The pump couldn't handle it last night because the pump wasn't on last night and don't talk to me about any downpour."

"Well there was one. You were asleep."

"You have no idea what you've done, do you? You don't even stick around to look at it. I have to look. I have to cope. I have to listen to that poor woman."

"Plug your ears."

"Shut up, you filthy moral idiot."

"I'm sorry. I was kidding. I'm sorry."

"Sorry. You're bloody sorry. This is the mess you made and I told you you'd made and you're bloody sorry."

"I have to go to a seminar. I am sorry. I can't talk now, it's no good talking to you now, I don't know what you're trying to get me to say."

"I'm just trying to get you to *realize*."

"All right, I realize. Though I still think it happened this morning."

"You don't realize. You never realize."

"You dramatize."

"*I* dramatize!"

Our luck held. Dotty's mother was not so likely as Dotty to do without explanations and it was, after all, her floor tiles and wallboard that were ruined. But Dotty's mother was sick, the cold wet weather had undermined her too, and she was taken to hospital with pneumonia that very morning. Dotty went to live in her mother's house to look after the boarders. The basement had a disgusting, mouldy smell. We moved out too, a short time later. Just before Clea was born we took over a house in North Vancouver, belonging to some friends who had gone to England. The quarrel between us subsided in the excitement of moving; it was never really resolved. We did not move much from the positions we had taken on the phone. I said you don't realize, you never realize, and he said, what do you want me to say? Why do you make such a fuss over this, he asked reasonably. Anybody might wonder. Long after I was away from him, I wondered too. I could have turned on the pump, as I have said, taking responsibility for both of us, as a patient realistic woman, a really married woman, would have done, as I am sure Mary Frances would have done, did, many times, during the ten years she lasted. Or I could have told Dotty the truth, though she was not a very good choice to receive such information. I could have told somebody, if I thought it was that important, pushed Hugo out into the unpleasant world and let him taste trouble. But I didn't, I was not able fully to protect or expose him, only to flog him with blame, desperate sometimes, feeling I would claw his head open to pour my vision into it, my notion of what had to be understood. What presumptuousness, what cowardice, what bad faith. Unavoidable. "You have a problem of incompatibility," the marriage counsellor said to us a while later. We laughed till we cried in the dreary municipal hall of the building in North Vancouver where the marriage counselling was dispensed. This is our problem, we said to each other, what a relief to know it, incompatibility.

I did not read Hugo's story that night. I left it with Clea and she as it turned out did not read it either. I read it the next afternoon. I got home about two o'clock from the girls' private school where I have a part-time job teaching history. I made tea as I usually do and sat down in the kitchen to enjoy the hour before the boys, Gabriel's sons, get home from school. I saw the book still lying on top of the refrigerator and I took it down and read Hugo's story.

The story is about Dotty. Of course, she has been changed in some unimportant ways and the main incident concerning her has been invented, or grafted on from some other reality. But the lamp is there, and the pink chenille dressing gown. And something about Dotty that I had forgotten: when you were talking she would listen with her mouth slightly open, nodding, then she would chime in on the last word of your sentence with you. A touching and irritating habit. She was in such a hurry to agree, she hoped to understand. Hugo has remembered this, and when did Hugo ever talk to Dotty?

That doesn't matter. What matters is that this story of Hugo's is a very good story, as far as I can tell, and I think I can tell. I had to admit, I was moved by Hugo's story; I was, I am, glad of it, and I am not moved by tricks. Or if I am, they have to be good tricks. Lovely tricks, honest tricks. There is Dotty lifted out of life and held in light, suspended in the marvellous clear jelly that Hugo has spent all his life learning how to make. It is an act of magic, there is no getting around it; it is an act, you might say, of a special, unsparing, unsentimental love. A fine and lucky benevolence. Dotty was a lucky person, people who understand and value this act might say (not everybody, of course, does understand and value this act); she was lucky to live in that basement for a few months and eventually to have this done to her, though she doesn't know what has been done and wouldn't care for it, probably, if she did know. She has passed into Art. It doesn't happen to everybody.

Don't be offended. Ironical objections are a habit with me. I am half-ashamed of them. I respect what has been done. I respect the intention and the effort and the result. Accept my thanks.

I did think that I would write a letter to Hugo. All the time I was preparing dinner, and eating it, and talking to Gabriel and the children, I was thinking of a letter. I was thinking I would tell him how strange it was for me to realize that we shared, still shared, the same bank of memory, and that what was all scraps and oddments, useless baggage, for me, was ripe and usable, a paying investment, for him. Also I wanted to apologize, in some not-outright way, for not having believed he would be a writer. Acknowledgement, not apology; that was what I owed him. A few graceful, a few grateful, phrases.

At the same time, at dinner, looking at my husband Gabriel, I decided that he and Hugo are not really so unalike. Both of them have managed something. Both of them have decided what to do about everything they run across in this world, what attitude to take, how to ignore or use things. In their limited and precarious ways they both have authority. They are not *at the mercy*. Or think they are not. I can't blame them, for making whatever arrangements they can make.

After the boys had gone to bed and Gabriel and Clea had settled to watch television, I found a pen and got the paper in front of me, to write my letter, and my hand jumped. I began to write short jabbing sentences that I had never planned:

This is not enough, Hugo. You think it is, but it isn't. You are mistaken, Hugo.

That is not an argument to send through the mail.

I do blame them. I envy and despise.

Gabriel came into the kitchen before he went to bed, and saw me sitting with a pile of test papers and my marking pencils. He might have meant to talk to me, to ask me to have coffee, or a drink, with him, but he respected my unhappiness as he always does; he respected the pretence that I was not unhappy but preoccupied, burdened with these test papers; he left me alone to get over it.

Alice Munro (1931-) was born in Wingham, Ontario. Her first collection of stories, *Dance of the Happy Shades,* won the Governor General's Award for fiction. Her more recent works include a novel, *Lives of Girls and Women,* and a second collection of stories, *Something I've Been Meaning to Tell You.*

Ethel Wilson
The Window

The great big window must have been at least twenty-five feet wide and ten feet high. It was constructed in sections divided by segments of something that did not interfere with the view; in fact the eye by-passed these divisions and looked only at the entrancing scenes beyond. The window, together with a glass door at the western end, composed a bland shallow curve and formed the entire transparent north-west (but chiefly north) wall of Mr. Willy's living-room.

Upon his arrival from England Mr. Willy had surveyed the various prospects of living in the quickly growing city of Vancouver with the selective and discarding characteristics which had enabled him to make a fortune and retire all of a sudden from business and his country in his advanced middle age. He settled immediately upon the very house. It was a small old house overlooking the sea between Spanish Banks and English Bay. He knocked out the north wall and made the window. There was nothing particular to commend the house except that it faced immediately on the seashore and the view. Mr. Willy had left his wife and her three sisters to play bridge together until death should overtake them in England. He now paced from end to end of his living-room, that is to say from east to west, with his hands in his pockets, admiring the northern view. Sometimes he stood with his hands behind him looking through the great glass window, seeing the wrinkled or placid sea and the ships almost at his feet and beyond the sea the mountains, and seeing sometimes his emancipation. His emancipation drove him into a dream, and sea sky mountains swam before him, vanished, and he saw with immense release his wife in still another more repulsive hat. He did not know, nor would he have cared, that much discussion went on in her world, chiefly in the afternoons, and that he was there alleged to have deserted her. So he had, after providing well for her physical needs which were all the needs of which she was capable. Mrs. Willy went on saying

"...and he would come home my dear and never speak a word I can't tell you my dear how *frightful* it was night after night I might say for *years* I simply can't tell you..." No, she could not tell but she did, by day and night. Here he was at peace, seeing out of the window the crimped and wrinkled sea and the ships which passed and passed each other, the seabirds and the dream-inducing sky.

At the extreme left curve of the window an island appeared to slope into the sea. Behind this island and to the north, the mountains rose very high. In the summer time the mountains were soft, deceptive in their innocency, full of crags and crevasses and arêtes and danger. In the winter they lay magnificent, white and much higher, it seemed, than in the summer time. They tossed, static, in almost visible motion against the sky, inhabited only by eagles and — so a man had told Mr. Willy, but he didn't believe the man — by mountain sheep and some cougars, bears, wild cats and, certainly, on the lower slopes, deer, and now a ski camp far out of sight. Mr. Willy looked at the mountains and regretted his past youth and his present wealth. How could he endure to be old and rich and able only to look at these mountains which in his youth he had not known and did not climb. Nothing, now, no remnant of his youth would come and enable him to climb these mountains. This he found hard to believe, as old people do. He was shocked at the newly realized decline of his physical powers which had proved good enough on the whole for his years of success, and by the fact that now he had, at last, time and could not swim (heart), climb mountains (heart and legs), row a boat in a rough enticing sea (call that old age). These things have happened to other people, thought Mr. Willy, but not to us, now, who have been so young, and yet it will happen to those who now are young.

Immediately across the water were less spectacular mountains, pleasant slopes which in winter time were covered with invisible skiers. Up the dark mountain at night sprang the lights of the ski-lift, and ceased. The shores of these mountains were strung with lights, littered with lights, spangled with lights, necklaces, bracelets, constellations, far more beautiful as seen through this window across the dark water than if Mr. Willy had driven his car across the Lions' Gate Bridge and westwards among those constellations which would have disclosed only a shopping centre, people walking in the streets, street lights, innumerable cars and car lights like anywhere else and, up the slopes, people's houses. Then, looking back to the south across the dark water towards his own home and the great lighted window which he would not have been able to distinguish so far away, Mr. Willy would have seen lights again, a carpet of glitter thrown over the slopes of the city.

Fly from one shore to the other, fly and fly back again, fly to a continent or to an island, but you are no better off than if you stayed all day at your own window (and such a window), thought Mr. Willy pacing back and forth, then into the kitchen to put the kettle on for a cup of tea which he will drink beside the window, back for a glass of whisky, returning in time to see a cormorant flying level with the water, not an inch too high not an inch too low, flying out of sight. See the small ducks lying on the water, one behind the other, like beads on a string. In the mornings Mr. Willy drove into town to see his investment broker and perhaps to the bank or round the park. He lunched, but not at a club. He then drove home. On certain days a woman called Mrs. Ogden came in to "do" for him. This was his daily life, very simple, and a routine was formed whose pattern could at last be discerned by an interested observer outside the window.

One night Mr. Willy beheld a vast glow arise behind the mountains. The Arctic world was obviously on fire—but no, the glow was not fire glow, flame glow. The great invasion of colour that spread up and up the sky was not red, was not rose, but of a synthetic cyclamen colour. This cyclamen glow remained steady from mountain to zenith and caused Mr. Willy, who had never seen the Northern Lights, to believe that these were not Northern Lights but that something had occurred for which one must be prepared. After about an hour, flanges of green as of putrefaction, and a melodious yellow arose and spread. An hour later the Northern Lights faded, leaving Mr. Willy small and alone.

Sometimes as, sitting beside the window, he drank his tea, Mr. Willy thought that nevertheless it is given to few people to be as happy (or contented, he would say), as he was, at his age, too. In his life of decisions, men, pressures, more men, antagonisms, fusions, fissions and Mrs. Willy, in his life of hard success, that is, he had sometimes looked forward but so vaguely and rarely to a time when he would not only put this life down; he would leave it. Now he had left it and here he was by his window. As time went on, though, he had to make an effort to summon this happiness, for it seemed to elude him. Sometimes a thought or a shape (was it?), grey, like wood ash that falls in pieces when it is touched, seemed to be behind his chair, and this shape teased him and communicated to him that he had left humanity behind, that a man needs humanity and that if he ceases to be in touch with man and is not in touch with God, he does not matter. "You do not matter any more," said the spectre-like wood ash before it fell to pieces, "because you are no longer in touch with anyone and so you do not exist. You are in a vacuum and so you are nothing." Then Mr. Willy, at first uneasy, became satisfied again for a time after being made uneasy by the spectre. A storm would get up and the wind, howling well, would lash the window sometimes carrying the salt spray from a very high tide which it flung against the great panes of glass. That was a satisfaction to Mr. Willy and within him something stirred and rose and met the storm and effaced the spectre and other phantoms which were really vague regrets. But the worst that happened against the window was that from time to time a little bird, sometimes but not often a seabird, flung itself like a stone against the strong glass of the window and fell, killed by the passion of its flight. This grieved Mr. Willy, and he could not sit unmoved when the bird flew at the clear glass and was met by death. When this happened, he arose from his chair, opened the glass door at the far end of the window, descended three or four steps and sought in the grasses for the body of the bird. But the bird was dead, or it was dying, its small bones were smashed, its head was broken, its beak split, it was killed by the rapture of its flight. Only once Mr. Willy found the bird a little stunned and picked it up. He cupped the bird's body in his hands and carried it into the house.

Looking up through the grasses at the edge of the rough terrace that descended to the beach, a man watched him return into the house, carrying the bird. Still looking obliquely through the grasses the man watched Mr. Willy enter the room and vanish from view. Then Mr. Willy came again to the door, pushed it open, and released the bird which flew away, who knows where. He closed the door, locked it, and sat down on the chair facing east beside the window and began to read his newspaper. Looking over his paper he saw, to the east, the city of Vancouver deployed over rising ground with low roofs and high buildings and at the apex the tall Electric Building which at night shone like a broad shaft of golden light.

This time, as evening drew on, the man outside went away because he had other business.

Mr. Willy's investment broker was named Gerald Wardho. After a time he said to Mr. Willy in a friendly but respectful way, "Will you have lunch with me at the Club tomorrow?" and Mr. Willy said he would. Some time later Gerald Wardho said, "Would you like me to put you up at the Club?"

Mr. Willy considered a little the life which he had left and did not want to re-enter and also the fact that he had only last year resigned his membership in three clubs, so he said, "That's very good of you, Wardho, but I think not. I'm enjoying things as they are. It's a novelty, living in a vacuum...I like it, for a time anyway."

"Yes, but," said Gerald Wardho, "you'd be some time on the waiting list. It wouldn't hurt—"

"No," said Mr. Willy, "no."

Mr. Willy had, Wardho thought, a distinguished appearance or perhaps it was an affable accustomed air, and so he had. When Mrs. Wardho said to her husband, "Gerry, there's not an extra man in this town and I need a man for Saturday," Gerald Wardho said, "I know a man. There's Willy."

Mrs. Wardho said doubtfully, "Willy? Willy who? Who's Willy?"

Her husband said, "He's fine, he's okay, I'll ask Willy."

"How old is he?"

"About a hundred...but he's okay."

"Oh-h-h," said Mrs. Wardho, "isn't there anyone anywhere unattached young any more? Does he play bridge?"

"I'll invite him, I'll find out," said her husband, and Mr. Willy said he'd like to come to dinner.

"Do you care for a game of bridge, Mr. Willy?" asked Gerald Wardho.

"I'm afraid not," said Mr. Willy kindly but firmly. He played a good game of bridge but had no intention of entering servitude again just yet, losing his freedom, and being enrolled as what is called a fourth. Perhaps later; not yet. "If you're having bridge I'll come another time. Very kind of you, Wardho."

"No no no," said Gerald Wardho, "there'll only be maybe a table of bridge for anyone who wants to play. My wife would be disappointed."

"Well thank you very much. Black tie?"

"Yes. Black tie," said Gerald Wardho.

And so, whether he would or no, Mr. Willy found himself invited to the kind of evening parties to which he had been accustomed and which he had left behind, given by people younger and more animated than himself, and he realized that he was on his way to becoming old odd man out. There was a good deal of wood ash at these parties — that is, behind him the spectre arose, falling to pieces when he looked at it, and said "So this is what you came to find out on this coast, so far from home, is it, or is there something else. What else is there?" The spectre was not always present at these parties but sometimes awaited him at home and said these things.

One night Mr. Willy came home from an evening spent at Gerald Wardho's brother-in-law's house, a very fine house indeed. He had left lights burning and began to turn out the lights before he went upstairs. He went into the living-room and before turning out the last light gave a glance at the window which had in the course of the evening behaved in its accustomed manner. During the day the view through the window was clear or cloudy, according to the weather or the light or absence of light in the sky; but there it was — the view — never quite the same though, and that is owing to the character of oceans or of any water, great or small, and of light. Both water and light have so great an effect on land observed on any scene, rural urban or wilderness, that one begins to think that life, that a scene, is an illusion produced by influences such as water and light. At all events, by day the window held this fine view as in a frame, and the view was enhanced by ships at sea of all kinds, but never was the sea crowded, and by birds, clouds, and even aeroplanes in the sky — no people to spoil this fine view. But as evening approached, and moonless night, all the view (illusion again) vanished slowly. The window, which was not illusion, only the purveyor of illusion, did not vanish, but became a mirror which reflected against the blackness every detail of the shallow living-room. Through this clear reflection of the whole room, distant lights from across the water intruded, and so chains of light were thrown across the reflected mantelpiece, or a picture, or a human face, enhancing it. When Mr. Willy had left his house to dine at

Gerald Wardho's brother-in-law's house the view through the window was placidly clear, but when he returned at 11.30 the window was dark and the room was reflected from floor to ceiling against the blackness. Mr. Willy saw himself entering the room like a stranger, looking at first debonair with such a gleaming shirt front and then—as he approached himself—a little shabby, his hair perhaps. He advanced to the window and stood looking at himself with the room in all its detail behind him.

Mr. Willy was too often alone, and spent far too much time in that space which lies between the last page of the paper or the turning-off of the radio in surfeit, and sleep. Now as he stood at the end of the evening and the beginning of the night, looking at himself and the room behind him, he admitted that the arid feeling which he had so often experienced lately was probably what is called loneliness. And yet he did not want another woman in his life. It was a long time since he had seen a woman whom he wanted to take home or even to see again. Too much smiling. Men were all right, you talked to them about the market, the emergence of the Liberal Party, the impossibility of arriving anywhere with those people while that fellow was in office, nuclear war (instant hells opened deep in everyone's mind and closed again), South Africa where Mr. Willy was born, the Argentine where Mr. Wardho's brother-in-law had spent many years—and then everyone went home.

Mr. Willy, as the months passed by, was dismayed to find that he had entered an area of depression unknown before, like a tundra, and he was a little frightened of this tundra. Returning from the dinner party he did not at once turn out the single last light and go upstairs. He sat down on a chair beside the window and at last bowed his head upon his hands. As he sat there, bowed, his thoughts went very stiffly (for they had not had much exercise in that direction throughout his life), to some area that was not tundra but that area where there might be some meaning in creation which Mr. Willy supposed must be the place where some people seemed to find a God, and perhaps a personal God at that. Such theories, or ideas, or passions had never been of interest to him, and if he had thought of such theories, or ideas, or passions he would have dismissed them as invalid and having no bearing on life as it is lived, especially when one is too busy. He had formed the general opinion that people who hold such beliefs were either slaves to an inherited convention, hypocrites, or nit-wits. He regarded such people without interest, or at least he thought them negligible as he returned to the exacting life in hand. On the whole, though, he did not like them. It is not easy to say why Mr. Willy thought these people were hypocrites or nit-wits because some of them, not all, had a strong religious faith, and why he was not a hypocrite or nit-wit because he had not a strong religious faith; but there it was.

As he sat on and on looking down at the carpet with his head in his hands he did not think of these people, but he underwent a strong shock of recognition. He found himself looking this way and that way out of his aridity for some explanation or belief beyond the non-explanation and non-belief that had always been sufficient and had always been his, but in doing this he came up against a high and solid almost visible wall of concrete or granite, set up between him and a religious belief. This wall had, he thought, been built by him through the period of his long life, or perhaps he was congenitally unable to have a belief; in that case it was no fault of his and there was no religious belief possible to him. As he sat there he came to have the conviction that the absence of a belief which extended beyond the visible world had something to do with his malaise; yet the malaise might possibly be cirrhosis of the liver or a sort of delayed male menopause. He recognized calmly that death was as inevitable as tomorrow morning or even tonight and he had a rational absence of fear of death. Nevertheless his death (he knew) had begun, and had begun — what with his awareness of age and this malaise of his — to assume a certainty that it had not had before. His death did not trouble him as much as the increasing tastelessness of living in this tundra of mind into which a belief did not enter.

The man outside the window had crept up through the grasses and was now watching Mr. Willy from a point rather behind him. He was a morose man and strong. He had served two terms for robbery with violence. When he worked, he worked up the coast. Then he came to town and if he did not get into trouble it was through no fault of his own. Last summer he had lain there and, rolling over, had looked up through the grasses and into — only just into — the room where this guy was who seemed to live alone. He seemed to be a rich guy because he wore good clothes and hadn't he got this great big window and — later, he discovered — a high-price car. He had lain in the grasses and because his thoughts always turned that way, he tried to figger out how he could get in there. Money was the only thing that was any good to him and maybe the old guy didn't keep money or even carry it but he likely did. The man thought quite a bit about Mr. Willy and then went up the coast and when he came down again he remembered the great big window and one or two nights he went around and about the place and figgered how he'd work it. The doors was all locked, even that glass door. That was easy enough to break but he guessed he'd go in without warning when the old guy was there so's he'd have a better chance of getting something off of him as well. Anyways he wouldn't break in, not that night, but if nothing else offered he'd do it some time soon.

Suddenly Mr. Willy got up, turned the light out, and went upstairs to bed. That was Wednesday.

On Sunday he had his first small party. It seemed inevitable if only for politeness. Later he would have a dinner party if he still felt sociable and inclined. He invited the Wardhos and their in-laws and some other couples. A

Mrs. Lessways asked if she might bring her aunt and he said yes. Mrs. Wardho said might she bring her niece who was arriving on Saturday to meet her fiancé who was due next week from Hong Kong, and the Wardhos were going to give the two young people a quiet wedding, and Mr. Willy said "Please do." Another couple asked if they could bring another couple.

Mr. Willy, surveying his table, thought that Mrs. Ogden had done well. "Oh I'm so glad you think so," said Mrs. Ogden, pleased. People began to arrive. "Oh!" they exclaimed without fail, as they arrived, "what a beautiful view!" Mrs. Lessways' aunt who had blue hair fell delightedly into the room, turning this way and that way, acknowledging smiles and tripping to the window. "Oh," she cried turning to Mr. Willy in a fascinating manner, "isn't that just lovely! Edna says you're quite a recluse! I'm sure I don't blame you! Don't you think that's the loveliest view Edna . . . oh how d'you do how d'you do, isn't that the loveliest view? . . ." Having paid her tribute to the view she turned away from the window and did not see it again. The Aunt twirled a little bag covered with iridescent beads on her wrist. "Oh!" and "Oh!" she exclaimed, turning, "my dear how *lovely* to see you! I didn't even know you were back! Did you have a good time?" She reminded Mr. Willy uneasily of his wife. Mr. and Mrs. Wardho arrived accompanied by their niece Sylvia.

A golden girl, thought Mr. Willy taking her hand, but her young face surrounded by sunny curls was stern. She stood, looking from one to another, not speaking, for people spoke busily to each other and the young girl stood apart, smiling only when need be and wishing that she had not had to come to the party. She drifted to the window and seemed (and was) forgotten. She looked at the view as at something seen for the first and last time. She inscribed those notable hills on her mind because had she not arrived only yesterday? And in two days Ian would be here and she would not see them again.

A freighter very low laden emerged from behind a forest and moved slowly into the scene. So low it was that it lay like an elegant black line upon the water with great bulkheads below. Like an iceberg, thought Sylvia, and her mind moved along with the freighter bound for foreign parts. Someone spoke to her and she turned. "Oh thank you!" she said for her cup of tea.

Mr. Willy opened the glass door and took with him some of the men who had expressed a desire to see how far his property ran. "You see, just a few feet, no distance," he said.

After a while day receded and night came imperceptibly on. There was not any violence of reflected sunset tonight and mist settled down on the view with only distant dim lights aligning the north shore. Sylvia, stopping to respond to ones and twos, went to the back of the shallow room and sat down behind the out-jut of the fireplace where a wood fire was burning. Her mind was on two levels. One was all Ian and the week coming, and one — no thicker than a crust on the surface — was this party and all these people talking, the Aunt talking so busily that one might think there was a race on, or news to tell. Sylvia, sitting in the shadow of the corner and thinking about her approaching lover, lost herself in this reverie, and her lips, which had been so stern, opened slightly in a tender smile. Mr. Willy who was serving drinks from the dining-room where Mrs. Ogden had left things ready, came upon her and, struck by her beauty, saw a different sunny girl. She looked up at him. She took her drink from him with a soft and tender smile that was grateful and happy and was only partly for him. He left her, with a feeling of beauty seen.

Sylvia held her glass and looked towards the window. She saw, to her surprise, so quickly had black night come, that the end of the room which had been a view was now a large black mirror which reflected the glowing fire, the few lights, and the people unaware of the view, its departure, and its replacement by their own reflections behaving to each other like people at a party. Sylvia watched Mr. Willy who moved amongst them, taking a glass and bringing a glass. He was removed from the necessities, now, of conversation, and looked very sad. Why does he look sad, she wondered and was young enough to think, he shouldn't look sad, he is well off. She took time off to like Mr. Willy and to feel sorry that he seemed melancholy.

People began to look at their watches and say good-bye. The Aunt redoubled her vivacity. The women all thanked Mr. Willy for his tea party and for the beautiful beautiful view. They gave glances at the window but there was no view.

When all his guests had gone, Mr. Willy, who was an orderly man, began to collect glasses and take them into the kitchen. In an armchair lay the bag covered with iridescent beads belonging to the Aunt. Mr. Willy picked it up and put it on a table, seeing the blue hair of the Aunt. He would sit down and smoke for a while. But he found that when, lately, he sat down in the evening beside the window and fixed his eyes upon the golden shaft of the Electric Building, in spite of his intention of reading or smoking, his thoughts turned towards this subject of belief which now teased him, eluded, yet compelled him. He was brought up, every time, against the great stone wall, how high, how wide he knew, but not how thick. If he could, in some way, break through the wall which bounded the area of his aridity and his comprehension, he knew without question that there was a light (not darkness) beyond, and that this light could in some way come through to him and alleviate the sterility and lead him, lead him. If there were some way, even some conventional way — although he did not care for convention — he would take it in order to break the wall down and reach the light so that it would enter his life; but he did not know the way. So fixed did Mr. Willy become in contemplation that he looked as though he were graven in stone.

Throughout the darkened latter part of the tea party, the man outside had lain or crouched near the window. From the sands, earlier, he had seen Mr. Willy open the glass door and go outside, followed by two or three men. They looked down talking, and soon went inside again together. The door was closed. From anything the watcher knew, it was not likely that the old guy would turn and lock the door when he took the other guys in. He'd just close it, see.

As night came on the man watched the increased animation of the guests preparing for departure. Like departing birds they moved here and there in the room before taking flight. The man was impatient but patient because when five were left, then three, then no one but the old guy who lived in the house, he knew his time was near. (How gay and how meaningless the scene had been, of these well-dressed persons talking and talking, like some kind of a show where nothing happened — or so it might seem, on the stage of the lighted room from the pit of the dark shore.)

The watcher saw the old guy pick up glasses and take them away. Then he came back into the room and looked around. He took something out of a chair and put it on a table. He stood still for a bit, and then he found some kind of a paper and sat down in the chair facing eastward. But the paper drooped in his hand and then it dropped to the floor as the old guy bent his head and then he put his elbows on his knees and rested his head in his hands as if he was thinking, or had some kind of a headache.

The watcher, with a sort of joy and a feeling of confidence that the moment had come, moved strongly and quietly to the glass door. He turned the handle expertly, slid inside, and slowly closed the door so that no draught should warn his victim. He moved cat-like to the back of Mr. Willy's chair and quickly raised his arm. At the selfsame moment that he raised his arm with a short blunt weapon in his hand, he was aware of the swift movement of another person in the room. The man stopped still, his arm remained high, every fear was aroused. He turned instantly and saw a scene clearly enacted beside him in the dark mirror of the window. At the moment and shock of turning, he drew a sharp intake of breath and it was this that Mr. Willy heard and that caused him to look up and around and see in the dark mirror the intruder, the danger, and the victim who was himself. At that still moment, the telephone rang shrilly, twice as loud in that still moment, on a small table near him.

It was not the movement of that figure in the dark mirror, it was not the bell ringing close at hand and insistently. It was an irrational and stupid fear lest his action, reproduced visibly beside him in the mirror, was being faithfully registered in some impossible way that filled the intruder with fright. The telephone ringing shrilly, Mr. Willy now facing him, the play enacted beside him, and this irrational momentary fear caused him to turn and bound towards the door, to escape into the dark, banging the glass door with a clash behind him. When he got well away from the place he was angry — everything was always against him, he never had no luck, and if he hadn'ta lost his head it was a cinch he coulda done it easy.

"Damn you!" shouted Mr. Willy in a rage, with his hand on the telephone, "you might have broken it! Yes?" he said into the telephone, moderating the anger that possessed him and continuing within himself a conversation that said It was eighteen inches away, I was within a minute of it and I didn't know, it's no use telephoning the police but I'd better do that, it was just above me and I'd have died not knowing. "Yes? Yes?" he said impatiently, trembling a little.

"Oh," said a surprised voice, "it *is* Mr. Willy isn't it? Just for a minute it didn't sound like you Mr. Willy that was the *loveliest* party and what a lovely view and I'm sorry to be such a nuisance I kept on ringing and ringing because I thought you couldn't have gone out so soon" (tinkle tinkle) "and you couldn't have gone to bed so soon but I do believe I must have left my little bead bag it's not the *value* but. . ." Mr. Willy found himself shaking more violently now, not only with death averted and the rage of the slammed glass door but with the powerful thoughts that had usurped him and were interrupted by the dangerous moment which was now receding, and the tinkling voice on the telephone.

"I have it here. I'll bring it tomorrow," he said shortly. He hung up the telephone and at the other end the Aunt turned and exclaimed "Well if he isn't the rudest man I never was treated like that in my whole life d'you know what he. . ."

Mr. Willy was in a state of abstraction.

He went to the glass door and examined it. It was intact. He turned the key and drew the shutter down. Then he went back to the telephone in this state of abstraction. Death or near-death was still very close, though receding. It seemed to him at that moment that a crack had been coming in the great wall that shut him off from the light but perhaps he was wrong. He dialled the police, perfunctorily not urgently. He knew that before him lay the hardest work of his life — in his life but out of his country. He must in some way and very soon break the great wall that shut him off from whatever light there might be. Not for fear of death oh God not for fear of death but for fear of something else.

Ethel Wilson (1890-) was born in Port Elizabeth, South Africa, and moved to Vancouver while still a child. Her novels include *Hetty Dorval, Swamp Angel,* and *Love and Salt Water.* Her stories have been collected in *Mrs. Golightly and Other Stories.*

Henry Kreisel
The Broken Globe

Since it was Nick Solchuk who first told me about the opening in my field at the University of Alberta, I went up to see him as soon as I received word that I had been appointed. He lived in one of those old mansions in Pimlico that had once served as town houses for wealthy merchants and aristocrats, but now housed a less moneyed group of people—stenographers, students, and intellectuals of various kinds. He had studied at Cambridge and got his doctorate there and was now doing research at the Imperial College and rapidly establishing a reputation among the younger men for his work on problems which had to do with the curvature of the earth.

His room was on the third floor, and it was very cramped, but he refused to move because he could look out from his window and see the Thames and the steady flow of boats, and that gave him a sense of distance and of space also. Space, he said, was what he missed most in the crowded city. He referred to himself, nostalgically, as a prairie boy, and when he wanted to demonstrate what he meant by space he used to say that when a man stood and looked out across the open prairie, it was possible for him to believe that the earth was flat.

"So," he said, after I had told him my news, "you are going to teach French to prairie boys and girls. I congratulate you." Then he cocked his head to one side, and looked me over and said: "How are your ears?"

"My ears?" I said, "They're all right. Why?"

"Prepare yourself," he said. "Prairie voices trying to speak French—that will be a great experience for you. I speak from experience. I learned my French pronunciation in a little one-room school in a prairie village. From an extraordinary girl, mind you, but her mind ran to science. Joan McKenzie—that was her name. A wiry little thing, sharp-nosed, and she always wore brown dresses. She was particularly fascinated by earthquakes. 'In 1755 the city of Lisbon, Portugal, was devastated. 60,000 persons died;

the shock was felt in Southern France and North Africa; and inland waters of Great Britain and Scandinavia were agitated.' You see, I still remember that, and I can hear her voice too. Listen: 'In common with the entire solar system, the earth is moving through space at the rate of approximately 45,000 miles per hour, toward the constellation of Hercules. Think of that, boys and girls.' Well, I thought about it. It was a lot to think about. Maybe that's why I became a geophysicist. Her enthusiasm was infectious. I knew her at her peak. After a while she got tired and married a solid farmer and had eight children."

"But her French, I take it, was not so good," I said.

"No," he said. "Language gave no scope to her imagination. Mind you, I took French seriously enough. I was a very serious student. For a while I even practised French pronunciation at home. But I stopped it because it bothered my father. My mother begged me to stop. For the sake of peace."

"Your father's ears were offended," I said.

"Oh, no," Nick said, "not his ears. His soul. He was sure that I was learning French so I could run off and marry a French girl. . . . Don't laugh. It's true. When once my father believed something, it was very hard to shake him."

"But why should he have objected to your marrying a French girl anyway?"

"Because," said Nick, and pointed a stern finger at me, "because when he came to Canada he sailed from some French port, and he was robbed of all his money while he slept. He held all Frenchmen responsible. He never forgot and he never forgave. And, by God, he wasn't going to have that cursed language spoken in his house. He wasn't going to have any nonsense about science talked in his house either." Nick was silent for a moment, and then he said, speaking very quietly, "Curious man, my father. He had strange ideas, but a strange kind of imagination, too. I couldn't understand him when I was going to school or to the university. But then a year or two ago, I suddenly realized that the shape of the world he lived in had been forever fixed for him by some medieval priest in the small Ukrainian village where he was born and where he received an education of sorts when he was a boy. And I suddenly realized that he wasn't mad, but that he lived in the universe of the medieval church. The earth for him was the centre of the universe, and the centre was still. It didn't move. The sun rose in the East and it set in the West, and it moved perpetually around a still earth. God had made this earth especially for man, and man's function was to perpetuate himself and to worship God. My father never said all that in so many words, mind you, but that is what he believed. Everything else was heresy."

He fell silent.

"How extraordinary," I said.

He did not answer at once, and after a while he said, in a tone of voice which seemed to indicate that he did not want to pursue the matter further, "Well, when you are in the middle of the Canadian West, I'll be in Rome. I've been asked to give a paper to the International Congress of Geophysicists which meets there in October."

"So I heard," I said. "Wilcocks told me the other day. He said it was going to be a paper of some importance. In fact, he said it would create a stir."

"Did Wilcocks really say that?" he asked eagerly, his face reddening, and he seemed very pleased. We talked for a while longer, and then I rose to go.

He saw me to the door and was about to open it for me, but stopped suddenly, as if he were turning something over in his mind, and then said quickly, "Tell me—would you do something for me?"

"Of course," I said. "If I can."

He motioned me back to my chair and I sat down again. "When you are in Alberta," he said, "and if it is convenient for you, would you—would you go to see my father?"

"Why, yes," I stammered, "why, of course. I—I didn't realize he was still . . ."

"Oh, yes," he said, "he's still alive, still working. He lives on his farm, in a place called Three Bear Hills, about sixty or seventy miles out of Edmonton. He lives alone. My mother is dead. I have a sister who is married and lives in Calgary. There were only the two of us. My mother could have no more children. It was a source of great agony for them. My sister goes to see him sometimes, and then she sometimes writes to me. He never writes to me. We—we had—what shall I call it—differences. If you went to see him and told him that I had not gone to the devil, perhaps. . ." He broke off abruptly, clearly agitated, and walked over to his window and stood staring out, then said, "Perhaps you'd better not. I—I don't want to impose on you."

I protested that he was not imposing at all, and promised that I would write to him as soon as I had paid my visit.

I met him several times after that, but he never mentioned the matter again.

I sailed from England about the middle of August and arrived in Montreal a week later. The long journey west was one of the most memorable experiences I have ever had. There were moments of weariness and dullness. But the very monotony was impressive. There was a grandeur about it. It was monotony of a really monumental kind. There were moments when, exhausted by the sheer impact of the landscape, I thought back with longing to the tidy, highly cultivated countryside of England and of France, to the sight of men and women working in the fields, to the steady succession of villages and towns, and everywhere the consciousness of nature humanized. But I also began to understand why Nick Solchuk was always longing for more space and more air, especially when we moved into the prairies, and the land became flatter until there seemed nothing, neither hill nor tree nor bush, to disturb the vast unbroken flow of land until in the far distance a thin, blue line marked the point where the prairie merged into the sky. Yet over all there was a strange tranquillity, all motion seemed suspended, and only the sun moved steadily, imperturbably west, dropping finally over the rim of the horizon, a blazing red ball, but leaving a superb evening light lying over the land still.

I was reminded of the promise I had made, but when I arrived in Edmonton, the task of settling down absorbed my time and energy so completely that I did nothing about it. Then, about the middle of October, I saw a brief report in the newspaper about the geophysical congress which had opened in Rome on the previous day, and I was mindful of my promise again. Before I could safely bury it in the back of my mind again, I sat down and wrote a brief letter to Nick's father, asking him when I could come out to visit him. Two weeks passed without an answer, and I decided to go and see him on the next Saturday without further formalities.

The day broke clear and fine. A few white clouds were in the metallic autumn sky and the sun shone coldly down upon the earth, as if from a great distance. I drove south as far as Wetaskiwin and then turned east. The paved highway gave way to gravel and got steadily worse. I was beginning to wonder whether I was going right, when I rounded a bend and a grain elevator hove like a signpost into view. It was now about three o'clock and I had arrived in Three Bear Hills, but, as Nick had told me, there were neither bears nor hills here, but only prairie, and suddenly the beginning of an embryonic street with a few buildings on either side like a small island in a vast sea, and then all was prairie again.

I stopped in front of the small general store and went in to ask for directions. Three farmers were talking to the storekeeper, a bald, bespectacled little man who wore a long, dirty apron and stood leaning against his counter. They stopped talking and turned to look at me. I asked where the Solchuk farm was.

Slowly scrutinizing me, the storekeeper asked, "You just new here?"

"Yes," I said.

"From the old country, eh?"

"Yes."

"You selling something?"

"No, no," I said. "I—I teach at the University."

"That so?" He turned to the other men and said, "Only boy ever went to university from around here was Solchuk's boy, Nick. Real brainy young kid, Nick. Two of 'em never got on together. Too different. You know."

They nodded slowly.

"But that boy of his—he's a real big-shot scientist now. You know them addem bombs and them hydrergen bombs. He helps make 'em."

"No, no," I broke in quickly. "That's not what he does. He's a geophysicist."

"What's that?" asked one of the men.

But before I could answer, the little storekeeper asked excitedly, "You know Nick?"

"Yes," I said, "we're friends. I've come to see his father."

"And where's he now? Nick, I mean."

"Right now he is in Rome," I said. "But he lives in London, and does research there.

"Big-shot, eh," said one of the men laconically, but with a trace of admiration in his voice, too.

"He's a big scientist, though, like I said. Isn't that so?" the storekeeper broke in.

"He's going to be a very important scientist indeed," I said, a trifle solemnly.

"Like I said," he called out triumphantly. "That's showing 'em. A kid from Three Bear Hills, Alberta. More power to him!" His pride was unmistakable. "Tell me, mister," he went on, his voice dropping, "does he remember this place sometimes? Or don't he want to know us no more?"

"Oh, no," I said quickly. "He often talks of this place, and of Alberta, and of Canada. Some day he plans to return."

"That's right," he said with satisfaction. He drew himself up to full height, banged his fist on the table and said, "I'm proud of that boy. Maybe old Solchuk don't think so much of him, but you tell him old Mister Marshall is proud of him." He came from behind the counter and almost ceremoniously escorted me out to my car and showed me the way to Solchuk's farm.

I had about another five miles to drive, and the road, hardly more now than two black furrows cut into the prairie, was uneven and bumpy. The land was fenced on both sides of the road, and at last I came to a rough wooden gate hanging loosely on one hinge, and beyond it there was a cluster of small wooden buildings. The largest of these, the house itself, seemed at one time to have been ochre-coloured, but the paint had worn off and it now looked curiously mottled. A few chickens were wandering about, pecking at the ground, and from the back I could hear the grunting and squealing of pigs.

I walked up to the house and, just as I was about to knock, the door was suddenly opened, and a tall, massively built old man stood before me.

"My name is. . ." I began.

But he interrupted me. "You the man wrote to me?" His voice, though unpolished, had the same deep timbre as Nick's.

"That's right," I said.

"You a friend of Nick?"

54

"Yes."

He beckoned me in with a nod of his head. The door was low and I had to stoop a bit to get into the room. It was a large, low-ceilinged room. A smallish window let in a patch of light which lit up the middle of the room but did not spread into the corners, so that it seemed as if it were perpetually dusk. A table occupied the centre, and on the far side there was a large wood stove on which stood a softly hissing black kettle. In the corner facing the entrance there was an iron bedstead, and the bed was roughly made, with a patchwork quilt thrown carelessly on top.

The old man gestured me to one of the chairs which stood around the table.

"Sit."

I did as he told me, and he sat down opposite me and placed his large calloused hands before him on the table. He seemed to study me intently for a while, and I scrutinized him. His face was covered by a three-days' stubble, but in spite of that, and in spite of the fact that it was a face beaten by sun and wind, it was clear that he was Nick's father. For Nick had the same determined mouth, and the same high cheek bones and the same dark, penetrating eyes.

At last he spoke. "You friend of Nick."

I nodded my head.

"What he do now?" he asked sharply. "He still tampering with the earth?"

His voice rose as if he were delivering a challenge, and I drew back involuntarily. "Why—he's doing scientific research, yes," I told him. "He's..."

"What God has made," he said sternly, "no man should touch."

Before I could regain my composure, he went on, "He sent you. What for? What he want?"

"Nothing," I said, "nothing at all. He sent me to bring you greetings and to tell you he is well."

"And you come all the way from Edmonton to tell me?"

"Yes, of course."

A faint smile played about his mouth, and the features of his face softened. Then suddenly he rose from his chair and stood towering over me. "You are welcome in this house," he said.

The formality with which he spoke was quite extraordinary and seemed to call for an appropriate reply, but I could do little more than stammer a thank you, and he, assuming again a normal tone of voice, asked me if I cared to have coffee. When I assented he walked to the far end of the room and busied himself about the stove.

It was then that I noticed, just under the window, a rough little wooden table and on top of it a faded old globe made of cardboard, such as little children use in school. I was intrigued to see it there and went over to look at it more closely. The cheap metal mount was brown with rust, and when I lifted it and tried to turn the globe on its axis, I found that it would not rotate because part of it had been squashed and broken. I ran my hand over the deep dent, and suddenly the old man startled me.

"What you doing there?" Curiosity seemed mingled with suspicion in his voice and made me feel like a small child surprised by its mother in an unauthorized raid on the pantry. I set down the globe and turned. He was standing by the table with two big mugs of coffee in his hands.

"Coffee is hot," he said.

I went back to my chair and sat down, slightly embarrassed.

"Drink," he said, pushing one of the mugs over to me.

We both began to sip the coffee, and for some time neither of us said anything.

"That thing over there," he said at last, putting down his mug, "that thing you was looking at—he brought it home one day—he was a boy then—maybe thirteen-year-old Nick. The other day I found it up in the attic. I was going to throw it in the garbage. But I forgot. There it belongs. In the garbage. It is a false thing." His voice had now become venomous.

"False?" I said. "How is it false?"

He disregarded my question. "I remember," he went on, "he came home from school one day and we was all here in this room—all sitting around this table eating supper, his mother, his sister and me and Alex, too—the hired man like. And then suddenlike Nick pipes up, and he says, we learned in school today, he says, how the earth is round like a ball, he says, and how it moves around and around the sun and never stops, he says. They learning you rubbish in school, I say. But he says, no, Miss McKenzie never told him no lies. Then I say she does, I say, and a son of mine shouldn't believe it. Stop your ears! Let not Satan come in!" He raised an outspread hand and his voice thundered as if he were a prophet armed. "But he was always a stubborn boy—Nick. Like a mule. He never listened to reason. I believe it, he says. To me he says that—his father, just like that. I believe it, he says, because science has proved it and it is the truth. It is false, I cry, and you will not believe it. I believe it, he says. So then I hit him because he will not listen and will not obey. But he keeps shouting and shouting and shouting. 'She moves,' he shouts, 'she moves, she moves!'"

He stopped. His hands had balled themselves into fists, and the remembered fury sent the blood streaming into his face. He seemed now to have forgotten my presence and he went on speaking in a low murmuring voice, almost as if he were telling the story to himself.

"So the next day, or the day after, I go down to that school, and there is this little Miss McKenzie, so small and so thin that I could have crush her with my bare hands. What you teaching my boy Nick? I ask her. What false lies you stuffing in his head? What you telling him that the earth is round and that she moves for? Did Joshua tell the earth to stand still, or did he command the sun? So she says to me, I don't care what Joshua done, she says, I will tell him what science has discovered. With that woman I could get nowhere. So then I try to keep him away from school, and I lock him up in the house, but it was no good. He got out, and he run to the school like, and Miss McKenzie she sends me a letter to say she will sent up the inspectors if I try to keep him away from the school. And I could do nothing."

His sense of impotence was palpable. He sat sunk into himself as if he were still comtemplating ways of halting the scientific education of his son.

"Two, three weeks after," he went on, "he comes walking in this door with a large paper parcel in his hand. Now, he calls out to me, now I will prove it to you; I will prove that she moves. And he tears off the paper from the box and takes out this—this thing, and he puts it on the table here. Here, he cries, here is the earth, and look, she moves. And he gives that thing a little push and it twirls around like. I have to laugh. A toy, I say to him, you bring me a toy here, not bigger than my hand, and it is supposed to be the world, this little toy here, with the printed words on coloured paper, this little cardboard ball. This Miss McKenzie, I say to him, she's turning you crazy in that school. But look, he says, she moves. Now I have to stop my laughing. I'll soon show you she moves, I say, for he is beginning to get me mad again. And I go up to the table and I take the toy thing in my hands and I smash it down like this."

He raised his fists and let them crash down on the table as if he meant to splinter it.

"That'll learn you, I cry. I don't think he could believe I had done it, because he picks up the thing and he tries to turn it, but it don't turn no more. He stands there and the tears roll down his cheeks, and then, sudden-like, he takes the thing in both his hands and he throws it at me. And it would have hit me right in the face, for sure, if I did not put up my hand. Against your father, I cry, you will raise up your hand against your father. Asmodeus! I grab him by the arm, and I shake him and I beat him like he was the devil. And he makes me madder and madder because he don't cry or shout or anything. And I would have kill him there, for sure, if his mother didn't come in then and pull me away. His nose was bleeding, but he didn't notice. Only he looks at me and says, you can beat me and break my globe, but you can't stop her moving. That night my wife she make me swear by all that's holy that I wouldn't touch him no more. And from then on I never hit him again nor talk to him about this thing. He goes his way and I go mine."

He fell silent. Then after a moment he snapped suddenly, "You hold with that?"

"Hold with what?" I asked, taken aback.

"With that thing?" He pointed behind him at the little table and at the broken globe. His gnarled hands now tightly interlocked, he leaned forward in his chair and his dark, brooding eyes sought an answer from mine in the twilight of the room.

Alone with him there, I was almost afraid to answer firmly. Was it because I feared that I would hurt him too deeply if I did, or was I perhaps afraid that he would use violence on me as he had on Nick?

I cleared my throat. "Yes," I said then. "Yes, I believe that the earth is round and that she moves. That fact has been accepted now for a long time."

I expected him to round on me but he seemed suddenly to gave grown very tired, and in a low resigned voice he said, "Satan has taken over all the world." Then suddenly he roused himself and hit the table hard with his fist, and cried passionately, "But not me! Not me!"

It was unbearable. I felt that I must break the tension, and I said the first thing that came into my mind. "You can be proud of your son in spite of all that happened between you. He is a fine man, and the world honours him for his work."

He gave me a long look. "He should have stayed here," he said quietly. "When I die, there will be nobody to look after the land. Instead he has gone off to tamper with God's earth."

His fury was now all spent. We sat for a while in silence, and then I rose. Together we walked out of the house. When I was about to get into my car, he touched me lightly on the arm. I turned. His eyes surveyed the vast expanse of sky and land, stretching far into the distance, reddish clouds in the sky and blue shadows on the land. With a gesture of great dignity and power he lifted his arm and stood pointing into the distance, at the flat land and the low-hanging sky.

"Look," he said, very slowly and very quietly, "she is flat, and she stands still."

It was impossible not to feel a kind of admiration for the old man. There was something heroic about him. I held out my hand and he took it. He looked at me steadily, then averted his eyes and said, "Send greetings to my son."

I drove off quickly, but had to stop again in order to open the wooden gate. I looked back at the house, and saw him still standing there, still looking at his beloved land, a lonely, towering figure framed against the darkening evening sky.

Henry Kreisel (1922-) was born in Vienna, came to Canada in 1940, and now lives in Edmonton, where he is University Professor at the University of Alberta, having been previously head of the English department, Dean of Graduate Studies, and Vice-President. He has published two novels, *The Rich Man* and *The Betrayal*. His short stories have appeared in a number of journals.

Margaret Atwood
Polarities

Gentle and just pleasure
It is, being human, to have won from space
This unchill, habitable interior...

MARGARET AVISON, "New Year's Poem"

He hadn't seen her around for a week, which was unusual: he asked her if she'd been sick.

"No," she said, "working." She always spoke of what she had been doing with organizational, almost military briskness. She had a little packsack in which she carried around her books and notebooks. To Morrison, whose mind shambled from one thing to another, picking up, fingering, setting down, she was a small model of the kind of efficiency he ought to be displaying more of. Perhaps that was why he had never wanted to touch her: he liked women who were not necessarily more stupid but lazier than himself. Sloth aroused him: a girl's unwashed dishes were an invitation to laxity and indulgence.

She marched beside him along the corridor and down the stairs, her short clipped steps syncopating with his own lank strides. As they descended, the smell of straw, droppings, and formaldehyde grew stronger: a colony of overflow experimental mice from the science building lived in the cellar. When he saw that she was leaving the building too and probably going home, he offered her a lift.

"Only if you're heading that way anyway." Louise didn't accept favours, she had made that clear from the start. When he'd asked her if she wanted to take in a film with him she said, "Only if you let me pay for my own ticket." If she had been taller he might have found this threatening.

It was colder, the weak red sun almost down, the snow purpling and creaky. She jumped up and down beside the car till he got the plug-in engine heater untangled and the door opened, her head coming out of the enormous second-hand fur coat she wore like a gopher's out of its burrow. He had seen a lot of gophers on the drive across, many of them dead; one he had killed himself, an accident, it had dived practically under the car wheels. The car itself hadn't held up either: by the time he'd made it to the outskirts—though later he realized that this was in fact the city—a fender had come off and the ignition was failing. He'd had to junk it, and had decided stoically to do without a car until he found he couldn't.

He swung the car onto the driveway that led from the university. It bumped as though crossing a metal-plated bridge: the tires were angular from the cold, the motor sluggish. He should take the car for long drives more often; it was getting stale. Louise was talking more than she normally did; she was excited about something. Two of her students had been giving her a hassle, but she told them they didn't have to come to class. "It's your heads, not mine." She knew she had won, they would shape up, they would contribute. Morrison was not up on the theories of group dynamics. He liked the old way: you taught the subject and forgot about them as people. It disconcerted him when they slouched into his office and mumbled at him, fidgeting and self-conscious, about their fathers or their love lives. He didn't tell them about his father or his love life and he wished they would observe the same reticence, though they seemed to think they had to do it in order to get extensions on their term papers. At the beginning of the year one of his students had wanted the class to sit in a circle but luckily the rest of them preferred straight lines.

"It's right here," she said; he had been driving past it. He crunched the car to a halt, fender against the rockbank, snowbank. Here they did not take the snow away; they spread sand on it, layer by layer as it fell, confident there would be no thaw.

"It's finished; you can come in and see it," she said, suggesting but really demanding.

"What's finished?" he asked. He hadn't been paying attention.

"I told you. My place, my apartment, that's what I've been working on."

The house was one of the featureless two-storey boxes thrown up by the streetful in the years after the war when there was a housing boom and materials were scarce. It was stuccoed with a greyish gravel Morrison found spiritually depleting. There were a few older houses, but they were quickly being torn down by developers; soon the city would have no visible past at all. Everything else was highrises, or, worse, low barrack-shaped multiple housing units, cheaply tacked together. Sometimes the rows of flimsy buildings—snow on their roofs, rootless white faces peering suspiciously out through their windows, kids' toys scattered like trash on the walks—

reminded him of old photographs he had seen of mining camps. They were the houses of people who did not expect to be living in them for long.

Her apartment was in the basement. As they went around to the back and down the stairs, avoiding on the landing a newspaper spread with the overshoes and boots of the family living upstairs, Morrison remembered vividly and with a recurrence of panic his own search for a place, a roof, a container, his trudges from address to address, his tours of clammy, bin-like cellars hastily done up by the owners in vinyl tile and sheets of cheap panelling to take advantage of the student inflow and the housing squeeze. He'd known he would never survive a winter buried like that or closed in one of the glass-sided cardboard-carton apartment buildings. Were there no real ones, mellowed, interesting, possible? Finally he had come upon an available second storey; the house was pink gravel instead of grey, the filth was daunting and the landlady querulous, but he had taken it immediately just to be able to open a window and look out.

He had not known what to expect of Louise's room. He had never visualized her as living anywhere, even though he had collected her and dropped her off outside the house a number of times.

"I finished the bookshelves yesterday," she said, waving at a wall-length structure of varnished boards and cement blocks. "Sit down, I'll make you some cocoa." She went into the kitchen, still with her fur coat on, and Morrison sat down in the leatherette swivel armchair. He swivelled, surveying, comparing it with the kind of interior he thought of himself as inhabiting but never got around to assembling.

She had obviously put a lot of energy into it, but the result was less like a room than like several rooms, pieces of which had been cut out and pasted onto one another. He could not decide what created this effect: it was the same unity in diversity he had found in the motels on the way across, the modernish furniture, the conventional framed northern landscapes on the walls. But her table was ersatz Victorian and the prints Picasso. The bed was concealed behind a partly drawn dyed burlap curtain at the end of the room, but visible on the bedside rug were two light blue fuzzy slippers that startled, almost shocked him: they were so unlike her.

Louise brought the cocoa and sat down opposite him on the floor. They talked as usual about the city: they were both still looking for things to do, a quest based on their shared eastern assumption that cities ought to be entertaining. It was this rather than mutual attraction which led them to spend as much time together as they did; most of the others were married or had been here too long and had given up.

The films changed slowly; the one theatre, with its outdated popular comedies, they had sneered at. They had gone to the opera together when it had come, though: local chorus and imported stars—*Lucia*, it had been, and really quite well done, considering. At intermission Morrison had glanced around at the silent, chunky audience in the lobby, some of the women still in early-sixties pointed-toe spike heels, and murmured to Louise that it was like tourist brochures from Russia.

One Sunday before the snow came they had gone for an impromptu drive; at her suggestion they had aimed for the zoo twenty miles from the city. After they made it through the oil derricks there had been trees; not the right kind of trees—he had felt, as he had on the way across, that the land was keeping itself apart from him, not letting him in, there had to be more to it than this repetitive, non-committal drabness—but still trees; and the zoo once they reached it was spacious, the animals kept in enclosures large enough for them to run in and even hide in if they wanted to.

Louise had been there before—how, since she had no car, he didn't ask—and showed him around. "They choose animals that can survive the winter," she said. "It's open all year. They don't even know they're in a zoo." She pointed out the artificial mountain made of cement blocks for the mountain goats to climb on. Morrison didn't as a rule like any animal bigger and wilder than a cat, but these kept far enough away to be tolerable. That day she had told him a little about herself, a departure: mostly she talked about her work. She had travelled in Europe, she told him, and had spent a year studying in England.

"What are you doing here?" he had asked.

She shrugged. "They gave me money; nobody else would."

Essentially it was his reason too. It wasn't the draft; he was really over-age, though here they kept wanting to think he was a dodger, it made his presence more acceptable to them. The job market had been tight back in the States and also, when he tried later, in what they called here the East. But in all fairness it hadn't been only the money or the dismalness of the situation back home. He had wanted something else, some adventure; he felt he might learn something new. He had thought the city would be near the mountains. But, except for the raw gully through which the brownish river curved, it was flat.

"I don't want you to think of it as typical," Louise was saying. "You ought to see Montreal."

"Are *you* typical?" he asked.

She laughed. "None of us is typical, or do we all look alike to you? I'm not typical, I'm all-inclusive."

She let her fur coat fall down from around her shoulders as she said this, and he wondered again whether he was expected to make a move, to approach her. He ought to approach someone or something; he was beginning to feel isolated inside his clothes and skin. His students were out of the question. Besides, they were so thick, so impermeable; the girls, even the more slender ones, made him think of slabs of substance white and congealed, like lard. And the other single women on staff were much older than he was: in

them Louise's briskness had degenerated into a pinpointing, impaling quality.

There must be a place where he could meet someone, some nice loosely structured girl with ungroomed, seedy breasts, more thing than idea, slovenly and gratuitous. They existed, he was familiar with them from what he had begun to think of as his previous life, but he had not kept in touch with any of them. They had all been good at first but even the sloppiest had in time come to require something from him he thought he was not yet ready to give: they wanted him to be in love with them, an exertion of the mind too strenuous for him to undertake. His mind, he felt, was needed for other things, though he wasn't quite sure what they were. He was tasting, exploring: goals would come later.

Louise wasn't at all like them; she would never lend him her body for nothing, even temporarily, though she had the fur spread out around her now like a rug and had raised one corduroy-trousered knee, letting him see in profile the taut bulge of her somewhat muscular thigh. She probably went skiing and ice skating. He imagined his long body locked in that athletic, chilly grip, his eyes darkened by fur. Not yet, he thought, raising his half-full cocoa cup between them. I can do without, I don't need it yet.

It was the weekend and Morrison was painting his apartment as he habitually did on weekends; he had been at it off and on since he moved in.

"You'll have to have it painted, of course," he'd said smoothly to the landlady when inspecting it, but he had already shown himself too eager and she'd outfoxed him. "Well, I don't know, there's another boy wants it says he'll paint it himself. . ." So of course Morrison had to say he would too. This was the third coat.

Morrison's vision of wall-painting had been drawn from the paint ads — spot-free housewives gliding it on, one-handed and smiling — but it wasn't easy. The paint got on the floor, on the furniture, in his hair. Before he could even begin he had to cart out the accumulated discards of several generations of previous tenants: baby clothes, old snapshots, an inner tube, heaps of empty liquor bottles, and (intriguingly) a silk parachute. Messiness interested him only in women; he could not live surrounded by it himself.

One wall of the living-room had been pink, one green, one orange and one black. He was painting them white. The last tenants, a group of Nigerian students, had left weird magic-looking murals on the walls: a sort of swamp, in black on the orange wall, and an upright shape, in pink on the green wall, was either a very poorly done Christ Child or — could it be? — an erect penis with a halo around it. Morrison painted these two walls first, but it made him uneasy to know the pictures were still there underneath the paint. Sometimes as he rollered his way around the room he wondered what the Nigerians had thought the first time it hit forty below.

The landlady seemed to prefer foreign students, probably because they were afraid to complain: she had been aggrieved when Morrison had demanded a real lock for his door. The cellar was a warren of cubbyholes; he was not sure yet exactly who lived in them. Soon after he had moved in a Korean had appeared at his door, hopefully smiling. He wanted to talk about income tax.

"I'm sorry," Morrison had said, "some other time, okay? I have a lot of work to do." He was nice enough, no doubt, but Morrison didn't want to get involved with someone he didn't know; and he did have work to do. He felt picayune about it later when he discovered the Korean had a wife and child down in his cubbyhole with him; often in the fall they had put fishes out to dry, stringing them on the clotheslines where they twirled in the wind like plastic gas-station decorations.

He was doing the ceiling, craning his neck, with the latex oozing down the handle of the roller onto his arm, when the buzzer went. He almost hoped it was the Korean, he seldom saw anyone on the weekends. But it was Louise.

"Hi," he said, surprised.

"I just thought I'd drop in," she said. "I don't use the phone any more."

"I'm painting," he said, partly as an excuse: he wasn't sure he wanted her in the house. What would she demand from him?

"Can I help?" she asked, as though it was a big treat.

"Actually I was about to stop for the day," he lied. He knew she would be better at it than he was.

He made tea in the kitchen and she sat at the table and watched him.

"I came to talk about Blake," she said. "I have to do a paper." Unlike him she was only a Graduate Assistant, she was taking a course.

"What aspect?" Morrison asked, not interested. Blake wasn't his field. He didn't mind the earlier lyrics but the prophecies bored him and the extravagant letters in which Blake called his friends angels of light and vilified his enemies he found in bad taste.

"We each have to analyse one poem in *Songs of Experience*. I'm supposed to do the 'Nurse's Song.' But they don't know what's going on in that course, he doesn't know what's going on. I've been trying to get through to them but they're all doing the one-up thing, they don't know what's happening. They sit there and pull each other's papers apart, I mean, they don't know what poetry's supposed to be *for*." She wasn't drinking her tea.

"When's it due?" he asked, keeping on neutral ground.

"Next week. But I'm not going to do it, not the way *they* want. I'm giving them one of my own poems. That says it all. I mean, if they have to read one right there in the class they'll get what Blake was trying to do with *cadences*. I'm getting it xeroxed." She hesitated, less sure of herself. "Do you think that'll be all right?"

Morrison wondered what he would do if one of his own students tried such a ploy. He hadn't thought of Louise as the poetry-writing type. "Have you checked with the professor about it?"

"I try to talk to him," she said. "I try to *help* him but I can't get *through* to him. If they don't get what I mean, though, I'll know they're all phonies and I can just walk out." She was twisting her cup on the table top, her lips were trembling.

Morrison felt his loyalties were being divided; also he didn't want her to cry, that would involve dangerous comforting pats, even an arm around her shoulder. He tried to shut out an involuntary quick image of himself on top of her in the middle of the kitchen floor, getting white latex all over her fur. *Not today*, his mind commanded, pleaded.

As if in answer the reverberations of an organ boomed from beneath their feet, accompanied by a high quavering voice: *Rock of a-ges, cleft for me. . . Let me* HIIIDE *myself. . .* Louise took it as a signal. "I have to go," she said. She got up and went out as abruptly as she had come, thanking him perfunctorily for the tea she hadn't drunk.

The organ was Hammond, owned by the woman downstairs, a native. When her husband and nubile child were home she shouted at them. The rest of the time she ran the vacuum cleaner or picked out hymn tunes and old favourites on the organ with two fingers, singing to herself. The organ was to Morrison the most annoying. At first he tried to ignore it; then he put on opera records, attempting to drown it out. Finally he recorded it with his tape recorder. When the noise got too aggravating he would aim the speakers down the hot air register and run the tape through as loudly as possible. It gave him a sense of participation, of control.

He did this now, admiring the way the tape clashed with what she was currently playing: "Whispering Hope" with an overlay of "Annie Laurie";"The Last Rose of Summer" counterpointing "Come to the Church in the Wildwood." He was surprised at how much he was able to hate her: he had only seen her once, looking balefully out at him from between her hideous flowered drapes as he wallowed through the snow on his way to the garage. Her husband was supposed to keep the walk shovelled but didn't.

Louise came back the next day before Morrison was up. He was awake but he could tell by the chill in the room — his breath was visible — and by the faint smell of oil that something had gone wrong with the furnace again. It was less trouble to stay in bed, at least till the sun was well risen, than to get up and try the various ways of keeping warm.

When the buzzer went he pulled a blanket around himself and stumbled to the door.

"I thought of something," Louise said tragically. She was in the door before he could fend her off.

"I'm afraid it's cold in here," he said.

"I had to come over and tell you. I don't use the phone any more. You should have yours taken out."

She stomped the snow from her boots while Morrison retreated into the living-room. There was a thick crust of frost on the insides of the windows; he lit the gas fireplace. Louise stalked impatiently around the uncarpeted floor.

"You aren't listening," she said. He looked out obediently at her from his blanket. "What I thought of is this: *The city has no right to be here.* I mean, why is it? No city should be here, this far north; it isn't even on a lake or an important river, even. Why is it here?" She clasped her hands, gazing at him as though everything depended on his answer.

Morrison, standing on one bare foot, reflected that he had often since his arrival asked himself the same question. "It started as a trading post," he said, shivering.

"But it doesn't *look* like one. It doesn't look like anything, it doesn't *have* anything, it could be anywhere. Why is it *here?*" She implored; she even clutched a corner of his blanket.

Morrison shied away. "Look," he said, "do you mind if I get some clothes on?"

"Which room are they in?" she asked suspiciously.

"The bedroom," he said.

"That's all right. That room's all right," she said.

Contrary to his fear she made no attempt to follow him in. When he was dressed he returned to find her sitting on the floor with a piece of paper. "We have to complete the circle," she said. "We need the others."

"What others?" He decided she was overtired, she had been working too hard: she had deep red blotches around her eyes and the rest of her face was pale green.

"I'll draw you a diagram of it," she said. But instead she sat on the floor, jabbing at the paper with the pencil point. "I wanted to work out my own system," she said plaintively, "but they wouldn't let me." A tear slid down her cheek.

"Maybe you need to talk to someone," Morrison said, over-casually.

She raised her head. "But I'm talking to you. Oh," she said, reverting to her office voice, "you mean a shrink. I saw one earlier. He said I was very sane and a genius. He took a reading of my head: he said the patterns in my brain are the same as Julius Caesar's, only his were military and mine are creative." She started jabbing with the pencil again.

"I'll make you a peanut-butter sandwich," Morrison said, offering the only thing he himself wanted right then. It did not occur to him until months later when he was remembering it to ask himself how anyone could have known about the patterns in Julius Caesar's brain. At the moment he was wondering whether Louise might not in fact be a genius. He felt helpless because of his own inability to respond; she would think him as obtuse as the others, whoever they were.

At first she did not want him to go into the kitchen: she knew the telephone was in there. But he promised not to use it. When he came out again with a piece of bread on which he had spread with difficulty the gelid peanut butter, she was curled inside her coat in front of the fire, sleeping. He laid the bread gently beside her as if leaving crumbs on a stump for unseen animals. Then he changed his mind, retrieved it, took it on tiptoe into the kitchen and ate it himself. He turned on the oven, opened the oven door, wrapped himself in a blanket from the bedroom and read Marvell.

She slept for nearly three hours; he didn't hear her get up. She appeared in the kitchen doorway, looking much better, though a greyish-green pallor still lingered around her mouth and eyes.

"That was just what I needed," she said in her old brisk voice. "Now I must be off; I have lots of work to do." Morrison took his feet off the stove and saw her to the door.

"Don't fall," he called after her cheerfully as she went down the steep wooden steps, her feet hidden under the rim of her coat. The steps were icy, he didn't keep them cleared properly. His landlady was afraid someone would slip on them and sue her.

At the bottom Louise turned and waved at him. The air was thickening with ice fog, frozen water particles held in suspension; if you ran a horse in it, they'd told him, the ice pierced its lungs and it bled to death. But they hadn't told him that till after he'd trotted to the university in it one morning when the car wouldn't start and complained aloud in the coffee room about the sharp pains in his chest.

He watched her out of sight around the corner of the house. Then he went back to the living-room with a sense of recapturing lost territory. Her pencil and the paper she had used, covered with dots and slashing marks, an undeciphered code, were still by the fireplace. He started to crumple the paper up, but instead folded it carefully and put it on the mantelpiece where he kept his unanswered letters. After that he paced the apartment, conscious of his own work awaiting him but feeling as though he had nothing to do.

Half an hour later she was back again; he discovered he had been expecting her. Her face was mournful, all its lines led downwards as though tiny hands were pulling at the jawline skin.

"Oh, you have to come out," she said, pleading. "You have to come out, there's too much fog."

"Why don't you come in?" Morrison said. That would be easier to handle. Maybe she'd been into something, if that was all it was he could wait it out.

He'd been cautious himself; it was a small place and the local pusher was likely to be one of your own students; also he had no desire to reduce his mind to oatmeal mush.

"No," she said, "I can't go through this door any more. It's wrong. You have to come out." Her face became crafty, as though she was planning. "It will do you good to get out for a walk." she said reasonably.

She was right, he didn't get enough exercise. He pulled on his heavy boots and went to find his coat.

As they creaked and slid along the street Louise was pleased with herself, triumphant; she walked slightly ahead of him as if determined to keep the lead. The ice fog surrounded them, deadened their voices, it was crystalliz- ing like a growth of spruce needles on the telephone wires and the branches of the few trees which he could not help thinking of as stunted, though to the natives, he supposed, they must represent the normal size for trees. He took care not to breathe too deeply. A flock of grosbeaks whirred and shrilled up ahead, picking the last few red berries from a mountain ash.

"I'm glad it isn't sunny," Louise said. "The sun was burning out the cells in my brain, but I feel a lot better now."

Morrison glanced at the sky. The sun was up there somewhere, marked by a pale spot in the otherwise evenly spread grey. He checked an impulse to shield his eyes and thereby protect his brain cells: he realized it was an at- tempt to suppress the undesired knowledge that Louise was disturbed or, out with it, she was crazy.

"Living here isn't so bad," Louise said, skipping girlishly on the hard- packed snow. "You just have to have inner resources. I'm glad I have them; I think I have more than you, Morrison. I have more than most people. That's what I said to myself when I moved here."

"Where are we going?" Morrison asked when they had acomplished several blocks. She had taken him west, along a street he was not familiar with, or was it the fog?

"To find the others, of course," she said, glancing back at him contemp- tuously. "We have to complete the circle."

Morrison followed without protest; he was relieved there would soon be others.

She stopped in front of a medium-tall highrise. "They're inside," she said. Morrison went towards the front door, but she tugged at his arm.

"You can't go in that door," she said. "It's facing the wrong way. It's the wrong door."

"What's the matter with it?" Morrison asked. It might be the wrong door (and the longer he looked at it, plate glass and shining evilly, the more he saw what she meant), but it was the only one.

"It faces east," she said. "Don't you know? The city is polarized north and south; the river splits it in two; the poles are the gas plant and the power plant. Haven't you ever noticed the bridge joins them together? That's how the current gets across. We have to keep the poles in our brains lined up with the poles of the city, that's what Blake's poetry is all about. You can't break the current."

"Then how do we get in?" he said. She sat down in the snow; he was afraid again she was going to cry.

"Listen," he said hastily, "I'll go in the door sideways and bring them out; that way I won't break the current. You won't have to go through the door at all. Who are they?" he asked as an afterthought.

When he recognized the name he was elated: she wasn't insane after all, the people were real, she had a purpose and a plan. This was probably just an elaborate way of arranging to see her friends.

They were the Jamiesons. Dave was one of those with whom Morrison had exchanged pleasantries in the hallways but nothing further. His wife had a recent baby. Morrison found them in their Saturday shirts and jeans. He tried to explain what he wanted, which was difficult because he wasn't sure. Finally he said he needed help. Only Dave could come, the wife had to stay behind with the baby.

"I hardly know Louise, you know," Dave volunteered in the elevator.

"Neither do I," said Morrison.

Louise was waiting behind a short fir tree on the front lawn. She came out when she saw them. "Where's the baby?" she said. "We need the baby to complete the circle. We *need* the baby. Don't you know the country will split apart without it?" She stamped her foot at them angrily.

"We can come back for it," Morrison said, which pacified her. She said there were only two others they had to collect; she explained that they needed people from both sides of the river. Dave Jamieson suggested they take his car, but Louise was now off cars: they were as bad as telephones, they had no fixed directions. She wanted to walk. At last they persuaded her onto the bus, pointing that it ran north and south. She had to make certain first that it went over the right bridge, the one near the gas plant.

The other couple Louise had named lived in an apartment overlooking the river. She seemed to have picked them not because they were special friends but because from their living-room, which she had been in once, both the gas plant and the power plant were visible. The apartment door faced south; Louise entered the building with no hesitation.

Morrison was not overjoyed with Louise's choice. This couple was foremost among the local anti-Americans: he had to endure Paul's bitter sallies almost daily in the coffee room, while Leota at staff parties had a way of running on in his presence about the wicked Americans and then turning to him and saying, mouth but not eyes gushing, "Oh, but I forgot—*you're* an American." He had found the best defence was to agree. "You Yanks are coming up and taking all our jobs," Paul would say, and Morrison would nod affably. "That's right, you shouldn't let it happen. I wonder why you hired me?" Leota would start in about how the Americans were buying up all the industry, and Morrison would say, "Yes, it's a shame. Why are you selling it to us?" He saw their point, of course, but he wasn't Procter and Gamble. What did they want him to do? What were they doing themselves, come to think of it? But Paul had once broken down after too many beers in the Faculty Club and confided that Leota had been thin when he married her but now she was fat. Morrison held the memory of that confession as a kind of hostage.

He had to admit, though, that on this occasion Paul was much more efficient than he himself was capable of being. Paul saw at once what it had taken Morrison hours, perhaps weeks, to see: that something was wrong with Louise. Leota decoyed her into the kitchen with a glass of milk while Paul conspired single-handedly in the living-room.

"She's crazy as a coot. We've got to get her to the loony bin. We'll pretend to go along with her, this circle business, and when we get her downstairs we'll grab her and stuff her into my car. How long has this been going on?"

Morrison didn't like the sound of the words "grab" and "stuff." "She won't go in cars," he said.

""Hell," said Paul, "I'm not walking in this bloody weather. Besides, it's miles. We'll use force if necessary." He thrust a quick beer at each of them, and when he judged they ought to have finished they all went into the kitchen and Paul carefully told Louise that it was time to go.

"Where?" Louise asked. She scanned their faces: she could tell they were up to something. Morrison felt guilt seeping into his eyes and turned his head away.

"To get the baby," Paul said. "Then we can form the circle."

Louise looked at him strangely. "What baby? What circle?" she said testing him.

"*You* know," Paul said persuasively. After a moment she put down her glass of milk, still almost full, and said she was ready.

At the car she balked. "Not in there," she said, planting her feet. "I'm not going in there." When Paul gripped her arm and said, soothingly and menacingly, "Now be a good girl," she broke away from him and ran down the street, stumbling and sliding. Morrison didn't have the heart to run after her; already he felt like a traitor. He watched stupidly while Dave and Paul chased after her, catching her at last and half-carrying her back; they held her wriggling and kicking inside her fur coat as though it was a sack. Their breath came out in white spurts.

"Open the back door, Morrison," Paul said, sergeant-like, giving him a scornful glance as though he was good for nothing else. Morrison obeyed and Louise was thrust in, Dave holding her more or less by the scruff of the neck and Paul picking up her feet. She did not resist as much as Morrison expected. He got in on one side of her; Dave was on the other. Leota, who had waddled down belatedly, had reached the front seat; once they were in motion she turned around and made false, cheering-up noises at Louise.

"Where are they taking me?" Louise whispered to Morrison. "It's to the hospital, isn't it?" She was almost hopeful, perhaps she had been depending on them to do this. She snuggled close to Morrison, rubbing her thigh against his; he tried not to move away.

As they reached the outskirts she whispered to him again. "This is silly, Morrison. They're being silly, aren't they? When we get to the next stoplight, open the door on your side and we'll jump out and run away. We'll go to my place."

Morrison smiled wanly at her, but he was almost inclined to try it. Although he knew he couldn't do anything to help her and did not want the responsibility anyway, he also didn't want his mind burdened with whatever was going to happen to her next. He felt like someone appointed to a firing squad: it was not his choice, it was his duty, no one could blame him.

There was less ice fog now. The day was turning greyer, bluer: they were moving east, away from the sun. The mental clinic was outside the city, reached by a curving, expressionless driveway. The buildings were the same assemblage of disparate once-recent styles as those at the university: the same jarring fragmentation of space, the same dismal failure at modishness. Government institutions, Morrison thought; they were probably done by the same architect.

Louise was calm as they went to the reception entrance. Inside was a glass-fronted cubicle, decorated with rudimentary Christmas bells cut from red and green construction paper. Louise stood quietly, listening with an amused, tolerant smile, while Paul talked with the receptionist; but when a young intern appeared she said, "I must apologize for my friends; they've been drinking and they're trying to play a practical joke on me."

The intern frowned enquiringly. Paul blustered, relating Louise's theories of the circle and the poles. She denied everything and told the intern he should call the police; a joke was a joke but this was a misuse of public property.

Paul appealed to Morrison: he was her closest friend. "Well," Morrison hedged, "she *was* acting a little strange, but maybe not enough to. . ." His eyes trailed off to the imitation-modern interior, the corridors leading off into god knew where. Along one of the corridors a listless figure shuffled.

Louise was carrying it off so well, she was so cool, she had the intern almost convinced; but when she saw she was winning she lost her grip. Giving Paul a playful shove on the chest, she said, "We don't need *your* kind here. *You* won't get into the circle." She turned to the intern and said gravely, "Now I have to go. My work is very important, you know. I'm preventing the civil war."

After she had been registered, her few valuables taken from her and locked in the safe ("So they won't be stolen by the patients," the receptionist said), her house keys delivered to Morrison at her request, she disappeared down one of the corridors between two interns. She was not crying, nor did she say goodbye to any of them, though she gave Morrison a dignified, freezing nod. "I expect you to bring my notebook to me," she said with a pronounced English accent. "The black one, I need it. You'll find it on my desk. And I'll need some underwear. Leota can bring that."

Morrison, shamed and remorseful, promised he would visit.

When they got back to the city they dropped Dave Jamieson off at his place; then the three of them had pizza and cokes together. Paul and Leota were friendlier than usual: they wanted to find out more. They leaned across the table, questioning, avid, prying; they were enjoying it. This, he realized, was for them the kind of entertainment the city could best afford.

Afterwards they all went to Louise's cellar to gather up for her those shreds of her life she had asked them to allow her. Leota found the underwear (surprisingly frilly, most of it purple and black) after an indecently long search through Louise's bureau drawers; he and Paul tried to decide which of the black notebooks on her desk she would want. There were eight or nine of them; Paul opened a few and read excerpts at random, though Morrison protested weakly. References to the poles and the circle dated back several months; before he had known her, Morrison thought.

In her notebooks Louise had been working out her private system, in aphorisms and short poems which were thoroughly sane in themselves but which taken together were not; though, Morrison reflected, the only difference is that she's taken as real what the rest of us pretend is only metaphorical. Between the aphorisms were little sketches like wiring diagrams, quotations from the English poets, and long detailed analyses of her acquaintances at the university.

"Here's you, Morrison," Paul said with a relishing chuckle. "'Morrison is not a complete person. He needs to be completed, he refuses to admit his body is part of his mind. He can be in the circle possibly, but only if he will surrender his role as a fragment and show himself willing to merge with the greater whole.' Boy, she must've been nutty for months."

They were violating her, entering her privacy against her will. "Put that away," Morrison said, more sharply than he ordinarily dared speak to Paul. "We'll take the half-empty notebook, that must be the one she meant."

There were a dozen or so library books scattered around the room, some overdue: geology and history for the most part, and one volume of Blake. Leota volunteered to take them back.

As he was about to slip the catch on the inside lock Morrison glanced once more around the room. He could see now where it got its air of pastiche: the bookcase was a copy of the one in Paul's living-room, the prints and the table were almost identical with those at the Jamiesons'. Other details stirred dim images of objects half-noted in the various houses, at the various but nearly identical get-acquainted parties. Poor Louise had been trying to construct herself out of the other people she had met. Only from himself had she taken nothing; thinking of his chill interior, embryonic and blighted, he realized it had nothing for her to take.

He kept his promise and went to see her. His first visit was made with Paul and Leota, but he sensed their resentment: they seemed to think their countrywoman should be permitted to go mad without witness or participation by any Yanks. After that he drove out by himself in his own car.

On the second visit Louise initially seemed better. They met in a cramped cubicle furnished with two chairs; Louise sat on the edge of hers, her hands folded in her lap, her face polite, withholding. Her English accent was still noticeable, though hard r's surfaced in it from time to time. She was having a good rest, she said; the food was all right and she had met some nice people but she was eager to get back to her work; she worried about who was looking after her students.

"I guess I said some pretty crazy things to you," she smiled.

"Well. . ." Morrison stalled. He was pleased by this sign of her recovery.

"I had it all wrong. I thought I could put the country together by joining the two halves of the city into a circle, using the magnetic currents." She gave a small disparaging laugh, then dropped her voice. "What I hadn't figured out though was that the currents don't flow north and south, like the bridge. They flow east and west, like the river. And I didn't *need* to form the circle out of a bunch of incomplete segments. I didn't even need the baby. I mean," she said in a serious whisper, dropping her accent completely, "I *am* the circle. I have the poles within myself. What I have to do is keep myself in one piece, it *depends* on me."

At the desk he tried to find out what was officially wrong with Louise but they would not tell him anything; it wasn't the policy.

On his next visit she spoke to him almost the whole time in what to his untrained ear sounded like perfectly fluent French. Her mother was a French Protestant, she told him, her father an English Catholic. "*Je peux vous dire tout ceci,*" she said, "*parce que vous êtes américain.* You are outside it." To Morrison this explained a lot; but the next time she claimed to be the daughter of an Italian opera singer and a Nazi general. "Though I also have some Jewish blood," she added hastily. She was tense and kept standing up and sitting down again, crossing and recrossing her legs; she would not look at Morrison directly but addressed her staccato remarks to the centre of his chest.

After this Morrison stayed away for a couple of weeks. He did not think his visits were doing either of them any good, and he had papers to mark. He occupied himself once more with the painting of his apartment and the organ music of the woman downstairs; he shovelled his steps and put salt on them to melt the ice. His landlady, uneasy because she had still not supplied him with a lock, unexpectedly had him to tea, and the tacky plastic grotesqueries of her interior decoration fuelled his reveries for a while. The one good thing in her bogus ranch-style bungalow had been an egg, blown and painted in the Ukrainian manner, but she had dismissed it as ordinary, asking him to admire instead a cake of soap stuck with artificial flowers to resemble a flowerpot; she had got the idea out of a magazine. The Korean came up one evening to ask him about life insurance.

But the thought of Louise out there in the windswept institution grounds with nothing and no one she knew bothered him in twinges, like a mental neuralgia, goading him finally into the section of the city that passed for downtown: he would buy her a gift. He selected a small box of water-colour paints: she ought to have something to do. He was intending to mail it, but sooner than he expected he found himself again on the wide deserted entrance driveway.

They met once more in the visitors' cubicle. He was alarmed by the change in her: she had put on weight, her muscles had slackened, her breasts drooped. Instead of sitting rigidly as she had done before, she sprawled in the chair, legs apart, arms hanging; her hair was dull and practically uncombed. She was wearing a short skirt and purple stockings, in one of which there was a run. Trying not to stare at this run and at the white, loose thigh flesh it revealed, Morrison had the first unmistakably physical stirrings of response he had ever felt towards her.

"They have me on a different drug," she said. "The other one was having the wrong effect. I was allergic to it." She mentioned that someone had stolen her hairbrush, but when he offered to bring her another one she said it didn't matter. She had lost interest in the circle and her elaborate system and did not seem to want to talk much. What little she said was about the hospital itself: she was trying to help the doctors, they didn't know how to treat the patients but they wouldn't listen to her. Most of those inside were getting worse rather than better; many had to stay there because no one would take the responsibility of looking after them, even if they were drugged into manageability. They were poor, without relations; the hospital would not let them go away by themselves. She told him about one girl from further north who thought she was a caribou.

She hardly glanced at the water-colour paints, though she thanked him sluggishly. Her eyes, normally wide and vivacious, were puffed shut nearly to slits and her skin appeared to have darkened. She reminded him of someone, though it took him several minutes to remember: it was an Indian woman he had seen early in the fall while he was still searching for a place to have a civilized drink. She had been sitting outside a cheap hotel with her legs apart, taking off her clothes and chanting, "Come on boys, what're you waiting for, come on boys, what're you waiting for." Around her a group of self-conscious, sniggering men had gathered. Morrison, against his will and appalled at her, the men, and himself, had joined them. She was naked to the waist when the police got there.

When he rose to say goodbye Louise asked him, as if it was a matter of purely academic interest, whether he thought she would ever get out.

On his way out to the car it struck him that he loved her. The thought filled him like a goal, a destiny. He would rescue her somehow; he could pretend she was his cousin or sister; he would keep her hidden in the apartment with all his dangerous implements, razors, knives, nailfiles, locked away; he would feed her, give her the right drugs, comb her hair. At night she would be there in the sub-zero bedroom for him to sink into as into a swamp, warm and obliterating.

This picture at first elated, then horrified him. He saw that it was only the hopeless, mad Louise he wanted, the one devoid of any purpose or defence. A sane one, one that could judge him, he would never be able to handle. So this was his dream girl then, his ideal woman found at last: a disintegration, mind returning to its component shards of matter, a defeated formless creature on which he could inflict himself like shovel on earth, axe on forest, use without being used, know without being known. Louise's notebook entry, written when she had surely been saner than she was now, had been right about him. Yet in self-defence he reasoned that his desire for her was not altogether evil: it was in part a desire to be reunited with his own body, which he felt less and less that he actually occupied.

Oppressed by himself and by the building, the prison he had just left, he turned when he reached the main road away from the city instead of towards it: he would take his car for a run. He drove through the clenched landscape, recalling with pain the gentle drawl of the accommodating hills east and south, back in that settled land which was so far away it seemed not to exist. Here everything was tightlipped, ungiving, good for nothing and nothing.

He was halfway to the zoo before he knew he was going there. Louise had said it was kept open all winter.

Not much of the day was left when he reached the entrance: he would be driving back in darkness. He would have to make his visit short, he did not want to be caught inside when they locked the gates. He paid the admission fee to the scarfed and muffled figure in the booth, then took his car along the empty drives, glancing out the side window at the herds of llama, of yak, the enclosure of the Siberian tiger in which only the places a tiger might hide were to be seen.

At the buffalo field he stopped the car and got out. The buffalo were feeding near the wire fence, but at his approach they lifted their heads and glared at him, then snorted and rocked away from him through the haunch-deep snowdunes.

He plodded along the fence, not caring that the wind was up and chilling him through his heavy coat, the blood retreating from his toes. Thin sinister fingers of blown snow were creeping over the road; on the way back he would have to watch for drifts. He imagined the snow rising up, sweeping down in great curves, in waves over the city, each house a tiny centre of man-made warmth, fending it off. By the grace of the power plant and the gas plant: a bomb, a catastrophe to each and the houses would close like eyes. He thought of all the people he barely knew, how they would face it, chopping up their furniture for firewood until the cold overcame. How they were already facing it, the Koreans' fishes fluttering on the clothesline like defiant silver flags, the woman downstairs shrilling "Whispering Hope" off-key into the blizzard, Paul in the flimsy armour of his cheap nationalism, the landlady holding aloft torchlike her bar of soap stuck with artificial flowers. Poor Louise, he saw now what she had been trying desperately to do: the point of the circle, closed and self-sufficient, was not what it included but what it shut out. His own efforts to remain human, futile work and sterile love, what happened when it was all used up, what would he be left with? Black trees on a warm orange wall; and he had painted everything white. . . .

Dizzy with cold, he leaned against the fence, forehead on mittened hand. He was at the wolf pen. He remembered it from his trip with Louise. They had stood there for some time waiting for the wolves to come over to them but they had kept to the far side. Three of them were near the fence now, though, lying in its shelter. An old couple, a man and a woman in nearly identical grey coats, were standing near the wolves. He had not noticed them earlier, no cars had passed him, they must have walked from the parking lot. The eyes of the wolves were yellowish grey: they looked out through the bars at him, alert, neutral.

"Are they timber wolves?" Morrison said to the old woman. Opening his mouth to speak, he was filled with a sudden chill rush of air.

The woman turned to him slowly: her face was a haze of wrinkles from which her eyes stared up at him, blue, glacial.

"You from around here?" she asked.

"No," Morrison said. Her head swung away; she continued to look through the fence at the wolves, nose to the wind, short white fur ruffled up on edge.

Morrison followed her fixed gaze: something was being told, something that had nothing to do with him, the thing you could learn only after the rest was finished with and discarded. His body was numb; he swayed. In the corner of his eye the old woman swelled, wavered, then seemed to disappear, and the land opened before him. It swept away to the north and he thought he could see the mountains, white-covered, their crests glittering in the falling sun, then forest upon forest, after that the barren tundra and the blank solid rivers, and beyond, so far that the endless night had already descended, the frozen sea.

Margaret Atwood (1939-) was born in Ottawa and now lives on a farm near Alliston, Ontario. She has published several volumes of poetry, including *The Circle Game,* which won the Governor General's Award for 1966; three novels, most recently *Lady Oracle;* a critical overview of Canadian literature, *Survival;* and a collection of short stories, *Dancing Girls and Other Stories.*

Sinclair Ross
One's a Heifer

My uncle was laid up that winter with sciatica, so when the blizzard stopped and still two of the yearlings hadn't come home with the other cattle, Aunt Ellen said I'd better saddle Tim and start out looking for them.

"Then maybe I'll not be back tonight," I told her firmly. "Likely they've drifted as far as the sandhills. There's no use coming home without them."

I was thirteen, and had never been away like that all night before, but, busy with the breakfast, Aunt Ellen said yes, that sounded sensible enough, and while I ate, hunted up a dollar in silver for my meals.

"Most people wouldn't take it from a lad, but they're strangers up towards the hills. Bring it out independent-like, but don't insist too much. They're more likely to grudge you a feed of oats for Tim."

After breakfast I had to undress again, and put on two suits of underwear and two pairs of thick, home-knitted stockings. It was a clear, bitter morning. After the storm the drifts lay clean and unbroken to the horizon. Distant farm-buildings stood out distinct against the prairie as if the thin sharp atmosphere were a magnifying glass. As I started off Aunt Ellen peered cautiously out of the door a moment through a cloud of steam, and waved a red and white checkered dish-towel. I didn't wave back, but conscious of her uneasiness rode erect, as jaunty as the sheepskin and two suits of underwear would permit.

We took the road straight south about three miles. The calves, I reasoned, would have by this time found their way home if the blizzard hadn't carried them at least that far. Then we started catercornering across fields, riding over to straw-stacks where we could see cattle sheltering, calling at farmhouses to ask had they seen any strays. "Yearlings," I said each time politely. "Red with white spots and faces. The same almost except that one's a heifer and the other isn't."

Nobody had seen them. There was a crust on the snow not quite hard enough to carry Tim, and despite the cold his flanks and shoulders soon were steaming. He walked with his head down, and sometimes, taking my sympathy for granted, drew up a minute for breath.

My spirits, too, began to flag. The deadly cold and the flat white silent miles of prairie asserted themselves like a disapproving presence. The cattle round the straw-stacks stared when we rode up as if we were intruders. The fields stared, and the sky stared. People shivered in their doorways, and said they'd seen no strays.

At about one o'clock we stopped at a farmhouse for dinner. It was a single oat sheaf, half thistles, for Tim, and fried eggs and bread and tea for me. Crops had been poor that year, they apologized, and though they shook their heads when I brought out my money I saw the woman's eyes light greedily a second, as if her instincts of hospitality were struggling hard against some urgent need. We too, I said, had had poor crops lately. That was why it was so important that I find the calves.

We rested an hour, then went on again. "Yearlings," I kept on describing them. "Red with white spots and faces. The same except that one's a heifer and the other isn't."

Still no one had seen them, still it was cold, still Tim protested what a fool I was.

The country began to roll a little. A few miles ahead I could see the first low line of sandhills. "They'll be there for sure," I said aloud, more to encourage myself than Tim. "Keeping straight to the road it won't take a quarter as long to get home again."

But home now seemed a long way off. A thin white sheet of cloud spread across the sky, and though there had been no warmth in the sun the fields looked colder and bleaker without the glitter on the snow. Straw-stacks were fewer here, as if the land were poor, and every house we stopped at seemed more dilapidated than the one before.

A nagging wind rose as the afternoon wore on. Dogs yelped and bayed at us, and sometimes from the hills, like the signal of our approach, there was a thin, wavering howl of a coyote. I began to dread the miles home again almost as those still ahead. There were so many cattle straggling across the fields, so many yearlings just like ours. I saw them for sure a dozen times, and as often choked my disappointment down and clicked Tim on again.

And then at last I really saw them. It was nearly dusk, and along with fifteen or twenty other cattle they were making their way towards some buildings that lay huddled at the foot of the sandhills. They passed in single file less than fifty yards away, but when I pricked Tim forward to turn them back he floundered in a snowed-in water-cut. By the time we were out they were a little distance ahead, and on account of the drifts it was impossible to put on a spurt of speed and pass them. All we could do was take our place at the end of the file, and proceed at their pace towards the buildings.

It was about half a mile. As we drew near I debated with Tim whether we should ask to spend the night or start off right away for home. We were hungry and tired, but it was a poor, shiftless-looking place. The yard was littered with old wagons and machinery; the house was scarcely distinguishable from the stables. Darkness was beginning to close in, but there was no light in the windows.

Then as we crossed the yard we heard a shout, "Stay where you are," and a man came running towards us from the stable. He was tall and ungainly, and, instead of the short sheepskin that most farmers wear, had on a long black overcoat nearly to his feet. He seized Tim's bridle when he reached us, and glared for a minute as if he were going to pull me out of the saddle. "I told you to stay out," he said in a harsh, excited voice. "You heard me, didn't you? What do you want coming round here anyway?"

I steeled myself and said, "Our two calves."

The muscles of his face were drawn together threateningly, but close to him like this and looking straight into his eyes I felt that for all their fierce look there was something about them wavering and uneasy. "The two red ones with the white faces," I continued. "They've just gone into the shed over there with yours. If you'll give me a hand getting them out again I'll start for home now right away."

He peered at me a minute, let go the bridle, then clutched it again. "They're all mine," he countered. "I was over by the gate. I watched them coming in."

His voice was harsh and thick. The strange wavering look in his eyes steadied itself for a minute to a dare. I forced myself to meet it and insisted, "I saw them back a piece in the field. They're ours all right. Let me go over a minute and I'll show you."

With a crafty tilt of his head he leered, "You didn't see any calves. And now, if you know what's good for you, you'll be on your way."

"You're trying to steal them," I flared rashly. "I'll go home and get my uncle and the police after you — then you'll see whether they're our calves or not."

My threat seemed to impress him a little. With a shifty glance in the direction of the stable he said, "All right, come along and look them over. Then maybe you'll be satisfied." But all the way across the yard he kept his hand on Tim's bridle, and at the shed made me wait a few minutes while he went inside.

The cattle shed was a lean-to on the horse stable. It was plain enough: he was hiding the calves before letting me inside to look around. While waiting for him, however, I had time to reflect that he was a lot bigger and stronger than I was, and that it might be prudent just to keep my eyes open, and not give him too much insolence.

He reappeared carrying a smoky lantern. "All right," he said pleasantly enough, "Come in and look around. Will your horse stand, or do you want to tie him?"

We put Tim in an empty stall in the horse stable, then went through a narrow doorway with a bar across it to the cattle shed. Just as I expected, our calves weren't there. There were two red ones with white markings that he tried to make me believe were the ones I had seen, but, positive I hadn't been mistaken, I shook my head and glanced at the doorway we had just come through. It was narrow, but not too narrow. He read my expression and said, "You think they're in there. Come on, then, and look around."

The horse stable consisted of two rows of open stalls with a passage down the centre like an aisle. At the far end were two box-stalls, one with a sick colt in it, the other closed. They were both boarded up to the ceiling, so that you could see inside them only through the doors. Again he read my expression, and with a nod towards the closed one said, "It's just a kind of harness room now. Up till a year ago I kept a stallion."

But he spoke furtively, and seemed anxious to get me away from that end of the stable. His smoky lantern threw great swaying shadows over us; and the deep clefts and triangles of shadow on his face sent a little chill through me, and made me think what a dark and evil face it was.

I was afraid, but not too afraid. "If it's just a harness room," I said recklessly, "why not let me see inside? Then I'll be satisfied and believe you."

He wheeled at my question, and sidled over swiftly to the stall. He stood in front of the door, crouched down a little, the lantern in front of him like a shield. There was a sudden stillness through the stable as we faced each other. Behind the light from his lantern the darkness hovered vast and sinister. It seemed to hold its breath, to watch and listen. I felt a clutch of fear now at my throat, but I didn't move. My eyes were fixed on him so intently that he seemed to lose substance, to loom up close a moment, then recede. At last he disappeared completely, and there was only the lantern like a hard hypnotic eye.

It held me. It held me rooted, against my will. I wanted to run from the stable, but I wanted even more to see inside the stall. Wanting to see and yet afraid of seeing. So afraid that it was a relief when at last he gave a shame-faced laugh and said, "There's a hole in the floor — that's why I keep the door closed. If you didn't know, you might step into it — twist your foot. That's what happened to one of my horses a while ago."

I nodded as if I believed him, and went back tractably to Tim. But regaining control of myself as I tied the saddle girths, beginning to feel that my fear had been unwarranted, I looked up and said, "It's ten miles home, and we've been riding hard all day. If we could stay a while — have something to eat, and then get started — "

The wavering light came into his eyes again. He held the lantern up to see me better, such a long, intent scrutiny that it seemed he must discover my designs. But he gave a nod finally, as if reassured, brought oats and hay for Tim, and suggested companionably, "After supper we can have a game of checkers."

Then, as if I were a grown-up, he put out his hand and said, "My name is Arthur Vickers."

Inside the house, rid of his hat and coat, he looked less forbidding. He had a white nervous face, thin lips, a large straight nose, and deep uneasy eyes. When the lamp was lit I fancied I could still see the wavering expression in them, and decided it was what you called a guilty look.

"You won't think much of it," he said apologetically, following my glance around the room. "I ought to be getting things cleaned up again. Come over to the stove. Supper won't take long."

It was a large, low-ceilinged room that for the first moment or two struck me more like a shed or granary than a house. The table in the centre was littered with tools and harness. On a rusty cook-stove were two big steaming pots of bran. Next to the stove stood a grindstone, then a white iron bed covered with coats and horse blankets. At the end opposite the bed, weasel and coyote skins were drying. There were guns and traps on the wall, a horse collar, a pair of rubber boots. The floor was bare and grimy. Ashes were littered around the stove. In a corner squatted a live owl with a broken wing.

He walked back and forth a few times looking helplessly at the disorder, then cleared off the table and lifted the pots of bran to the back of the stove. "I've been mending harness," he explained. "You get careless, living alone like this. It takes a woman anyway."

My presence, apparently, was making him take stock of the room. He picked up a broom and swept for a minute, made an ineffective attempt to straighten the blankets on the bed, brought another lamp out of a cupboard and lit it. There was an ungainly haste to all his movements. He started unbuckling my sheepskin for me, then turned away suddenly to take off his own coat. "Now we'll have supper," he said with an effort at self-possession. "Coffee and beans is all I can give you — maybe a little molasses."

I replied diplomatically that that sounded pretty good. It didn't seem right, accepting hospitality this way from a man trying to steal your calves, but theft, I reflected, surely justified deceit. I held my hands out to the warmth and asked if I could help.

There was a kettle of plain navy beans already cooked. He dipped out enough for our supper into a frying pan, and on top laid rashers of fat salt pork. While I watched that they didn't burn he rinsed off a few dishes. Then he set out sugar and canned milk, butter, molasses, and dark heavy biscuits that he had baked himself the day before. He kept glancing at me so apologetically all the while that I leaned over and sniffed the beans, and said at home I ate a lot of them.

"It takes a woman," he repeated as we sat down to the table. "I don't often have anyone here to eat with me. If I'd known, I'd have cleaned things up a little."

I was too intent on my plateful of beans to answer. All through the meal he sat watching me, but made no further attempts at conversation. Hungry as I was, I noticed that the wavering, uneasy look was still in his eyes. A guilty look, I told myself again, and wondered what I was going to do to get the calves away. I finished my coffee and he continued:

"It's worse even than this in the summer. No time for meals—and the heat and flies. Last summer I had a girl cooking for a few weeks, but it didn't last. Just a cow she was—just a big stupid cow—and she wanted to stay on. There's a family of them back in the hills. I had to send her home."

I wondered should I suggest starting now, or ask to spend the night. Maybe when he's asleep, I thought, I can slip out of the house and get away with the calves. He went on, "You don't know how bad it is sometimes. Weeks on end and no one to talk to. You're not yourself—you're not sure what you're going to say or do."

I remembered hearing my uncle talk about a man who had gone crazy living alone. And this fellow Vickers had queer eyes all right. and there was the live owl over in the corner, and the grindstone standing right beside the bed. "Maybe I'd better go now," I decided aloud. "Tim'll be rested, and it's ten miles home."

But he said no, it was colder now, with the wind getting stronger, and seemed so kindly and concerned that I half forgot my fears. "Likely he's just starting to go crazy," I told myself, "and it's only by staying that I'll have a chance to get the calves away."

When the table was cleared and the dishes washed he said he would go out and bed down the stable for the night. I picked up my sheepskin to go with him, but he told me sharply to stay inside. Just for a minute he looked crafty and forbidding as when I first rode up on Tim, and to allay his suspicions I nodded compliantly and put my sheepskin down again. It was better like that anyway, I decided. In a few minutes I could follow him, and perhaps, taking advantage of the shadows and his smoky lantern, make my way to the box-stall unobserved.

But when I reached the stable he had closed the door after him and hooked it from the inside. I walked round a while, tried to slip in by way of the cattle shed, and then had to go back to the house. I went with a vague feeling of relief again. There was still time, I told myself, and it would be safer anyway when he was sleeping.

So that it would be easier to keep from falling asleep myself I planned to suggest coffee again just before we went to bed. I knew that the guest didn't ordinarily suggest such things, but it was no time to remember manners when there was someone trying to steal your calves.

When he came in from the stable we played checkers. I was no match for him, but to encourage me he repeatedly let me win. "It's a long time now since I've had a chance to play," he kept on saying, trying to convince me that his short-sighted moves weren't intentional. "Sometimes I used to ask her to play, but I had to tell her every move to make. If she didn't win she'd upset the board and go off and sulk."

"My aunt is a little like that too," I said. "She cheats sometimes when we're playing cribbage — and, when I catch her, says her eyes aren't good."

"Women talk too much ever to make good checker players. It takes concentration. This one, though, couldn't even talk like anybody else."

After my long day in the cold I was starting to yawn already. He noticed it, and spoke in a rapid, earnest voice, as if afraid I might lose interest soon and want to go to bed. It was important for me too to stay awake, so I crowned a king and said, "Why don't you get someone, then, to stay with you?"

"Too many of them want to do that." His face darkened a little, almost as if warning me. "Too many of the kind you'll never get rid of again. She did, last summer when she was here. I had to put her out."

There was silence for a minute, his eyes flashing, and wanting to placate him I suggested, "She liked you, maybe."

He laughed a moment, harshly. "She liked me all right. Just two weeks ago she came back — walked over with an old suitcase and said she was going to stay. It was cold at home, and she had to work too hard, and she didn't mind even if I couldn't pay her wages."

I was getting sleepier. To keep awake I sat on the edge of the chair where it was uncomfortable and said, "Hadn't you asked her to come?"

His eyes narrowed. "I'd had trouble enough getting rid of her the first time. There were six of them at home, and she said her father thought it time that someone married her."

"Then she must be a funny one," I said. "Everybody knows that the man's supposed to ask the girl."

My remark seemed to please him. "I told you, didn't I?" he said, straightening a little, jumping two of my men. "She was so stupid that at checkers she'd forget whether she was black or red."

We stopped playing now. I glanced at the owl in the corner and the ashes littered on the floor, and thought that keeping her would maybe have been a good idea after all. He read it in my face and said, "I used to think that too sometimes. I used to look at her and think nobody knew now anyway and that she'd maybe do. You need a woman on a farm all right. And night after night she'd be sitting there where you are — right there where you are, looking at me, not even trying to play—"

The fire was low, and we could hear the wind. "But then I'd go up in the hills, away from her for a while, and start thinking back the way things used to be, and it wasn't right even for the sake of your meals ready and your house kept clean. When she came back I tried to tell her that, but all the family are the same, and I realized it wasn't any use. There's nothing you can do when you're up against that sort of thing. The mother talks just like a child of ten. When she sees you coming she runs and hides. There are six of them, and it's come out in every one."

It was getting cold, but I couldn't bring myself to go over to the stove. There was the same stillness now as when he was standing at the box-stall door. And I felt the same illogical fear, the same powerlessness to move. It was the way his voice had sunk, the glassy, cold look in his eyes. The rest of his face disappeared; all I could see were his eyes. And they filled me with a vague and overpowering dread. My own voice a whisper, I asked, "And when you wouldn't marry her — what happened then?"

He remained motionless a moment, as if answering silently; then with an unexpected laugh like a breaking dish said, "Why, nothing happened. I just told her she couldn't stay. I went to town for a few days — and when I came back she was gone."

"Has she been back to bother you since?" I asked.

He made a little silo of checkers. "No — she took her suitcase with her."

To remind him that the fire was going down I went over to the stove and stood warming myself. He raked the coals with the lifter and put in poplar, two split pieces for a base and a thick round log on top. I yawned again. He said maybe I'd like to go to bed now, and I shivered and asked him could I have a drink of coffee first. While it boiled he stood stirring the two big pots of bran. The trouble with coffee, I realized, was that it would keep him from getting sleepy too.

I undressed finally and got into bed, but he blew out only one of the lamps, and sat on playing checkers with himself. I dozed a while, then sat up with a start, afraid it was morning already and that I'd lost my chance to get the calves away. He came over and looked at me a minute, then gently pushed my shoulders back on the pillow. "Why don't you come to bed too?" I asked, and he said, "Later I will — I don't feel sleepy yet."

It was like that all night. I kept dozing on and off, wakening in a fright each time to find him still there sitting at his checker board. He would raise his head sharply when I stirred, then tiptoe over to the bed and stand close to me listening till satisfied again I was asleep. The owl kept wakening too. It was down in the corner still where the lamplight scarcely reached, and I could see its eyes go on and off like yellow bulbs. The wind whistled drearily around the house. The blankets smelled like an old granary. He suspected what I was planning to do, evidently, and was staying awake to make sure I didn't get outside.

Each time I dozed I dreamed I was on Tim again. The calves were in sight, but far ahead of us, and with the drifts so deep we couldn't overtake them. Then instead of Tim it was the grindstone I was straddling, and that was the reason, not the drifts, that we weren't making better progress.

I wondered what would happen to the calves if I didn't get away with them. My uncle had sciatica, and it would be at least a day before I could be home and back again with some of the neighbours. By then Vickers might have butchered the calves, or driven them up to a hiding place in the hills where we'd never find them. There was the possibility, too, that Aunt Ellen and the neighbours wouldn't believe me. I dozed and woke — dozed and woke — always he was sitting at the checker board. I could hear the dry tinny ticking of an alarm clock, but from where I was lying couldn't see it. He seemed to be listening to it too. The wind would sometimes creak the house, and then he would give a start and sit rigid a moment with his eyes fixed on the window. It was always the window, as if there was nothing he was afraid of that could reach him by the door.

Most of the time he played checkers with himself, moving his lips, muttering words I couldn't hear, but once I woke to find him staring fixedly across the table as if he had a partner sitting there. His hands were clenched in front of him, there was a sharp, metallic glitter in his eyes. I lay transfixed, unbreathing. His eyes as I watched seemed to dilate, to brighten, to harden like a bird's. For a long time he sat contracted, motionless, as if gathering himself to strike, then furtively he slid his hand an inch or two along the table towards some checkers that were piled beside the board. It was as if he were reaching for a weapon, as if his invisible partner were an enemy. He clutched the checkers, slipped slowly from his chair and straightened. His movements were sure, stealthy, silent like a cat's. His face had taken on a desperate, contorted look. As he raised his hand the tension was unbearable.

It was a long time — a long time watching him the way you watch a finger tightening slowly on the trigger of a gun — and then suddenly wrenching himself to action he hurled the checkers with such vicious fury that they struck the wall and clattered back across the room.

And everything was quiet again. I started a little, mumbled to myself as if half-awakened, lay quite still. But he seemed to have forgotten me, and after standing limp and dazed a minute got down on his knees and started looking for the checkers. When he had them all, he put more wood in the stove, then returned quietly to the table and sat down. We were alone again; everything was exactly as before. I relaxed gradually, telling myself that he'd just been seeing things.

The next time I woke he was sitting with his head sunk forward on the table. It looked as if he had fallen asleep at last, and huddling alert among the bed-clothes I decided to watch a minute to make sure, then dress and try to slip out to the stable.

While I watched, I planned exactly every movement I was going to make. Rehearsing it in my mind as carefully as if I were actually doing it, I climbed out of bed, put on my clothes, tiptoed stealthily to the door and slipped outside. By this time, though, I was getting drowsy, and relaxing among the blankets I decided that for safety's sake I should rehearse it still again. I rehearsed it four times altogether, and the fourth time dreamed that I hurried on successfully to the stable.

I fumbled with the door a while, then went inside and felt my way through the darkness to the box-stall. There was a bright light suddenly and the owl was sitting over the door with his yellow eyes like a pair of lanterns. The calves, he told me, were in the other stall with the sick colt. I looked and they were there all right, but Tim came up and said it might be better not to start for home till morning. He reminded me that I hadn't paid for his feed or my own supper yet, and that if I slipped off this way it would mean that I was stealing, too. I agreed, realizing now that it wasn't the calves I was looking for after all, and that I still had to see inside the stall that was guarded by the owl. "Wait here," Tim said, "I'll tell you if he flies away," and without further questioning I lay down in the straw and went to sleep again. . . . When I woke coffee and beans were on the stove already, and though the lamp was still lit I could tell by the window that it was nearly morning.

We were silent during breakfast. Two or three times I caught him watching me, and it seemed his eyes were shiftier than before. After his sleepless night he looked tired and haggard. He left the table while I was still eating and fed raw rabbit to the owl, then came back and drank another cup of coffee. He had been friendly and communicative the night before, but now, just as when he first came running out of the stable in his long black coat, his expression was sullen and resentful. I began to feel that he was in a hurry to be rid of me.

I took my time, however, racking my brains to outwit him still and get the calves away. It looked pretty hopeless now, his eyes on me so suspiciously, my imagination at low ebb. Even if I did get inside the box-stall to see the calves—was he going to stand back then and let me start off home with them? Might it not more likely frighten him, make him do something desperate, so that I couldn't reach my uncle or the police? There was the owl over in the corner, the grindstone by the bed. And with such a queer fellow you could never tell. You could never tell, and you had to think about your own skin too. so I said politely, "Thank you, Mr. Vickers, for letting me stay all night," and remembering what Tim had told me took out my dollar's worth of silver.

He gave a short dry laugh and wouldn't take it. "Maybe you'll come back," he said, "and next time stay longer. We'll go shooting up in the hills if you like—and I'll make a trip to town for things so that we can have better meals. You need company sometimes for a change. There's been no one here now quite a while."

His face softened again as he spoke. There was an expression in his eyes as if he wished that I could stay on now. It puzzled me. I wanted to be indignant, and it was impossible. He held my sheepskin for me while I put it on, and tied the scarf around the collar with a solicitude and determination equal to Aunt Ellen's. And then he gave his short dry laugh again, and hoped I'd find my calves all right.

He had been out to the stable before I was awake, and Tim was ready for me, fed and saddled. But I delayed a few minutes, pretending to be interested in his horses and the sick colt. It would be worth something after all, I realized, to get just a glimpse of the calves. Aunt Ellen was going to be skeptical enough of my story as it was. It could only confirm her doubts to hear me say I hadn't seen the calves in the box-stall, and was just pretty sure that they were there.

So I went from stall to stall, stroking the horses and making comparisons with the ones we had at home. The door, I noticed, he had left wide open, ready for me to lead out Tim. He was walking up and down the aisle, telling me which horses were quiet, which to be careful of. I came to a nervous chestnut mare, and realized she was my only chance.

She crushed her hips against the side of the stall as I slipped up to her manger, almost pinning me, then gave her head a toss and pulled back hard on the halter shank. The shank, I noticed, was tied with an easy slip-knot that the right twist and a sharp tug would undo in half a second. And the door was wide open, ready for me to lead out Tim — and standing as she was with her body across the stall diagonally, I was for the moment screened from sight.

It happened quickly. There wasn't time to think of consequences. I just pulled the knot, in the same instant struck the mare across the nose. With a snort she threw herself backwards, almost trampling Vickers, then flung up her head to keep from tripping on the shank and plunged outside.

It worked as I hoped it would. "Quick," Vickers yelled to me, "the gate's open — try and head her off" — but instead I just waited till he himself was gone, then leaped to the box-stall.

The door was fastened with two tight-fitting slide-bolts, one so high that I could scarcely reach it standing on my toes. It wouldn't yield. There was a piece of broken whiffle-tree beside the other box-stall door. I snatched it up and started hammering on the pin. Still it wouldn't yield. The head of the pin was small and round, and the whiffle-tree kept glancing off. I was too terrified to pause a moment and take careful aim.

Terrified of the stall though, not of Vickers. Terrified of the stall, yet compelled by a frantic need to get inside. For the moment I had forgotten Vickers, forgotten even the danger of his catching me. I worked blindly, helplessly, as if I were confined and smothering. For a moment I yielded to panic, dropped the piece of whiffle-tree and started kicking at the door. Then, collected again, I forced back the lower bolt, and picking up the whiffle-tree tried to pry the door out a little at the bottom. But I had wasted too much time. Just as I dropped to my knees to peer through the opening Vickers seized me. I struggled to my feet and fought a moment, but it was such a hard, strangling clutch at my throat that I felt myself go limp and blind. In desperation then I kicked him, and with a blow like a reflex he sent me staggering to the floor.

But it wasn't the blow that frightened me. It was the fierce, wild light in his eyes.

Stunned as I was, I looked up and saw him watching me, and, sick with terror, made a bolt for Tim. I untied him with hands that moved incredibly, galvanized for escape. I knew now for sure that Vickers was crazy. He followed me outside, and, just as I mounted, seized Tim again by the bridle. For a second or two it made me crazy too. Gathering up the free ends of the rein I lashed him hard across the face. He let go of the bridle, and, frightened and excited too now, Tim made a dash across the yard and out of the gate. Deep as the snow was, I kept him galloping for half a mile, pommelling him with my fists, kicking my heels against his sides. Then of his own accord he drew up short for breath, and I looked around to see whether Vickers was following. He wasn't — there was only snow and the hills, his buildings a lonely little smudge against the whiteness — and the relief was like a stick pulled out that's been holding up tomato vines or peas. I slumped across the saddle weakly, and till Tim started on again lay there whimpering like a baby.

We were home by noon. We didn't have to cross fields or stop at houses now, and there had been teams on the road packing down the snow so that Tim could trot part of the way and even canter. I put him in the stable without taking time to tie or unbridle him, and ran to the house to tell Aunt Ellen. But I was still frightened, cold and a little hysterical, and it was a while before she could understand how everything had happened. She was silent a minute, indulgent, then helping me off with my sheepskin said kindly, "You'd better forget about it now, and come over and get warm. The calves came home themselves yesterday. Just about an hour after you set out."

I looked up at her. "But the stall then — just because I wanted to look inside he knocked me down — and if it wasn't the calves in there —"

She didn't answer. She was busy building up the fire and looking at the stew.

Sinclair Ross (1908-) was born near Shellbrook, Saskatchewan, and now lives in Spain. Out of his experience as a banker in the West during the 1930s and 1940s came the novel *As for Me and My House*. His short stories have been collected in *The Lamp at Noon and Other Stories*.

Rudy Wiebe
Tudor King

"Will he be all right?" the boy asked again. Against the cold his breathing came in short gasps and his normally round face was pinched together expectantly to the huge parka-ed figure beside him.

"I told you—we'll see when we get there." His brother Frank flipped the reins gently against the flanks of the horses. Encouraged, they butted their way into another drift driven behind the brush skirting the road. "Don't talk. Just stop wriggling, keep the robe up—tight."

Immediately the boy settled back and resolved again not to make another move until they got there. The question, however, ran on through his mind in circular repetition, like Little Black Sambo's tigers around and around the tree. Remembering that naked little fellow, the boy involuntarily hunched lower into the blankets for warmth, eyes squinting at the storm-wasted world. His father had said it had been the worst storm to ever hit the district. For five days the blizzard had whipped the pellet-snow across the land; one evening only the ropes they had strung between house and barn had brought Frank safely in from feeding the stock. But last night when the boy awoke there had been no storm whine. What he heard as he lay, limp from sleep and staring at the red bulge of the heater, was the sad howl of the wolves, hunger-desperate after the storm. He had heard, and felt something finger down his spine even as he curled up more tightly, pulling the wool quilt up and over, and then he had heard his father just beyond the bedroom partition make a sound in his sleep and the long moans had lost their hold and he had lain snug, his eyes wide again to the cheery heater. Abruptly he had remembered the old man, thought of all the after-blizzard nights he must have lain in his sagging cabin, hearing the wolves. With no father to clear his throat in the darkness.

Now, the team ploughing steadily ahead, the boy shuddered again. He sensed Frank looking at him and to cover up he rubbed his nose fast with the back of his mitten. Somehow that did not seem enough; he crouched lower in the seat of the cutter and lifted the heavy robe over his head. The musty smell of the cow-hide brought him back to the old man again because that was his cabin smell too. Mixed with some others.

His father had said the old man was already there when they came to their homestead. Probably he had always lived there, bent, scum-grey hair projecting from his face and under his cap, pants held up by twine, stitched together with string, old. On warmer days in spring and summer he shuffled past their farm every week towards the store which was also post office, his hands folded behind his back, a greyish sack held in place by cord over his shoulder. And at his heels followed the dog, small, brownish, and always bald at varying spots from his truceless battle with fleas. Like the other children of the settlement, the boy stared at the stooped figure almost apprehensively from behind a tree or barn-corner. The name, hissed at bed-time, was enough to quiet any restless youngster.

But once, last summer, the boy had faced him. On a long Sunday after-noon the boy and two friends, daring each other into a corner beyond their courage, had inched up to the cabin where the old man lived. Someone, with gritted teeth, knocked. And then the door squeaked open and they were inside where the litter, gathered home over years in the greyish sack, left them barely room to shuffle their feet. The dog, squatting on the sack-heaped bedstead too, looked more miserable than ever, but something had happened to the old man. In the darkness under the robe the boy, now as then, saw him in awe. And heard his voice.

"Think I'm in bad shape, huh? You," jabbing a finger at the tallest of the three, "you taken history?" He said it as if there were only one bit of history to be known and it could be taken like a pill.

Henry nodded hastily.

"It says the Tudors was once kings of England. Eh!" The last was not a question; his whole body jerked as he shot it out.

Henry, whose head was still bobbing slightly from the previous question, said quickly, "Uh-huh!" because that was one bit he did seem to know.

"Well, what's my name?" The boys could say nothing, quite floundered that the old man should ask such a thing. Even the dog had stopped scratch-ing. "Eh!"

Henry ventured, very gently, "Mr—Tudor."

"Eh!" The ejaculation snapped at them like a whip; in the gathering wonder of that moment the three suddenly comprehended. Under the robe, the boy could again see the flash of the grey eyes and again he was mes-merized. "That means I come from them same Tudors that was kings of England. You know what that means?" The voice, not creaking now but great, "I'm a Tudor. I should be king of England."

As if suddenly aware of their numb comprehension, the old man relented a little, but the flame in his eye did not die. "Now I ain't saying I'm against the King. I ain't really, no, only I don't think he's running the war right. Look at what that Hitler's doing to the people. Even bombing them! I ain't against him, but if George was to come out from England and say, 'Tudor, will you take over?' why, I wouldn't refuse him. Eh!"

As on that summer day, the boy heard no more of the voice but in the musty, seeping coldness under the robe he again saw the old man before him. And the dingy flesh obvious through the rags, the bedraggled whiskers, the rotting shoes, even the dog with his ceaseless scratch, were transformed. If before him was the nadir of humanity, the flashing eyes and the compulsive spirit moving there revealed the stuff of majesty. The lined face was no longer directed toward the palpable ambitions of youth; no longer toward an actuality or even a probability. Whatever had crushed any fulfillable ambition had not been able to erase a fragment of history, or prevent it from blossoming in the failing mind of the old man.

The boy had not actually known this on the last summer afternoon as he and his friends stood dumb in the cabin. He did not even know it now under the robe on his way to see how the old man had weathered the storm; if asked directly, he could have shaped no words to explain himself. He simply knew what he had seen in the wreck before him, and the two miles home had vanished under his feet as he sped to tell all he could put in words: I saw a king! And the disappointment struck him again as he remembered how Frank had laughed.

"Ah, Andy. That's his dream. Told me years ago. Dream — what else can he do, now?"

He stood sullen in the warm dust of the barnyard. The Tudors *had* been kings of England; it was in a book at school. And the old man's name *was* Tudor. So he must be from the same family, and so the throne belonged as much to him as King George VI. And the way he had looked and the way he had spoken —

Frank put down the book he was reading and leaned back against the haystack. "Sorry, Andy, I didn't think you really believed him." He looked over the trees into the sky and added slowly, "But you're almost ten. You've got to learn sometime that you can't believe everything. It's okay to dream about chasing wolves and flying planes — every boy does — but you can't go around believing every old tramp that says he's a king. Even if his name happens to fit something, four hundred years ago."

Seeing the boy stare wordlessly at the ground, he insisted, "Kid, you can tell. He's not really right anymore, up here. He's lived alone and with that dog too long. A man can become low and cheap if he just lives with himself too long. He can become no man at all. How can a man live as he does — in a shack full of junk and that filthy runt. That's what you saw. Listen. Just last week Ted Martin was missing some eggs again. He had a good idea where they were going, so when he met old Tudor on the road he said, 'You know, I've been losing eggs out of my barn again."

"'Oh,' says old Tudor, 'Say, there must be a snitcher around. Just yesterday I was missing some—'

"'Yah,' Ted interrupted, 'but I'm fixing him. I'll plant some poisoned eggs in that barn and we'll see what's what.'

"Ted said Tudor's eyes got all big and scared, 'Hey Ted, you wouldn't do a thing like that to an old friend, would you?'"

After a moment Frank said heavily, "All these years he's lived alone, in dirt. Too long. All the truth and pride in him—everything's rotten away. What can you believe him?"

But no logic or facts could budge the idea caught in the gleam of the old man's eye as he sat enthroned among the sacks of his bed. The boy could no more deny it than he could understand it. But it was there.

He heard Frank shout "Haw!" and he felt the cutter lurch to the left. He thrust his head above the robe; they were turning off the main road up the drifted track to the cabin now, the greys steaming, heaving themselves forward together. The jack-pine and scrawny outline poplars crowded closer here. It was too cold for wind or even clouds; there was just one massive inhuman concentration on cold. The sunlight blazing on the drift-driven snow only added ironical emphasis.

But the cold, sting as it might, could not hold his thoughts. *Around the copse and then we'll see,* he thought, keeping even the cold at arm's length. *Just around the corner. A few more steps—that one more big drift, and there it will be—*

Only it was not. When they rounded the last pine they saw no cabin in the clearing. The boy jerked to his feet. Where the cabin should have been hunched in the lee of a small hill there was only the straight waste of a giant drift that had levelled the clearing to lose itself at the edge of the spruce. Then, his eyes skipping back over the drift, he saw the bit of stove-pipe sticking up and he knew that the wind had only buried the shack and that beneath the hard surface it was snug and—then he looked at the stove-pipe again.

"Frank," he said.

His brother was standing too, huge, his weathered face rimmed by the frost on his parka. "Yah," he said.

The horses fought their way a bit closer, then halted at a word. Frank muttered, "Hang on here," giving the boy the reins, and stepped out to pull the blankets over the hot horses. "I agreed to watch him, but the Mounties can't blame me. Not for a five-day blizzard."

"Frank—"

"Stay in the cutter! Get under there and stay warm. Y'hear!" The boy, knowing his brother was rough because he had just said what he need not have said, and yet having been compelled to say it though useless, sat down slowly and watched him bull himself into the deepening snow. From this angle the boy could see that the wind had eddied the snow clear within a few feet of one side of the cabin, leaving a curving rift in the drift. He saw the iceless glass of one small window; he looked at the stove-pipe. No smoke. He remembered the look of the old man. He dropped the reins and was out, his legs churning along the straggled trail. Frank wheeled at him, mouth open to thunder, then after an instant stooped without a word to continue clearing the door.

The inner door ground a cracking protest on its leather hinges. Beyond the flash of snow the interior was black as Frank pushed back his hood and stepped in. He completely blocked the opening, but the boy, hunching over, slipped past his legs. As he stood there facing the gloom he could feel the old trunk against his leg and he knew from the shadows that the clutter of pottery and worn-out harness of the summer before was still upon it. Through a corner of the east window the sunlight now managed a faint reflection, outlining in ragged silhouette the heaps of things crowding the room. The stove-pipe stood above the hump of the heater against the middle of the low ceiling. The boy's mittened hand reached up to the edge of Frank's parka in the silence of their breathing.

"Uh—Tudor," Frank cleared his throat gruffly. Then more loudly, "Tudor, you here?" His voice bounced about.

After a moment Frank started into the room. "He saw a hundred storms—had enough wood for four days if he skimped." He leaned forward in the gloom about the heater. "Maybe he tried to go out for more—there's none h—Oh."

He straightened instantly, brushing away the boy's hand. "Andy, you better get back to the cutter, and..." but there was no need to finish. More accustomed to the half-light, the boy had already seen the figure curled tight against the heater, the back cramped against it as though to plead some touch of warmth from its rigid flank. They both leaned closer as sunlight from the door fell on the granite face. An icicle of saliva had frozen the mouth and beard to the floor.

Frank said, "Wonder, where's the dog."

The boy, still gripping the parka, pointed.

"Huh?" Frank's glance moved slowly around the room, ending on the bed bare to its rope springs. His hands fumbled slightly as he thrust his mitts more firmly onto them, then, with an abrupt movement he bent down. Rigidly, as a welded iron framework, the whole shape moved. He half-straightened and said strangely, "No weight to it." Then quickly he reached in and pulled the dog from where it had been cradled, hugged, in the nest of rags. It seemed at that moment to be turning stiff. Even as Frank pushed something aside and eased it to the floor, the hairless limbs stretched rigid also.

Frank said slowly, "He tried his best for the dog. Knowing we'd come when the storm dropped, Old Man Tudor."

Then he suddenly turned. The boy felt himself lifted up in his brother's strong arms, held close as he had not been since he was a small child. But he did not find that strange. Something was breaking through his numbness, painful and wet, and he pushed his face against his brother's hard, cold shoulder; as if he were already remembering his own fierce happiness at once having recognized the fleeting stuff of human majesty.

Rudy Wiebe (1934-) was born in Saskatchewan and has lived in Edmonton since 1967. When not writing, he is professor of English and Creative Writing at the University of Alberta. He has written five novels, including *The Temptation of Big Bear* and *The Scorched-Wood People*. His stories have been collected in *Where Is the Voice Coming From?*

Robert Kroetsch
That Yellow Prairie Sky

I was looking at the back of a new dollar bill, at that scene of somewhere on the prairies, and all of a sudden I was looking right through it and I wasn't in Toronto at all any more — I was back out west. The clouds were moving overhead as if we were travelling and I pointed to that fence that's down and I said, "Look't there, Julie, that must be Tom's place. He hasn't fixed that piece of fence these thirty years." And then I noticed the elevator wasn't getting any closer.

It never does.

My brother Tom, he was quite a guy for women. I'll bet he was the worst for twenty miles on either side of the Battle River. Or the best, whichever way you look at it. I guess I wasn't far behind. Anyway, we spent the winter courting those two girls.

The way it happened, we met them in the fall while we were out hunting. I mean, we knew them all our lives. But you know how it is, eh? You look at some girl all your life, and then one day you stop all of a sudden and take another look and you kind of let out a low whistle.

Well, Tom was twenty-three then, with me a year younger, and we'd grown up together. He taught me how to play hockey and how to snare rabbits and anything new that came along. Out on the prairies you don't have neighbours over your head and in your back yard, and a brother really gets to be a brother.

When it rained that fall and the fields got too soft for threshing we decided to go out and take a crack at some of the ducks that were feeding on our crop. We built a big stook that would keep us out of view, facing the slough hole and the setting sun, and we crawled inside. I can still see it all in my mind...

A thousand and a thousand ducks were milling black against the yellow sky. Like autumn leaves from the tree of life they tumbled in the air; a new flock coming from the north, a flock, circling down, a flock tremulous above the water, reluctant to wet a thousand feet. And silhouetted on the far horizon was a threshing machine with a blower pointed at a strawpile, and nearer was the glint of the sun on the slough, and then a rush of wings from behind, overhead, going into the sun, and with a sudden jolt the autumn-sharp smell of a smoking gun.

I let go with both barrels at a flock that was too high up, and before I could reload there was a scream that left my jaw hanging as wide open as the breech of my old 12-gauge.

"I swear," Tom said, "now ain't that the prettiest pair of mallards that ever came close to losing their pinfeathers?"

I pushed my way out of the stook, and Tom was right.

I guess they didn't see us. I mean, Kay and Julie.

They were standing back of our stook, looking scared, with their skirts tucked into—tucked up—and nobody thought of it in the excitement, or at least they didn't.

"Are you trying to kill us?" Julie asked, pushing back a blond curl and pretending she was only mad and not scared at all.

"Can't you see we're shooting ducks?" Tom said.

"I can't by the number that fell," she said.

That's when I spoke up. "They were too high and I was too anxious."

Julie looked at me and my gun and she blushed. "I didn't mean to insult your shooting. I've heard folks say you're one of the best shots around."

Funny thing. I was pretty good, but just about then I could've told a battalion of the Princess Pats to back up and drop their guns.

It was then that the redhead, Kay, spoke up. "Really, I'm glad you missed. I hate to see things get killed."

Tom looked up at the distant ducks for a minute, and then said, "As a matter of fact, I hate it myself." It was the first time I ever heard Tom say a thing like that. Most of the time you couldn't hold him.

There was a kind of a loss for words. Then Kay explained, "We're making boxes for the box social in the church hall tonight, and we're taking the short cut over to Rittner's place to borrow four little wheels that the Rittners have left over from the little toy wagon that Halberg's new automobile ran into."

"We're in a terrible hurry," Julie said, "so instead of going around by the road we're going to wade across Rittner's slough—"

And then they noticed it too, and before Tom could say he figured as much, they were in the slough wading above their knees.

"A nice pair of shafts," Tom commented.

"A dandy pair," I said. But I soon found out I was talking about a different pair.

That night at the box social Tom paid three dollars and a half for the lunch box that looked like a pink Red River oxcart with toy wagon wheels on it. He figured it was Kay's because she had red hair, and in a pinch we could make a switch.

Some religious fellow caught on to me and ran me up to five and a quarter on the yellow one. It was a great help to the church committee, and it looked like a fair enough investment otherwise. Sure enough, I got Kay's and I wanted Julie's, so Tom and I switched and the girls never caught on; or at least they never let on that they did.

Through the rest of the fall and during the winter Dad had to do the chores quite a few times by himself. Tom and I didn't miss a dance or a hay-ride or a skating party within trotting range of the finest team of dapple greys in the country. We didn't have all the fancy courting facilities that folks here in the east have, but we had lots of space and lots of sky. And we didn't miss much on a frosty night, the old buffalo robe doing whatever was necessary to keep warm...

The northern lights in the winter sky were a silent symphony: flickering white, fading red and green, growing and bursting and dying in swirls and echoes of swirls, in wavering angel-shadows, in shimmering music. And on one edge of the wide white prairie shone a solitary light, and toward it moved a sleigh with the jingle of harness, the clop of hoofs, the squeak of runners on the snow; and the jingling, clopping, squeaking rose up like the horses' frozen breath to the silent music in the sky.

I guess we did pretty well. I remember the night we were driving home from a bean supper and dance, and Julie said, "You're getting pretty free with your behaviour."

"Well, you're going to be my wife soon enough," I said.

"It can't be soon enough," she whispered, and she pushed my arm away. Women are always contrary that way.

Tom and Kay were curled up at the back of the sleigh and they couldn't hear us.

"Let's get out and run behind for a ways," I said. "My feet are getting cold. And I can clap my hands."

"My feet are warm," she said.

"But mine aren't."

"You're just making that up because you're mad."

"Why would I be mad?"

"You're mad because I stopped you."

"Stopped me what?"

She didn't want to say it. "Nothing," she said.

"I think I'll get out and run behind by myself," I said. "Should I?"

She reached up and kissed me right on the mouth, cold and yet warm, and that was that as far as running behind went.

"Let's talk," she said. "We've only been engaged since midnight, and here you want to act like we're married already."

"Who, me?" I said, trying to sound like I didn't know what she was talking about.

"Let's talk," she said.

98

"Talk?" I said. "I'm all ears."

"Don't you want to talk?"

"Sure I want to talk. If I can get a word in edgewise."

"I can't get used to being engaged," she said. "I want to talk."

"What'll we talk about?" I said. "It seems to me we've done nothing but talk since last fall."

"Let's plan," she said.

That was the end of my plans.

"We're going to get married, remember?" she went on. "You asked me and I said yes before you had hardly asked the second time."

"You weren't so sure I'd ask a third time."

She soon changed that subject. "Kay said that she and Tom are going to build a house this fall."

"It's a good idea. Living on the home place is no good for them and no good for Ma and Dad."

"Why can't we build a house?"

"We got a shack on our place."

"Shack is right. One room and a lean-to."

"It's a roof."

"Kay and Tom are going to get a new bedroom suite and a new stove, and Kay is going to start making new curtains. I could start making new curtains too if we were going to have a new house with lots of windows."

"If we get a good crop, okay. But I got enough stashed away to get married on and put a crop in, and that's it."

"I want to make a nice home for you. We'll have a family."

"We might," I said. "But things'll have to pick up."

"Promise," she said.

"Sure enough," I said.

"I mean promise we'll have a new house."

"Don't you think it would be better to wait and see?"

She didn't answer.

"We might flood out or dry out or freeze out. How do I know?"

She still didn't answer.

"What if it's a grasshopper year? What about wireworms and wild oats and rust and buckwheat?"

"Promise me," she said. "I don't even think you love me."

That was her final word.

I talked for another ten minutes about wireworms and rust, and after that things got quiet. We sat in that sleigh for an hour, our breath freezing in our scarves (twenty-seven below, it was), wrapped in a buffalo robe and in each other's arms and never once did she speak. To a young fellow twenty-two years old it didn't make much sense. But I didn't push her away. She was soft and warm and quiet; and I thought she had fallen asleep.

"Okay," I said, finally. "Okay okay okay. I promise."

She snuggled closer.

We had a double wedding in the spring.

Tom's father-in-law fixed up two granaries near the house and we held the reception at his place. Everybody was there. My cousin had trouble with the pump, and while everybody was watching him trying to tap the keg, Tom came over to where I was watching the sky for a nice day and he shook my hand.

"We're the luckiest pair of duck hunters this side of the fourth meridian," he said. "We've each got a half section that's almost paid for, we've got a big crop to put in that'll put us on our feet, and we've each got the prettiest girl in the country. How do you like being a married man?"

"Yes, sir," I said. I had one eye on a couple of my old sidekicks who were kissing the bride for the second time. "This here love business is the clear McCoy."

I remember that my cousin drew the first pitcherful just then, and it was all foam. But we were only just married...

The sky was the garment of love. It was a big sky, freckled with the stars of the universe; a happy sky, shrouding all the pain. It was the time of spring, and spring is love, and in the night sky arrow after arrow of honking geese winged across the yellow moon, driving winter from the world.

Right after the wedding we moved into the shack and really went to work. I was busy from morning till night putting in a big crop, while Julie helped with the chores and looked after her little chicks and put in a big garden. When the crop was in we started on the summer fallow, and before that was done it was haying time.

At noon she brought dinner out to me in the field, out in the sun and the wind, and we sat side by side and talked and laughed, and the dust from my face got on hers sometimes, and sometimes I didn't get started quite on time. And the weather was good too...

In the evening a black cloud towered up in the west and tumbled over the land, bringing lightning and rain and hope. In the morning there was only a fragment of cloud; the dot worn on a woman's cheek beside a pair of beautiful eyes, and the beautiful sun in the fair blue sky sent warmth and growth into the earth, and the rain and the sun turned the black fields green, the green fields yellow.

I remember one Sunday we went over to Tom's for a chicken supper. Tom and Dad and I talked about the way the crops were coming along and where to get binder repairs, and we made arrangements to help each other with the cutting and stooking.

The womenfolk talked about their gardens and their chickens until Julie mentioned the drapes she was sewing.

"I'm going to have one of those living-room parlours," she said, "one of those living-room parlours with lots of windows, like in the magazines, and I'm making drapes for that kind of window."

"I think I will too," Kay said. "Tom cut some of the nicest plans out of last week's *Free Press*. I hope the fall stays nice."

"My husband is even getting enthusiastic," Julie said, giving me a teasing smile. "I caught him holding up the drapes one day and looking at them."

Ma said she was crocheting some new pillow covers for all the pillows and easy chairs that seemed to be coming up, and she thought they all better get together and do some extra canning. Entertaining takes food.

Kay said, "Ma," meaning her mother-in-law, "you'll soon have your house all to yourself again. And since Tom is afraid he'll have to help with the washing, he's going to get me a new washing machine."

"We might pick up a secondhand car," Julie said, "if the crop on our breaking doesn't go down because it's too heavy."

I had mentioned it'd be something to tinker on during the winter.

It wasn't long before Julie was talking about the washing machine and Kay was talking about a second-hand car. Wheat was a good price that year.

We menfolk laughed at the women and we found a few things in the Eaton's catalogue that we could use ourselves. It seemed that somebody was always coming up with something new that we couldn't possibly do without.

After supper we all walked out to have a look at Tom's crop. Tom could even make a gumbo patch grow wheat.

I guess it happened a week later. I mean, the storm. Julie was working on her drapes. It was a hot day, too hot and too still, and in the afternoon the clouds began to pile up in the west. . .

The storm came like a cloud of white dust high in the sky: not black or grey like a rain cloud, but white; and now it was rolling across the heavens with a brute unconcern for the mites below, and after a while came the first dull roar. The hot, dead air was suddenly cool, stirring to a breeze, and then a white wall of destruction bridged earth and sky and moved across the land and crashed across the fields of ripening grain.

Old man Rittner saw it coming west of us, and he went out and drove his axe in the middle of the yard, figuring to split her. But she didn't split.

In fifteen minutes it was all over and the sun was shining as pretty as you please. Only there was no reason for the sun to shine. Our garden and our fields were flat, and the west window was broken, and half the shingles were gone from the shack. The leaves were half stripped from the trees, and the ground was more white than black and, I remember, the cat found a dead robin.

My wife didn't say a word.

I hitched up old Mag to the buggy and Julie and I drove over to Tom's place.

Tom was sitting on the porch steps with his head in his hands, and Kay was leaning on the fence, looking at her garden. It looked like they hadn't been talking much either.

I got out and walked over to Tom, and Julie stayed in the buggy.

"A hundred per cent," I said.

"The works," he said. "And all I got is enough insurance to feed us this winter or to buy a ticket to hell out of here."

"The same with me," I said.

We couldn't think of much to say.

All of a sudden Tom almost shouted at Kay: "Say it and get it over with. If you want we'll go to the city and I'll get a job. I can get on a construction gang. They're paying good now. We'll get a washing machine and a second-hand car." He looked at his wheat fields, beaten flat. "We'll make a payment and get our own house."

He kicked at a hailstone.

"A house with big windows for my new drapes," Kay added.

Tom got up and he walked to the gate where Julie sat in the buggy. Kay and I, we stood there watching him, almost afraid of the storm in his eyes, and Kay looked at me as if I should stop him before he went and grabbed a pitchfork or something.

"Tom, I was joking," Kay said. "I don't need fancy curtains and a washing machine. And we never needed a car before. Did we, Tom? We got enough for us and Ma and Dad. Haven't we, Tom? And we got next year."

Tom snorted at that idea. He kicked open the gate and walked out toward the barn. There was so much helpless anger in him he couldn't talk.

Kay called after him. "We still got this, Tom." She was kind of crying. She was pointing at the black dirt that showed through the broken grass. "Look, Tom, we still got this."

Tom, he stopped in the middle of the yard and he turned around. For a long time he was only looking at Kay's empty hand.

All of a sudden he bent down like he was going to say a prayer or something. And he scooped up a handful of hailstones, and he flung them back at the sky.

Like I say, my wife; she didn't say a word.

Robert Kroetsch (1927-) was born in Heisler, Alberta. He has published five novels, three collections of poems, and a travel book on Alberta. His third novel, *The Studhorse Man,* received the Governor General's Award for 1969. He is professor of English at the University of Manitoba.

Gabrielle Roy
*A Tramp at the Door**

My mother was expecting something or other. She kept going to the door, drawing back from the windowpane the white curtain hemmed in red linen and staring long and vaguely out at the drenched countryside. Suddenly she gave a start, one hand going up to her forehead.

"Somebody's coming," she announced, and went on, her voice filled with surprise: "Coming here, it looks like!"

Rain was rattling on the roof. On either side of the house we could hear water from the spouts splashing down from the overflowing rain barrels. Evening was falling. From the ditches, filled to their banks, a white steam went up. Beyond the slope of the rye field you could see no more than a few blackened, bare treetops emerging soaked from the mist. For two days we hadn't seen a living soul pass by. "Not a cat, not even a beggar," my mother had sighed.

The man pushed the gate open. We could see him tip back his head and try to smile as he saw the two gable windows of the house and perhaps the smoke from the chimney. With every step he had to fight the wind, pulling his dark coat tight around him. The garden shrubs near him were twisted and tousled by the wind. Because of the shadow that already lay dark beneath the hedge, the man was on top of Farouche's kennel before he saw our German shepherd about to spring.

My mother stifled a cry.

Almost at once we saw Farouche wagging his tail, wiggling his body and crouching in front of this man whose strangely gentle, coaxing tone we in the house could catch between the gusts of the storm.

My mother breathed a great sigh, even more astonished than she was relieved.

*Translated by Alan Brown

"Well," she said, "that's the first time I ever saw Farouche make friends that fast!"

The man straightened up and seemed to be surveying all the ways of entering the house. Finally, overcoming his hesitation, he made a half-turn and came rapping on the back door which looked out on the farmyard.

My father, sitting by the fire, was in the grip of the unbearable boredom he suffered with each return of the wet season to our country of the plains. The whole day long he hadn't said a word. You wondered if he really felt he belonged there with the rest of us. Buried in his thoughts, he hadn't seen the stranger coming, and even the sound of our voices had most likely not come through to him.

"It's somebody who doesn't know his way around here." This was my mother again as she gestured to me to open the door.

As soon as autumn came we lived in the big room. The small lean-to that served as a kitchen in the summertime now turned into a kind of storage space where we could pile furniture and tools no longer needed. I went through this freezing space and with difficulty lifted the rusty latch. A wallop of rain took me in the face. The man's head appeared, feebly lit by a vestige of light coming from the big puddles around the pump. All in all, it was a rather nice tramp's face, the kind that isn't any particular age and asks for a bowl of soup and will go on his way right afterwards if he isn't offered an attic for the night. We didn't see those people often in our out-of-the-way parts, maybe one or two a year, if that. But this one seemed to have a certain dignity and wasn't in a hurry to beg. A short, reddish, frizzy beard, pearled with great raindrops, invaded half his cheeks; the peak of his cap threw a clean line of shadow on his forehead. His eyes, very gentle and smiling, almost tender, sparkled under the wet fringe of his lashes.

"Well! My little cousin!" he cried in a voice that was as soft and flexible and unsettling as his gaze. "You must be my little cousin Alice!" he went on, laughing.

I shook my head

"No? Must be Agnes, then!"

"No," I said, irritated. "I'm Ghislaine."

"Of course, just what I thought! Of course you're Ghislaine. I should have known it, even if I never saw you."

As he spoke, his hands made as if they were drying each other, and he laughed behind his beard and his foot cleverly pushed at the door I was holding slightly open.

Somehow he was inside.

"This is the Rondeaus' house, I guess?" he asked, and his incredible, friendly smile swept around the interior of the damp, cold shed as if he found it welcoming and filled with people.

"No," I said, "we're the Trudeaus."

"Why, sure, just as I was going to say," he went on coolly. "Rondeau, Trudeau, names as like as peas. Right, cousin?"

He gave me a little nudge, and I saw his eyes shining with satisfaction.

"Now, little girl, you just go and tell your father there's a cousin here from the land of Quebec."

I went before him into the big room — he was right on my heels — and blurted out to my father, as if in mocking reproach: "He says he's a cousin from Quebec."

My father stood up and made an odd gesture, as if to take the stranger in his arms, but the impulse failed him. Yet his handsome, aging, peaceful face betrayed not so much a withdrawal as the vagueness of someone suddenly awakened from a dream.

"Well, now! What part of Quebec? Saint-Alphonse?"

"Saint Alphonse," said the man.

He approached the stove. His clothes were starting to steam. My mother brought the Aladdin lamp. She lifted it a little above the stranger and you could see great rips in his clothing, some held together by bits of string, others gaping to reveal glimpses of his red shirt.

But the man directed at my mother a gaze so filled with friendship that she set down the lamp and busied herself elsewhere without speaking. We could see that she was excited from the way she opened all the drawers of the sideboard without finding what she wanted.

For a moment the man stood alone in the middle of the room, trying to catch our eyes, which fled his. He drew up a chair by the stove, sat down and breathed a great sigh of well-being.

Then in the silence, two or three times, we could hear his soft, rather drawling voice: "Saint-Alphonse, yes sir. That's where I come from. Saint-Alphonse . . ."

My father took out his tobacco pouch. He was about to fill his pipe when the stranger held out a hand and, unabashed, helped himself to the tobacco. Then, after lighting a short clay pipe, he settled back in his chair and murmured distinctly: "Thank you. Much obliged."

The two men smoked. My mother fussed among her pots with an unusual amount of noise. And sometimes her lips opened as if she were about to say some wounding word. The stranger looked around at us children sitting in the corners, observing one after the other, and smiled out of his beard. He made little jabs with his chin, winked at each of us, then started the rounds again. A badger that we had tamed, still highly suspicious of strangers, actually slipped under the man's chair. He took it by the scruff of its neck and laid it in his lap. The little animal, far from protesting, licked his wet beard and, its claws retracted, allowed itself to be rocked like a baby. As wild and speechless as our only friends — our animals — we were astounded to see that two of them had taken up with this stranger. Even my mother seemed impressed, and that must have aggravated her ill humour. Little by little we slid off our chairs to come nearer. The strange man gave us signs of encouragement in the manner of the magician our parents had once taken us to see at the rodeo in the next village.

My father had stood up. He was pacing to and fro in the room, his hands behind his back. Then, planting himself in front of the vagabond, he asked: "But whose boy would you be then?"

"Me?" said the man. "Why, the one that disappeared."

A glimmer of interest showed beneath my father's lowered eyelids.

"Gustave?"

"Yep. Gustave."

"But they thought he was dead!"

"He wasn't dead. He went to the States. I'm his boy."

"Oh!" said my father. "You're his boy!"

"I'm his boy," the stranger repeated in a voice that was soft and stubborn.

And he turned his smiling face to where my mother was beating her pancake batter. He seemed determined to drag from her a look, a smile, a word. But she was speeding up her supper preparations so as to stay out of the conversation. It wasn't long before the first spoonful of batter dropped into the hot frying pan. A pleasant odour filled the room. Outside, darkness spread over the desolate, naked landscape. All that could still be seen through the windowpanes was the vague glimmer of water accumulated in great pools between the patches of brush, in the hollows of the plain or running in streams. The man stretched out his legs. He took time to look around the room, low-ceilinged, large, furnished with an oak sideboard and old, modest, but solid pieces so well-polished and softened by use that they reflected a long contentment. Then, without moving, he began smiling at nothing again, to himself.

"But what put you onto our trail?" my father asked suddenly.

The stranger raised his blue eyes, which shone in the direct rays of the lamp.

"In Saint-Alphonse."

"Oh!"

My father gave a long sigh.

"It's been a mighty long time since I saw hide or hair of any of them from Saint-Alphonse."

It was his turn to look toward my mother, so tiny, so much younger than he. A big apron tied around her waist, she was leaning attentively above her pan and the flame at times leapt perilously close to her face.

"How long is it now, Albertine, since I was in those parts?"

And indeed it was she who was charged with refreshing his memory on events he had described to her about people she had never seen.

She took a little while to reflect, mentally juggling dates, her pretty eyebrows arched high and her mouth a little open.

"You told me you were fourteen when you left home and you hadn't set foot there since. You figure it out. About fifty years, if you were telling the truth."

She always ended up with that reservation, as if to throw back the error, if error there was, solely upon my father.

Then, sulking a little, and because the stranger's presence doubtless irritated her, she added: "What's more, you haven't written the folks at home for fifteen years. It's a real shame!"

"Yes," said my father, ignoring his wife's last remark. "It'll be fifty years. I wouldn't even know them back there anymore."

He looked down, his face lit up by distant, melancholy memories.

My mother placed her fists on her hips. Quickly, without looking at the stranger, she said: "It's ready! Come on, children. Come and eat, Arthur."

The tramp too stood up gaily. He chose a seat by the wall, slid in, pulling his wretched jacket tight around him, and, once established, seized his fork.

"Yes," my father mused, "there's a lot of things back there I never heard a word about."

The man speared a large slice of bread with his fork. He bit the bread in the middle, then, smiling, his mouth full, he promised: "I'll tell you all about it after."

II

After supper he actually did begin to tell us about the relatives, helped along by my father who would situate things in time by his questions: "Marcelline, now, you must have found she'd aged? And I suppose Eustache took over the farm . . ."

We knew very little about my father's people. He'd never told us at one time how many brothers and sisters he had. On occasion, and as his reveries would have it, he would let a name drop: Marcelline, Philomène, Aristide. His tone changed, too, according to his mood.

One day, for example, when the soup was too salty, he had grumbled: "Albertine, are you going to start making salty soup like Philomène?"

"Who is Philomène?" we asked.

My father seemed more disconcerted at having provoked the question than by our breathless curiosity. Philomène, he finally admitted, was his father's second wife. A sign from my mother at that moment advised us not to push our researches any further. So it was that my father managed to keep the shades of his childhood for himself alone. At times, though, he himself renewed this singular aura of mystery attached to our uncles and aunts in Quebec. He spoke of ill-defined figures and always in the past tense, as if they had ceased to exist. That's why we were surprised that evening to hear him say, "Marcelline, now, she must have aged?"

Marcelline had made her entry into our family one evening when my father, seeing my mother patching old clothes, protested: "Now don't you start going on like that penny-pincher Marcelline!" The moment his sister's name had slipped out he walled himself in silence.

Others popped up, as faceless as Marcelline. They seemed incredibly far away yet, like that Marcelline, they would suddenly become attached to our lives through their penchant for patching old rags or because of a dreamy warmth that would spread at twilight through the house. And we never knew how many shadowy beings would rise up at our next question, behind Philomène or Marcelline, or if they'd be revealed thanks to some irritation of my father's or in a moment of more tender feeling. One thing we did know: you had to wait for these confidences, never push.

Well, that evening my father sat close to our strange visitor and, behold, names were flying from his lips, those associated with his ill humour as well as the ones we heard on feast days — and others we had never heard at all: Uncle France, Aunt Eléonore, Cousin Brault. You'd have thought a dike that had stood too long against the past had given under the flood of hurrying memories. The visitor gave little signs of approval. His eyes followed my father with an attentiveness that was ingratiating, sustained and encouraging, an attentiveness I have in later life observed in very few human beings. Truly, we might have imagined that it was my father who had just arrived from his travels and that the other one was there only to corroborate the facts or testify to them.

At last, when my father gave the other his turn, our visitor started in with his own stories. He spoke in a restful voice that he seldom raised. He dipped into his memories as into a heap of thick and rustling leaves, fallen at the trees' roots, in autumn.

We, the Trudeaus, were, according to him, a family out of the ordinary. The old couple, alas! had died working, on land that was richer in stones than pasture. But they had left behind them solid testimonials to their ingenuity, a thousand things well done, well carried out, if it was no more than a fence, a barn door or a delicately sculptured weathercock on the roof of that same barn. Whereas nowadays . . .

Several times he stopped to make sure that my father was listening with pleasure. In fact, my father seemed to have changed, to have emerged from a kind of penumbra as he renewed touch, so to speak, with his family, divided and scattered to all corners of the country by obscure misfortunes or obstinacies. In one swift glance our visitor would seize the trace of an emotion; then, sure of his trail, he would take off again without more emphasis but as if animated by a great desire to please.

What began to strike us then about this singular creature was that from the depths of his solitude he accused no one but seemed rather to assume all faults himself.

On the subject of family, however, it can't be said that he gave us many important details that first evening. Apart from that, he described minutely Christmas parties, New Years' parties, winter-evening parties, wedding parties, and suddenly Montreal, the great city, and suddenly Joliette, the small city, where the people of Saint-Alphonse went shopping. Then he'd comment on pioneer days, only to drift unexpectedly to meals of buckwheat cakes and wild honey or memories of square dances in the kitchen; and we'd see my father tapping lightly on the floor with toe and heel.

But already, through our visitor's account, these vague, far-off relatives of ours all seemed to have changed their characters—even Marcelline, who was no longer grasping, only provident. Eustache had inherited the paternal land and made it bear fruit; he raised children courageously. Anais, now, there was nobody like her for spinning the local wool and filling the cupboard with bolts of homespun. Devout she was, too, never missed her weekday mass. Uncle France had made it to a hundred, and they'd had a fine Christian birthday for him with all the children and grandchildren, of whom two were attending the seminary and three had taken vows. Family was something sacred: nothing could be as touching as the members of a single family knowing each other by their voices and opening their arms. Alas, people sometimes rejected their own flesh and blood when it turned up from afar, especially if it wasn't very clean or a particularly shining case.

This was said in a tone of resignation that made us all hang our heads, except my mother who, on the contrary, raised hers defiantly. She was sewing, a little off to one side, sticking her needle so impatiently into the cloth that she often pricked herself. Then we could hear her groan softly as she put her lips to the finger where a drop of blood was forming.

In the middle of a silence my father said: "Marcelline, now . . . did she ever mention me, sometimes?"

The man assured him warmly: "Oh, for sure! She often talked about her brother . . ."

"Arthur." My father completed the sentence.

"That's it, Arthur."

My father pulled up his chair until his foot almost touched the stranger's muddy boots. He lit his pipe for the fourth time and asked a question that astonished us greatly.

"Did they know back there that I'd been appointed justice of the peace?"

"They knew it," affirmed the vagabond. "Marcelline was very proud."

A happy silence followed, broken by my mother's noisy sigh.

The man turned in her direction: "What about you, cousin, which parish are you from? Maybe I know your people too . . ."

My mother rose up, all round and little and trembling at this mode of address, as if the stranger's hand had touched her.

"She's from the prairies," my father hastened to explain. "I married her out here."

"What of it?" the man insisted. "I've drifted around every which way at harvest times. Maybe I knew her folks."

No one took him up on it. The man seemed hurt. A little later his pale-blue gaze grew fixed and we could see that he was close to sleep. For a second his eyelids would drop, his eyes would glaze, and before they closed you could see in them a vague smile of apology and a slightly crestfallen expression.

It had just struck eleven. But my mother was acting as if the evening had just begun. My father, for his part, kept looking at the clock, pulling out his watch and comparing the two. The stranger dozed in his chair for minutes at a time, then awoke with a start, trying to cover up by winking at each of us in turn and changing posture.

My father said suddenly: "Hey, children! It's bedtime!" Then, without waiting for my mother's approval, he suggested: "Maybe you could make up a bed, Albertine..." He hesitated, then concluded: "...for our cousin..."

"Gustave. After my father," explained the stranger, yawning. "Gustave, that's me."

My mother stood up without a word, took the lamp and left us in shadows and then in darkness as she went up the steps leading to the attic. We could hear her moving a cot around, opening trunks. Through the half-open trap door a cold draught swept on our shoulders, soon bearing with it the odour of fresh linen.

Later, having awakened, I could hear my mother speaking in a low voice to my father: "You always told me your brother Gustave was built like a giant, tall and broad, the strongest one in the family. This one's a puny runt..."

"Far as that goes," my father replied, "you take any family around here. The big men don't always have the big sons. Maybe he takes after his mother," he added after a pause.

"That may be, but couldn't you see he was at a loss for an answer when you asked him for news of Marcelline and Philomène?"

"That's only natural. He's been on the road a lot. It couldn't all come back at once."

"Oh, that's the excuse, is it?" exclaimed my mother in a hostile, discouraged tone.

In the next room to theirs the man was snoring peacefully. Once he mumbled a few words in his sleep. Then I thought I heard, at the end of a jovial little laugh: "Good day! Good day, dear cousin!"

III

He stayed at our house three weeks. My mother gave him some clothes left by a former hired man, and they were about Gustave's size. Early in the morning, he used to wash in the kitchen sink, and comb his beard, and turn out quite presentable.

During the day he tried to make himself useful and took special pains to anticipate my mother's wishes. He'd bring in wood, run to the well as soon as the pail was dry, repair the traps. One day when she complained there'd been no mail for a week because of the roads, he went off on foot to the village. He came back at day's end with a letter which he held out to her in the hope, no doubt, of getting a friendly word.

In spite of everything we couldn't get used to the idea that he was supposed to be our cousin. We ordered him around like a farm hand. "Better get the wood in before the rain soaks it." In the daytime we called him "you" or "the man" or "him." My mother, above all, because she was afraid of having him with us all winter, would say each morning, looking out at the road unwinding toward the dark, dank woods: "There's going to be a big snowstorm before long. A person won't even be able to get out of here."

The man seemed not to hear. In the daytime we paid little attention to him. But in the evening, as soon as the lighted lamp stood on the table, this strange creature, through what kind of spell we didn't know, became indispensable to us. Every evening he again turned into "Cousin Gustave."

He appeared sensitive to this kind of disgrace, of which we absolved him every evening. Silent the whole day long, he regained the use of words as soon as our eyes, grown softer, consented to look at him again. Then, in his quiet, unchanging voice, he would once more tell the story of Marcelline's second wedding, or Uncle France's hundredth birthday, but always adding fresh details. "Hey, you didn't mention that last time!" my father would cry. And Gustave would look at him with a vague reproach in his eyes, as if he wanted to say: The things I know are too vast, too many-sided. You can't get all that out at once.

"Well, go on," my father would hurry him.

Gustave, cut adrift from his vision, would set off again, but on a new tack.

His stories proceeded by short stages, often interrupted at the most touching or fascinating part, so that we were always inclined to give him another day of hospitality in order to hear the end. And finally we had to admit it to ourselves: if Gustave's story the previous night had been a good one, we were polite and well-disposed toward him the following day. But when he'd disappointed us, we had ways, unconsciously but cruelly, of showing him.

Well, this fellow Gustave grew very skilful. He spun his stories out. He cut them into little slices in a way that later became familiar to us through the radio. Everything was used to stretch them out. The landscape would be painstakingly described. The village teacher, the notary, and the doctor had their parts to play. Jumping from one family to the next, it might happen that he got into events that barely concerned us but livened up his story immeasurably. There was one about the son of Magloire the blacksmith who hanged himself in the barn with his own belt; and one about Fortunat who, at the age of twenty, married a rich widow of fifty.

One evening, when I pointed out that all this had nothing to do with us, he turned toward me a look that was courageous and untamed: "Come now! Who's related to who? There's a question: where it starts, where it stops, who knows?"

Then, as if he realized that our suspicions could be nourished by this odd remark, he gave a little strangled laugh and went patiently back to the tale that especially pleased my father, about Marcelline's second wedding. Little by little he grew lively again, and treated us to the fiddler who had made Marcelline, at fifty-five, dance for the first time in her life.

"What! She got up and danced?" asked my father.

"Yes, sir, she danced!" Gustave affirmed.

And in his eyes as pale as water we thought we saw Marcelline's cotton lustre skirt whirl and pass by.

"So she got up and danced!" repeated my father, delighted.

One night my father mentioned two of his brothers who had also settled out West, Uncle Alfred in Saskatchewan and Uncle Edouard in Alberta. In a sentimental mood, he admitted his regret that he had failed to keep in touch at least with these two.

Gustave let my father go on for some time, then he promised, in that spell-binding voice which sometimes sang through our house like the winds of the wide world: "Who knows, maybe I'll drop in and see them one of these days! You just give me the right address and if the good Lord wills, I'll give them your regards."

That was all that was said about our western uncles, whom we had seen only once, Alfred when he had started off from Montreal and stopped to see us on the way, and Edouard when he had arrived from Quebec with his family and almost settled nearby.

As Gustave could give us no news of these two, my father asked for more news from Quebec, in particular about a charlatan he had known in his youth and who, it seemed, had made a fortune.

"Oh, yes! Ephrem Brabant!" said Gustave.

And that evening he began a story that lasted almost a week.

This charlatan, Ephrem Brabant by name, had started off by handing out samples of his cough syrup to the congregation as they left the chilly church on Sunday mornings. But the remedy that someone had taken for his cold had miraculously cured him of another much more serious illness. Thanks to an early spring, the news of the cure spread rapidly around the countryside. It was at once attributed to Ephrem, who was a "seventh son."

Now Ephrem wasn't about to belittle the powers and properties of his remedy any more than he denied the supernatural gifts attributed to him. A pious man, gentle and charitable, he was quite ready to admit that faith helped medicine along. So, as he enjoined his customers to prayer, he sold them more and more little bottles. The same herbal product with different labels and in different containers brought relief to stomach cramps, asthma and rheumatic pains.

Ephrem's renown spread beyond the limits of the village. Soon he had a little covered cart and a horse as black as night, and he went from farm to farm leaving brown bottles wherever he stopped. People in perfect health tried his remedy and declared they felt none the worse, which added to Ephrem Brabant's prestige as much as the cures themselves. He had grown a beard, which he trimmed to a point, and wore a black, wide-rimmed hat. His photo appeared on the bottles of syrup. Everyone in the area called him Dr. Brabant. It was at this time that he had the notion of writing and distributing an almanac to publicize the testimonials of people cured by his attentions. It was to contain, as well, practical advice for people of various ages, the interpretation of dreams, and all the known signs of good or inclement weather. The fellow could neither read nor write, but he had immense practical knowledge based on direct observation of rural life. For the spelling and fine phrases he depended on a son he had sent to school. He moved to Montreal, to a luxurious house, and despite being hauled to court, he accumulated a tidy fortune.

This was the story Gustave told us. Or, rather, this was the version we created with the passage of time and according to our desire to draw our own conclusions. Gustave must have told it more simply, and perhaps with more indulgence. For he blamed no one, judged no one. Almost every creature found mercy before him. If some really bad ones turned up, Gustave had them die off quickly, which in the end appeased my mother.

IV

Now that I think of it, it's true he talked very little about the members of our own family, apart from saying they were fine people. The unforgettable ones he managed to dig up elsewhere. After the story of Brabant, he told us about Roma Poirier who murdered her husband by putting ground glass in his soup day after day. Oh, the strange, cruel, and fascinating beings he brought to our place in the evenings, when the pails swung and rattled on the fence posts outside and from the woodland's edge coyotes yapped incessantly.

Long after he had left, as unexpectedly as he had come, long after his features had blurred in our memories, or his gentle way of smiling as he

talked of the most sinister events, it would happen that those characters—
the charlatan, the murderess, the old man of a hundred and I don't know
how many more—would turn up in our thoughts. A whole unconnected
cohort, the friends of Gustave the tramp, who revealed them to us perhaps
less through his words than through a certain slow way of pulling back his
coat as he reflected on their lives, or by an occasional amused smile at the
troop of them.

He knew the great wickedness of the world quite well but he neither
judged it nor renounced it. Nor the great distress of the world. Of that he
sometimes gave us a glimpse beneath his heavy eyelids, as he stared at a
windowpane whipped by rain and branches.

But, above all, it was the great piety of the world that he had seen and
recognized.

And through this, in the end, he found grace even in my mother's eyes.

One night he was telling about the pilgrims flocking to the sanctuary of
Sainte-Anne-de-Beaupré. The nave appeared before us, filled with votive
offerings, with longboats and schooners for lamps. Thousands of crutches
hung between the stations of the Cross, as if the lame, on their march
toward God, had recovered their agility and taken off for heaven through
the pale openings of the stained-glass windows. A pious murmur rose in the
shadows; our house was too small to contain the piety of the pilgrims, their
thanksgiving, their wild hope. Gustave led us beyond all the paths we knew.
We followed his blue gaze, a pool of water in the night, toward a dim region
through which he led us to the sound of chants and organs.

There was always someone who sighed loudly when Gustave's voice fell
silent and we came back to the reality of our house.

Of course he mixed up times and persons, but which of us, living on the
prairie, far from the beaten path, could have told true from false in his
accounts?

He had quickly seen that the mistress of the house appeared to listen only
when he talked of miracles and pilgrimages. From that moment we could
get him to speak of nothing else. He carried us to the places of prayer up and
down the length of the St. Lawrence. At the very words "St. Lawrence," we
were captured at once, for he had given us such a gripping vision of the
river. He talked of it as a living creature, a tumultuous force, and yet at
times so kind that its flow made no more than a murmur. He had described
it has having its source in the Niagara cataracts (he was a little careless
about geographical accuracy). Then he showed us how it fled toward the
sea, encircling a great island whose name we loved: Anticosti.

Then one evening he ran out of places of prayer on the St. Lawrence.
And he began to describe St. Joseph's Oratory, built stone after stone with
the people's offerings. My mother (she had a special devotion for Brother

André) stopped sewing and for the first time spoke directly to Gustave. She normally addressed him through the mediation of one of the children. "Ask him," she'd say, "if he's seen the hammer"; or, "Was he the one that took the shovel? See if you can find out..." For in the process of making himself useful he mislaid things, and my mother, who would have had scruples about accusing him directly, didn't hesitate to burden him with a latent guilt.

But this time she looked him in the eye and said: "Tell me, did you ever see him? Brother André?"

Perhaps Gustave felt the full risk of a careless answer. My mother, depending on her mood, would give him a heaping plateful at dinner, or nothing but the less tasty scraps. Did he understand the thirst for spiritual adventure that lived in this serious little woman, sentimental and deprived of the joys of church? Could he conceive of her longing for "back home," she who had been born out here in the plains? And maybe, after all, he *had* seen Brother André, for had he not assured us that he'd seen the Prince of Wales and Sarah Bernhardt? In any case, he described him to us so faithfully that much later, when we received a calendar from Quebec bearing a lithograph of the saintly Brother, we all exclaimed, "that was him, sure enough!"

For greater effect he assured us at the end, after his accumulation of evidence: "I saw him the way I see you now...Madame!"

He no longer dared to say "Cousin" to her, but could not pronounce "Madame" without a perceptible hesitation and a note of regret.

From that moment on he grew in my mother's esteem. Henceforth, she gave him an attention which if not always benevolent was at least sustained.

V

But this state of affairs didn't last long. This little devil of a man, who could down plates of porridge in the early morning and fried pork piled up on his plate at other meals without putting on a pound, this "puny runt," as my mother called him, for she still doubted at times whether he had really seen the faces of saints and sanctuaries, this tranquil old soul, perhaps he was waiting for nothing more than to tame my mother, and then away he'd go, leaving the fireside, the set table, and the lamp that shone in the window on rainy nights.

One morning we caught him at the door, staring at the scrubby copses that cut the horizon beyond the swollen coulee. The rain was still falling. Soon it was mixed with snow, and before the day's end the prairie, under its puffy vestment, seemed quite round. Only once did we see him at the door. But we knew he wanted to be on his way, as we had known three weeks before, just from seeing him sit down and sniff the smells of the house, that he wanted to stay. He was just like a big, skinny dog we'd had when we were small, who would beg to come in when the weather was bad and beg to go out when it was worse.

It was no use, my father's going back to the stories of Marcelline and France and Cousin Brault the fiddler, who left by himself for Montreal with his violin and played in orchestras there to the great shame of the family: Gustave's face had darkened. He looked at the door, nothing but the door, the one through which he had made such a joyous entrance. He looked nowhere else and seemed to be pining away each day. For we were witnesses to a strange phenomenon: the clothes my mother had given him seemed to be his own as long as he was happy to stay among us, but then we saw them collapse, hang loose about his shoulders, getting in his way. And what about the stories, the wonderful stories forever extinguished in his eyes! As the sky of our prairies is empty when all the wings have flown south, so Gustave's eyes grew bleak and, as it were, uninhabited. That was perhaps what we held against him most: not having any stories in reserve behind the farther mists of his pale smile.

One evening my father went so far as to offer him a little pay if he wanted to work. My mother showed no offence. Gustave's eyes were grateful, but he gave no other reply.

Next day he was gone. He must have slipped off at night, raising the latches cautiously. Farouche hadn't barked.

My mother flew into a rage. She ran to the silver drawer, to the relic box, to the crockery pot where the change was kept; nothing was missing anywhere. She counted the knives, the spoons, the candlesticks, but had to admit they were all there. Then she was even more humiliated.

"What did we do to make him leave like that?"

My father, for his part, inspected the barn, the granaries, the sheds. He came back discomfitted. The shadows on his mute face revealed a regret that did not fade away. From time to time he sighed. At last one evening we heard him complaining, or accusing us: "We didn't receive him the way he deserved. He showed us: he went away."

But we had news of him the following year. In the mail one evening, along with the catalogue from the store in town and the weekly newspaper, was an envelope covered with an unknown handwriting, awkward and blotted with ink spots. My mother opened it at once. Leaning over her shoulder we read along with her. From the wet smell of the paper I cried out before reading a word: "It's from Gustave!"

A skip to the laborious and childish signature confirmed it. It was Gustave's.

He'd made it to Uncle Alfred's place in Saskatchewan and said he'd been asked to send regards. He said very kind things about the three girls, Emilie,

Alma and Céline, whom my father, by the way, had described as hard to marry off: "Too fancy." From the lines a certain gaiety emanated. You could feel that Gustave was happy. No doubt he was telling his funniest stories in the evenings. A thin smell of tobacco clung to the paper. Crosses at the bottom were meant for kisses.

A little daring, this last familiarity! My mother didn't fail to be offended. My father grew cheerier and we often heard him prophesy in a satisfied tone: "You'll see, he'll be back one of these days."

The following year Gustave was in Alberta. He told us about it in a letter written at Uncle Edouard's place. Uncle Ed and Aunt Honora were working three-quarters of a section with their son. Gustave had helped with the harvest, which had been a good one. They had had him driving the truck, and he'd delivered the grain to the village. One girl was getting married this fall (he didn't say which one, and this unsettled point was the subject of many discussions among us). Another was taking orders. (My mother, to shut us up, said that could only be Paule, because of an old photo that showed her as rather scrawny, her eyes turned heavenward.) Anyway, all were well, including Gustave, except Honora who had stomach trouble. But he was sending for some of Ephrem Brabant's remedy to cure her. He didn't know yet if he'd spend the winter with the "relatives" or go and see a brother of Honora's who'd settled "across the big mountains."

My mother made a few objections, not so much to shake our convictions as to put her own to the test. Aunt Honora, who was such a cold, suspicious fish...how could she have given Gustave a welcome like this? That remained to be seen. You'd have thought my mother felt a little resentful.

We were certainly glad to get the news, in any case. Lazy about writing, we had never, for all our good resolutions, renewed a correspondence (which in fact had never begun) with our western uncles. And it seemed that Gustave, by taking this duty over, took our bad conscience with it.

This was all very well, but my mother took the opportunity of giving a little lesson to my father, indirectly, as she well knew how to do.

Her head thrown back, shaking a mat, she remarked one day: "I must say, there's strangers that have more family feeling than...than...."

My father refused to take offence. He smiled the serene smile of one whose confidence is sheltered from all doubt.

And so time passed. We had another letter six months later, not from British Columbia but from the Yukon, where Gustave vaguely gave us to understand he had turned trapper. Years passed. We might even have forgotten him had he not, by coming to see us long ago, awakened that mysterious thing: interest in one's family, that bewildering affinity that makes a Marcelline, unknown though she may be, less of a stranger than any other old woman in the village. Or, above all, if he hadn't left in our house the memory of so many places and things and people that still carried us through the long evenings, when boredom was not far and we grasped at dreams to drive it off. At those times, rising behind our hazy imaginings, the slightly drawling voice of Gustave would come back from the depths of our recollections.

We no longer talked of him, but thought of him often, each of us, in the evening when a shadow grew long on the road outside.

VI

He came back on a foggy, rainy night like the first one. And Farouche was the only one that knew him, from the smell of wet leaves and mud that his clothing gave off. They recognized each other, the man and the dog, the one perhaps luckier than the other because he had obeyed the mysterious call of the roads and the moonlit nights. But the man seemed weary. Leaning over the anxious dog, patting his head, you would have said he was advising him to appreciate the comfort of his kennel and perhaps even the benevolent servitude of the chain.

He straightened up, examined with the same slow, sad smile the roof of our house and the smoking chimney.

My mother uttered a few excited words: "Good Lord! It looks like..."

The man hesitated, then, as he had the first time, detoured around to tap on the back door.

I went to open it. His eyes, deep in their sockets, shone for a second. There was no more gaiety in those eyes, not even in their depths. The lustreless blue of water sleeping on the road after heavy storms!

But he exclaimed: "Ghislaine! I'd have known you anywhere, but my land, you've grown!"

I showed him into the big room. He followed me. He was just raising his arms in a great gesture to the reunited family when suddenly we saw him totter, then stagger against the stove and fall, his thin face turned toward us, a little spittle at his lips, his eyes fixed on the shadows like trickles of stagnant water.

My mother touched his reddened forehead. She said: "He has a high fever."

My father took Gustave's feet, my mother his shoulders, and they carried him to their bed.

Then his delirium began.

"I'm Barthélémy," he said. "Son of your brother Alcide. I come from Saint-Jerome. Yep, from Saint-Jerome."

Then he sighed.

"You've got to be friends with your folks, even if they're not always up to the mark."

Then again, in a wheezing voice, between coughing fits: "Come on! You don't know me? I'm Honoré, old man Phidime's boy, the one they thought was dead. I'm his Honoré!"

And suddenly he was muttering about tapers, the monstrance on the altar, the great piety of the world. In the middle of a brisk little laugh he exclaimed: "Good day to you, cousin Anastasie! Well, hello there!"

My father and mother exchanged a long look, then one after the other pulled banket over the sick man's body.

It snowed that night, and the next day too, and then another whole day. Then it blew. You could hear the coyotes that had ventured right to the doors of the barns, hear them howling and fighting over the carcass of a white hare that had fallen into their ambush. At times, from the growls that shook Farouche's kennel, we concluded that a great wolf was stalking around the house. Powerful gusts swept the prairie, piled the snow high near the stables, sheds and all the buildings of the farm, which next morning would be half-buried. Snow was already up to our windows. Suddenly a great gust hurled itself against them as if to have a try through glass at blowing out our lamp, last visible sign of life struggling against the unleashed passion of the blizzard.

"No use talking," said my father. "We'll have to try and get out before all the roads are blocked. He could die, that fellow. At least we need some medicine."

He spoke with no warmth. You could feel that his grave affection for the poor wretch had not outlasted the confessions murmured in his delirium; he was being torn by an inner tempest as powerful as the one outside.

Just then, as if mysteriously aware of our concern and his own great danger, Gustave murmured among other unintelligible phrases: "Ephrem Brabant!"

Inspired, my mother fumbled in the pockets of his old overcoat hanging on a nail in the wall. She discovered a small brown bottle. On its label, the face with the white beard, that of the charlatan of Saint-Alphonse, seemed to us familiar and reassuring.

"It can't do him any harm, anyhow," said my mother.

She gave the poor man a gulp of the elixir.

"After all, he believed in it," she added.

My father was getting ready to go out just the same. He wrapped himself in a heavy coat with a fur collar and, to calm my mother, assured her he was just going to the nearest neighbour who had a phone.

My mother calculated: "Six miles there and back. I'll be worried."

A few minutes later we heard a faint sound of sleigh bells whipped by the wind, then the horse whinnying as it plunged past the fence into an immense, tumultuous tempest.

Gustave was quieter after he had swallowed Ephrem Brabant's remedy.

Soon he was sleeping deeply, his hands open on the white sheet.

"Now who'd have thought it!" my mother sighed.

Several times she went to sniff at the few drops of brown syrup left in the bottle.

"Just because he believed in it."

Her remark, however, seemed to refer less to the remedy than to a possible thought that arose in her, illuminating her solitary wonderment. She resisted it still at times, as you could see from her restive look; then, with a little shrug of her shoulders, she seemed to give in to the undeniable evidence.

The hours passed. The sick man was still asleep. My mother had finally dozed off. But, waking suddenly, she looked at the clock with growing anguish. Then she struggled to keep awake, and watched over Gustave as she had watched over us, her children, through our illnesses.

Then came the crunching of the cutter's runners in the snow, as if it were still far off, though it was in fact close by the house. A little later my father came in. He was pale, despite the cold, and in a shaking rage.

"How is he?" he asked.

My mother pointed to Gustave, sleeping, and indicated that it was all right to talk.

Then my father turned on her violently as if he were going to accuse her: "The very idea!...Albertine...Who'd have thought it? Do you know the police may be here tomorrow because of him?"

"What! He's not a criminal? Oh, no!" stammered my mother, her hands fluttering to her heart.

"No. Maybe worse."

"Is he crazy? Sick?" she asked, pressing her hands to her heaving breasts.

"No. But I'd just as soon it was that."

"What then? Tell me, Arthur."

My father strode across the room, darting wounded glances to one side and the other. His thick overcoat, which he had forgotten to take off, gave an impressive form to his shadow on the wall.

"Oh," he shouted, with lively rancour, "he'd be just as well off dead, that fellow. Imagine, Albertine, and you looked after him so well! Imagine, he passed himself off for a Lafrenière at the Lafrenières below the big hill. And for a Poirier at the Poiriers. And so on. He hasn't one name, that man, he has ten, twenty, as many families as he likes."

"What then?" asked my mother. She had grown strangely calm.

"An impostor!" my father exploded. "Don't you realize, Albertine? An impostor!"

He tried to control his voice: "Somebody reported him. The police have started an inquiry. When people find out he's here..."

"What then, Arthur?"

120

My mother had taken up her stand at the door of the bedroom as if to forbid all entry. Tiny as she was, when she stood this way, her head high, her eyes flashing with determination, not many would have dared defy her.

"Well?" she said. "Don't we know what to say? Don't we know it?" she repeated, questioning each of us in turn with her clear, open gaze.

Suddenly the violence that had seized my father was broken. He seemed infinitely tired. Almost feeling his way, he sought out his chair in the corner by the fire and sank down in it. And at last we understood the disenchantment, worse than anger, that he had to bear. A Marcelline who could laugh and dance at her second wedding; Eustache, attached to the memory of his parents; a tender, affectionate Philomène; these characters, like a mirage that had for some time fed my father's dreams, had already disappeared from before his eyes. They were replaced by a dried-up, hardened little woman, by the bad son who had deceived his parents, by Philomène, frightful and graceless. In my father's eyes we saw the return of that absence of love with which he had had to live for so long.

"Good gracious now!" my mother said in a curiously persuasive tone. "Who's to prove it isn't true? He has to be somebody's relative. What's to prove to us it isn't true?"

Next morning Gustave awoke practically cured. He accepted the warm clothing my mother had taken from the trunks for him. He thanked her without effusiveness. You'd have thought he'd left a few of his things with us, and was grateful to get them back clean and mended. Gradually our wrath, our shame at having liked him, quieted down.

That day the sky swept the snow away with great waves of sunlight. The buildings, the cutters with their shafts pointed skyward, the buckets and barrels, all our everyday things, projected only the flimsiest of shadows in the immense plain all trembling with light. In the distance, on the hardened crust of the prairie, tiny tracks made their way toward the woods. At dawn, when the storm grew still, the wolves and coyotes had again sought the refuge of the trees.

Gustave was getting ready to go. He went to the door, downcast, but paused, his hand on the latch. My mother was preparing a splendid stew of jack rabbit and beef.

"There's no rush," she said, paying no attention to my father's silence. "You were a sick man. There's no rush at all."

Gustave made a despairing gesture with his arms. Then a shiver passed through his whole body. He seemed to be struggling against the temptation of warmth and the odour of the stew. Had some echo of our words of yesterday floated up in his memory? Or was it his old mania taking over again? He began to lift the latch.

"I suppose you have to get along to see some relatives?"

My mother had spoken in a friendly and reassuring voice. The man pricked up his ears. His stooped shoulders straightened. He looked back at the room. Greedily, as if to make a memory of it, he comtemplated a ray of sunlight slanting through it, delicately lighting up the steam from the pots simmering on the stove. Finally he glanced up at my mother. His old eyes with their worn gaze were shining again.

"Yes," he said.

"Well! And which way are you heading this time?"

"I have some folks on my mother's side . . . in Ontario . . . " he began uncertainly.

"Would that be down Hawkesbury way?" asked my mother, with every sign of lively interest. "They say there's a lot of our people there still speak French."

She had thrown a shawl over her shoulders. She went with the man past the threshold. She encouraged him with her eyes. He went off, walking backward a few steps, as if he couldn't decide whether to give up my mother's accepting gaze. Then he turned to face the naked, empty plain.

Farouche, straining at his leash, was whining, almost choking himself in the attempt to leave with that miserable silhouette.

"Quiet, Farouche, quiet!" said my mother.

Then she did something so simple, so splendid. Cupping her hands to her mouth, she shouted loudly into the wind, her apron flying around her: "Take care! Take good care . . . Cousin Gustave!"

Did he hear? Perhaps. In any case, he had cut a branch in our garden for a walking stick.

Gabrielle Roy (1909-) was born in St. Boniface, Manitoba, and now lives in Quebec City. Her novels that have been translated into English include *The Tin Flute, Where Nests the Water Hen,* and *The Road Past Altamont.* She has won two Governor General's Awards, for *Bonheur d'occasion (The Tin Flute)* and for *Ces enfants de ma vie* (1977).

Margaret Laurence
A Gourdful of Glory

You could walk through the entire market and look at every stall, but never would you see calabashes and earthen pots any better than those sold by Mammii Ama. She was honest—true as God, she really was. You might claim that there were as many honest traders here as there were elephants, and Mammii Ama would understand your meaning, and laugh, and agree with you. But she would let you know she was the one old cow-elephant that never yet died off.

She was a petty trader. A few market women grew rich, and became queen mammies, but Mammii Ama was not one of these. She got by. She lived. Nobody ever got the better of her, but she wasn't one to cheat her customers. She handled good stock. She wasn't like some of those shifty mammies who bought cheap and sold at the regular price the gourd with the faint seam of a crack right in the bottom where you wouldn't notice it until the soup began to leak out. She never sold flawed pots and bowls, either, a bit damaged in the firing so that they broke if you laughed in the same room with them. Such a trick was not Mammii Ama's way. The odd cull, maybe, she would admit. A few could always slip into a lot. You know how it is. A trader woman has to live, after all.

The cockerels, piercing the dawn grey with shrill and scarlet voices, awoke no earlier than Mammii Ama. Expertly, she bunched her fish-patterned cloth around her, bound on a headscarf of green and glossy artificial silk, and was ready for the day. She puffed the charcoal embers into flame, plonked on the tin kettle, brewed tea, and ate some cold boiled yam.

Comfort was still lying curled up on the straw mat. One always hated to waken a sleeping child. Mammii Ama gently shook her granddaughter, and Comfort sat up, dazed, like a parrot with all its feathers ruffled. She was soon dressed; not yet five years old, she wore only a shamecloth, a mere flutter of red and beaded rag around her middle and between her legs.

Then they were off. Wait—a last thought. Did Adua sleep peacefully? Was she covered? If you sweated, sleeping, you got a chill in your belly and you had pain passing water for evermore. Quiet as a watch-night, Mammii Ama padded across the hut to the iron cot where her snoring daughter lay. Adua was properly covered—the blanket was drawn up to her neck, and all you could see of her was her head with its wiry hair that she was always straightening with hot pull-irons, and her face, breathing softly and brown under its matting of white powder from the night before. Mammii Ama did not understand why her daughter daubed herself with talcum until she looked like a fetish priestess in a funeral parade. Many things about Adua were difficult to comprehend. The high-heel shoes, for instance, which hurt and were all but impossible to walk on. Teeter this way, lurch that—a fine business. The woman's ankle-bones would snap one of these days—but try to tell her. And the palaver about the name—a lunacy. Adua called herself Marcella, and insisted that everyone else do the same. It was not like the granddaughter's name. Comfort—a decent name. A mission name, true, but it had lived here a long time, until it seemed to have been African always. But Marcella—who ever heard of such a name? Mammii Ama couldn't bring herself to speak it. She called her daughter "moon woman" or "choice of kings," and Adua, who was—you had to admit it—very vain, liked to hear those names as she preened herself.

Still, she was a good daughter. She brought home money—worked all night for it. A club girl, she was, at the Weekend In Wyoming, and Mammii Ama loved her more dearly than life, and felt for her a shy and surprised pride, for the daughter was certainly a beauty, not a cow-elephant like her mother.

Mammii Ama looked once more on the powdered and sleeping face, then she was gone, shutting quietly behind her the packing-case door of the mudbrick shanty.

Mammii Ama took the child's hand while they clambered onto the crowded bus. She paid her fare, and the bus, with a rumble like the belly of a giant, jolted off down the road and into the city.

The market was already filling with sellers. The best hunter got an early start, Mammii Ama would say. You'd never catch a fat cutting-grass by sleeping late. As she spread out her wares in front of her stall, Mammii Ama sang. She sang in pidgin, so that every passer-by, whatever his language, would understand.

"*Mammii Ama sell all fine pot,*
  Oh oh Mammii Ama
She no t'ief you, she no make palavah,
  Oh oh Mammii Ama—"

And the girl child, squatting in dust as she arranged just-so the stacks of brown earthen bowls, the big-bellied black cooking-pots, added to the refrain her high and not-quite-true-pitched voice.

"Oh oh Mammii Ama—"

Everywhere there were voices, and sweet singing bodies. Everywhere the market women's laughter, coarse and warm as the touch of a tongue. It was still early, and the morning cooks had not yet arrived to buy vegetables and meat for the Europeans.

Moki was already perched atop his firewood. He wiped the rheum from his eyes with an end of his dirty turban. He was old, and his eyes ran mucus, especially in the morning. He was not a Muslim, but his nephew, who died of a worm in the guts, had been one, so Moki always wore a turban in memory of him. No one knew where Moki came from. He didn't know himself. He knew the name of his village, but not the country where it was, and he knew the names of his people's gods. He had come here who knows how long ago, with a Hausa caravan, and had somehow lost the trader who hired him to carry headload. Now he sold pieces of firewood, which he gathered each evening in the bush.

"Morny, Mistah Moki! I greet you!" Mammii Ama called, and the old man fake-bowed to her as though she were a queen mother.

On the other side, a Hausa man was hanging up his white and black wool mats and huge pointed hats and long embroidered robes which only men tall as the Hausas could wear. Sabina the cloth-seller snapped at a small boy who pissed beside her stall, complaining that he was spraying her second-best bolts, draped outside to catch the eye. The small boy's mother threw a coconut husk which caught him on the ear, and he ran off, leaking and howling.

T'reepenny, who looked more ancient than the gods, creaked and trembled up to Mammii Ama's stall. Her hands, bony as tree roots and frail as grass, lugged along the bucket of gourd spoons, half of them broken. She had no stall. She had no money to rent one, so Mammii Ama allowed her to sit beside the calabash-and-pot stall with her bucket. She only said one word, ever. Maybe she only knew one. "T'reepenny," she would quiver and quaver. "T'reepenny, t'reepenny," over and over like a brainfever bird, as she held up the gourd spoons for all to admire. She was pleased if she got one penny. Only from white women, rich and gullible, had she ever received as much as three.

With the wares arranged, Mammii Ama was light in heart. Now she began to recall last night's rally. She had gone with the others in the Association of Market Women. They all wore new cloth, in the party's colours, red and white and green. What a thing it had been! Her well-fleshed hips remembered their jigglings and marvellous convolutions in the parade. Her shoulders and hearty arms remembered the touch of others' arms and shoulders as the market women marched. Four abreast, they entered the

125

meeting-place like a charging army, like an army with spears of fire, with rifles fashioned of power and glory. And they all shouted together—loud as a thousand lorry horns, loud as the sea—"Free-Dom!"

And he had been there, the lovely boy they loved so well, the Show-Boy. He spoke to them of the day that was coming, the day of freedom. And they shouted with one voice, and they cheered with one voice. They were his women, his mothers and his brides.

"Hey, you Sabina!" Mammii Ama shouted. "Were you at the rally?"

"Naturally," the shriek came back. "Didn't you see me, Mammii Ama? I was at the back, in between Mercy Mensah and that old Togo woman, whatever her name is."

"I was at the front," Mammii Ama said loudly, but with modesty.

"I was there, too," Moki chipped in.

Everyone laughed.

"Wha-at? I never knew you were a market woman, Moki," Mammii Ama bellowed.

"When you get to my age, it's all the same," Moki replied evenly. "Man—woman—what does it matter? We all eat. We all die."

An outburst of chitter-chatter. "Don't tell me that story, Moki!" "Maybe it's an old muzzle-loader, but I'll bet it still fires!" And so on.

"What did you think of it, Sabina, the rally?" Mammii Ama continued, when the gust of ribaldry faded.

Sabina shrugged. She was thin, and her mouth always turned down, as though she had just swallowed a piece of rotten fish.

"Well, it's a lot of talk, if you ask me," she said. "Free-Dom. Independence. All right—the white men go. So, then? We'll still be haggling over tuppence at our stalls, my friends."

Mammii Ama jumped to her feet and shook her head and both fists at Sabina.

"Ei! Somebody here is like a crocodile! Yes, somebody acts like the crocodile who crawls in the mud of the river. He lives in the river mud—and he thinks the whole world is only river mud. Oh, blind! Blind!"

She appealed to the others.

"Free-Dom—it's like the sun," she cried. "You have to crawl out of the river mud or you can't see it."

Moki muttered and went on cleaning his eyes. Old T'reepenny nodded her head. She agreed in this way with everything Mammii Ama said. She didn't understand, but she agreed. Whatever Mammii Ama said must be right. The Hausa man stared—he spoke no Ga.

Sabina went on shrugging, and Mammii Ama grew so furious she rushed over to Sabina's stall and burst into fresh argument. She grew inspired. She no longer cared about Sabina. Around her, the market women gathered.

They cried "Ha—ei!" when she paused for breath. They swayed and chanted to the rhythm of Mammii Ama.

"Go call all de market woman!" Mammii Ama cried, this time in pidgin, to captivate a wider audience. "Tell dem say 'Free-Dom'! Go call all de market woman—say, you no go sell befoah five minute. You sell Free-Dom dis time. What dis t'ing, what dis Free-Dom? He be strong, he be fine too much. Ju-ju man he no got such t'ing, such power word. Dis Free-Dom he be sun t'ing, same sun he be shine. Hey, you market woman, you say 'Money sweet—I be poor woman, nothing with, on'y one penny. I no'gree dis Free-Dom, I no be fit for chop him.' Oh—oh—I t'ink you be bush woman, no got sense. I no 'gree for you. I tell you, dis Free-Dom he be sweet sweet t'ing. You wait small, you see I tell you true. Market woman all dey be queen mammy den."

Moki stopped his eye-wiping and waved a piece of firewood, roaring encouragement to his friend Mammii Ama. The Hausa man uttered sombre cries in his own tongue— "Allah knows it! Has not the Prophet himself said the same? It will be shown at the Last Day!" T'reepenny, carried away by excitement, grasped a gourd spoon in either hand and executed a sort of dance, back bent and stiff-kneed, all by herself, until her unsteady breath gave out and she sank down beside her bucket once more, chirping her mournful word.

Sabina, feeling herself outnumbered, began to weep, begging them all not to forget her unfortunate past. If she seemed sour, she sobbed, they knew why.

Mammii Ama immediately grew sympathetic. She broke off and put an arm around Sabina's shoulder. A terrible thing it must have been, she agreed. Enough to mark a person for life.

Sabina had once had a wealthy lover—well, not wealthy, perhaps, but certainly nicely fixed. A clerk, he was, a man in a government office. He always seemed healthy, Sabina used to say. He seemed so strong, so full of life, so full of love. How that man would do it! Again and again—why, half a dozen times in a single night, that was nothing to him, Sabina said, simply nothing.

Then one night, his heart swelled and burst, and he died, just like that. He was with Sabina at the time. They had gone to sleep, still together. At least, she had gone to sleep. A little later, feeling cramped and trying to turn, she had wakened to find a dead man there. Dead as a gutted fish, and his eyes wide open. Sabina got a baby that night, it turned out, and she went around saying her child had been given her by a dead man. She was sure of it. She screeched and cried. A child begotten by a corpse—who could stand the thought? No one was surprised when the baby was born dead.

The women clucked softly. Mammii Ama, ashamed of her attack, soothed and soothed in her full mother-voice.

"There, my red lily. Cry, then. It is nothing. I am a fool; I have a head like calabash, empty."

Into the hush-hushing throng of women ran Comfort. Her face was frightened and excited.

"Mammii Ama! Mammii Ama! A white woman has come to your stall.!"

And Mammii Ama looked amazed, dumbfounded, only partly in mockery of the child. Hastily she hitched her cloth up around her and flew back.

"Ei—what a madness!"

She went running like a girl, like a young girl at her first outdooring. She carried her weight lightly, and her breasts bounced as she bounded over gutter and path, over smouldering charcoal burner, over the sleeping babies with blackflies at their nostrils' edge.

"Who is the young virgin fleeing from her seducer?" Moki shouted, as she approached. "Oh oh Mammii Ama!"

The white woman was thin and tall. She had very little flesh on her, just yellow hide over bones, and her eyes were such a pale blue they seemed not to be there at all—only the jelly of the eyeball, nothing to see with. She was holding a brown earthen bowl in her hands.

Mammii Ama regained her breath.

"Madam—I greet you," she said with hoarse cheerfulness.

The white woman smiled uncertainly and looked over her shoulder. Mammii Ama looked, too, and it was Ampadu standing there.

Ampadu was a clerk. He had a good job. One heard he had influence. He was a really educated man—he knew not only reading and writing, but also the work of account-books and typewriters. Mammii Ama, who could neither read nor write, and who kept her accounts in her head with never a mistake in twenty-four years, was greatly impressed with Ampadu's power over words and numbers. She did not tell him so—in fact, she constantly made fun of him. They were distantly related, and Ampadu, who understood her unexpressed pride in this relationship, took her jibs in an easy-natured way.

She clapped him on the shoulder. He was neatly dressed in a white shirt and grey flannel trousers. How prosperous he looked. And his rimmed spectacles, how well they suited him.

"Ampadu! I greet you!" she cried in Ga. "How are you, great government man? Do they still say your pen is more active than your love-branch? Hey—you, Moki! Did you know this? When the old chief's young wife wanted a lover, she sent for Ampadu's pen!"

The clerk laughed, but not wholeheartedly. He patted his stomach in embarrassment. Mammii Ama, realizing Ampadu was accompanying the white woman, began to roll her eyes and pretended to stagger.

"What's this, Ampadu? What's this? What's all this about?"

Ampadu held up his hand, like a policeman stopping a lorry.

"She wants to see the market," he hissed. "She's the wife of my new boss. Mammii Ama, please be sensible, I implore you. She wants to buy a calabash, God knows why."

The white woman was growing impatient.

"Ampadu — ask her what she'll take for this bowl, please."

"Ten shilling," Mammii Ama replied without hesitation.

"Ten shillings!" the white woman cried, and even Ampadu looked stunned.

Mammii Ama seized the bowl from her hands.

"See, madam — dis one, he be fine too much. No be bad one. Look — put you fingah heah — you feel? All fine — nevah broke, dis one. Ten shilling, madam."

"How much is the usual price?" the white woman asked Ampadu.

Ampadu scuffed his shoes in the dust. Mammii Ama felt quite sorry for him, but she had to try hard not to laugh.

"Usual price?" Ampadu appeared to search his memory. "Let me see, what is the usual price? I am sorry, madam — I am afraid I don't really know. My wife, you see, buys all the cooking-pots — "

"Ten shilling!" shouted Mammii Ama in a huge voice. "All time, meka price he be ten shilling! I tell you true, madam. I no t'ief you."

"Five shillings," the white woman offered.

"Nine shilling sixpence — for you."

They settled at length on six shillings, to Mammii Ama's well-disguised delight. The white woman then bought a black cooking-pot and two calabashes. Mammii Ama was amazed. What could such a woman want with cooking-pots and calabashes? Were Europeans living like poor Africans all of a sudden? Mammii Ama felt excited and confused. The order of things was turning upside down, but pleasurably, in a way that provided food for speculation and gossip.

When the white woman was gone, they all discussed it. Who could understand such a thing? Mammii Ama, dusting and re-arranging her stock of pots and bowls, began one of her speeches.

"Hey! Stranger woman, listen to me. Do you feed your man from a calabash you bought in the market? Does your man eat from a bowl made of river clay? Ei! The gourd-vine dances — he shakes his leaves with laughter. Ei! The river fish drown in their laughter. Your own dishes — are they not white as a silver shilling? They are white as the egret's feathers, when he sleeps in the baobab tree. If the fine vessels displease you, give them to my granddaughter. Yes! Give them to Comfort, the lovely and dear one — "

Mammii Ama turned the last bit into a song, and sang it all day. Some of the others joined the refrain, varying it from time to time for amusement.

> *"Yes! Give them to the woodseller,*
> *Give them to Moki, the lovely one—"*

Mammii Ama added a stanza in pidgin, so everyone around would know she was no longer cross at Sabina.

> *"Meka you dash dem for Sabina,*
> *She fine too much, same been-to gal,*
> *She like all fine t'ing—"*

A week later, the white woman returned, this time alone. Mammii Ama greeted her like an old friend. The white woman bought a gourd spoon from T'reepenny, and haggled with Mammii Ama over the price of another bowl. Finally, Mammii Ama could restrain her curiosity no longer . . .

"Madam — why you buy African pot?"

The white woman smiled.

"I want to use them for ashtrays."

"Ashtrays! For dem cig'rette?" Mammii Ama could not believe her ears. "You no got fine one, madam?"

"Oh — I have lots of others," the woman said, "but I like these. They're so beautifully shaped."

Mammii Ama could not credit it.

"An' dem calabash? Madam chop *fu-fu* now?"

"I use the shallow ones to put groundnuts in," the woman explained. "For small-chop with drinks. The big ones I'm using for plants."

"Free-Dom time, meka all African get dem fine dish," Mammii Ama mused. "I look-a dem na Kingsway store. Fine dish, shine too much."

She stopped herself. It would not do, for business, to admit she would like to use fine white dishes. She even felt a little guilty at the thought. Were not her calabashes and bowls the best in the market? But still —

The white woman was looking at her oddly.

"You don't mean to tell me that you think you'll all be given — what did you say — shiny dishes, when Independence comes?"

Mammii Ama did not know whether she believed it or not. But she grew stubborn.

"I tell you true!" Speaking the words, she became immediately convinced of their absolute truth. "Market woman, all dey be same queen mammy den."

"Is that what freedom means to you?" the woman asked.

Mammii Ama felt somehow that she was being attacked at her very roots.

"What dis t'ing, what dis Free-Dom? You no savvy Free-Dom palavah, madam. He be strong, dis Free-Dom, he be power word."

"You're free now," the woman said. "We give you justice. I'll wager you won't have it then."

The woman did not speak pidgin. Mammii Ama could not follow every word, but she detected the meaning. The white woman was against Free-Dom. Mammii Ama was not surprised, of course. Nor was she angry. What else would you expect of Europeans? When she spoke, it was not to the white woman. It was to the market, to the city, to every village quiet in the heat of the sun.

She spread her arms wide, as though she would embrace the whole land. She felt the same as she had once long ago, when she went to meet her young man in the grove. She was all tenderness and longing; she was an opening moonflower, filled with the seeds of life everlasting.

"Dis Free-Dom he be sun t'ing," she cried. "Same sun, he be shine. I no 'gree for Eur'pean. I 'gree for Free-Dom."

The woman looked thoughtful.

"Your leader seems popular among the market women."

"Ha—aah! He fine too much. He savvy all t'ing. He no forget we. Market woman all dey come queen mammy. All—all—"

She stuttered and stopped. The Free-Dom speech seemed to have lost something of its former grandeur. Now, Mammii Ama's words would not rise to her heights. Earthbound, she grasped for the golden lightning with which to illumine the sky. She found it.

"Dat time, you t'ink we pay wen we deah go for bus?" she cried. "We no pay! At all! Nevah one penny."

The white woman still peered. Then she laughed, a dry sound, like Moki breaking firewood.

"You really think the buses will be free after Independence?"

"I hear so," Mammii Ama said, truthfully. Then, feeling her faith not stated with sufficient strength, "Be so! Meka come Free-Dom nevah one penny for we. We go for bus free, free, free!"

Her words had the desired effect. The white woman was staring at her, certainly, staring with wide eyes. But in her face was an expression Mammii Ama did not understand. Who was this stranger, and why did she come here with her strange laughter and strange words and a strange look on her skull-face? Why didn't she go away?

Mammii Ama frowned. Then she heaved her shoulders in a vast shrug and turned back to her stall.

"Hey, you Comfort! Hasn't the village woman come yet with the new calabashes?"

Soon, with the white woman gone, everything was in order, everything was itself once more, known and familiar.

"Mammii Ama sell all fine pot,
  Oh Oh Mammii Ama!
She no t'ief you, she no make palavah,
  Oh Oh Mammii Ama!"

The white woman did not come again for a long time, and Mammii Ama forgot about her. Things weren't going so well. Both Adua and the child got sick—skin burning all over, belly distended. Mammii Ama went to a dealer in charms. Then she went to a dealer in roots and herbs. She spent, altogether, six pounds four shillings and ninepence. But it did no good. Adua wouldn't drink the brew the herb-dealer concocted, nor would she allow Mammii Ama to give it to the child. When the fetish priest came to the shanty, Adua lay with her head covered by the blanket, not wanting to see him, but afraid to send him away. Then Adua insisted that Mammii Ama take Comfort to the hospital to see the doctor. Mammii Ama was very much opposed to the idea, but one did not dare argue with a sick person. She took the child. They waited three days before they could see the doctor, and Mammii Ama was in a panic, thinking of her empty market stall, and no money coming in. She had a little money saved, but it was almost gone now. Finally, the doctor gave Comfort a bottle of medicine, and Mammii Ama, when they arrived home, gave some of it to Adua as well. Slowly, the sickness went away, withdrawing a speck of its poison at a time. Adua went back to work, but Comfort was still too weak to help in the market.

That was always the way—sometimes you had luck; you were well; the coins in the wooden box grew; you bought a little meat, a little fish, a bowl of lamb's blood for the stew. Then—bam! Fever came, or somebody robbed you, or nobody needed pots and calabashes that month. And you were back where you started, eating only *garri* and lucky to have anything. You got by somehow. If you couldn't live, you died, and that was that.

But then a great thing happened. Not in the ordinary run of exciting things, like Moki killing a small python, or Sabina getting pregnant again, this time by a live man. No—nothing like that at all. This was a great thing, the greatest of all great things.

Independence.

The time came. Everyone was surprised when the time actually came, although they'd been expecting it for so long. It was like a gift—a piece of gold that somebody dashed you for nothing.

Mammii Ama was so excited she could hardly breathe. The night before the Day, everyone gathered at the Parliament building, everyone who could dance or walk or totter, even old T'reepenny, who nearly got broken like a twig by the crowd, until Mammii Ama staunchly elbowed a path for her. And there at midnight, the white man's flag came down, and the new flag went up—so bright, and the black star so strong and shining, the new flag of the new land. And the people cried with one voice—"Now—now we are Free!"

The Day—who could describe it? Commoners and princes, all together. The priest-kings of the Ga people, walking stately and slow. The red and gold umbrellas of the proud Akan chiefs, and their golden regalia carried aloft by the soul-bearers, sword-bearers, spokesmen, guards. From the northern desert, the hawk-faced chiefs in tent-like robes. The shouting young men, the girls in new cloth, the noise and the dancing, the highlife music, the soldiers in their scarlet jackets. The drums beating and beating for evermore. The feasting. The palm wine, everybody happy. Free-Dom.

Mammii Ama sang and shouted until her voice croaked like a tree toad's. She drank palm wine. She danced like a young girl. Everybody was young. Everybody's soul was just born this minute. A day to tell your grand-children and their children. "Free-Dom shone, silver as stars—oh, golden as sun. The day was here. We saw it. We sang it and shouted."

The day, of course, like any other day, had to finish sometime. Mammii Ama, exhausted, found her way home through the still-echoing streets. Then she slept.

The next morning Mammii Ama did not rise quite so early. The tea and boiled yam tasted raw in her mouth. She swallowed her cold bile and marched out.

Only when the bus drew to a stop did she remember. She climbed on, cheerful now, full of proud expectancy. She was about to push her way through the standing people near the door, when the driver touched her arm.

"Hey—you! You no pay yet."

She looked at him shrewdly.

"Wey you say? You t'ief me? I no pay now."

"So? Why you no pay?"

Mammii Ama folded her arms and regarded him calmly.

"Free-Dom time, meka not one penny for we. I hear it."

The driver sighed heavily.

"De t'ing wey you hear, he no be so," he said crossly. "Meka you pay you fare. Now—one-time!"

Some of the other passengers were laughing. Mammii Ama scarcely heard them. Her eyes were fixed on the driver. He was not deceiving her—she could read it in his tired, exasperated face.

Without a word, she took out the coin and dropped it in the metal fare-box.

That day the white woman visited the market again. Mammii Ama, piling bowls in neat stacks, looked up and saw her standing there. The white woman held up a calabash and asked how much.

"Twelve shilling," Mammii Ama said abruptly, certain that would be enough to send the woman away.

To her utter astonishment, however, the woman paid without a murmur. As Mammii Ama reached out and took the money, she realized that the calabash was only an excuse.

"How were your Independence celebrations?" the white woman smiled. "Did you have a good time?"

Mammii Ama nodded but she did not speak.

"Oh, by the way—" the white woman said in a soft voice." How did you get on with the bus this morning?"

Mammii Ama stared mutely. She, the speech-maker, was bereft of speech. She was more helpless than T'reepenny. She did not have even one word. She could feel her body trembling. The fat on her arms danced by itself, but not in joy. The drummer in her heart was beating a frenzy. Her heart hurt so much she thought she would fall down there in the dust, while the yellow skull of the woman looked and tittered.

Then, mercifully, the word was revealed to her. She had her power once more. Her drumming heart told her what to do. Snake-swift, Mammii Ama snatched back the calabash, at the same time thrusting the coins into the woman's hand.

"You no go buy from Mammii Ama! You go somewhere. You no come heah. I no need for you money."

She felt a terrible pang as she realized what had happened. She had parted with twelve shillings. She must be going mad. But she would not turn back now. She took another belligerent step, and the yellow menacing skull retreated a little more. She spoke clearly, slowly, emphasizing each word.

"I no pay bus dis time," she said. "Bus—he—be—free! You hear? Free!"

Inspired, Mammii Ama lifted the gourd vessel high above her head, and it seemed to her that she held not a brittle brown calabash but the world. She held the world in her strong and comforting hands.

"Free-Dom he come," she cried, half in exultation, half in longing. "Free-Dom be heah now, dis minute!"

The sun rolled like an eye in its giant socket. The lightning swords of fire danced in the sky.

She became calm. She knew what was what. She knew some things would happen, and others—for no reason apparent to her—would not. And yet, there was a truth in her words, more true than reality. Setting down the calabash, she re-adjusted her fish-patterned cloth above her breasts. She looked disinterestedly at her former customer. The white woman was only a woman—only a bony and curious woman, not the threatening skull-shape at all.

She watched the white woman go, and then she turned back to her stall. She picked up the calabash and set it with the rest. An ordinary calabash, nothing in it. Where was the glory she had so certainly known only a moment before? Spilled out now, evaporated, gone. The clank of the coin in the fare-box echoed again in her head, drowning the heart's drums. She felt weary and spent as she began stacking the earthen pots once more. A poor lot—she would be lucky to get ninepence apiece. They seemed heavy to her now—her arms were weighted down with them. It would continue so, every day while her life lasted. Soon she would be an old woman. Was death a feast-day, that one should have nothing else to look forward to?

Then a voice, hoarse as a raven's, began to sing. It was Moki the wood-seller, and as he sang he beat out the rhythm with one of his gnarled sticks. Nearby, others took up the song. Sabina, singing, wrapped her cover-cloth more tightly and swaggered a little in front of her stall so they could see her belly was beginning to swell with the new, good child. The Hausa man donned one of his gilt-beaded hats and waggled his head in mock solemnity. Ancient T'reepenny shuffled in her solitary dance.

Mammii Ama, looking from one to the other, understood their gift and laughed her old enduring laughter and sang with them.

> "Mammii Ama sell all fine pot,
>   Oh Oh Mammii Ama—"

She was herself again, known and familiar. And yet—there was something more, something that had not been before. She tried to think what it was, but it eluded her. She could feel it, though. So that the others might know, too, she added to her old chant a verse no one had ever heard her sing before.

> "Mammii Ama, she no come rich.
> Ha—ei! Be so. On'y one penny.
> She nevah be shame, she no fear for nothing.
> D'time wey come now, like queen she shine."

And they caught the rhythm, and the faith, and the new words. Mammii Ama straightened her plump shoulders. Like a royal palm she stood, rooted in magnificence, spreading her arms like fronds, to shelter the generations.

Margaret Laurence (1926-) was born in Neepawa, Manitoba, and now lives at Lakefield, near Peterborough, Ontario. Her novels include *The Stone Angel, A Jest of God,* which won a Governor General's Award, and *The Diviners.* She has published two collections of stories, *The Tomorrow-Tamer* and *A Bird in the House.*

Dave Godfrey
On the River

"What is it? Really."

"There's nothing. It's nothing. Or you know what it is. The country's lovely. You'd better watch for the sign."

"Christ, you know I'm watching for the sign. But I need it like these crops
need rain, not at all. Some of the most miserable moments of my youth were
spent here. Summers. Even after ten years you don't forget roads."

"It's more like a trail."

"I'm going as slow as I can. You can't really expect gravel to stay long on
top of straight granite."   .

"I'm sorry. I know you're taking it easy."

"It's the odds, isn't it? The fifty-fifty."

"No."

They parked the car by the barn. He knocked on the door of the house but
nobody answered. He went out into the thin wedge of soil that made the
vegetable garden and dug some worms. He felt the poverty of the land in the
thinness of the mossy soil. The meadow was gone to weeds and he had to
remember where the path had been. Age had worn it into the ground,
though, and once he could feel its pattern he could not stray, no matter how
thick the weeds were. They were both damp almost to their knees by the
time they reached the dock.

The boat was half-full of water and green with thin slime even after he
had tipped all the water out by hauling the boat partially up on the dock.
The near part of the bay was full of stumps and shore birds, but beyond that
the river was clear and fresh looking.

"Let's just forget about it all, babe," he said. "Here I can promise you fish
for sure."

Her face was beautiful and yet when he had turned from it for a minute its outlines and clarity blurred and he couldn't bring even a photograph of it back into his mind. It started to rain and she pulled a rain hat out of her pocket and adjusted it to cover as much of her hair as possible. Her gestures were still shy and cautious as though she were yet a girl. He pulled on the oars and took careful glances at her, measuring the angle of her cheekbones and the grace of her lips. Her eyes followed carefully the bobber as it danced on the water. If you took fine green glass, and filled it full of paraffin and a wick, and lit a flame that jogged and flickered as wind blew over the lip of the glass, that would be somewhat like her eyes. Her body was only beginning to bulge with this troublesome child and he realized that she was more appropriately dressed than he. The entire shore was totally familiar except where the brush had been cleared from what were hopefully cottage lots. It wasn't likely that people would come this far, he thought. Yet here was he with his city man's raincoat rowing in an almost water-logged boat. The oars dipped into the spools of fallen rain and he moved the boat farther from the shore.

They fished and let the boat drift. She used only a child's line with the worms he had dug from near the old farmhouse, and she caught, as he knew she would here at this time of year, whether it rained or not, innumerable small sunfish. She hooked a small bass from time to time and he carefully released those. He cast his own plugs farther and farther out, looking for something larger. They moved across the river and tried the deeper shore and then moved farther up to where a rocky point jutted out and where he remembered there would be bass and there were and she caught some more sunfish while he boated several bass—large enough to keep, if the season were open.

"You're getting cold," he said.

"No, I'm fine. I'm really fine."

"We're just compounding our illegalities, we'd better go in."

"If you insist."

He felt he should return the fish to their own cold depths, but he saw her face glisten with rain and a smile and he realized he wouldn't forget the way she looked there, so determined to keep herself under control despite everything and to enjoy their time on the water. It was a long row back to the dock, but the movement warmed him and the rain didn't get any worse and he was glad they hadn't drowned in the leaky, decrepit boat.

They carried their catch in the bailing-bucket up the path to the barn. It had stopped raining and they began to feel the cold. He said that they ought to make a fire and she asked if she had not always been his furnace and pulled him towards her to kiss her, and their bodies, draped in clothes still wet from the river, met. He set down the bait bucket. They climbed into the loft which was full of dusty straw and they made love pleasantly and he could feel the fires within him and stronger within her and nothing was imperfect about it, except that he could not lose himself in his desire as he had once been able, he couldn't somehow get beyond the world and he felt that they were not as close as they had once been.

He told her he was going to clean the fish and bake them on sticks against a fire and she said that was fine. He could tell that her anguish had caught her again and he did not mention what he had felt after the lovemaking nor ask her about that which she was choosing to hide from him. Her body was half hidden by the dusty straw and the lack of light from the rainy day. The first time she had been pregnant she had been awed by the changes in her body and had done a long series of sketches as her breasts slowly swelled and her hips widened and the child pushed her belly forward. She had made no sketches this time. He envied her ability to draw and kept his eyes upon the shapes of her body as long as he could without letting her know he was observing her.

He started a fire outside with dry straw from the barn and pieces of an old wagon seat which was rotting near the door. He cleaned the fish and set them on sticks in the ground so that they leaned near the fire and the fillets began to twist and curl about the sticks.

He didn't hear his uncle come up behind him.

"You the fellows that were out in my boat?"

"George. Hey, I thought you were the warden there for a minute. How've you been?"

"It's a dollar an hour for the boat and fifty cents for the worms. I seen you digging through the window."

He stood up and looked at the old man. His eyes were still clear, his skin was dark, yet faded from the bright red of old sun-burning haying days.

"There's better boats, but it's a dollar an hour."

He argued with this suddenly strange old man for four or five minutes, reminding him of family ties, asking after his wife Martha, even telling him the name of the horse that had once pulled the mowing machine that sat rusting in the barn. The old man blinked his eyes unnaturally, but did not seem to be listening at all.

"Martha left of cancer some time back," the old man said. "It's a dollar an hour for the boats."

"I'm your nephew, uncle George. For God's sake, I used to come here every summer for four or five years. I know you. You should know me. You must know me. I helped you caulk that very boat once. I've been to America and I've come home. I remember you. I remember you used to laugh at old Jenkins down the road who'd only been here twenty years and got taken for his suspenders and his drawers when he bought a piece of land down near the locks. Once I came up in the winter and helped you fill the ice-house.

138

I've looked up the family records. I know which regiment your grandfather was disbanded from when he settled here and how all the men felt cheated when they saw how much rock there was in the land and demanded larger allotments. Remember that? You may not know me, but I know who you used to be. I know where you came from. I know who you are now."

But the old man only looked at him somewhat queerly as if he couldn't understand why anyone would raise his voice at an old man. He realized that he had been shouting and he pulled out his wallet quickly and paid this old man three dollars for the time they had been out on the river and fifty cents for the worms. Because he didn't want his wife any more worried than she was now. The old man walked back up to the house and tried to lock the gate behind him, but it swung open and blew in the wind which was coming up after the storm.

She had come out to the door of the barn and was standing there with her eyes full of sorrow for him, that sorrow which he had always searched for when he was a young man and for which he had fallen so deeply in love with her, but he was sure of himself now, he didn't need that any more, and he wanted suddenly to hurt her, or to make her at least present her weakest side in acknowledgement of submission.

"It's not the same," he said. "Nothing's the same." He glared at her for a moment but he couldn't sustain that confrontation. "Let's get the hell home. The fish is so charred nobody'll be able to tell what kind it is. I don't know why you keep bashing away at me. My whole life is flowing away looking after you."

She held herself stiffly and distant from him, as though she were willing the body which was softening for the child to a new hardness. The heater dried their clothes but she was careful to keep them neat about her as though she were a young virgin afraid of exposing herself.

When they got back to the city there was no bread in the house so he went around the corner to the College Bakery to get some challah.

He took number 66, although he saw 65 had already been replaced, but there was a blond man in front of the cash register who seemed to be taking all of Mrs. Mier's time. He was obviously begging from her and she was shrugging her shoulders at him as though he were one of thousands she turned away every day. The two of them argued in a language he didn't try to listen to, and then Mrs. Mier took a loaf of bread from the counter and gave it to the blond man. Then she took ten dollars from the cash register and gave that to him also. The blond man walked out. He had been quite handsome obviously, but his face was flushed red with years of wine and his eyes looked as though they were looking away from the objects in the store, away from the ice cream freezer, the wedding cakes, the spiced meats, the displays of small delicacies.

"Ah," Mrs. Mier sighed. "What can I do for you?"

He ordered a loaf each of challah, rye, and whole wheat.

"You've been away," she said. "I don't see your wife so much anymore. To the country? All the English go up north for the summer. My husband he was always going to buy a little cottage, but the store took all the money and then he was gone."

"I'm not English."

"You're not Jewish?"

"I'm not Jewish."

"So what are you?"

"I'm an Indian," he said. She looked very unhappy and he wanted to joke with her and cheer her up.

"Sure, sure. You're dark, your wife's dark, and your little boy's got blond hair. Indians. You can never tell what's happening. You saw that man who was just in? John? He frightened your wife last time. His hair is not really blond. What can you do? He's from the same city in Europe as my husband, my own city. So we keep together here, you know. And my husband always took care of him. At first we just gave him money; and when we had none we gave too. But then, you know, he was drinking; the world knew he was drinking. It was like pouring silver into a well. But my husband he never quit. He would just pay John's rent for him direct to the landlord, and take groceries over and try to get him jobs. But you just look at him now, he's not like ordinary. He would always quarrel, and fight even. Who fights? What's to do? My husband would be feeding and sheltering him, and he would take the welfare money or from the United and spend that on wine. Sweet wine. Ah, then he was sick. And now vodka. He would argue even with my husband. What's your reason? my husband would shout at him. We knew that, we knew that. He saw the Germans kill his whole family. You can't deny him reasons for being like that. But we all did — see horror. It gets too much for me sometimes and I just go up to my bedroom and cry for four or five hours. I can't do anything except that and each time I feel that it won't work, that I'm going to fall apart from sorrow this time. But after four or five hours my children bring me a little something to eat and I go on. It's hard for them to understand and we drive them so and give them too much. They can't understand why we give them so much and take so little ourselves, but then sometimes later they do, they find out that we don't believe in all the things we collect about ourselves. And now it's worse for the ones up in the high part of the city. If the children understand that, sometimes they're all right; otherwise they go bad and we get drugs and disrespect for our troubles. Who can understand drugs? My son he says John would be better off with marijuana. Can you believe that? But I think he's getting worse. I just give him money now. I don't know what to do. 'Mrs. Mier, you're rich,' he says. 'Look at all this about you; and three women in the back doing the baking. You're rich, Mrs. Mier. I have nothing.' And ah, he frightened your wife. I can't understand that. She is so beautiful, and with the small boy. *Ich bin Yetzer Hara*, he said to her. I didn't want to give him anything, it seemed so useless, and then she came in and he said that to her and laughed at her. *Ich bin Yetzer Hara*. I thought that's why you were going to Dominion for your bread."

"My wife is pregnant," he said as he paid. "She's been having a bad time and the doctors say there's a good chance she'll lose the child."

"Ah, I didn't know. Why shouldn't she tell me? But if she's not sure. Ah, that John. Did he know? He is getting worse. It cannot be denied. How do you think he escaped? That is what he torments himself with. How do you think I escaped? Because I gave them up? Some did that, you know. Just to save their own skins. Ah, he is worse. Here, take. Take for the child. All will be well. Ah. I'm sorry for John. Tell that to your wife. That a man from my own city should say such a thing."

She gave him an extra loaf of challah and he took it and left the clean store.

When he got home he put one of the loaves in the freezer compartment.

His son was kicking a many-coloured ball between the two brick walls which surrounded their garden. Though the boy was young, he could kick it hard enough so that it bounced from wall to wall and he could lose himself following it, turning and spinning and chasing after its flight. He wanted to go out and comfort his wife and have her drive out of him the fear that Mrs. Mier's story had brought, but the telephone rang. It was his broker and he stood there in the kitchen, staring through the windows at his wife and son, while this man who dealt in shares of other men's business and distant mines spoke to him about rising inflation and defending one's position. He listened to him, but he watched his own son, and he thought of his uncle George, and he remembered himself when he was not much older than his own son, skipping stones from the point where today he had caught the fish. Three of his friends had been caught in a sudden storm and drowned and he had developed a game where he skipped stones at death.

The waves were paperchases in furrows of blue questionings. The stones skipped between them.

Hello death, are you a porcupine?

Three skips.

Are you a Lancaster bomber carved of balsa?

Seven skips. Flat.

Are you the spring where deer come, half a mile beyond the *cnr* station, where the water has made the ground all mushy and you have to walk on a board path to get to the place where it fountains among the rocks?

One skip. Overconfidence. Beware.

Are you the men who hung Mussolini by his heels?

Four skips. Caught in a crest.

Do you like blueberries?

Three skips. First repeater. He is not a porcupine

Hello death. Do you have trouble getting through the locks that join this lake to the next? Do you know what it means to portage? Is it you who turns the lightning to thunder? Does 7-Up like you? May I cross the river?

Ten skips. Second time. The answer to the tenth question is no. Come back again tomorrow. Try me tomorrow.

Goodbye child.

Goodbye death.

He went outside into the garden they had built in the midst of the city. There was only twenty-two feet between the wall of the funeral chapel and the wall of the coach house that had been turned from an artist's studio into two apartments, but they had filled the small space with grass and marigolds and odd pieces of stonework, angels and ornate stone flowers, which the mason who had built the house in the previous century had been unwilling to sell.

"The doctor phoned while you were out."

"Good news?"

"He said it was sixty-forty now."

"Well, that's better."

"I guess so."

"I shouldn't have been so sharp at the barn."

"I hope you're going to do something about your uncle."

"God, I don't know. I really don't know. He's my great-uncle really. There's nobody left of his generation, but that's not an excuse at all."

"I don't understand your family."

"They're solitary, that's true. The only thing that held them together was the queen, I used to think, and of course that's absurd now. Now nothing holds them together. The land still frightens them. And poverty. I think everybody who came here was poor and is still afraid of it."

He lay down on the sheet in the late sun beside her, filled with an overwhelming love of her endurance.

"I don't understand you," she said, her anger breaking out. "I used to think I did, but I don't. Sometimes I think you want not to see me. Or to see me only as I used to be four or five years ago, when we were first together. When we used to spend all that time outdoors, running away from things. I get sick of it. I don't see why I should be afraid of saying it; I get sick of it.

He wanted to tell her that everything had been changed. That she was right. That he was sorry for how the blond man had frightened her. That he loved her for her courage of endurance, but he couldn't get those words to come out.

"I bought you some fresh challah—so your traditions don't die out in a new land. That was my broker on the phone. I'm even changing my opinions about them, the older ones. Somebody sent me some information about Levy Industries—which will double for sure—and I asked him about it. He told me I wouldn't want to get rich out of the war. Surprised the hell out of me. He said the money was really coming from war contracts, helicopter gears or something. You just can't escape it, I guess. Anyhow, I put the challah in the freezer. Mrs. Mier says hello and hopes you'll stop going to the Dominion."

"I'm not the same to you as I used to be. That's it, isn't it? That's what you said to me by the barn?"

"Look," he said, "you're right. I'm not arguing with you. Let's put the kid to bed and then we'll come back out here and lie on the sheet and watch the stars and ignore the bloody soot."

She agreed, her body loosening, and he realized that he had given in and by doing so had won a small victory. He knew he could never talk to her of the blond man, but he would be able to talk to her of how his gnawing desire for her had lessened as his fear of life had disappeared, as his acceptance of change and imperfection had increased almost miraculously, so that he no longer constantly desired to escape somewhere but was willing to accept everything, Mrs. Mier, the blond man from her city, his uncle George, the doctor's fluctuating odds, Levy Industries, everything, and still allow desire to overtake his body, and he realized somehow that what he had always desired had happened and that he had got, somehow, beyond certain desires which had blinded his early life.

In the evening, once the child was asleep, they would come out and lie on the sheet on the grass and be protected by the ugly brick walls which rose on all four sides of the small garden and he would be able to talk to her and reassure her. In the winter the new child would come, safely.

"Did the doctor say why the odds were better?"

"No. I don't know how he can tell without seeing me. He just said that if time goes by and nothing happens that even that is an improvement."

"Okay. Okay."

Dave Godfrey (1938-) was born in Toronto and now lives in Victoria, where he is chairman of the Creative Writing department at the University of Victoria. Formerly a partner in two publishing houses, Anansi and New Press, he is now president of Press Porcépic. His novel *The New Ancestors* won a Governor General's Award, and he has published two collections of stories, *Death Goes Better with Coca-Cola* and *Dark Must Yield*.

Leo Simpson
The Lady and the Travelling Salesman

Patricia had been expecting Harry since five o'clock, when somebody had called long distance and asked for him. He was apparently the kind of important — or maybe self-important — businessman who gave people schedules of addresses and phone numbers so that he could be reached when he went on a trip. Now Patricia was on the phone to Penny Neal and speaking firmly because Penny was trying to dodge.

"No, it isn't demeaning in the least, it's exactly the opposite," Patricia said. "You see we're helping a good cause and at the same time we're being ironical about the role of woman in the kitchen. Ironical, yes. Men had this *mystique* about home-made bread and cakes and things. But of course it isn't complicated, it's easy. For goodness sake, two years ago you graduated with an honours degree in chemistry. All I want is four cherry cheesecakes. Yes, today, because I have to pick up everything tomorrow morning. Our stand is just inside the door, beside the Indian Craft stand. No, you can't do brownies, Julia Dempsey is doing brownies. We had far too many volunteers for brownies. Me? Well of course I am, Penny, I'm doing strawberry flans. We're all pitching in together."

She listened for a few more minutes to Penny's reluctance and evasions. Patricia went back to the kitchen counter and looked without enthusiasm at a bowl of custard cream filling. "Ecch," Patricia said. She had to separate out four egg whites, and she put the yolks in Heathcliff's dish since she could think of no immediate use for eggs without whites. As she was rolling out the first strip of sweet flan pastry she saw a man through the kitchen window, on his way up the drive. He was about forty, and he had a weather-worn face and untidy brown hair. Harry, thought Patricia. He moves like an actor. My, that's a casual and confident walk.

"Come in here, would you," Patricia said. "I'm baking something but I've been looking forward to meeting you for ages and I want to talk. What will you drink?"

Heathcliff, with raw egg yolk on his face, ran between her legs and in a late performance of duty barked at Harry, who perched himself with loose grace on the kitchen stool. As it happened Patricia was wearing cut-off cord shorts and just a jersey top. Pouring from the whisky bottle, she felt Harry's examining eyes. He would be pretending to look at the dog and sneaking a look at the backs of her legs, she thought. When she turned with the drink Harry wasn't pretending to look at Heathcliff, he was looking directly at her legs and, what was more, at her bare midriff, and so on.

"Thanks," he said. "My plane leaves at noon tomorrow. Africa, and other distant countries. I've just come from Chicago. This is a detour, since I haven't seen old Robert in, oh it must be three years. What a nice little kitchen, Mrs. Douglas."

She looked at him quickly, but he was innocently taking a sip from his whisky.

"I'm not emotionally involved with the kitchen," Patricia said. She didn't care what his opinion of her might be, and just to make that fact clear she returned to her pastry-rolling with her back to Harry. He could assume, if he wanted to, that she did meaningless baking every day and took empty-headed pride in it. Neither did she see why she should be forced into the role of frightened maiden, merely because he was on the make—it had crossed her mind that she might change into jeans—so she said: "You must call me Patricia, please."

"More of a bedroom girl, are you, Patricia?" Harry said.

The crassness of that made Patricia pause for a second or so. From debonair visitor on the make to a smirking little adolescent in one crass sentence, and she waited until she knew her tone of voice would be right.

"I'm sorry Robert isn't here to meet you. I'm expecting him home soon. He'll be very impressed by what you're doing," Patricia said, and hardly paused, "making a detour of a thousand miles to see an old friend."

"Well, a thousand miles doesn't mean so much these days."

"Oh but it does, it's a long way to travel to see a male friend." This was the manner Patricia had used for lecturing in her graduate-student days. "You know, Harry, I've always been interested in that particular relationship, the great male province of friendship, the buddy relationship. Sometimes it seems to be stronger than marriage. I've been listening to Robert's stories of Harry Connors for years. I think I know how it feels to be a second wife," she said, laughing easily. "I'd say that the basis of the good old buddy relationship is probably homosexual, wouldn't you, on one side at least?"

"Wait a minute," Harry said. Well, I've got a vicious charmer by the tail this time, he thought. It bites and scratches.

"The other interesting part is the illusion," said Patricia, who hadn't finished with him. "The whole *mystique* of hearsay, do you know what I mean? When you keep hearing about somebody over a long period of time you begin to imagine a person much larger than life size. I had a picture in my mind of a Harry Connors who was eight feet tall, a reckless free spirit like Zorba the Greek. A creature as bright as Apollo." She became concerned with a speck of foreign matter in her pastry. "And now here you are," she said with a little frown of distaste, using a spoon to pick the speck out.

The wall phone by the kitchen door rang and Patricia wiped her hands and went to answer it.

A very good attacking style, Harry told himself. He searched in his mind for a synopsis of what was happening, in the form of a newspaper headline describing his position. "CONNORS IS CRUELLY SMITTEN UNDER THE FIFTH RIB," he decided. Heathcliff stood with two front paws on one of Harry's shoes, furiously wagging his tail. "CHAMP ON THE ROPES IN ROUND ONE," Harry said. He patted the dog. Harry had always been a dog man.

Patricia was receiving some news that surprised her on the telephone.

"But that's awful," she said. "He's gone, he's left her for sure, has he? But they've only been married a year, why would he suddenly run off like that? Oh it can't be true, Stephanie's dramatizing. You know how she dramatizes everything. Well, I can't believe it, sending a postcard from the airport, my God that's barbaric. You know, I never completely trusted Ludwig. He was so vague, and he did far too much smiling. No, I have somebody here now. I'll call Stephanie later, after Robert gets home. Yes, I'll see you tomorrow."

Patricia had four strips of pastry ready and she began to roll a fifth. "That's the most surprising news," she said, with a faraway glance at Harry which didn't see him. In fact Harry was watching the way her hips moved when she leaned forward on the rolling pin. She kept her knees together so there was that rhythmic in-and-out movement. "It's about these friends of ours. He just packed up and left her. No explanation, no regrets. He sent her a postcard from the airport."

"I may be old-fashioned..."

"Yes, I agree. We're living in an age of freedom but at least the courtesy of an explanation..."

"I may be old-fashioned," Harry said with sincerity, "but to me there's something—what's the word I want—something heartwarming in this cosy domestic scene. There you are, a pretty young wife, obviously well educated but still uncontaminated by fashionable politics, by all this shrill nonsense about women being the same animals as men. Happy in your kitchen, baking something nice for your husband, who's a respected doctor no less, and breaking off every now and then to have little gossipy chats on the telephone. The good old ways," said Harry, shaking his head as he pondered them, and their erosion by foolishness, "I don't know, there's something there of value—heartwarming."

Patricia was staring at Harry, uncertain and wide-eyed, as if he had gone mad without warning. She said: "Would you like more whisky?"

"Yes, please. Bitch?"

"I beg your pardon?"

"The dog."

"No. No, it's a male dog." Patricia poured Harry's whisky and gave it to him. As an afterthought she took down another glass for herself. "His name is Heathcliff. He seems to like you."

"All dogs like me."

"Yes? Tell me something, Harry. In the business of making a living, that great *mystique* of the male breadwinner who is so important, while we're at home in our happy little kitchens, what exactly do you do?"

"Whenever that subject comes up," Harry said, animated. "Every time the conversation turns to jobs, roles, positions, the great *mystique* of earning a living so to speak, I always find myself envying old Robert. I mean, what could be finer than what he's doing?"

"You haven't told me what you do."

"Did you know that we were at medical school together?"

"Yes."

"Anatomy, that's what finished me, cutting up the dead bodies. You should have seen us together. There's Robert, sawing away inside a stomach or something, eating a bologna sandwich at the same time. And there I am, barely able to keep my breakfast down. They were great old days. I remember once he got so interested in a tubercular ankle that he took it home to study it."

"What is it that you do for a living, Harry?" asked Patricia. She was used to bringing evasive people to the mark.

"Oh, nothing very important. Sort of a travelling salesman."

This was not a satisfactory answer but the phone rang right then and Patricia went to answer it, and Harry said to Heathcliff: "What do you say, Heathcliff? Do you think we should behave until Robert gets home, or should we try another round with this — very beautiful possession of his?"

"Oh for goodness sake, Julia, you got the brownies, they're the very easiest things to do," said Patricia on the telephone. "Julia, I'd give you something easier than brownies, but there isn't anything. Everybody wanted brownies. Of course I'm doing something myself, I'm doing strawberry flans, and they're difficult. You can't even use the blender, you have to do everything by hand. I'm beginning to feel like a Victorian kitchen-maid. Yes, I heard. Imagine sending a postcard from the airport, the bastard. Poor Stephanie. She was doing four dozen taffy tarts for us too. Yes. Well, I hope so. Fine, Julia."

Harry asked: "Is Robert at the hospital?"

"No, he's down at the city hall with a delegation. They're trying to re-zone one of his slum districts for industry."

"Sounds as if Robert hasn't changed much. Bucking authority and fighting the good fight."

"He's marvellous," Patricia said warmly, indeed with some intimacy to Harry, enlisting him in a conspiracy of affection for Robert. "A delegation is hopeless, he knows that, but it's better than doing nothing. The mandatory smoke-stack height in this city is just criminal. I forget, a hundred feet or something, and they have no fuel regulations. You can burn whatever you damn well like. There are children in Robert's wards with lungs about forty years old."

"Non-smokers too, I suppose," Harry said sympathetically.

"I was like everybody else before I met Robert. Just shrugging my shoulders and saying, well we live in a rotten world and there's nothing to be done about it. Robert is doing something about it. He has that fantastic energy. He never gets more than six hours' sleep a night. What do you think of this house?"

"Well, it's unpretentious . . ."

"At least unpretentious. Robert earns $25,000 a year. For two months every year we go to a mission-house in Mexico and work there for nothing. It's at a place named Guanabaja, in the lowlands, a town built near a swamp, if you can imagine it. We pay our own expenses. Robert buys all the medicine for the mission dispensary. He works just as hard there as he does here. That's our annual holiday."

"What do you do there, Patricia?"

"I help him. I'm in my second year of medical school."

"You're okay with the dead bodies?"

"Oh yes. I'm one of the bologna eaters."

Harry got down from the stool and began to pace back and forth with enthusiasm in the small kitchen. He slapped his fist into his palm a few times. "I wish to God I could be the same sort of man," Harry said. "A man of mercy, a giver. His idea is that if he works hard enough he can cure the world all by himself, and who's to say that he won't succeed? It's a career of total use, clean and healthy dedication, that's what it is."

This time when the phone rang Patricia answered it with a misty smile. Harry had stopped in front of the refrigerator, and he addressed the blank white door portentously. "Yes," he said, "in the great scraped elbow that we call life, good old Robert is the soothing band-aid."

"It's a man named Gus for you, long distance," Patricia said.

"That's the office. I'll take it on the extension."

"We don't have an extension."

Harry became unaccountably shy. "Well, all right," he said, having thought about it.

Instead of continuing her work with the rolling-pin, which made a growling noise on the counter, Patricia began to lay her strips of pastry in a neat stack on a plate, so that she could listen to what Harry was saying.

"Yes, Gus," he said. "Eighty thousand rounds, no we can't use them. Sure it's cheap, but .426 is a ridiculous calibre. I see. They probably make the rifles out of bamboo or something, Gus. No, that's the M14 automatic rifle, American. We're bidding on the West German Schmeisser MP 50. That's right, they ordered 400 Suomi SMGs, nine mill. Well, the advantage is that you can also use nine mill in a Sten gun, and it's a much cheaper machine. Sure. You can stamp 'em out with a cookie cutter. Bury 'em for a hundred years and dig 'em up and they'll fire under water for you. They're a beautiful weapon. That's the Ecuador shipment, is it? Guatemala. I see. Right, Gus."

Harry hung up the phone, expecting uncomfortably that Patricia would have a question about his business. He didn't expect her to be standing directly in front of him, smiling into his eyes with strange, sleepy passion. For a moment he thought she wanted a kiss, then he saw she was in a fearful rage.

"Are you a salesman for the government, Harry?" she asked, more or less through her teeth.

"No, we're a private outfit. We buy surpluses and obsolete . . . armament. For sale abroad."

"You're allowed to do that?"

"Of course. It's a perfectly legitimate business. We have proper licences for every transaction."

Patricia went and got her glass of whisky and swallowed the drink. She held the empty glass in her left hand, thinking, then threw it away on the floor behind her without turning. It smashed at Harry's feet. "Why, you miserable bastard," she said, speaking to the window. "You foul miserable bastard. You're a *gun* salesman. Robert is working eighteen hours a day, trying to save one or two lives. My God, I'm making filthy pastry here, I'm humiliating myself, just to earn a few stinking dollars for bandages, a few stinking dollars for drugs." She took down another glass from the cupboard and poured a tot of whisky into it. She poured the whisky from the glass into the sink, and replaced the glass in the cupboard. "I actually thought I was doing some good," Patricia said. "I actually . . . My God, two months every year in a mosquito swamp, living in misery, and the rest of the time in a house so . . . so unpretentious, so *fucking* unpretentious, so small and mean that I can't even invite my friends for a meal. And all the time I'm hearing about Harry, Harry, *Harry*," she said, beginning to shout and searching with her eyes for something up and down the counter, "until I start to believe that I'm the small person, me, I'm the only grubby person in the whole stinking world." Not finding what she was looking for on the counter, she took a glass down again and quite carefully poured a measure of whisky into it. "And Harry is a travelling salesman selling machine guns. You awful pig, they're killing women and children with your guns, do you know that?"

"Hold on now, they kill a lot of men with those guns too . . ."

Attempts to dominate him always stirred up Harry's resentment anyway, but right then her sincerity, the cleanness of her sincerity and youth, was the salt in the wound. What a performance, he thought, what passion. She's having a little catharsis, a self-satisfied temper tantrum at my expense. I'm a big villain. My God, I've stood toe-to-toe with people she wouldn't even believe existed on the face of the earth. I've seen acts of men that would turn her heart to stone.

"Get out. Get out of my house."

And now I'm being exorcised I suppose. Harry shouted too, right into her face. "Look, you're a child. Do you think I came all the way here to listen to sophomore morality, do you?"

Patricia closed her eyes so she could scream better. "Get out of my *house*." The phone rang.

It's wasted on fatuity, Harry thought. There should be a way of harnessing all this passion to a mattress. "What are you presiding over, the Day of Judgement?" he shouted. "Do you think I came here just to be judged by you?"

"You murdering swine, I won't have you in my house."

Heathcliff dashed urgently around the kitchen, yelping at both of them while the phone continued ringing. Harry stood over the plate of pastry, looking from it to Patricia with a squinted eye.

"Good God, the new breed of conscience, the sheer brutal arrogance, we won't survive all these pretty consciences, you mark my words. Stupid little bitch, you can't even make a decent strawberry flan. I've never seen such messy goddamn pastry in my life. Come here," Harry raged, pointing a terrible accusing finger at the plate. "Look at that. What is it supposed to be? Tell me. What is it?"

"That's flan pastry and it's good, damn you, that's exactly the way it's supposed to be."

"Well, it looks like Heathcliff's mess."

"You have a pig's mind. You have a gutter mind."

"I have a human mind," Harry told her vehemently, and still squinting. "I don't make a competition out of righteousness. I'm not trying to elbow my way into somebody else's career, and I'm not pretending to save the world by playing with mud pies."

Harry picked the phone up and listened and said: "Yes, Charlie, speaking." Patricia seemed disposed to wait until he had finished, then she changed her mind. She took four eggs from the refrigerator and threw them at Harry one by one. Two hit him in the chest and slid down his shirt. She filled a pitcher with water and heaved it at him but most of the water went by when he ducked because she was hopping mad and not aiming. "No, no bother, Charlie," Harry said, with his unsquinted eye warily on Patricia. "Make it snappy, though, I'm having a little trouble here. Some woman throwing stuff. No, not a customer, she's a pacifist. Yes. All right, that completes the shipment. We already have a restricted licence for Ecuador. Yes, we'll buy anything Israeli in operational use, that's policy. Tell him we'll take 200 Uzis at that price. If it's Israeli and operational, yes. Charlie, I don't care if it's a bow and arrow, we'll take it. Yes, I cleared it with them." Something cold and flaccid struck Harry on the forehead and he said: "Look, I have to ring off. It's getting a bit slapstick here, she's started throwing pastry. Thanks, Charlie."

"I won't *have* you conducting your filthy business on my telephone."

"Everything in this house is so pure. Good God almighty, even the telephone is pure."

Short of breath and breathing hard, Patricia surveyed the debris on the floor and said: "I want you out of here." Heathcliff went past, with gobbets of pastry as well as egg on his face now, and stood on one of Harry's shoes wagging his tail. Patricia said: "No, I don't want you out of here either. I'm going to kill you." She hefted the rolling pin and swung at Harry. She was an athletic girl, a swimmer and a golfer, and she played squash occasionally too, so it wasn't a flustered ladylike attack. Left foot shifting slightly forward, she brought the rolling pin toward Harry's head in a murderous swipe, following through with her right shoulder. Harry danced sideways, his eyes bright with fear, and the weapon whistled by his shoulder. Having missed, Patricia's common sense told her that she might injure him seriously and she felt frustrated, because she wanted to. So she just flung the rolling pin away, toward the counter, and put her face down in her hands to relieve the frustration in tears. Unluckily, Harry had tried to dodge again, a sort of low dive behind the counter for protection. In fact he didn't feel much pain when the rolling pin bounced on the counter and struck him, and he was beginning to entertain a sense of gratitude—for his deliverance—when the light in his head was rudely switched off.

Patricia sobbed into her hands. Everything is so frustrating for me, she thought, every tiny event in my life is a frustration. This is how Cinderella felt. The silence gave her the impression that Harry had left, and when she looked up presently the kitchen was empty and unrewarding and demanding. The difference is that if a prince came in that door to take me away he'd probably be a white-slave trafficker. I'll tell Robert the truth, exactly as it happened, Patricia decided. But then he'll say, but why didn't you say this, and why didn't you say that. Yes, and he'll be bewildered because I don't share his admiration for the great Harry. Oh God, the poor innocent. The poor innocent man.

Heathcliff went behind the counter and came out again, tilting his head in inquiry. He went behind the counter again, a busy little dog. "Oh, Heathcliff, you're tracking all over the floor," Patricia said, at the telephone. She dialled, brooding over the telephone mouthpiece like a sullen child while she waited. "Stephanie, what can I say, I was so shocked," she said. "If there's anything I can do. . . What did Ludwig write on the postcard? Made out of what? Tired of living a life made out of plastic, that's very strange. No, I mean it's a strange thing to write on a postcard. Stephanie dear, I know it's not the time to ask, but before you got the postcard did you manage to make the taffy tarts? Oh that's wonderful, you're a darling. I'll pick them up tomorrow. Well, we're being ironical about a woman's role, you see." Patricia said this with a sigh. "Yes, take off your frilly little apron, it's time to put on your black lace nightie. Our stand is just inside the door, beside the Indian Craft stand. And Stephanie, please call if you think of anything I can do. I'm very sorry, we all are. . ."

She swept up the glass first, and then the water and pastry with broom and mop. Her mind was on Robert again. Suddenly she noticed Heathcliff's front paws, tipped with blood, and she went down on one knee to look, concerned. On the counter's far side four fingers of one hand appeared on the formica, then the other hand and Harry's head, and one elbow and then the other, as he shakily heaved himself up like a creature of dark intent emerging from a fissure in the earth's crust.

"Mine, that's my blood," Harry said. His voice was shaky too. "Dog's been standing on my forehead, you see. Standing on my forehead and licking my nose, it hurt like hell." And indeed Harry had bits of dried egg yolk and pastry on his face, and there was also a bloody crescent-shaped gash, an ugly gape of red, just above his left eyebrow. Patricia was startled by this appearance. With a gasp she put the back of her hand against her mouth.

"Here are the headlines," Harry said. He used a thumb and forefinger to scribe a newspaper headline in the air. "ROLLING PIN FELLS CONNORS. A woman with a rolling pin is no joke, victim tells our reporter."

"Why are you still here?" Patricia asked peremptorily.

"I was unconscious," Harry explained, gesturing loosely toward the floor behind the counter, "down there. The dog brought me round." Harry came out slowly and made it to the stool. This time he didn't lounge gracefully, he slumped on the seat with his chin down, supporting his body by resting both elbows on the counter behind, staring straight ahead with a beaten and dull-eyed stare. Patricia was at the telephone again, ignoring him.

"Are you phoning for an ambulance?" Harry asked.

"No. I'm calling a friend about some cherry cheesecakes she's baking."

"When you finish doing that, would you call me an ambulance?"

Penny's line was busy, which to Patricia was bad news. Patricia knew her Penny—a good-hearted girl and reasonably loyal friend, but a mistress of tricks and evasions. Also very lazy and a terrible liar. It would be like Penny to take the phone off the hook so that nobody could check on her, and then call in at the last minute with a wild excuse about the cherry cheesecakes.

What Patricia was doing was pretending that Harry didn't exist. But then she saw the gash on his forehead. She went to him without hesitation, showing as much concern as she had for Heathcliff's paws.

She said: "Oh gosh, that's a bad cut. Oh I'm very sorry. You need two stitches."

"Two stitches, all right. Can you put them in?"

"I'm not supposed to," Patricia said. She held Harry's head in both hands, turning it this way and that carefully to examine the wound. Harry thought her eyes were the prettiest he had seen in years of womanizing. "*May I* put them in, though?" Patricia asked. "They're just apposition stitches. I can get the autoclave ready in a minute."

"Go ahead."

Patricia was pleased and surprised, like a child who has asked for coffee at breakfast and got it. "Don't worry, I'm very dainty with a needle and thread," she said. She wasn't able to resist saying that. The phone rang as she went past it toward the surgery.

"It's a man named Charlie for you. Can you walk?"

"Of course I can't walk. I can't even stand."

"He can't come to the telephone right now, Charlie," said Patricia to Charlie on the telephone. "What is it? Fifty dollars a thousand sounds cheap enough. Wait, though, are they the .426s? I see, Chinese. Yes, except that .426 is a ridiculous calibre. They probably make the rifles out of bamboo, Charlie. Very well, I'll tell him. Twenty 81-mill mortars. Seventy us standard 300-pound napalm. Yuck," said Patricia, with fastidious disgust. "I did not, I said yuck. Well, how would you like somebody to drop one on you?"

"Patricia, please," Harry said.

"Where do the fragmentation grenades come from? Are they operational? Yes, take them. I *said yes*, didn't I? Hold on a minute." She turned to Harry with an efficient frown, as if asking to be reminded of something she had recently known. "What's a *Sturmgewehr?*"

"It's German for assault rifle. A submachine gun."

Harry had been behaving before this pretty much from force of habit, and lust of course, but now he sincerely wanted to take Patricia to bed. He felt that if he didn't he would be missing an unrepeatable event in his life.

"And the number would be the particular model, would it?"

"That's right, usually it has an mp letter prefix, for *Maschinenpistole*."

"Well, yes, but not if it uses 7.92 mill," said Patricia to the telephone, speaking patiently, having apparently encountered some stubbornness on the other end of the line. "I don't care about that, we don't want them. I don't understand why you keep asking me to ask him, I know he'll say no. All the other submachine guns he likes use nine mill. *All right,* I will." She said to Harry: "There's an auction in Milan of 2000 surplus MP 44s. Do you want them?"

"No, we can't get ammunition for those old 44s."

"He says no. I told you he would. Yes, I'm the lady who was throwing the pastry. No, he needs a stitch or two in his scalp, that's all. Of course not with pastry. I'm not telling you what it was, it's none of your business," said Patricia, resisting Charlie's question morosely. "For God's sake, my telephone is being polluted with napalm bombs and submachine guns... I'm sick and tired of this whole heroic *mystique* of weapons and violence, we're all so polite and businesslike, and meanwhile people are screaming and dying." She listened and her expression became gentler. She cuddled the phone nearer with a reluctant smile. "Well, all right, if you promise not to laugh," she said. "A rolling pin." Then she said: "It isn't that funny!" and banged the telephone back on the cradle.

Several minutes later, while Patricia was cleaning Harry's forehead with a swab on forceps, he asked: "How many frag grenades did we buy?"

"Five hundred, at $4 each."

He looked worried. Patricia said: "This will sting." She wondered how he would react to pain, a man in the business of providing pain and death. Harry didn't flinch, which made it easy for her to work. He did put a hand on her shoulder, and Patricia thought: we all need support when we're weak. He was pale. The operation was just finished when to her surprise Harry's hand went from her shoulder to her bare waist and then upward under her jersey top.

The way Harry had assessed the situation, it was a matter of timing. Patricia could hardly jump away, as a medical person, while she was attached to him by catgut. He found himself dizzily fondling a naked breast, plump as a partridge. Patricia's eyes closed and her chin rose until her throat was practically in a straight line. Her lower lip curled down from her teeth, which were tightly clenched. Oh boy, she's mad as a hornet, Harry thought. Nevertheless he allowed his hand to wander dizzily here and there under the top because he couldn't stop it. Her head came down again, and she looked into his eyes with an expression of strange, sleepy passion that Harry recognized, or imagined he recognized. *Jesus*, he told himself, she's really infuriated now. But he couldn't command his tranced hand. Possibly because of the rise in his blood pressure, Harry lost consciousness again just then. Patricia caught him in time, and she was able to ease him to the floor.

She wasn't happy with herself. Great, Patricia, she chided, he had you dancing merrily to his tune, didn't he. She turned his head sideways so that he wouldn't swallow his tongue, and taped gauze on Harry's wound. Heathcliff put his front paws on Harry's head and started licking his nose, and Patricia shooed the dog away. Bastard was playing me like a violin, she complained, in two minutes we would have been in bed or something for God's sake.

154

Harry opened his eyes. "I went out again, did I?" he said. "Look, shouldn't I be in bed?"

"No," Patricia said, still remonstrating with herself. How come I'm suddenly a pushover, she asked herself. For crying out loud, now it takes an act of God to save me, a bolt from heaven to strike enterprising seducers senseless. Stray men who come in off the street to see my husband. "I knew the minute I saw you what kind of man you were," she said, and she explained briskly, to diminish the incident: "The kind of man who slurps his soup. Instead of making an appeal to a woman's mind and attention he reaches for her tits or whatever . . ."

"The new emancipated woman," said Harry. He had recovered well. "She's something I haven't figured out yet. Talks like a longshoreman, and she's as touchy as a nun. Would you help me up, please?"

"Yes. Just be careful where you put your hands."

"The whole male world is trying to ravish her," Harry said. He sat on the stool again, uprightly this time. "Be careful where you put your hands, that's wonderful. Can't I even hold you for a little support?"

"Harry, I know the difference between a hand that's holding me for support and one that's trying to feel me up."

"Charming language," said Harry, shaking his head.

"The whole world of morality and loyalty is *terra incognita* to you, isn't it Harry?" said Patricia. She took an aerosol can of Lysol from under the sink and gave the kitchen two or three long bursts and put it back. Her mind had been on asepsis, she knew, and she also knew that she needed to be doing something ordinary. She also knew that she was unconsciously trying to disperse a compliant atmosphere in the kitchen. "You're loyal when it's expedient to be loyal, but that's all."

"You mean to Robert?" Harry asked waving the Lysol away. He thought: there's a part of this woman that thinks of me as a nasty smell.

"Certainly I mean to Robert. You don't have any loyalty to Robert. You're the friend of his youth, and the hero of all his stories. So you travel a thousand miles to see him, and the first thing you do is try to lay his wife. How do the stitches feel?"

"I feel as if my scalp is gathered into one big knot. I think my ears are higher."

"You're an attractive man, in a way."

"I don't know how I'm going to look with high ears and all my loose scalp in a bun."

"I don't mean good-looking. What I'm talking about is your attitudes to life." Patricia decided that she would raise this subject, so that she could dismiss it. "I can understand how some women, certain kinds of women, would be attracted to you. A footloose adventurer, with no morals to speak of but with strong and basic appetites."

"Christ, we're back to ideas again, are we?" Harry wanted to know, with plain discouragement. "We're sitting around the cafeteria table between classes drinking coffee and getting excited about ideas. Look, Robert knows me, can you get that into your head? If you tell him that I haven't made any kind of grab at you he won't believe you. Or else he'll think I've changed for the worse."

Patricia was interested in this thought about her husband. "He doesn't expect loyalty from you?"

"Loyalty," Harry said, "is a word. I'm not talking about words. I'm talking about the way people behave. Robert expects me to behave as I behave. He expects Heathcliff to be a dog, and I'd say he expects Patricia to be Patricia."

"I have to make more pastry," Patricia said.

"Did you throw the whisky bottle at me?"

"No."

"Then would you mind pouring me a drink?"

Their relationship for the next half hour or so was polite, with conversation about Robert, and new movies and good places to go for a holiday. It was the kind of conversation they should have had from the beginning, as Patricia saw it. "There are rationalizations for everything, that's what's so frightening," she happened to say, though. "You travel around the world selling guns. But if you didn't somebody else would, is that right?"

"Oh yes. It's a competitive business."

"So you're not *causing* death and maiming, and so on. You're not responsible personally for things that would happen anyway. People having their arms and legs blown off. Children starving to death." She was rolling the last of her pastry, half turned away from Harry.

"Death," Harry said queasily. "I've always had a bad feeling about death, and I'm fond of children. Where do you suppose Robert's got to?"

"And you're not responsible for the dirty side of humanity. The dirty side would be there anyway. It's what creates demands for your guns and bombs."

Harry wasn't comfortable with this drift of talk. He said: "Well, it isn't civilized, that's for sure."

"I think I see your dilemma, Harry. People blame you, but blaming you is mistaking the symptom for the disease. We should blame the dirty side of humanity. Like everybody else you wish it didn't exist but—"

Harry said sharply: "Wait a minute, I didn't say anything about wishing it didn't exist. If it didn't exist I'd be out of business, for God's sake."

"And you don't want to be out of business?"

"What's the matter with you?" Harry asked. He was squinting at Patricia again. He got off the stool and paced the kitchen behind her. "Why the hell should I want to be out of business? I have a living to make. I'm not trying to be Jesus Christ, I'm trying to make a living." She had stopped working and was looking at him without comprehension, bleakly. He tapped her shoulder with his forefinger. "I know what you're doing, you're trying to forgive me. I hate it when people do that. Tell me this, how would *you* feel if some man took a liking to you, and then felt so guilty that he had to do a big white-washing job, that he had to *clean you up* before he could be happy with his own feelings?"

She slapped the finger away violently. "Why, you conceited pig. Where on earth did you get the idea that I've taken a liking to you?"

Harry picked up the telephone, which had started ringing. "Let me tell you something else," he said to Patricia. "When I want forgiveness I'll apologize! Got that?" He said to the telephone: "Hello? Yes, she's here. No, I'm not Robert. Well, I'm a friend of Robert's. Did you want to speak to her? Pleased to meet you, mine's Harry Connors. I'll ask her." He put the phone on his shoulder. "Julia Dempsey wants to come over and borrow some brown food colour. Is that okay?"

"Oh for goodness sake she's doing brownies," said Patricia, much distracted. "She doesn't need brown food colour for brownies."

"You don't need brown food colour for brownies, Julia," Harry said to Julia on the telephone. "What colour are they coming out? Well, are you using chocolate? That could account for it, you see. They're coming out white because you're not using chocolate. I've never actually made any myself, no, but I imagine if you use chocolate, flour, eggs, maybe some chopped nuts . . ."

Patricia brushed past Harry saying "Heaven grant me patience!" and he heard her going upstairs. Gone to sulk in the bathroom, he guessed. He chatted amiably with Julia Dempsey.

In the bathroom Patricia cleaned the tub and sink and tiles, a job she had meant to do that morning and would not be able to do next day because of the bake sale. She was not sulking as such; she merely had a lot of energy to use. She could vacuum upstairs too, she thought. When she went down to get the vacuum cleaner she heard Harry on the phone again in the kitchen.

"Yes, Stephanie, you left the paper bag on the hall stand," Harry was saying. He saw Patricia and smiled, grimacing at the telephone then to indicate that something unusual was afoot. "You made the taffy tarts," he said for Patricia's benefit, "and you put them in a box and put the box in a paper bag, and you left the paper bag on the hall stand."

"Stephanie?" Patricia said. "What about the taffy tarts?"

"She's lost them."

"She can't have!" Patricia said. "How could she lose four dozen taffy tarts? I don't believe it!" .

"All right, now when Ludwig came home he had a paper bag. He put that in his study. Yours was on the hall stand, his was in his study. Suppose it happened this way, suppose Ludwig was on his way out, on his way to the airport, and saw the paper bag on the hall stand and took it. No no, Stephanie, it isn't a question of why he would steal your taffy tarts. Ludwig thought he was taking his own paper bag. So go in his study and see what's in Ludwig's paper bag."

Patricia said, distressed: "I'm sorry her husband ran away. I'm sorry he sent her a postcard saying his life was made out of plastic. But she told me she'd baked those taffy tarts. I wish people would be honest once in a while. And Penny's phone is off the hook. I just know she's going to call at the last minute with some wild excuse about the cherry cheesecakes. Why tell lies? Why tell lies about something so — so utterly childish, and *ironical*..."

"Hold on a sec, Stephanie," Harry said. He said to Patricia: "Will you shut up, please? I'm trying to get to the bottom of this."

"Oh great," Patricia said. "This is my lucky day. I have a big businessman in the house. He'll take charge. He'll find my taffy tarts for me."

"How many bundles?" Harry said to Stephanie. "Wow, that's a lot of money, maybe twenty thousand dollars. Well, he came home from the bank with it, Stephanie, didn't he? And he thought he was taking the money with him when he ran away. No, it was no trouble. Glad to be of service. I hope we do too. 'Bye now."

"What's that about taking money?"

"Ludwig stole money from the bank," said Harry. He was amused. He chuckled happily to himself. "And I can tell you where your taffy tarts are. They're in South America or somewhere, if he hasn't eaten them. Here are the headlines," Harry said. "BANK MANAGAER STILL AT LARGE. Flees country with four dozen taffy tarts!"

"Surely that isn't funny?" Patricia said.

"Of course it's funny. It's hilarious. That Ludwig now, he's a man who blames everybody else for the kind of life he's leading. He's having a lousy time, and whose fault is it? Why, everybody else's! So he decides to make a break for freedom. Nobody tells him what to do any more, right? He'll be the master of his fate, he'll be the captain of his soul. Then the first thing he does under his own gas is to run away with a bag of pastry instead of a bag of money. For God's sake, if he told his wife what he was doing she would have made sure he took the right bag."

"Stephanie dramatizes everything."

"Do you blame her? She had this Ludwig for a husband. She says she's sorry he took your taffy tarts, by the way. How about this," said Harry, using a big boyish grin on Patricia. "Say Ludwig gets in a taxi at the other end, and he gives a taffy tart to the driver. The driver looks at the taffy tart, and what does he say?"

"What do you mean?" asked Patricia. She understood that Stephanie was now without a husband, however unsatisfactory he had been, and that Ludwig had committed a serious crime, and would be put in jail when he was caught.

"The cab-driver says: *haven't you got anything smaller?*"

For a while Patricia frowned, trying to grasp this idea. A crazy picture gathered in her mind then. Ludwig, a vague and smiling man, was sitting in a foreign taxi, and a foreign driver with a big black moustache was looking dubiously at the taffy tart Ludwig was offering him. The driver had a handful of cookies, sorting through them for change.

Patricia tried to withhold a laugh, with three fingers at her mouth. Harry said solemnly: "Are you ready for this? Ludwig takes his loot to a bank to deposit it. He says to the manager, what's the official rate on these, and the manager looks in the bag and says: *We're never sure, sir, there's been a lot of speculation in taffy tarts recently!*"

This silly thought, and Harry's solemn face, provoked a sort of sudden paroxysm in Patricia, something that hadn't happened to her since she was very young and giggly. She laughed and laughed helplessly. Her hair came loose and she put her hand up to hold it back. Harry took Patricia in his arms, and Patricia submitted, laughing into his shoulder. Presently she went quiet. She stayed in Harry's arms, though.

"You're a delight, Patricia," said Harry. "I could kiss you."

"I know," Patricia said, into his shoulder. "I want you to."

"Now that's a beautiful thought, you see," Harry said.

"Harry, do you really like me?" Patricia asked unexpectedly. "I mean, you're not just looking for some quick sex before Robert comes, are you? I'm not just a thing?"

"I really like you, Patricia," Harry said, which was actually true.

"I'd better get the phone," Patricia said, almost as soon as it began to ring. "It may be Robert. I don't understand why he's so late."

Harry stood there, bereft, for an age it seemed, immobilized by his rotten luck. He didn't listen to Patricia. She was receiving upsetting and perplexing news. Heathcliff came and stood on one of Harry's shoes and wagged his tail. "I don't even believe this," Harry said finally to the dog. "Here is a sports headline. CONNORS IS STOPPED NEAR THE END ZONE. Injured player fails in touchdown bid."

"Yes, of course," Patricia said on the telephone. "Thank you for what you're doing, Ben. Please, please call me as soon as you know." She said to Harry: "That was a friend of ours. He's a lawyer. God, it's despicable. It was the delegation. Some of the people started shouting and throwing things. Robert's at the police station. He's been arrested!"

"You're kidding? Robert?"

"Robert! It's so unfair," Patricia said. "People were throwing stones and bottles, and they sent for the police, and Robert was arrested because he was leading the delegation."

"All right," Harry said at once. "Let's get the hell down there and bail him out."

"No. Ben says I'm to stay here. He's with Robert now. It's incredible. Robert!"

"So they've got old Robert in the dungeons. For being a good guy. How about that?" Harry poured a couple of whiskies, as if celebrating. "You have an intelligent town here, you know. On Tuesday afternoon the bank manager absconds with his wife's baking. Wednesday evening the cops are over at City Hall, busting philanthropists."

"Today is unusually dramatic," Patricia said. "The days are usually dull. You wouldn't understand what dull means, Harry. Dullness is a punishment you receive for doing the right things. I don't so much mind the bad reputation you get—people saying you're too good to be true, or you must be hiding something, or atoning for something. It's the filthy monotony I can't stand. The deadly dull routine of responsibility and good works and humane endeavour..."

"The heavy weight of the halo," Harry said.

Patricia looked at Harry and shrugged, and smiled a little although she didn't feel like smiling. "Well, make fun if you like, but that's precisely it," she said. "I have this enormous craving to break out, to escape from the whole goddamn *mystique* of compassion and all the rest of it...and then of course I feel like a hypocrite, so I can't even have the satisfaction of a clear conscience while I'm killing myself being so goody-goody."

"Well, I'm afraid I can't help you with advice Patricia. I don't know much about consciences, they puzzle me."

"I wish I could make an honourable compromise. All I want is some freedom. I just want what Heathcliff has, some simple animal freedom. I'm suffocating!"

"That shouldn't be out of reach, should it? A little freedom never hurt anybody. A few laughs. Maybe a bit of innocent fooling around now and then..."

Patricia smiled, still without amusement however. But she looked at Harry fondly. She could never talk like this to Robert. Robert would be baffled. He would be full of solicitude, and love, and incomprehension. He lived within the proprieties like a fish in water. "Do you know what else it does to you?" she said. "It changes you. Yes, no more open friendly faces because we must always be on guard. I can tell. I can feel it, when my mouth tightens up because I disapprove of something. I'm getting a mouth the shape of a prune. I find myself holding my back stiff too, and lately I've noticed that I've a habit of putting my knees together. I can't sit down any more without putting my knees together. Do you know why, Harry? It has nothing to do with being afraid of men. It has to do with me, it's because I'm afraid I might *loll* all over the damn place, that I might suddenly decide to demonstrate that I'm a woman, and that I have as many desires and needs as everybody else . . ."

"You're wasting yourself," Harry told her. "You know you're wasting yourself, don't you?"

"Of course I know. I'll die of boredom before I'm thirty. Or I can see myself secretly watching people and disapproving of them, with my knees together and my mouth all pursed up as if I'd been sucking lemons."

"Anyway, Robert will be delayed," Harry said, very casually indeed. "Could be that he'll spend the night in the cells."

"Ben says there's a chance he won't be charged. The police haven't charged anybody yet."

"Well, we were doing this," Harry said, taking Patricia in his arms. But Patricia looked at him in surprise.

"Harry, you said you liked me," she said, and pushed him away.

"I do like you."

"Then why aren't you helping me?"

"If we could do anything for Robert—"

"I'm not *talking* about Robert, I'm talking about *me*." Patricia searched Harry's face closely, studying him. "You don't understand anything I said, do you?" she asked, interested. "You're still thinking about a tumble in bed, aren't you, and that's what you really mean when you say I'm wasting myself, that I'm not tumbling around in bed with everybody?"

"I was talking in my own interests, and not for everybody," Harry said honestly. "I mean, self-denial and sacrifice," he said, looking around at Patricia's inadequate kitchen, "and poverty and all that shit, where does it get you? Well, it gets you a mouth like a prune and bony knees, is that the deal? All right, what does it do? I suppose that's your important question. I can't see it doing a goddamn thing. Take that Mexican nonsense of yours, Patricia. I have a couple of Mexican customers, and believe me those fellows are killing Mexicans and torturing them faster than you're patching 'em up and giving 'em aspirins. They have a higher turnover, you see. Mind you, they're working for the betterment of humanity too. You're wasting yourself all along the line. I'd like us to get back to where we were before. I said I could kiss you, and you said yes."

"I did not say yes. I said I want you to."

"What's the difference?"

"The difference?" Patricia said, beginning to be angry again. "The *difference* is all the difference in the world, it's between what I want to do and what *I do*. I thought you understood that. I'm not prejudiced against you for being evil . . ."

"Evil?" said Harry, squinting.

"Yes, evil for God's sake, there is such a thing," said Patricia, shouting. "You're an evil man, Harry: You grab at everything you want like a greedy child. Now you want to get me into bed, and you don't give a damn what you destroy. So Robert expects you to, does he? And what do you think he expects of me? Robert is delighted, is he, does he bring us coffee in bed in the morning and say, nice to see you Harry, old buddy, and maybe he pokes me in the ribs and says, he's a dog, old Harry, isn't he?"

"Let's forget everything," Harry said. "I don't enjoy these shouting matches as much as you do. I don't have a need for them." He turned away discouraged. Something flew past his ear and shattered glass rained on the floor. With horror, Harry saw the neck of the whisky bottle ricocheting from the wall into the sink. "Christ," he said.

"You're a destroyer," Patricia shouted. "You'll sacrifice anything, anything at all, for a minute of pleasure. You're prepared to destroy your great friendship with Robert, damn you, and you're prepared to destroy *me*. Off you go to Africa tomorrow selling your filthy guns and bombs, and you don't even care what happens in this house after you leave . . ."

While she shouted at Harry, Patricia seized harmless objects from the counter and flung them at him, as a way of releasing emotional energy apparently. She threw two spoons and a plastic salt shaker and an oven mitt. Harry could see, though, that she was seizing blindly and not actually choosing lightweight missiles. He noticed a Chinese cleaver within her reach, for instance, and a wrought-iron trivet and an omelet pan, and also the rolling pin as before.

"The great prince of freedom," Patricia shouted, "the man of laughter and song, as bright as Apollo, and he thinks I should fall down at his feet just because he condescends to come into my filthy dull little house all blazing with freedom —"

"I didn't say anything about dull," said Harry, who was watching Patricia's hands and experiencing genuine fear. "You're the one who keeps talking about dull."

"It is dull! It's dull! Yes, Robert is ten times duller than you are. And he's ten times more of a man! You haven't got the guts to be as dull as Robert is. You haven't got the soul, you haven't got the *character* to be as dull as Robert is."

Harry tried a fast appeal to the housewife in Patricia, the daily inhabitant of the kitchen. "Hey, stop throwing things," he said, shrugging off a spatula. "Look at the mess here. I can help you clean up if I'm not injured." It worked fine as an inhibiting ploy. Patricia had started to spend her feelings in tears, just crying silently with a distraught hand across her eyes and forehead, when Harry unluckily added: "There's no call for violence all the time. You don't want to go to bed with me. Very well, I'll accept that."

162

She took her hand away and stared at Harry, blinking large tears. "You're stupid too, aren't you?" she said. "By God, I've never met anybody so stupid and insensitive...Of course I want to go to bed with you! What do you think I've been explaining and shouting about? I want to go to bed with you so badly that I have a headache!"

It was here that Patricia's groping blind hand encountered the rolling pin. Harry went into a crouch instantly, one elbow protectively raised and his mouth slack with anticipation of pain. "Don't throw it, Patricia," he said. "You could kill me, you know."

Things like needle-sharp prongs began to sink agonizingly into the flesh above Harry's ankle. This was Heathcliff, who was standing on one of Harry's shoes with his head sideways and his mouth viciously fastened on Harry's leg. When Patricia threw the rolling pin Harry had gone into the shape of a pretzel, the leg with the dog attached to it lifted against the other leg, trying to scrape the dog off, and the elbow still shielding his head. He said: "Good God Almighty, what a day!" The rolling pin cartwheeled by his head so closely that he felt a little breath of displaced air, just before he lost his balance and fell down. Heathcliff retreated, and went behind Patricia and menacingly growled from there at Harry. "I'm bleeding again," Harry said, sitting on the floor and turning down his sock to examine his fanged ankle.

Patricia was wet-eyed and plaintive. "It's so unfair. Robert likes you because you're fun, because you make him laugh, and he doesn't often get a chance to laugh. He's so innocent. He doesn't know what a swine of a person you are."

The polite conversation they had had before did not recur. They were separated by their private thoughts, but curiously closer too, like old lovers who meet by chance and find some of the dream still alive. There was palpable intimacy while Patricia swabbed Harry's leg and put a pad on it. Domesticity, Harry thought, as he gathered up the glass from the broken whisky bottle, without saying anything except: "Are you finished with the dust-pan?" and "Don't walk in your bare feet in here for a while." Patricia said nothing at all to Harry. When they were finished she called Penny again and listened to the busy signal, conscious of deliberately creating a delay. The daylight was fading. "Oh Harry, I don't know what you must think of me," Patricia said to Harry then. "I'm sorry I called you a swine. It isn't completely true." She held Harry's eyes steadily.

Harry's resilience was decimated but he was pleased to realize, meeting Patricia's eyes, that it was by no means routed. Twilight was on the window and he had seen that steady look in women's eyes before. And Harry was by nature venturesome, and he hadn't found it an unwise trait. "Well, look, I apologize," he said. "I didn't try to understand you." He put a hand out, and Patricia took the hand. Harry pulled her toward him. Reeling me in like a played-out fish, Patricia thought, I wonder if he'll be successful this time. There was the sound of a car turning into the driveway. I guess not, she thought, poor Harry, and poor me too. "That's Robert's car," she said. "He's home."

In the event, the chagrin on Harry's face seemed to have a softening of relief in it.

Harry and Robert had been talking and laughing merrily for more than an hour. Patricia stayed with them until she heard all the details of Robert's arrest. But then she found herself excluded, by their repertoire of jokes and experiences which they recalled in a kind of shorthand or code, a phrase or even a single word being good for a chortle or a mad howl of mirth. When they explained a few of the jokes Patricia thought they were funny enough but hardly funny enough for hysteria.

So she just pretended to be with them in the living-room, sitting for a few minutes and smiling along, then returning to the kitchen. She was pleased with her strawberry flans, and a little annoyed with herself for being pleased. They were perfect. Just as she thought of calling Penny again, the phone rang and it was Penny. Her phone had been out of order, Penny said. "I'm sorry, I've been misjudging you," said Patricia to Penny, and laughed. "I thought you'd taken the phone off the hook, and that you'd call with some excuse for not baking the cherry cheesecakes." From where Patricia stood at the telephone she could see a corner of the living-room, and Robert. He was sitting forward, eagerly listening to Harry. It was a story about selling weapons to both sides during the civil war in Paraguay. He's like a little boy at story-time, Patricia told herself, secretly watching her husband, he's lovely, I could love him to death right now. He's not a boy either, he's hard as rock, a man, more mature than Harry will ever be and a good deal younger than Harry too.

"What, you mean your new Dalmatian?" Patricia said to Penny. "For goodness sake, Penny, that dog is still a pup. How could he eat four cheesecakes?" Wait a minute, what does Robert think he's doing, she asked herself, troubled. Patricia was suddenly troubled by Robert's enjoyment of Harry's war story, all blood and jokes. Is that honest of Robert, Patricia wanted to know, since he hates wars so definitely? Is it even fair to Harry, keeping oneself lily-white, letting Harry do the dirty stuff and then taking second-hand pleasure in it? "If you say so I believe you, Penny, you don't have to swear." she said. Well, it's cheap at the very least, it's cheap and vicarious, a cheap compromise to have things both ways. "Yes, I suppose we can manage without the cheesecakes. All right, Penny, thank you anyway," Patricia said with as much disapproval as she dared to express in a tone of politeness. You either do a thing or you don't do it, that was how Patricia felt, putting the phone back on the cradle and still watching Robert. *I* was prepared to go to bed with Harry or not to go to bed with him. And I wasn't sneaky, apart from the time I let him feel me up a little, and that was only for a minute and it wasn't really my fault. My prune-shaped mouth of the future, Patricia thought, becoming conscious of her pursed lips. I'm prune-mouthed now because of Robert, my dedicated husband knight, the man I love so much. Although I imagine it wouldn't be difficult to convince myself that it's because Penny Neal didn't bake the cherry cheesecakes and has the gall to insult my intelligence with the most far-fetched lie I've ever heard from her.

Leo Simpson (1934-) was born in Limerick, Ireland, and came to Canada in 1961. He now lives in Madoc, Ontario. He has published two novels, *Arkwright* and *The Peacock Papers,* and his short stories have been collected in *The Lady and the Travelling Salesman.*

Gwendolyn MacEwen
House of the Whale

Of course I was never a whale; I was an Eagle. This prison is a cage for the biggest bird of all. I'm waiting for them to work their justice, you see, and while I'm waiting I'm writing to you, Aaron, good friend, joker. The hours pass quickly here, strange to say; I have all kinds of diversions. The nice fat guard with the bulbous nose and the starfish wart at the tip often greets me as he makes his rounds. I make a point of waiting at the front of the cell when I know he's coming. And then there's Mario in the next cell who taps out fascinating rhythms at night with his fingernails against the walls.

I don't have an eraser with me, Aaron, so any mistakes I make will have to stay as they are, and when the pencil wears down, that will be that.

I can't help thinking how young I still am—23. Twenty-three. Can I tell you about my life again? It was normal at first. I wrenched my mother's legs apart and tore out of her belly, trailing my sweet house of flesh behind me. I lay on a whaleskin blanket and watched the water; I sucked milk; I cried. I was wrapped up in thick bearskin in winter. I was bathed in the salt water of the sea. My mother was taller than all the mountains from where I lay.

There were the Ravens and the Eagles. You already know which I was. When I was old enough to take notice of things around me, I saw the half-mile line of our houses facing the waters of Hecate Strait. And I saw the severe line of the totems behind them, guarding the village, facing the sea—some of them vertical graves for the dead chiefs of old. Some totems, even then, had fallen, but our Eagle still looked down on us from the top of the highest one, presiding over the angular boats on the beach, the rotting cedar dugouts and black poplar skiffs. (Someone ages before had suggested getting motors for them—the boats, that is—and the old men of the village almost died.)

I was turned over to my uncle's care after I passed infancy, and he spoke to me in the Skittegan tongue and told me tales in the big cedar-plank house. I've long since forgotten the language, you know that, but the stories remain with me, for stories are pictures, not words. I learned about the Raven, the Bear, the Salmon-Eater and the Volcano Woman—just as your children someday will learn all about Moses or Joshua or Christ.

I never knew my father; after planting me in my mother's belly he left to go and work in the Commercial Fisheries on the Mainland. He forsook the wooden hooks and cuttlefish for the Canneries—who could blame him? Secretly, I admired him and all those who left the island to seek a fortune elsewhere, to hook Fate through the gills. But he never came back.

Our numbers had once been in the thousands but had dwindled to hundreds. My grandfather, who was very old, remembered the smallpox that once stripped the islands almost clean. He remembered how the chiefs of the people were made to work in the white man's industries with the other men of the tribe, regardless of their rank; he remembered how the last symbols of authority were taken away from the chiefs and *shamans*. A chief once asked the leader of the white men if he might be taken to *their* island, England, to speak with the great white princess, Victoria—but he was refused.

Sometimes I heard my grandfather cursing under his breath the Canneries and hop fields and apple orchards on the mainland. I think he secretly wished that the Sacred-One-Standing-and-Moving who reclined on a copper box supporting the pillar that held the world up would shift his position and let the whole damn mess fall down.

When I was young some of our people still carved argillite to earn extra money. It was a dying art even then, but the little slate figures always brought something on the commercial market. The Slatechuk quarry up Slatechuk creek was not far from Skidegate; and there was an almost inexhaustible supply of the beautiful black stone, which got shaped into the countless figures of our myths. I remember having seen Louis Collison, the last of the great carvers, when I was still a child. I watched his steady gnarled hands creating figures and animals even I didn't know about, and I used to imagine that there was another Louis Collison, a little man, who lived inside the argillite and worked it from the inside out.

(The fine line, Aaron, between what is living and what is dead...what do I mean, exactly? That party you took me to once in that rich lady's house where everyone was admiring her latest artistic acquisition—a *genuine Haida* argillite sculpture. It illustrated the myth of Rhpisunt, the woman who slept with a bear and later on bore cubs, and became the Bear Mother. Well, there were Rhpisunt and the bear screwing away in the black slate; Rhpisunt lay on her back, legs up, straddling the beast, her head thrown back and her jaws wide open with delight—and Mrs. What's-Her-Name kept babbling on and on about the "symbolic" meaning of the carving until I got mad and butted in and told her it was obviously a bear screwing a woman, nothing more, nothing less. She looked upset, and I was a little

167

drunk and couldn't resist adding, "You see, I too am *genuine Haida*." And as the party wore on I kept looking back at the elaborate mantelpiece and the cool little slate sculpture, and it was dead, Aaron, it had *died*—do you see?)

My mother wove baskets sometimes and each twist and knot in the straw was another year toward her death. And she sometimes lit the candlefish, the *oolakan*, by night, and we sat around its light, the light of the sea, the light of its living flesh. Sometimes the old *shaman* would join us, with his dyed feathers and rattles, and do magic. I saw souls and spirits rising from his twisted pipe; I saw all he intended me to see, though most of the people left in the village laughed at him, secretly of course.

My grandfather was so well versed in our legends and myths that he was always the man sought out by the myth-hunters—museum researchers and writers from the mainland—to give the Haida version of such-and-such a tale. My last memory of him, in fact, is of him leaning back in his chair and smoking his pipe ecstatically and telling the tale of Gunarh to the little portable tape recorder that whirred beside him. Every researcher went away believing he alone had the authentic version of such-and-such a myth, straight from the Haida's mouth—but what none of them ever knew was that grandfather altered the tales with each re-telling. "It'll give them something to fight about in their books," he said. The older he got, the more he garbled the tales, shaking with wicked laughter in his big denim overalls when the little men with tape recorders and notebooks went away.

Does he think of me now, I wonder? Is he still alive, or is he lying in a little Skidegate grave after a good Christian burial—a picture of an eagle on the marble headstone as a last reminder of the totem of his people? Is he celebrating his last *potlache* before the gates of heaven; and has the *shaman* drummed his long dugout through waves of clouds? Are the *ceremonial* fires burning now, and is my grandfather throwing in his most precious possessions—his blue denim overalls, his pipe?

(Remember, Aaron, how amazed you were when I first told you about the *potlache*? "Why didn't the chiefs just *exhibit* their wealth?" you argued, and I told you they felt they could prove their wealth better by demonstrating how much of it they could *destroy*. Then you laughed, and said you thought the *potlache* had to be the most perfect parody of capitalism and consumer society you'd ever heard of. "What happened," you asked, "if a chief threw away everything he owned and ended up a poor man?" And I explained how there were ways of becoming rich again—for instance, the bankrupt chief could send some sort of gift to a rival chief, knowing that the returned favour had to be greater than the original one. It was always a matter of etiquette among our people to outdo another man's generosity.)

Anyway, I lie here and imagine grandfather celebrating a heavenly *potlache*—(heaven is the only place he'll ever celebrate it, for it was forbidden long ago by the government here on earth) — and the great Christian gates are opening for him now, and behind him the charred remains of his pipe and his blue denims bear witness to the last *potlache* of all.

Some of my childhood playmates were children of the white teacher and doctor of Skidegate, and I taught them how to play *Sin*, where you shuffle marked sticks under a mat and try to guess their positions. They got sunned up in summer until their skins were as copper as mine; we sat beneath the totems and compared our histories; we sat by the boats and argued about God. I read a lot; I think I must have read every book in the Mission School. By the time I was fifteen I'd been to the mainland twice and come back with blankets, potato money, and booze for the old *shaman*.

I began to long for the mainland, to see Vancouver, the forests of Sitka spruce in the north, mountains, railroads, lumber camps where Tsimsyan and Niskae workers felled trees and smashed pulp. My uncle had nothing to say when I announced that I was going to go and work at "the edge of the world" — but my grandfather put up a terrific fight, accusing me of wanting to desert my people for the white man's world, accusing my mother of having given birth to a feeble-spirited fool because on the day of my birth she accepted the white man's pain-killer and lay in "the sleep like death" when I came from her loins. And then he went into a long rambling tale of a day the white doctor invited the *shaman* in to witness his magic, and the *shaman* saw how everything in the doctor's room was magic white, to ward off evil spirits from sick flesh, and he saw many knives and prongs shining like the backs of salmon and laid out in neat rows on a white sheet; from this he understood that the ceremony wouldn't work unless the magical pattern of the instruments was perfect. Then the doctor put the sick man into the death-sleep, and the *shaman* meanwhile tried to slip the sick soul into his bone-box, but he couldn't because the doctor's magic was too powerful to be interfered with. It was only when the doctor laid out exactly four knives and four prongs onto another white sheet, that the *shaman* realized the doctor had stolen the sacred number four from us to work his magic.

I worked north in a lumber camp for a while; we were clearing a patch of forest for an airplane base. In one year I don't know how many trees I killed — too many, and I found myself whispering "Sorry, tree" every time I felled another one. For *that* I should be in prison — wouldn't you think? Wasn't it worse to destroy all those trees than do what I did? Oh well, I can see you're laughing in your beer now, and I don't blame you. Anyway, I really wanted to tell you about Jake and the other guys in the bunkhouse, and what a great bunch they were. I learned a lot about girls and things from them, and since I didn't have any stories of my own like that to tell them, I told them the myth of Gunarh — you know the one; you said the first part of it is a lot like a Greek myth — and all the guys gathered round, and

Jake's mouth was hanging open by the time I got to the part about Gunarh's wife eating nothing but the genitals of male seals...

"Then she took a lover," I went on, "and her husband discovered her infidelity and made a plan."

"Yea, yea, go on, he made a *plan!*" gasped Jake.

"He—"

"SHADDUP YOU GUYS, I'M TRYING TO LISTEN!"

"When they were asleep after a hard night, the lover and the wife..."

"Hear that, guys—a HARD night!"

"Jake, will ya SHADDUP!"

"—Gunarh came in and discovered them together. He killed the lover and cut off his head and his—"

"Jesus CHRIST!"

"Jake will ya SHADDUP!"

"—and put them on the table..."

"Put *what* on the table?"

"It ain't the *head*, boys!"

"Jesus CHRIST!"

"So the next morning his wife found her lover gone, and she went to the table for breakfast—you remember what she usually ate—and instead of..."

"O no! I'm sick, you guys, I'm sick!"

"SHADDUP!"

"—well, she ate *them* instead."

"Jake, will ya lie down if you can't take it?"

I never did finish the story, because they went on and on all night about what Gunarh's wife ate for breakfast, and Jake kept waking up and swearing he was never going to listen to one of my stories again, because it was for sure all Indians had pretty dirty minds to think up things like that.

Almost before I knew it, my year was up and I was on a train heading for Vancouver; the raw gash I'd made in the forest fell back behind me.

At first I spent a week in Vancouver watching the people carry the city back and forth in little paper bags; I stayed in a strange room with a shape like a big creamy whale in the cracked plaster on the ceiling, and curtains coloured a kind of boxcar red which hung limply and never moved. I drank a lot and had some women and spent more money than I intended, and after standing three mornings in a row in a line-up in the Unemployment Office, I bumped into you, Aaron, remember, and that was the beginning of our friendship. You had a funny way of looking at a person a little off-centre, so I was always shuffling to the left to place myself in your line of focus. I can't remember exactly what we first talked about; all I know is, within an hour we'd decided to hitch-hike to Toronto, and that was that. At first I hesitated, until you turned to me, staring intently at my left ear, and said, "Lucas George, you don't want to go back to Skidegate, you're coming east." And it was that careless insight of yours that threw me. You always knew me well, my friend. You knew a lot, in fact—and sometimes I was sure you kept about fifty percent of your brain hidden because it complicated your life. You were always a little ahead of yourself—was that the reason for your nervousness, your impatience? You could always tell me what I was thinking, too. You told me I was naive and you liked me for that. You predicted horrible things for me, and you were right. You said my only destiny was to lose myself, to become neither Indian nor white but a kind of grey nothing, floating between two worlds. Your voice was always sad when you spoke like that...

Hey Aaron, do you still go through doors so quickly that no one remembers seeing you open them first?

My grandfather's tales, if he's still alive, are growing taller in Skidegate. My mother's baskets, if she's still alive, are getting more and more complicated—and the salmon are skinnier every season. My time's running out, and I'd better finish this letter fast.

You were silent in B.C. but you talked all the way through Alberta and Saskatchewan; we slept through Manitoba and woke up in Ontario. The shadows of the totems followed me, growing longer as the days of my life grew longer. The yellow miles we covered were nothing, and time was even less.

"Lucas," you turned to me, "I forgot to tell you something. In B.C. you were still something. Here, you won't even exist. You'll live on the sweet circumference of things, looking into the centre; you'll be less than a shadow or a ghost. Thought you'd like to know."

"Thanks for nothing," I said. "Anyway, how do *you* know?"

"I live there too, on the circumference," you said.

"What do you do, exactly?"

"I'm an intellectual bum," you answered. "I do manual work to keep my body alive. Sometimes I work above the city, sometimes I work below the city, depending on the weather. Skyscrapers, ditches, subways, you name it, I'm there..."

Aaron, I only have a minute left before they turn the light out for the night. I wanted to ask you...

Too late, they're out.

"Well," you said, the first day we were in the city, "Welcome to the House of the Whale, Lucas George."

"What do you mean?" I said.

"Didn't you tell me about Gunarh and how he went to the bottom of the sea to rescue his wife who was in the House of the Whale?"

"Yes, but—"

"Well, I'm telling you *this* is the House of the Whale, this city, this place. Ask me no questions and I'll tell you no lies. This. This is where you'll find your *psyche*."

"My *what*?"

"This is where you'll find what you're looking for."

"But, Aaron, I'm not looking for anything really!"

"Oh yes you are . . ."

We stood looking at City Hall with its great curving mothering arms protecting a small concrete bubble between them. Behind us was Bay Street and I turned and let my eyes roll down the narrow canyon toward the lake. "That's the Wall Street of Toronto," you said. "Street of Money, Street of Walls. Don't worry about it; you'll never work there."

"So what's down there?" I asked, and you pointed a finger down the Street of Walls and said, "That's where the whales live, Lucas George. You know all about them, the submerged giants, the supernatural ones . . ."

"The whales in our stories were gods," I protested. And you laughed.

"I wish I could tell you that this city was just another myth, but it's not. It smacks too much of reality."

"Well *what else*!" I cried, exasperated with you. "First it's a whale house, then you want it to be a myth—couldn't it just be a city, for heaven's sake?"

"Precisely. That's precisely what it is. Let's have coffee."

We walked past the City Hall and I asked you what the little concrete bubble was for.

"Why that's the egg, the seed," you said.

"Of *what*?"

"Why, Lucas George, I'm surprised at you! Of the *whale*, of course! Come on!"

"Looks like a clamshell to me," I said. "Did I ever explain to you where mankind came from, Aaron? A clamshell, half open, with all the little faces peering out . . ."

"I'll buy that," you said. "It's a clamshell. Come on!"

I got a job in construction, working on the high beams of a bank that was going up downtown. "Heights don't bother you Indians at all, do they?" the foreman asked me. "No," I said. "We like tall things."

He told me they needed some riveting work done on the top, and some guys that had gone up couldn't take it—it was too high even for them. So I went up, and the cold steel felt strange against my skin and I sensed long tremors in the giant skeleton of the bank, and it was as though the building was alive, shivering, with bones and sinews and tendons, with a life of its own. I didn't trust it, but I went up and up and there was wind all around me. The city seemed to fall away and the voices of the few men who accompanied me sounded strangely hollow and unreal in the high air. There were four of us—a tosser to heat the rivets and throw them to the catcher who caught them in a tin cup and lowered them with tongs into their holds—a riveter who forced them in with his gun, and a bucker to hold a metal plate on one end of the hole. They told me their names as the elevator took us to the top—Joe, Charlie, Amodeo. I was the bucker.

Amodeo offered me a hand when we first stepped out onto a beam, but I couldn't accept it, although the first minute up there was awful. I watched how Amodeo moved; he was small and agile and treated the beams as though they were solid ground. His smile was swift and confident. I *did* take his hand later, but only to shake it after I had crossed the first beam. I kept telling myself that my people were the People of the Eagle so I of all men should have no fear to walk where the eagles fly. Nevertheless when we ate lunch, the sandwich fell down into my stomach a long long way as though my stomach was still on the ground somewhere, and my throat was the elevator that had carried us up.

I found that holding the metal plate over the rivet holes gave me a kind of support and I was feeling confident and almost happy until the riveter came along and aimed his gun and WHIRR-TA-TA-TAT, WHIRR-TA-TA-TAT! my spine was jangling and every notch in it felt like a metal disc vibrating against another metal disc.

After a while, though, I got the knack of applying all sorts of pressure to the plate to counteract some of the vibration. And when the first day was over I was awed to think I was still alive. The next day I imagined that the bank was a huge totem, or the strong man Aemaelk who holds the world up, and I started to like the work.

I didn't see you much those days for I was tired every night, but once I remember we sat over coffee in a restaurant and there was an odd shaky light in your eyes, and you looked sick. A man at a nearby table was gazing out onto the street, dipping a finger from time to time into his coffee and sucking it. I asked you why he was so sad. "He's not a whale," you answered.

"Then what is he?" I asked.

"He's a little salmon all the whales are going to eat," you said. "Like you, like me."

"Where are you working now, Aaron?"

"In a sewer. You go up, Lucas, and I go down. It fits. Right now I'm a mole and you're the eagle."

Aaron, I've got to finish this letter right now. I don't have time to write all I wanted to, because my trial's coming up and I already know how it's going to turn out. I didn't have time to say much about the three years I spent here, about losing the job, about wandering around the city without money, about drinking, about fooling around, about everything falling round me like the totems falling, about getting into that argument in the tavern, and the fat man who called me a dirty Indian, about how I took him outside into a lane and beat him black and blue and seeing his blood coming out and suddenly he was dead. You know it all anyway, there's no point telling it again. Listen, Aaron, what I want to know now is:

Is my grandfather still telling lies to the history-hunters in Skidegate?

Are the moles and the eagles and the whales coming out of the sewers and subways and buildings now it's spring?

Have all the totems on my island fallen, or do some still stand?

Will they stick my head up high on a cedar tree like they did to Gunarh?

Will the Street of Walls fall down one day like the totems?

What did you say I would find in the House of the Whale, Aaron? Aaron? Aaron?

Gwendolyn MacEwen (1941-) was born in Toronto, where she still lives. She has published a collection of short stories, *Noman;* two novels, *Julian, the Magician* and *King of Egypt, King of Dreams;* and several volumes of poetry, including *The Shadowmaker*, which won a Governor General's Award.

Morley Callaghan
A Wedding-Dress

For fifteen years Miss Lena Schwartz had waited for Sam Hilton to get a good job so they could get married. She lived in a quiet boarding-house on Wellesley Street, the only woman among seven men boarders. The landlady, Mrs. Mary McNab, did not want woman boarders; the house might get a bad reputation in the neighbourhood, but Miss Schwartz had been with her a long time. Miss Schwartz was thirty-two, her hair was straight, her nose turned up a little, and she was thin.

Sam got a good job in Windsor and she was going there to marry him. She was glad to think that Sam still wanted to marry her, because he was a Catholic and went to church every Sunday. Sam liked her so much he wrote a cramped homely letter four times a week.

When Miss Schwartz knew definitely that she was going to Windsor, she read part of a letter to Mrs. McNab, who was a plump, tidy woman. The men heard about the letter at the table and talked as if Lena were an old maid. "I guess it will really happen to her all right!" they said, nudging one another. "The Lord knows she waited long enough."

Miss Schwartz quit work in the millinery shop one afternoon in the middle of February. She was to travel by night, arrive in Windsor early next morning, and marry Sam as soon as possible.

That afternoon the downtown streets were slushy and the snow was thick alongside the curb. Miss Schwartz ate a little lunch at a soda fountain, not much because she was excited. She had to do some shopping, buy some flimsy underclothes and a new dress. The dress was important. She wanted it charming enough to be married in and serviceable for wear on Sundays. Sitting on the counter stool, she ate slowly and remembered how she had often thought marrying Sam would be a matter of course. His love-making had become casual and good-natured in the long time; she could grow old with him and be respected by other women. But now she had a funny aching feeling inside. Her arms and legs seemed almost strange to her.

Miss Schwartz crossed the road to one of the department stores and was glad she had on her heavy coat with the wide sleeves that made a warm muff. The snow was melting and the sidewalk steaming near the main entrance. She went light-heartedly through the store, buying a little material for a dress on the third floor, a chemise on the fourth floor, and curling-tongs in the basement. She decided to take a look at the dresses.

She took an elevator to the main floor and got on an escalator because she liked gliding up and looking over the squares of counters, the people in the aisles, and over the rows of white electric globes hanging from the ceiling. She intended to pay about twenty-five dollars for a dress. To the left of the escalators the dresses were displayed on circular racks in orderly rows. She walked on the carpeted floor to one of the racks and a salesgirl lagged on her heels. The girl was young and fair-haired and saucy-looking; she made Miss Schwartz uncomfortable.

"I want a nice dress, blue or brown," she said, "about twenty-five dollars."

The salesgirl mechanically lifted a brown dress from the rack. "This is the right shade for you," she said. "Will you try it on?"

Miss Schwartz was disappointed. She had no idea such a plain dress would cost twenty-five dollars. She wanted something to keep alive the tempestuous feeling in her body, something to startle Sam. She had never paid so much for a dress, but Sam liked something fancy. "I don't think I like these," she said. "I wanted something special."

The salesgirl said sarcastically, "Maybe you were thinking of a French dress. Some on the rack in the French room are marked down."

Miss Schwartz moved away automatically. The salesgirl did not bother following her. "Let the old maid look around," she said to herself, following with her eyes the tall commonplace woman in the dark coat and the oddly shaped purple hat as she went into the grey French room. Miss Schwartz stood on a blue pattern on the grey carpet and guardedly fingered a dress on the rack, a black canton crèpe dress with a high collar that folded back, forming petals of burnt orange. From the hem to the collar was a row of buttons, the sleeves were long with a narrow orange trimming at the cuff, and there was a wide corded silk girdle. It was marked seventy-five dollars. She liked the feeling it left in the tips of her fingers. She stood alone at the rack, toying with the material, her mind playing with thoughts she guiltily enjoyed. She imagined herself wantonly attractive in the dress, slyly watched by men with bold thoughts as she walked down the street with Sam, who would be nervously excited when he drew her into some corner and put his hands on her shoulders. Her heart began to beat heavily. She wanted to walk out of the room and over to the escalator but could not think clearly. Her fingers were carelessly drawing the dress into her wide coat sleeve, the dress disappearing steadily and finally slipping easily from the hanger, drawn into her wide sleeve.

She left the French room with a guilty feeling of satisfied exhaustion. The escalator carried her down slowly to the main floor. She hugged the parcels and the sleeve containing the dress tight to her breast. On the street-car she started to cry because Sam seemed to have become something remote, drifting away from her. She would have gone back with the dress but did not know how to go about it.

When she got to the boarding-house she went straight upstairs and put on the dress as fast as she could, to feel that it belonged to her. The black dress with the burnt orange petals on the high collar was short and loose on her thin figure.

And then the landlady knocked at the door and said that a tall man downstairs wanted to see her about something important. Mrs. McNab waited for Miss Schwartz to come out of her room.

Miss Schwartz sat on the bed. She felt that if she did not move at once she would not be able to walk downstairs. She walked downstairs in the French dress, Mrs. McNab watching her closely. Miss Schwartz saw a man with a wide heavy face and his coat collar buttoned high on his neck complacently watching her. She felt that she might just as well be walking downstairs in her underclothes; the dress was like something wicked clinging to her legs and her body. "How do you do," she said.

"Put on your hat and coat," he said steadily.

Miss Schwartz, slightly bewildered, turned stupidly and went upstairs. She came down a minute later in her coat and hat and went out with the tall man. Mrs. McNab got red in the face when Miss Schwartz offered no word of explanation.

On the street he took her arm and said, "You got the dress on and it won't do any good to talk about it. We'll go over to the station."

"But I have to go to Windsor," she said, "I really have to. It will be all right. You see, I am to be married tomorrow. It's important to Sam."

He would not take her seriously. The street lights made the slippery sidewalks glassy. It was hard to walk evenly.

At the station the sergeant said to the detective, "She might be a bad egg. She's an old maid and they get very foxy."

She tried to explain it clearly and was almost garrulous. The sergeant shrugged his shoulders and said the cells would not hurt her for a night. She started to cry. A policeman led her to a small cell with a plain bed.

Miss Schwartz could not think about being in the cell. Her head, heavy at first, got light and she could not consider the matter. The detective who had arrested her gruffly offered to send a wire to Sam.

The policeman on duty during the night thought she was a stupid silly woman because she kept saying over and over, "We were going to be married. Sam liked a body to look real nice. He always said so." The unsatisfied expression in her eyes puzzled the policeman, who said to the sergeant, "She's a bit of a fool, but I guess she was going to get married all right."

At half past nine in the morning they took her from the cell to the police car along with a small wiry man who had been quite drunk the night before, a coloured woman who had been keeping a bawdy-house, a dispirited fat man arrested for bigamy, and a Chinaman who had been keeping a betting-house. She sat stiffly, primly, in a corner of the car and could not cry. Snow was falling heavily when the car turned into the city hall courtyard.

Miss Schwartz appeared in the Women's Court before a little Jewish magistrate. Her legs seemed to stiffen and fall away when she saw Sam's closely cropped head and his big lazy body at a long table before the magistrate. A young man was talking rapidly and confidently to him. The magistrate and the Crown attorney were trying to make a joke at each other's expense. The magistrate found the attorney amusing. A court clerk yelled a name, the policeman at the door repeated it and then loudly yelled the name along the hall. The coloured woman who had been keeping the bawdy-house appeared with her lawyer.

Sam moved over to Miss Schwartz. He found it hard not to cry. She knew that a Salvation Army man was talking to a slightly hard-looking woman about her, and she felt strong and resentful. Sam held her hand but said nothing.

The coloured woman went to jail for two months rather than pay a fine of $200.

"Lena Schwartz," said the clerk. The policeman at the door shouted the name along the hall. The young lawyer who had been talking to Sam told her to stand up while the clerk read the charge. She was scared and her knees were stiff.

"Where is the dress?" asked the magistrate.

A store detective with a heavy moustache explained that she had it on and told how she had been followed and later on arrested. Everybody looked at her, the dress too short and hanging loosely on her thin body, the burnt orange petals creased and twisted. The magistrate said to himself. "She's an old maid and it doesn't even look nice on her."

"She was to be married today," began the young lawyer affably. "She was to be married in this dress," he said, and good-humouredly explained that yesterday when she stole it she had become temporarily a kleptomaniac. Mr. Hilton had come up from Windsor and was willing to pay for the dress. It was a case for clemency. "She waited a long time to be married and was not quite sure of herself," he said seriously.

He told Sam to stand up. Sam haltingly explained that she was a good woman, a very good woman. The Crown attorney seemed to find Miss Schwartz amusing.

The magistrate scratched away with his pen and then said he would re-mand Miss Schwartz for sentence if Sam still wanted to marry her and would pay for the dress. Sam could hardly say anything. "She will leave the city with you," said the magistrate, "and keep out of the department stores for a year." He saw Miss Schwartz wrinkling her nose and blinking her eyes and added, "Now go out and have a quiet wedding." The magistrate was quite satisfied with himself.

Miss Schwartz, looking a little older than Sam, stood up in her dress that was to make men slyly watch her and straightened the corded silk girdle. It was to be her wedding-dress, all right. Sam gravely took her arm and they went out to be quietly married.

Morley Callaghan (1903-) was born in Toronto, where he has lived most of his life. Since the appearance of his first novel, *Strange Fugitive*, he has published numerous short stories, collected in *Morley Callaghan's Stories*. His novels include *Such is My Beloved, More Joy in Heaven, The Loved and the Lost* (which won a Governor General's Award), and, most recently, *A Fine and Private Place*.

Margaret Gibson
Ada

"I can so think. I can so and don't you ever say that again Alice. I can draw
and I can so think. Go ask—ask the nice people here—can so think and I
draw pretty pictures." It was only crazy Ada, crazy half-brain Ada and
everybody in the communal bathroom ignored her. She had a lobotomy
years ago in this place and now no one even knows she exists. She's not much
trouble any more since she had that operation. I remember her before the
operation and she was a lot of trouble back then, seven years ago. She used
to bite people if they said certain words that were magic in her mind and she
would walk in mad, fast circles, round and round in the hallway shouting
poetry at the top of her lungs. I remember some of it—*Slow bleak awakening from the morning dream, Brings me in contact with this sudden day. I
am alive—this I*. And then there was something more but all I can
remember is—*While memory begins recording, coding*. Monro! She would
scream at the end and begin another poem—*The Conqueror Worm*—
screaming Poe! at the end of it. I had never known anyone who knew so
many poems by heart but the poetry merely added to her frenzy and violence
and so one day they took Ada away, somewhere downstairs, and she came
back the way she is now. She paints little stick figures and sings nursery
rhymes to herself. Most everybody ignores her except Alice who likes to tor-
ment her even though everyone on the ward is always telling Alice to screw
off.

I guess I remember some of her poetry because I was younger then—
twenty-two—and I thought the poetry quite beautiful and she was so majes-
tic in her frenzy, a tall, thin, big-boned woman, with short bobbed black
hair that used to fly all over the place as she recited her poetry. She was
thirty then and her eyes were keen and dark, looking far beyond the age of
thirty. Oh yes, she was something to watch. I guess too, that I'm thankful
I'm not half-brained like Ada. For a while I was a lot like Ada and refused to
take my pills because I wanted a clear head to plan my escape, but that was

in the beginning and after they gave me thirty shock treatments something went ping in my head and I didn't mind taking the pills so much and I became much quieter and so everyone on the staff leaves me alone now so I guess I won't end up a lobotomy like Ada, not after that little ping in my head.

All the women are waiting in the bathroom, waiting to get their toothbrushes and hair brushes unlocked from the little cabinets, we push forward to the dented mirrors like cattle. Everybody was pushing and elbowing each other and saying "screw off" or "watch it, will you!" Sometimes I think the bathroom must be hell itself with the dented mirrors and the keys hitting the latches of the cabinets and the stink from the toilets and all those women in rumpled bathrobes and slept-upon hair and unclean teeth pushing and groaning their way toward the two mirrors, sleep in their eyes, veins protruding on the feet of the thin ones. But I am one of those women, I have been for seven years. I hardly ever think about escaping anymore.

The sweaty, sleep-drenched, and drugged bodies move like a wave to the sinks. Not everyone washes, not everyone cares to, or even bothers to brush their hair. Myself, I wash and brush my hair, I don't want to end up a lobotomy like poor Ada. Everything is counted in points, I used to add up my points and say to myself—in three hundred more points I'll be out of here but it never turned out that way, as I've said I've been here seven years, back in the old days when Ada had a whole brain and an incandescent frenzy. Sometimes I find it difficult to look at Ada because I remember the old days but Ada is always coming up to me and tugging at my sleeve smiling a big wet smile and asking, "Just a few pennies, Jenny, just a few for my chocolate." I usually give her a few pennies—what the hell—what am I going to spend my money on anyway besides cigarettes? Most of us here have parents or husbands that send the office a certain amount of money each month, which is doled out to us by the office, but Ada has nobody, she must have had someone once but they are long gone, perhaps they left with that little piece of Ada's brain and so she has no one to give her chocolate money except the other patients. Ada is very fat now, with round white calves like a plump child, and one of her few pleasures left in life besides her calendar and her stick figures is chocolate bars. And so when she pulls my sleeve and says please for the chocolate money I have to say yes because I remember Ada when she was Ada.

By 7.15 we're all herded back into the dorm where the student nurses wait for us with the pill trays. Candy time we call it. I take the two grey pills and the three blue ones in one swallow and wait for the closets to be unlocked so I can get dressed. Some people lie sprawled on the floor, the ones that won't get up when the aides come to make the beds. The aides with a sense of duty and rightness throw them on the floor. I used to think that was funny when I was first here, seeing the shocked expressions on their sleepy faces, but it doesn't amuse me any more. No joke can endure seven years. And besides, sometimes I long to stay in bed past seven, till eight, maybe, till nine, oh Christ make it noon. On the Outside before I was sent here I never got out of bed. Everyone in the dorm sits on the side of their beds, rolling up stockings and putting on dresses that all look like baggy shifts since we're not allowed belts, everyone that is except the Virgin. She gets dressed behind a screen. By 7.30 we're all lined up in the chain gang in front of the heavy wood locked doors waiting for the aides to come with their jingling keys. I don't know who first named it the chain gang, it may even have been me but I've forgotten a lot of things from the past ever since that little ping came into my head. Most things around here are easy to remember though because everything is so repetitive, the same things happen year after year. The same type of people get to leave here after a year or six months or four months and other types of people like myself just stay and stay.

The aide unlocks the door and we walk in twos down the great, grey staircase and through A-1, the open ward for men. The men wait for us each morning lining the hallway in striped pyjamas and blue jeans or terry-cloth bathrobes, smoking cigarettes in a careful, calculated way meant to impress the aides with their relative freedom and us too, I suppose. "Hey Jenny, how's it going up there?" and they reach out and try to grab my long red hair. "Come up and see for yourself," I say. Sometimes I give different answers like doing a Mae West and saying "C'mon up and see me some-time." I don't want my speech to become as predictable as everything else in this place. Most everybody knows me and so I don't mind them touching my hair because I know they like to touch it but I remember a world where touching was soft and full, not like this world of half touches, calculated, stolen quickly in front of the eyes of the ever-watchful aides. The men talk to a lot of the women but the one they are really watching for is the Virgin.

The Virgin is older than I am, nearly forty I think, but the years have not marred her beauty one bit. The Virgin has long, thick black hair, the kind that poets write about (Ada might have had a poem for that once, long ago). She wears it in a long blue-black tail down her back where it falls about her waist, her hair is drawn severely away from her face. Her skin is pale as an eggshell and just as fragile-looking with enormous opaque blue eyes beneath her high pale forehead. Her hands are thin and pale like egg-shells too and she holds them in front of her like a nun. The Virgin is just two inches short of six feet and so even if she's at the end of the line the men can still see her coming. They never touch the Virgin though — once, about two years ago, someone reached out and touched her hair and her face just for a moment and the Virgin became so upset that she had to be placed in seclusion for two days and all we heard for those two days was, "Contamina-tion! Contamination! Get away, get away!" No one has touched the Virgin since then.

The Virgin and I are friends of a sort if one can have friends in a place such as this. We only talk at night in whispers, lying in beds side by side. "Do you think Dostoyevsky was a deeply religious man?" she will whisper to me. "I don't know. He railed against the sky because it was either too full or too empty." "Ah," she sighs. "Have you read Dostoyevsky?" "No, but he comes to me in dreams asking for supplication and I haven't decided yet." "Decided what?" "Oh, nothing, nothing. It is of no importance. My dreams must bore you, they bore Dr. Gordon." "How do you know that?" "He no longer takes down notes, he only pretends to," she says softly. "Mine too." And then the discussion is over. The Virgin will not or cannot talk for any great length of time. Nor can I any longer, but sometimes I wonder if I can't or just won't. I think it's that little ping in my head that makes it difficult for me to know.

In the dining-room we sit in fours at little round tables with white table-cloths on them, we call it the Holiday Inn. I sit with the Virgin and Ada and Leslie who eats glass, so our table is watched very carefully. Just one month ago Leslie began to eat her water glass and the blood spurted out onto the white table-cloth and down my legs and onto the scrambled eggs. "Eat your plate too, Leslie," Alice shouted from her table. Christ, how I hate that Alice, almost everyone does. Leslie didn't seem to hear and kept right on chewing the glass, her eyes blank and far away. The aides seized Leslie and tried to pry the broken glass out of her mouth with their fingers but their fingers got cut and more blood spurted onto the table-cloth, no longer white but pinkish. Someone pressed the emergency buzzer and in a moment there were four male aides with a gurney and a strait-jacket and a hypo. Leslie was still chewing the glass as they lifted her onto the gurney and strapped her down. "At least it wasn't a light-bulb like the last time. The glass in light-bulbs is much finer and much more difficult to get out," said Isabel, one of the aides, in a tired, bored voice. "Thank God for His mercies," said another aide in a sarcastic voice.

There's still a water glass at Leslie's place, so our table is watched very carefully, but then it always has been. I suppose they figure if Leslie insists on eating glass it might as well be right out in the open where they can catch her at it immediately, unlike the time they didn't know she'd eaten it until they discovered cigarette butts with blood on them. The other patients call our table the Last Chance because the four of us are figured to be the craziest in this place even though Leslie has only been here two years. Ada began to cry when Leslie ate her water glass but the Virgin was very serene and just smiled a quick smile and drew her finger through the blood on the table-cloth. I can't remember how I reacted, I think I just said oh Christ when the blood spurted onto my leg. Leslie was toying with her water glass trying to make the aides nervous, but she was in good spirits this morning. "Dr. Kincaid wants to sleep with me," she confided. The Virgin winced.

"How do you know that?" I asked. "He is drawn to sex and destruction. I told him that I was caught in a giant spider web, not like an ordinary spider's web but strong, strong as rope, and this giant spider was making love to me, all his black, hairy legs wrapped around me and after he was finished he bit me on the neck and blood came gushing out all over the web and the spider drowned in my blood and that's one of the nicer dreams I've told him." Leslie laughed. "Sounds icky," said Ada. "And Kincaid really like that?" I said. "You should have seen his face. It was all flushed and excited as he wrote down his notes and he's had me in for two sessions this week instead of one. Oh yes, he liked it all right. I'm his destruction and when he sleeps with me I'll bleed all over him like I did the spider."

"What?" said the Virgin, startled. "I said I'll bleed all over him like..." "You couldn't bleed on him you little slut because you're not capable of it, not capable!" The Virgin was screaming. "I suppose if it ever happened to you, you'd bleed over the entire goddamn world, you've been saving it up for so long!" Leslie shouted back, quite enjoying herself. "It will not happen, it will not happen! I am the Virgin!" By this time her screams were a wail and the aides came over and picked her up like a rag doll saying, "There, there, girl, come along with us like a good girl." The Virgin was half carried, half dragged out of the dining-room, her face had gone even paler than eggshell. "You shouldn't talk to the Virgin like that," I said. "Icky," said Ada. "I think it's ridiculous the way you all call her the Virgin. You're not so deluded that you don't know she has a husband and a seventeen-year-old son. I'd sure as hell like to be around when she loses that little piece of skin," Leslie laughed. "I have skin too, just like everybody," said Ada. I was going to say something more to Leslie but the winged darkness had set in surrounding me and I could hear the soft flutter of Their wings, beating, beating, close to my eardrums and I couldn't speak again for a long time.

The next thing I remember was Nurse Jamie shaking me gently by the shoulder. Everyone likes Nurse Jamie. She's tough and honest and the only nurse I know who is so unafraid of us that she will even joke with us as we sit on the hall floor smoking cigarettes. "Jenny, Jenny, are you okay?" "What day is it?" I asked. "It's tomorrow already." "Tomorrow since breakfast?" "Yes, Jenny. Here, sit up, I've got a cigarette for you from the nursing station." "Thanks. Was I very bad?" "Not as bad as a lot of other times. I think it was the thing between Leslie and the Virgin, an altercation shall we say, that set you off. You like the Virgin more than you care to admit and now you feel you've jeopardized yourself by defending her. To come to the defence of a friend is not a reprehensible act the way you think it is, Jenny. It's a good thing." "A human thing I suppose you're going to tell me." "I was but you said it." "Then why the hell won't they let me out of here?" Nurse Jamie laughed. "Someday maybe, Jenny. I know it's been a long time but they're doing some great things with chemo-therapy and if they find a drug

184

that can control you. . . ." "I know, calm the cerebral ridges." "You're tough, Jenny, and that's good. Do you know how many people in here can't even think anymore?" "Like Ada," I said. "Ada was an accident. They didn't mean to do so much, I'm sure they didn't." "That's right, stick up for the butchers," I said angrily. "Jenny, you forget, I remember Ada too, way back then, and I'm just as sorry as you are." "Yeah, I guess." The cigarette tasted terrific.

"Your mother is here, Jenny." "Christ!" "Try and be nice to her, Jenny. She comes twice a month and a lot of people here never see their families again. She brought your brother with her." "Double Christ!" "Now brush your hair and wash your face, they're in the sunroom." "Okay, Jamie, okay."

I brushed my hair very slowly and washed my face with care. I didn't want to face them, I never do. My mother has the manufactured sweetness of a volunteer worker. I walked slowly to the sunroom with a couple of cigarettes that I'd gotten from Jamie. My mother was sitting looking abstractedly out of the barred windows, trying to treat them casually as if it meant nothing at all. My brother who is about six foot five was sitting slumped down in an armchair. "Hello Mother, hello Robert." My mother tried to kiss me but I turned my cheek so that her lips barely brushed my face. "Hello dear. You are looking well. Doesn't she look well, Robert?" "Yeah, sure," Robert mumbled. My mother gave him an anxious look. "Yeah Jen, you really do look well. Great. I mean that." Robert fumbled with a cigarette. I guess that's the only thing my family and I have in common, we all smoke excessively. My mother looked like a nervous sparrow in her new pale-blue spring suit and white heels. She crossed her thin legs and settled back in her chair, lighting up a cigarette. "Well. . ." Robert slunk lower in his chair. He hates coming to this place, the place he calls the nuthouse, but every so often Mother drags him out here because—as she says— you and I are the only family Jenny's got and we must be supportive of her. He told me that once, smirking. "Well, Jenny, don't stand there like a nervous cat. Come, sit down and let's have a nice chat, the three of us." I sat down on the edge of a wicker chair. Mary-Anne, the whirling dervish, was whirling round and round on one foot a few yards away from us. "I see you got a new volleyball court in this joint," Robert said finally. "Yes." "Isn't that lovely dear, in the summer you can get outside and play volleyball and get some fresh air. Won't that be nice?" "I guess." "How's the food, Jen?" asked Robert, who is four years younger than me and has just two main interests in life—food and screwing. "The same." "I couldn't eat crap like that for seven years, not even for seven days." "Robert!" Mother said sharply. "You know that this is a good institution, one of the best, and I'm sure their food reaches nutritional standards, doesn't it Jennifer?" "Who cares about eating anyway?" I said. "I sure as hell do," said Robert. "Among other activities," I said drily. Robert was about to say something nasty but Mother cut him short.

"Remember Mrs. Higgins from next door, dear?" "Yes," I said, though I didn't. The whirling dervish was spinning closer. "Well, since her husband died she's had a lot of time on her hands and she's doing the most marvellous thing. She's working as a volunteer at a hospital. She's what they call the book lady and she wheels around this little cart full of books to patients who are too ill to get out of bed. She says they're so grateful for their books and it just does her heart good, it's so rewarding, such rewarding work. But she likes the maternity ward best because everybody up there is so happy and cheerful with all those beautiful little babies in the nursery. She goes up there sometimes even without her book cart just to look at the babies and talk to all those happy mothers. Of course, nowadays they only keep them in the hospital for five days, in my day it was two weeks but medicine is so advanced." "I know a woman who went insane from childbirth," I said. "I'm sure that was an isolated case," Mother huffed, "women are so grateful, so overjoyed when they have their babies." "We're all isolated cases here," I said. Robert smirked. "Jennifer," sternly now, "I have never, never given up hope that one day you will get well and be able to come home to a family that loves you very, very much. I imagine a lot of these poor women here don't have a soul in the world to care about them so don't give me that sarcastic smile, young lady." "I'm not so young anymore Mother. I'm twenty-nine. You forget. You still like to think it's still the first year when I was twenty-two." "I do no such thing!" "All Mother talks about is you, Jen. How bright you were, how pretty, how smart, and how you started to talk when you were six months old in sentences. Me—I'm the dummy," said Robert complacently. "I still have your old room for you, Jennifer. The same bedspread, everything, the little china figurines, the same yellow curtains." Mother's voice has a slight tremour to it as it so often does on visiting days. It always ends up that way and I always end up feeling terribly sad for her. Hers is the life filled with pathos, not mine. Mine is predictable. "I know, Mother, I know. It's all right." "Well, I just want you to know that I haven't forgotten you like a lot of people here have been forgotten. You're still my own little girl." Oh Mother, oh Mother, what can I say? What is left to say after all these years? "You have Robert." "Yes, he's a blessing with your father gone and everything."

"Lookee—here she comes," Robert said, almost visibly licking his lips. It was the Virgin, of course. She was walking slowly down the hall, her hands before her in the familiar nun position. Her eyes were staring at some far-off place beyond Robert's head. She walked slowly into the sunroom past the whirling dervish and to the window. She stood with her hands clasped in front of her, staring out, her lips moving silently. "Forget it, Robert." "I know, I know all that virgin crap but boy could I take care of all that."

"Robert!" said Mother, clenching her hands to control herself. Mother doesn't like to think or hear about sex. "Okay, okay. Say Jen, do they let you listen to the Rolling Stones in here?" "What's that?" "Forget it. You've been here longer than I thought," and he smirked at his joke.

"Well, Robert, we mustn't tire your sister out. I think it's been a most pleasant visit. The reports they send us are quite good, Jennifer," Mother added as she picked up her purse and gloves. "Yeah. See ya, Jen."

They were out of the sunroom and into the hall by the time I caught up to them. I didn't want to ask her but I had to. "Mother," I said. "Yes, dear?" She turned, a little alarmed, it was not part of the routine to speak beyond the confines of the sunroom without four nurses lining the walls. "Mother, I want to ask you something." "Of course, dear." She pulled on her white gloves nervously. "Were you glad, were you grateful, joyful when I was born?" "Of course dear, what a strange question." "You know what I would like to do, Mother, more than anything. I'd like to stay in bed till noon. Past noon, till one, till two even!" I was nearly shouting. "Wouldn't we all, dear," she said nervously and smiled a quick good-bye and began to walk in short, fast, clipped steps down the hall with Robert, her white heels clicking against the hall floor. Wouldn't we all, dear! She hadn't even listened to me and I felt pity for her. Pity! Their wings began to beat softly, far off, in some far corner of the ward and the floor beneath me heaved and sighed. Beating, beating, closer and closer. I began to laugh. I buried my face in my arms so that no one could see me laughing, and between the laughter and the beating wings and the breathing floor it's a wonder that I heard the Virgin at all. She placed her hand on my shoulder, light as a butterfly wing. "We are grains of sand in a dust bowl," she said and drifted off down the hall toward the dorm. I shouted above the beating wings, "If there were enough of us couldn't we *be* the dust bowl?" She didn't turn or reply. The whirling dervish was upon me, "I'm a top, I can't stop, I'm a top, I can't stop," it sang, the arms flailing like a windmill. "To hell with it," I said to the whirling dervish and went into the dorm just a beat away from Their wings and lay down on my bed, the winged, furry darkness engulfing me.

"A few pennies please, for my chocolate, please, please, Jenny." Ada was sitting on the edge of my bed in a yellow nightgown with flowers on it that billowed out around her. I looked out the dormitory window. It was dark outside. "What day is it, Ada?" Ada got up and went over to her bed and opened the drawer to her night table and brought out her large calendar. The calendar is Ada's pride. It's a large calendar and above each month is a very pretty scene depicting the month and amazingly Ada manages to keep track of the days by drawing huge red circles around each day just before she goes to bed. She came back to my bed proudly carrying her calendar. She sat heavily on the side of my bed and held the calendar out before her, studying the page for a long time. "Wed-nes-day," she said at last, triumphantly. "Are you sure?" "I—I am not stupid. Don't you ever say that!" Ada was close to tears. "I didn't say you were stupid, Ada. A lot of people here don't know what day it is but you always know. "Yes, I always know," she said with great pride. "I mark them off, see, like this, with my crayon. Look at that pretty picture. Isn't it pretty?" I looked at the calendar. Above the big, bold, black capital letters of April was a picture of a little girl with blond hair in pigtails wearing bright red boots and a bright red sweater, skipping rope on a sidewalk in front of a white clapboard house with huge green trees surrounding it and little yellow flowers on the lawn. A brown dog with a turned-up tail was trying to catch the rope in his teeth. "I hope he bites her," I said. "Oh no, he's a nice doggie. Can I please have some chocolate money, Jenny, please. I told you what day it was, please." Her wet mouth went into a pout. "The tuck shop is closed now, Ada." "One of the nurses will get it for me. They will. I know they will, they're nice." "Yeah, sure, Ada." I lit a forbidden cigarette, forbidden because we're only sup- posed to smoke in the halls or the sunroom. I used a paper cup for the ashes. "Here's some chocolate money." "Thank you. You're the best friend I got." Ada said it as if she really meant it and I wondered if she remembered the old days at all when she and I used to sit smoking in the hallway discussing the possibility of madness in *The Great Gatsby* and exchanging plays by Chekhov.

"Ada, wouldn't you like a calendar with poetry on it instead of pictures?" "Poetry? I can't read very well. I like the pictures, they're pretty." "I know, but so is poetry." "You're making fun of me again," said Ada, two big tears rolling down her plump face. "No, Ada, no, I'm not. Don't cry. I was just asking. I thought maybe sometimes you got tired of the pictures and would like something new." "I—I can't read too good. What's poetry anyway? Like those rhymes, called nursery rhymes?" "Yes, that's it, Ada, like nursery rhymes." "Goodie. I can so think. You see. People think I don't know anything." "Only Alice and she's full of crap." "Shouldn't swear," said Ada, counting her pennies with difficulty. *And I shall rage, rage against the dying light.* She remembered nothing. "There's ten pennies there," I said to Ada who was moving her lips, counting over and over again. "Thank you, Jenny, you're the best friend. Will you live here with me always?" "I don't know. It seems that way. It's been a long time, hasn't it Ada?" "Oh, I don't know. Can't remember. Were you here before—before I came here to live?" "Just a little after you. Don't you remember?" "Yeah, sure I do. You were nice like you are now." "You remember that, Ada?" "I know you're nice, that's all. You shouldn't talk to me like Dr. Applebee. He's always asking me funny things, if I 'member stuff or not. What am I s'pose to remember? Is it impor- tant like my calendar?" "No, it's not important, Ada. Get your chocolate and go to bed." "Okay. Thank you for my chocolate money." She shuffled off, a ridiculous figure in her yellow nightgown and yellow slippers with little furry puffs on them, a great, waddling half-brain. Ada, Ada, I can't find you anymore and I shall rage, rage, and then I fell asleep.

Thursdays are group therapy days. I hate them, almost everyone here does except Alice, and it was with the same feeling of predictable dread that I awoke Thursday morning. In the bathroom it was the same as it is every morning, sleep-drugged women pressing forward to the dented mirrors and porcelain sinks. Leslie wasn't allowed a comb or brush this morning—she had scraped some of her skin off with a comb the day before and though it wasn't much they decided to withhold the comb and brush from Leslie. "Shit," Leslie said, walking in a circle in the bathroom. "Shit, shit, shit! I'll have to go to group looking like the typical madwoman and Dr. Kincaid is going to be there and my hair is sticking out all over the place. It's all tatty. Shit!" "You certainly do look like destruction this morning," said the Virgin with a half smile on her face and then she drifted serenely out of the bathroom. I had never heard the Virgin so flippant, I had never before heard her make a joke, however small, and the dread in me increased, higher on the barometer than the usual Thursday morning dread. "What's with her?" said Leslie. "I didn't notice anything," I said, pretending to be immersed in the task of washing my face. "Like hell you didn't," said Leslie. "Shouldn't swear," said Ada. Alice had elbowed her way past Ada and a few others to the front of the mirror and was carefully brushing her long blond hair. Alice has only been here a few months and no one can figure out why she was sent here in the first place, although Leslie did tell me that Alice took some drug on the Outside that made her go crazy but she doesn't seem crazy and perhaps that is why we all hate her.

At ten o'clock all the chairs are arranged in a big circle in the living-room, twenty-five chairs for the patients, six chairs for the nurses, and four chairs for the attending doctors. The coffee tray is wheeled in as we begin to assemble from different parts of the ward, cigarettes light up and are extinguished like fireflies. Ada is already seated eating a chocolate bar with her coffee and the doctors are assembled in a tight safe group talking about their golf scores. The Virgin is sitting serenely in a chair by the corner window and I am a little to the left of her, wearing sunglasses and smoking like crazy. Alice is one of the last to come in, her hair gleaming from her one hundred strokes per day. (Who ever heard of a crazy person doing a hundred strokes on their hair?) Alice is wearing a white cotton dress, white sandals, and a clear and innocent scrubbed face (only the watery blue eyes ruin Alice's opinion of herself as a sex symbol). Dr. Kincaid is here today and Dr. Rogers and Dr. Applebee and Dr. Billings. Dr. Billings is the youngest doctor, with a collegiate haircut, horn-rimmed glasses, and a pipe. Alice is hot for him, Leslie says. Dr. Billings has only been here six months and pictures himself as the new boy wonder around this joint. Alice is the only one here that thinks there's anything wonderful about him. Dr. Applebee is older, about fifty, and he too remembers Ada when she was Ada — and yet as her doctor he must have ordered that operation that took away the little piece of Ada's brain. He has a grey beard and smokes cigarettes from the States and is totally unaware of the horror of his butcher job on Ada. Dr. Kincaid is about forty, with a nervous tic under his left eye and a small, carefully clipped brown moustache.

"Well," says Dr. Billings enthusiastically, moving back and forth on the balls of his feet, rubbing his hands together and smiling a great deal, "are we all here, ready to begin, to explore, to go on this adventure all together?" "Everyone is here except Mrs. Jones who had insulin shock this morning," said Nurse Fisher with her usual efficiency, clutching her clipboard to her big bosom. "Good, good, have some coffee, ladies, and then we can all settle back and begin our exploration." Even Dr. Kincaid looked a little pained with this last utterance from Dr. Billings. Everyone got their coffee except Leslie who was frantically trying to pat down her mat of hair. "Well, who's going to begin?" said Billings, rubbing his hands together.

There was a long silence while everyone pulled frantically on their cigarettes. "I had a dream," said Alice proudly. "Well we would all certainly like to hear your dream," and Billings smiled. Like hell, I thought. Leslie made a horrible face and mouthed the word slut. "I dreamt that I was back in Toronto with the rest of the kids smoking up and we were listening to some great music, Alice Cooper, and everyone was getting good vibrations and high on the smoking up and the music and we were all talking about the ultimate trip, trying to figure out what the ultimate trip would be and then suddenly. . . ." Alice paused, blushing a demure little blush, and then hurried on, "Dr. Billings was there in the dream and he told me that where I was going was the ultimate trip. He said it so calm and nice and took my hand and said come with me and I said I've always liked the smell of a pipe and then I woke up and I was here and I knew that this was the ultimate trip and you know it is!" She was very flushed and excited by the end of her recitation and through my sunglasses I could see that the group looked dangerous. No one said a word except Dr. Billings. "That's very interesting, Alice. By the ultimate trip, which I understand is slang but has far deeper meanings than you may realize, by the ultimate trip I take it you have been travelling a very long time in search of this awakening and now that you've found it you find some relevance to your life?" "Exactly!" gushed Alice. "And so when you get out of here you will no longer need to experiment with drugs because you have found it all out by yourself by being here and recognized the foolishness of such experimentation and with this new insight — "

"Crap!" shouted Leslie. "Now that's interesting, Leslie, that you should be so offended by Alice's new insight into herself and her problems." Leslie was toying dangerously with the china coffee cup. "Crap!" she shouted again. "Now, Leslie — " said Dr. Kincaid, taking the coffee cup out of her hand.

"What I mean, my dear Dr. Billings, what I mean by crap is that Alice is full of it. She didn't even dream that, she made it up for you for God's sake, she's hot for you, sweetie, and secondly she shouldn't even be here. She doesn't belong here. Get her the hell out of here, inflict her on an open ward but not on us or better yet send her home where she can get high on smoking up and that damn music. We don't need manufactured insanity here. Take a pill like Alice in Wonderland, grow small, grow tall, go crazy, how bloody convenient." Leslie was pacing the circle now, waving her cigarette around. "So we're dear little Alice's ultimate trip, what are we, a zoo on display?" "Leslie, I think you are over-reacting to Alice's insight into your difficulties. As I recall Laing said—" "Bullshit!" Leslie screamed. "I don't want to be in a zoo," Ada sobbed. "Don't put me in a zoo." "Bullshit!" I shouted too. "Bullshit what, Jennifer?" Dr. Billings said with affected calm. "I agree with Leslie. Alice is full of crap and you needn't quote Laing to me about having to go crazy to become sane, why, we on this ward are the sanest group you could find. I know Laing backwards and forwards and it's Alice who realizes nothing. Don't you see, we're her high, all us poor crazies, we're her goddamned entertainment. We don't want her here. She doesn't fit Laing's qualifications. Ger her out of here. She doesn't belong."

The whole group began to mutter bullshit and get rid of her. "We cannot release a sick girl into society," said Billings, "however clear her insights may be into her problems, we are not out of the woods yet." "Adler would puke," said Leslie. "Save it for your finals," I said. Billings didn't know what to say to that, he had not yet written his final examinations. "At least get the bitch to lay off Ada," said Leslie. "Do you have any complaints, Ada?" Dr. Applebee asked her in a calculated soft voice. "No," whimpered Ada, who hates to be noticed in group in case anyone should find anything she says dumb. "I don't bother Ada, she said so herself," said Alice, regaining her composure and running her hand down her long blond hair, smoothing it out. "You bastard, you know damn well Ada won't say anything in group!" I shouted. "Ada is quite capable of speech," said Dr. Applebee. "No thanks to you," I screamed. Applebee blanched. "Bravo, bravo!" shouted Leslie jumping up and down. "Girls, girls," said Nurse Fisher in her clipped, efficient voice. Almost everyone was shouting something or other by this point. "Do you girls want to lose privileges?" Everyone quieted. Nurse Fisher smiled a brisk, everything-is-in-order smile. "She is not one of us, she does not belong here," said the Virgin quietly. Everybody looked at the Virgin, surprised. The Virgin never spoke in group. "I think we shall call this meeting to an end now," said Dr. Kincaid quietly. People began to get slowly out of their chairs, unwilling to leave. There hadn't been so much excitement in group since I kicked Marion in the leg two years ago and broke it. But then we had never had a foreigner in our midst before. We didn't know it then on that Thursday but excitement had been set off in a chain reaction. In the days that followed there was going to be much more than anyone could have imagined.

Friday morning was grey and bleak, rain pounding against the barred windows, and when I went into the bathroom the day got even worse. Alice had just pushed Ada away from the mirror with a hard dig of her elbow into Ada's side and she was saying. "Thanks for not squealing on me, though I guess the only reason you didn't is because you're an idiot." "I—I am not an idiot. I'm not!" "Are too," said Alice preening herself in front of the dented mirror. "Am not," Ada whimpered. "And your pictures stink," said Alice. "They're pretty pictures and I always know what day it is," Ada was crying now, curled up on the floor in her yellow nightgown weeping on the tiles. "A three-year-old could draw better than you do," Alice said gleefully, setting in for the kill. "I always know what day it is," Ada wailed. "Sure, you half-wit. You're a joke, an idiot and a joke, no one here even knows you're alive." "Am too alive," Ada's body heaved in great tortured sobs.

"You stop that!" I screamed so suddenly that Alice dropped her hairbrush and moved a little fearfully away from me. It was only we three in the bathroom and surely Alice had heard of my propensity toward violence. Few secrets can be kept on a locked ward. I grabbed Alice by the arm. "You're the one that's the half-wit, the idiot, the joke on mankind. You're the foreigner here and this is a strange land and strange things can happen to foreigners here!!" "Are you threatening me?" said Alice. "Are you threatening me?" I mimicked. "Those are the words used on the Outside, not in here, you ass. You don't have half the brains, not a quarter of the brains that Ada had when she had a whole brain. Ada was incandescent and you're a piece of turd. Do you know Tolstoy? Dostoyevsky? Fitzgerald? Well, do you?" I was screaming now and my nails were digging into her arm. "No," she whined. "Ada knew them all, all of them, and knew hundreds of poems by heart, poems you couldn't begin to understand. Recite a poem for me, Alice. I would very much like to hear a recitation from the great fund of knowledge you have in your head. Recite *Hickory, Dickory, Dock,* or is that beyond you?" "You're hurting me." "Not half as much as you hurt Ada and you better be careful not to act too crazy, otherwise you might end up like Ada only worse because you never had any brains to begin with!" I let go of her arms then because I saw that she was staring past me at the doorway. I turned to see the Virgin standing there, her hands folded in front of her, smiling. "Jenny, you have made up the mind of my forces," said the Virgin softly. "Is that good or bad?" "We may never know," she said and drifted away.

Alice took this moment as a chance to escape from the bathroom and I squatted down on the tiled floor beside Ada. I lit another forbidden cigarette. "Want a drag, Ada?" "No," said Ada, sobbing. "Want some chocolate money?" "No." I think some chocolate might make you feel better." Ada didn't reply but I remained squatting on the floor listening to her sobs and the dripping of a tap. "She—she said I was an idiot. That means I'm stu-pid," Ada said at last, still sobbing. "Oh, Ada, how can you say that? You always know what day it is, I hardly ever know what day it is and you always know what day it is. Don't I have to come to you sometimes and ask what day it is, well don't I?" "Yes," said Ada in a small voice. "Why do you take that bitch seriously? No one else does." "She said my pictures stink," Ada said somewhere into the tiles. "What the hell does she know? She doesn't know any nursery rhymes." "She doesn't?" said Ada sitting up a lit-tle. "No, not one." "I know lots of nursery rhymes. I don't know as many as you do." "But you're so smart, Jenny. You're really smart." "Maybe, but I don't know half the nursery rhymes you do." "She said my pictures stink," Ada said again. "That's ridiculous. You draw pictures of where we'd all like to be. Remember once you drew a lake with a little person swimming in it, a nice blue lake and when we saw it we all wished we were there." "Really and truly?" "Really and truly," and as I said it I realized it wasn't a lie. Ada's simple pictures had the magic of a child in them. "Remember when I had my birthday last year and the staff made me a special coffee cake but of course that isn't nearly as good as a real birthday cake and you drew me a real birthday cake with pink frosting and candles. You gave me my birthday cake, Ada." "Did you really like it?" "It was a terrific present, Ada." "My pictures don't stink then?" "No, Ada, they don't stink. Here, here's some chocolate money, maybe Jamie will take you downstairs to the tuck shop." "Thank you, Jenny. You're the best friend I got, the best. I can say *Hickory, Dickory, Dock*, do you want to hear it?" "Sure, Ada." *Hickory, dickory, dock, the mouse ran up the clock,* Ada began to sing in a small voice and I squatted there beside her on the tiles smoking and listening to the childish voice singing a nursery rhyme, and I put my head between my legs and began to weep for all that had been Ada.

On Saturday night about midnight we all heard the emergency buzzer go off—hurry hurry! it screamed into the half-lit regions of the dorm. It was then we heard the Virgin's moans and screams. It only took them a few moments to strap her on the gurney and wheel her into seclusion but it was enough for all of us to know what had happened. "Rape! Rape!" she screamed over and over again and then "You have murdered me, murdered me." A wail like a banshee rose from her lips. The Virgin at long and bitter last had lost her little piece of skin.

I guess it was because of the excitement over the Virgin that no one noticed the other thing for quite a while. It took a while to get the dorm settled down and we could still hear the Virgin screaming rape from her seclusion room but finally the ward quieted and people began to drift into sleep. I was nearly asleep myself when I heard it, at first I thought I was dreaming, a dream of long ago—it was like a chant, an endless chant as if in a ritual—*Slow bleak awakening from the morning dream, I am alive—this I.* "Ada," I whispered. *Slow bleak awakening. . .* I got out of bed and went over to Ada's bed but it was empty, perhaps it had been a dream, but then I saw her crouched at the farthest and darkest end of the dorm, crouched over Alice's bed. I think I knew even before I reached the bed. Ada was in her yellow nightgown, moving her body back and forth to her chant, beside Ada was the lifeless body of Alice. It was something so simple, something all the nurses and all the patients had overlooked for years, that piece of coiled wire that held Ada's calendar together, sharp wire. Alice's throat had tiny puncture marks in it and the blood was streaming down over her white nightgown and her long blond hair was drenched in it. Ada was holding the bloody bit of wire. "Ada," I said. *I am alive—this I.* "Ada, It's me, Jenny." The chant stopped. She looked at me, a look of true recognition. "You remember, Ada," I said. "Sometimes words come to me like a dream but I don't tell anyone, so don't tell on me Jenny." "I won't, Ada." *Slow bleak awakening from the morning dream, Brings me in contact with this sudden day. I am alive—this I.* I looked down at Ada and Alice and the blood and I knew that someone would have to be told soon but for the moment, for the moment I just wanted to listen to the Ada of long ago.

Margaret Gibson (1948-) was born in Toronto and lives with her son Aaron in the Toronto borough of Scarborough. Her first collection of stories, *The Butterfly Ward*, shared the 1977 City of Toronto Book Award. Her second collection is *Considering her Condition*.

Hugh Hood
Three Halves of a House

East of Kingston the islands — more than eleven hundred of them — begin to sprout in and all around the ship channel, choking and diverting the immense river for forty amazing miles, eastward past Gananoque, almost down to Stoverville. But a third of the continent leans pushing behind the lakes and the river, the pulse, circulation, artery, and heart, all in one flowing geographical fact, of half the North Americans, the flow we live by all that long way from Minnesota to the Gulf.

Saint Lawrence's Gulf, martyr roasted on a gridiron, Breton saint, legend imported by the French to name the life's current of a hundred million industrious shore dwellers, drinking the water, lighting their houses by it, floating on it in numberless craft. "Seas of Sweet Water," the Indians called the lakes, and to the east the marvellous Saint Lawrence with the weight of the American Northeast inclining to the Gulf.

So the channel must be cut, though the islands press against the current in resistance, cut sometimes through needles' eyes and wearing deep, deep, through solid pressed ancient rock a hundred and fifty feet down, two hundred, icy-cold ten feet below the surface. A holidaying swimmer floats up half frozen in the narrow channel from a shallow drive of the current, lucky to catch an exposed tree-root at the edge of a corroded island and haul himself ashore, the water sliding and driving beneath him two hundred feet down to the anonymous rock.

Try to swim upstream, brother, at Flowerlea! And feel yourself carried backward through your best stroke, feel yourself whipped out of yourself as the river pulls at your thighs, hauling you down away eastward as though you were falling helpless down a chute. Then grab at the skeletal roots, hang on, swing in the water and ride an eddy ashore! Fight the weight of eleven states and half of Canada, something to think about swinging on your sodden shredded branching root while fifty feet away — not an inch more — a ship seven hundred and fifty feet long glides ghostly past, soundless, what a thing to meet on a holiday beach! Not a thing to swim too close to, glistening black walls rising out of the water above you like an apartment building—*Scott Misener* on the bows and the name of the line reading backward to the stern in letters twice your height, swimmer, and not a sound from the ship, the current moving the ship as easily as it moves you. A deckhand leans incuriously at the rail, lifting a friendly hand, and is gone, whirled away eastward while he lowers his arm.

Scott Misener, Erika Hamburg, Tosui Maru, Bristol City, Mooremacglen—they hail from everywhere, upper lakers, tankers, the few remaining canallers, ocean-going freighters built by thrifty Danes for the lakes trade, drawing twenty-seven feet precisely, up and down all day and all night with their myriad of sirens sounding the whole range of the tempered scale. The shipmaster confers anxiously with his pilot through the forty perilous miles, threading needle after needle. At Flowerlea the channel is so narrow the summer cottagers can lean over and assess the deckhands' breakfast bacon. In the fall the last of the cottagers sit around their barbecue pits with a liner in the front yard, the shipmaster pacing about above them, cursing them and their hot dogs, the handiest things to curse. He is afraid of the Flowerlea channel, so narrow, and of the weight of waters astern hurrying him along, the navigation season waning and his insurance rate about to jump sky-high if he doesn't clear the locks by the appointed day.

Late last autumn a shipmaster drove aground off Stoverville at the end of the season; he lost the closing date at the locks and passed the winter iced into the river with a ruined cargo. Each day the sailors walked to Stoverville over the three feet of ice, but the captain, a ruined man, brooded in solitary humiliation all winter in his cabin. He was never seen in Stoverville, although hysterical cables addressed to him arrived daily from Oslo.

He was unlucky, mistrusted his pilot, didn't know the river, hated it, and the river ruined him. He missed all the signs, the waning of the islands, the widening of the channel, the three trees—tamaracks with fifty feet of bare trunk and perky coronas on top—that stand on the promontory west of Stoverville. Making his move to starboard toward the New York shore minutes too late, he felt the current drive his bows so deep into the river bottom he knew he'd never haul her off. He stared at the three tamaracks all winter, counting them and counting them and there were never more than three. This summer, in Oslo, he killed himself.

The tamaracks mark the end of the islands, the beginning of the river's free run from Stoverville to the Atlantic, nothing in the way but mammoth new locks, then Montreal, Quebec, wider and wider until you can't see across, at last the sleety Gulf. But at Stoverville the river's freedom is a newborn thing, the mass of water has just begun to run, eroding, finding the fastest way down. At Stoverville it's hardly two miles across.

Over there on the New York shore are the old resort towns, fading now, the gingerbread hotels coming down, their gilt furnishings sold off. Now and then a welterweight contender trains here and sometimes a powerboat regatta invites the curious. But the real tourist money goes to Europe or Montego Bay and the old millionaires, who found their way upstate in the seventies from Saratoga, are dead and gone. Between Watertown and Plattsburg, back a few miles from the river, there's nothing. An Army camp, a NIKE site, trees and woods and dunes and the snow belt. And that's it.

On the Canadian side there's Highway Number Two, the worst main highway in the world, with the small river towns dotted along it — Kingston, Gananoque, Stoverville, Prescott — dreaming their dreams dating from the eighteen-thirties of a prosperity which never came. Yet they sleep there along the shore waiting for things to pick up when the hundred and fifty years' slack season shall be over, an occasional coal boat putting in and water buses running thrice-daily tours of the islands up to the bridge and back.

Twenty miles north of the riverfront strip the towns begin to shrink in size — Tincap, Newboro, Athens; the farms are scrubbier and smaller and hillier. You still see television aerials but now the rocks begin to stick up through the thin topsoil and you are into the Laurentian Shield with a rocky uninterrupted thousand miles clear to James Bay of round old rock, polished by the last Ice Age. Saint Lawrence again but this time choking off life, not conferring it. And from this hinterland, from the little towns like Athens, people have been moving back down to the shore for sixty years, as soon as they broke their first ploughshares on the intractable rock humping up out of the hillsides. They come back to Stoverville and cherish their disappointments, the growth of their numbers limited by their situation between the river and the rock, the same smooth incredibly ancient rock which beds the river. Life and power flowing beside them and old impregnable rock, out of which nothing can be forced to grow, above them northerly, so they come back one by one into Stoverville from Athens and the other little towns, and here they fashion their lamentations.

"They are painting the house," says Mrs. Boston vengefully, "green and white — so unoriginal. In the thirty years we lived there they never offered to paint it for us. Your father painted every four years, always green and white. He spent thousands on paint, and always the best white lead — money I might have had, or you, that has been absorbed into the walls of that place, with the Hungarians living in the other side."

"Hungarians must live somewhere," offers her daughter mildly.

"But need they live in Stoverville?"

"They make their choices unknowingly, the poor things," says Maura even more mildly, "and I suppose once here they must abide by the original choice. I must say, I think it kind of Grover to let them have the other half of the house."

"Most Stoverville people won't rent to them," says Mrs. Boston, "but Grover does, in preference to me."

"You didn't wish to stay in the smaller half. You had the opportunity."

"Taken a crumb from his table, you mean? Accepted the little half, and maintained it as we did the other side for thirty years until they pushed us out? That I should lie awake alone in my bedroom in the smaller half and listen to Grover rattling around on the other side of the wall! I don't know what he proposes to do with all that space, with just the two of them. Ellie, of course, doesn't go out any more, the poor unfortunate. Can you imagine it? Cooped up all day with that man, green and white? The very least he could have done would be to choose new colours. Green and white were your poor father's choice. Heavens, what it cost! It was that dirty grey, you know, but of course you couldn't know. You weren't five years old when we moved in. Your father had to pay for three coats of the finest white lead to cover the grey, the way they'd let it all run down, Ellie's crazy mother!"

"Was she crazy? I remember her."

"Undeniably, and her husband was worse. I tell you, Maura, there's a warped streak in that family somewhere, and it comes out, it comes out. I'm glad they're not my blood relations."

"But they were father's."

"He was a medical doctor, my dear," says Mrs. Boston stiffly, "and he understood these things."

"These things?" asks Maura delicately, lighting a cigarette. She does not wish to pass the entire weekend in these debates.

"Tubercular bone," says her mother, "congenital physical rot. And other things than physical for they've never been right, none of them. Your father at least went from Stoverville to the city, though in the end he came back. But these clumps of Phillipses — they move from the farm to Athens looking for the easy life, and from Athens to Stoverville believing they've found it because they don't have to rise at four in the morning. My dear girl, they infest the countryside, they're a positive plague."

"I'm one-eighth Phillips," says Maura with a faint apprehension.

"But you live in Montreal where medicine and science have penetrated."

"The weak drive out the strong, Mother," says Maura, "like vines driving through rock. You're better off away from either side of that house."

"But to be driven out! And then those Hungarians." She smiles maliciously. "I understand that the ships' sirens terrify the Hungarians, wake them up at night. They think of Russians, I expect." The sirens give everyone dreams, thinks Maura to herself, everyone in Stoverville. *Paaaaarrrrpppp* — I am going to starboard. *Mmeeeuuuhhhhhh* — I am going to port. They never collide in the channel, even at Flowerlea; they do not astonish us with freakish mishaps, sinkings, or grounding except for a single dead Norwegian, but they are all around us in the night. *Paaarrrrppp. Mmeeuuuuhhhh.* They give us dreams in Stoverville, but in Montreal, though they circumnavigate the city, no one notices them. I forget the river in Montreal or in New York while here it rolls through me, head to thighs. I dreamed as a child in my bed at the dark top of the house, their house, probably Grover's room now; he can't sleep with Ellie, she'd never allow it, so virginal at sixty. Poor Grover Haskell, sleeping in my bed in my room listening first to the sirens and then to the cranky breathing of his good wife who has done everything for him, according to Mother, subjugated herself entirely to him, yielded him up her house, for of course it's her house, not his—she's legitimately Phillips. I'm only one-eighth, thank God, so she has the house that was my father's by temporary arrangement because he was only a quarter Phillips and had the house at a nominal rent while Ellie, disguised as Mrs. Grover Haskell, tried to get away to other parts of the world. What is a nominal rent? Daddy never complained of the rent and we knew that one day the Haskells would drift back, allowing Daddy the smaller side while they all four enjoyed a polite Stoverville retirement, except that they didn't. Daddy is dead and Ellie is dying slowly and Grover is not. And my dear mother flourishes.

The year we moved in, the tamarack trees were lonely and beginning to lean over the river, earthfall exposing part of their roots on the promontory's side.

"We'll fix that," Daddy said, and he poured in cement and fill, so the trees are still there. "Those tamaracks look lonely," he said to me, "and they're important. Did you know, Maura," he said, talking as if I were an adult, "that sailors talk about our three trees from here to Duluth?" Then he told me where Duluth was and I remember it still. I think of the sailors at the Lakehead, talking about our three tamaracks, only of course they were never really ours at all but belonged first to her grandfather, who was the town saddler and unsuccessful, and then the town magistrate—and tubercular. Then they were her mad father's, whom I knew, who moved into the little half of the house to rent us the larger and to resent us—we paid a nominal rent for the privilege of becoming an object of resentment to that frustrated painter.

When I was five he would beckon to me from his side of the porch to show me his new picture, clutching at his brushes with arthritic paws and aiming unsteadily to pat me where he had no business to. "It's a schooner, Maura, do you see?" he said, pulling at the frill on my sleeve. "It's a schooner on the river."

"I like the steamers, Uncle Wallace," I said, and he changed colour. "But I can't help it, I like them."

"This is a schooner, don't you see?"

"But I like the steamers' horns better."

Then Ellie came onto the porch, calming the morning with her still face. She picked up her father's pencils which were rolling hastily away along the porch toward the shrubbery, and, handing them to him, kissed him while he stormed at me.

"The child's difficult, Ellie! She abuses my pictures. Everyone always does, everyone but you." She patted him and was silent, listening to his vacuities and smiling secretly at me from her still face around her lashes, drawing her father's sting as he went on rebuking me, not directly—he said nothing to me directly, but he let me hear. "My house, my house. I let them have my house, which I love, and their child must criticize. Let her stay on her side of the porch. Edward Boston is a young fool and his wife is malicious. When I asked him what was the matter with me, he declined to say, the coward—he knows all right but he daren't say. Only he sends his little girl around the corner of my house to make sure that my hands aren't right, that they shake, that my schooners look like steamers because I can't hold my pencil straight, a poor old man; they laugh at me. I'll raise his rent!"

Sitting on the arm of the deep chair in which her father crouches, mouthing his poison, she smiles sweetly along her lashes at me, frightened and trembling, five years old, misunderstanding it all because my father, young and poor as he is, worries about rent, cement, and fill and the three trees.

"Look at the new white paint," I wail, starting to cry. "Daddy painted your old house for you." But old Mr. Phillips can't hear as he begins to slide into a soothed nearly senile sleep. Ellie tucks his blanket around him, watches him slide away, and takes me by the hand, walking me back around the corner of the porch to our front door.

"I only said I like the steamers. I didn't mean to make him mad."

"It's all right, darling, he's an old man. It's nothing you've said, he's an old man. He's been disappointed and he's sick."

"But he'll be all right, won't he?"

She stands with me at the door to our half of the house. We look through the screen into the hall, and at the back of the house my mother bustles, moving kitchen furniture with a cheerful scraping noise.

"He'll be all right soon," says Ellie full of comfort, placing her hand on her forehead and drawing me down after her onto the porch swing, which rocks gently with a creak of chains as we look into each other's eyes, hers the Phillips eyes, rapt, violet, staringly intense, and her face so sweet and still; mine the brown eyes my mother imported into the family, round and direct, eyes I hated as a child, so agatelike and unblinking, my mother's and mine, not glancing and vivid like Ellie's. All at once she hugs me and whispers secretly, "I wish you were mine."

I am appalled by the notion. "I belong to Daddy."

Ellie kisses me briskly and for a moment we stare together at the tamarack trees on the point. "We love our fathers," she says absently, and turning gives me again her ineffable saint's gaze, visionary, violet, preoccupied. "Find your mother, sweetheart," she tells me, and I trot into the house vaguely disappointed.

"If you were not such an intractable mule," says Mrs. Boston, fixing her agate eyes in a persuasive stare, "you might do well in Stoverville. There are four distinct pieces of house property you might inherit if only you'd be nice to people." She holds up her fingers, beginning to itemize them. "There's our house, to begin with."

Maura emerges from her reverie, balking at this projected deathwatch which jerks her suddenly over nearly thirty years to her pallid present prospects. What had been the frill on the arm of a child's frock becomes a table napkin across which she's thrown a suddenly adult arm, plumper and hairier than a five-year-old's.

"I've stayed away too much."

"Then come home more often!"

"This is home? Pardon me, Mother, but the only thing that brings me to Stoverville is you. And this isn't your home, any more than Montreal is mine. You weren't born here."

"It has grown into my home. The thought makes me weep sometimes now that your father is three years' dead."

"You don't go back to your birthplace." Maura hopes to make a point.

"I do not. Nobody there remembers me or my family. We're obliterated. If I have any home, which is dubious, it's here in this crazy town beside these damned ships."

"What's the matter with the ships?"

"They're getting bigger and bigger. I don't know where it'll stop. It was never like this before."

"It's the new locks," says Maura. "The big ships used to stop at Montreal."

"You're past thirty, Maura," says Mrs. Boston. "Do you imagine that Montreal will provide you with a home?"

The faintest enlivening blush dabbles Maura's cheek as she folds and refolds a table napkin in her hands. "I meet men of my own age at the studios," she says reluctantly, "and you never can tell."

At this indecency her mother recoils, her life's scheme all at once readjusted. "You do not think of marriage?"

"I think of it all the time," says Maura, crossing her leg irritably, "all the blessed time and I wish somebody would ask me."

"A particular somebody?"

"Since you ask, yes." And then she grows defensive. "You were close to thirty when you married."

"But not past it."

"Thirty is no immutable barrier. Women past thirty have married before this, and will again."

"You mean that you will?"

"Given the chance!"

"Then think," says Mrs. Boston, adapting her tactics, "of the uses of our home as, perhaps, a summer place. Right on the river, a most desirable location."

"I thought that you disapproved of the location."

"I should disapprove less," says Mrs. Boston with regal dignity, "were the house legally mine."

"Ah!"

"There is no need to be ironic, Maura. I am your mother, after all, and I have your best interests at heart."

Maura thinks this over solemnly, seeming from her attitude to fancy a world in which fewer people have her interests more personally at heart. Identification with her interests, not cool appraisal of them, is the desideratum.

"I mean to protect you from Grover and his schemes," her mother pursues. "It is not a Haskell house but a Phillips house, and should come to you. He has no children."

"The poor man," exclaims Maura involuntarily.

"Poor man, bosh!" says her mother with energy. "He never wanted them and Ellie gave in to him everywhere. Poor woman, rather! You know that Grover Haskell is a monster of selfishness."

"Has he the necessary wit and tenacity?"

"All that he requires. You remember how, three years ago, he brutalized me, wouldn't even let me go on clinging to the littler half, but insisted on what he calls 'a proper rent, considering.' That man had the audacity to ask me to move your father's workbench from one side of the cellar to the other as soon as it was convenient — the tools still warm from your father's palms. I offered him a cord of firewood that your father had stored in the cellar to dry — out of the purest neighbourly feelings — and he told me, as curtly as you please, that he meant to use the fireplaces ornamentally, to fit into their new décor."

"It is their house."

"It is her house, and will be yours, I tell you, if you behave properly. She must know by now what he is, even though she's sick. She has sacrificed everything to him, given in to him, followed him through all his failures like a saint, I tell you, like a saint, and now she's sick. She has never been well since her father died."

"When I was small," says Maura, remembering it with deep pleasure, "I really loved Ellie, she was so good."

"She is a saint. But queer, Maura, queer. She has these visions, you know." And Mrs. Boston begins a rambling account of the phenomenon called "second sight," by means of which events occurring at a distance in space or time may be observed directly by persons with certain particular spiritual equipment. "Your father's great-aunt had it," she concludes, "and I believe Ellie has it, or something like it. When I go to see her I have the feeling that there are other people in the room."

"You go to see her?"

"I do."

"When Grover isn't there?"

"He is always there. He daren't leave her, you know, for fear she'll die while he's out of the house. But I'll grant him one good grace. He usually goes down to the cellar while I'm there. Can't face me, I suppose.'

"How does she act?"

"Well, she wanders. She is sorry for what Grover has done to me; she is ashamed for him. She always asks for you, Maura, and you should go to see her, if only out of kindness."

"What's the matter with her?"

"She was always a visionary and religious, and of a self-sacrificing temperament, first her mother and father and now Grover. She seems to have gone completely religious, speaking in symbols and so on. She has been reading Revelation, I suspect."

"I'll go and see her," concedes Maura, not entirely reluctantly.

Peering through blue spruce and cedar, Grover studies the three tamaracks from the porch, trying to ignore the river below them which he has never loved, and assessing fondly the intervening plantings which have suddenly devolved upon Ellie and himself. When he courted his wife thirty years ago, coming fearfully to the old house because of the uncertainties of her father's temper, pausing on the front walk and studying the movement of dragonflies in the porch light, he had wished that it were warmer near the house, that someone might fill the space between the house and the tamaracks with sod, flowers, and other trees and vines, to take away something of the starkness of the house's situation, perched icily on the promontory unscreened from the winter reflection off the river's ice. He had been lucky. For most of the subsequent thirty years while he and Ellie tried their luck in Kingston, Belleville, and for a few desperate years in Toronto, they had had a caretaker who paid them for the privilege of keeping the property up and even improving it. A nominal rent but one that paid the taxes — and the house was regularly painted, heated, kept immaculate, ventilated, and the memory of Ellie's terrible father gradually expunged.

Grover had liked Dr. Boston, though he couldn't abide his widow, and had tried to deal fairly with him. He had accepted forty dollars a month from him for nearly thirty years and had never counted it up to see what it came to. Edward had had inexpensive living accommodation and had been free to improve the property for his own comfort if he wished. That the Bostons had come in time to think of his house as immutably their home was certainly natural enough but scarcely his concern. That Dr. Boston had planted and cultivated a perfectly splendid arbour, a lovely jungle of carefully selected trees and shrubs between the house and the tamaracks, that he had installed a darkroom and a new furnace, was his business, done with his eyes wide open. However much the Bostons might have resented their involuntary move into the smaller half of the house, they had been given fair — and more than fair, generous — notice of the event.

Grover knew that the enforced move was not what had killed Dr. Boston, although his death had certainly followed hard upon the move, coming three months after it had been accomplished. He didn't see why he shouldn't do over the house the way he and Ellie wanted it; but Dr. Boston had inconsiderately died and he was to be blamed for it, he supposed. The doctor's widow didn't seem at all interested to see what he was doing with so much unaffected delight to remodel the place according to his own ideas of comfort, his and Ellie's.

But they had gone ahead the way they'd planned during long years of living in inconvenient apartments, dreaming of the wealth of space they'd one day enjoy. They had saved, made sketches, eyed antique-stores, and scrabbled around in back-concession attics looking for curly-maple antiques, planning at length to reclaim the house and furnish their half with their painfully acquired and stored treasures. And when the time had come, despite Edward's inconvenient death, they had gone ahead with their plans. He had done it all for Ellie, had followed her in all things, had done everything for her because he'd cherished her and had hoped to exorcise the crazy memory of her parents.

"Softening of the brain" they'd called it when her mother died, the state of medical science being what it was in the Stoverville of thirty years ago. Like mother, like daughter, and like father, too. For Ellie was going the same way — he saw it though he tried not to — and here he was in a house, or half a house, that wasn't really his, had never been and would never be his, that now, watching her sicken prematurely, he hated and didn't want any more. He couldn't get out of the house, not even to go to the grocery store; there were razor blades lying loose in the medicine cabinets, mirrors that might be broken and wrists to slash. He didn't know what they might come to and couldn't leave the house for fear.

Light, not sunny light but cold white light, slides through the cedars and spruce, giving them a smoothly suave waxy sheen. Standing on the south corner of the porch, catching sharp gleams off the water through the glancing leaves, he wishes now that they'd kept their last mean apartment in Toronto. It is with a sense of felt physical release that he watches Maura push through a hole in the fence, enter the arbour, and make her way automatically, without pausing to place her feet safely on the springy over-grown turf, along winding paths aslant the promontory, coming to pay her call. Now he sees the oddness of their situation: Maura is a native of the place who's fled and felt no ties; he's an outsider who's gotten stuck fast in-side. "Softening of the brain." They have a hospital of a kind these days in Stoverville and he know what they'll call it.

Then the shrubbery shakes and parts and Maura stands revealed, mounting the sagging porch steps. Behind her the small green and copper leaves whisper together, and all at once, miles away to the east, a steamer hoots once.

"Hello," they say together, almost strangers, and again, with embarrass-ment, "well, hello!"

"I'm here for the wekend," she says with constraint, "and I wanted to see you both."

"You can see her," he says, forever an inside outsider. How the girl resembles her father! More and more he feels sixty-five and out of place.

"How is she? You know, Grover, she's the one person in Stoverville... well...she was a second mother to me."

"I wish we'd had children."

"You do?"

"Certainly I do. But her health was never up to it."

"Oh! How is she now?"

"Lying down," he says abruptly, with a shiver. "Come along, I'll show you what we've done with the house." He pauses. "You don't mind our doing it over, do you?"

"Of course not. It's yours, after all. But how is she?"

She won't be diverted, it seems. "When her mother died, you remember, it was the same thing. But they've a new name for it now, which sounds a lit-tle better."

"Most people said that old Mrs. Phillips was out of her mind."

"She wasn't, exactly. They called it 'softening of the brain.' That's the trouble. It runs in the family, don't you see?"

"But there isn't any such thing."

"They don't call it that any more. Now they call it" — and he rattles off the foolish phrase—"'premature senility induced by an insufficient supply of oxygen to the brain.' Her circulation is poor and the artery which feeds the brain is narrowing—like hardening of the arteries—I don't recollect the medical term."

"Sclerosis?"

"That's it. Arteriosclerosis affecting the brain, and hypertension, too, of course. She's all right sometimes but she wanders. And then she was always religious, you know."

"Is she still?"

"Worse, if anything. Good heavens, Maura, she sees ghosts. According to her the house is full of people. And I—I can't see anything. I tell you, it's frightening. Come inside, I'll show you around. You see on the floor here in the hall I've installed a parquet, black and white squares. Very cheerful, don't you think?"

He conducts her around the familiar rooms, exhibiting them in their novel guise. Soon they hear a voice calling from upstairs. Ellie's.

"I'm coming down. I've a housecoat here," she warbles with enthusiasm, "and I've had a good sleep, Grover."

She has no footfall. She had been soundless in Maura's memory, never letting the floorboards announce her coming. She had floated around her unfortunate father and mother like a creature from another world, a wraith. Now she floats down the quiet staircase more impalpable than ever, her face bloodless, her hair gone silver, white white white, like someone who lives in the river, Maura thinks, like somebody made of water. She stretches out her arms and floats along, singing that thin melody. What happens in her head, does she hear anything? She doesn't look at you but over your shoulder, seeing things beyond and to one side of you. Poor Grover. No wonder he's afraid that the house is full of people who can't be seen or heard. Her gaze closes around and behind you like water, and you aren't solid.

"My dear child," says Ellie moving soundlessly over the black and white squares while Maura, entranced, feels but doesn't see Grover melt away out of vision bound for his workbench, to feel the cutting edges of his chisels and wonder about them.

The two women embrace and Ellie is so weightless that Maura can hardly feel her hug. She, poor chunky brown-eyed girl, solidly there, whoever else vanishes, feels as if she's tearing an invisible tissue of air as she follows Ellie into the drawing room. So she takes good care to sit facing her across the room, not relishing the idea of that disturbing weightlessness at her side.

"You're always the same girl," says Ellie, plucking at the sleeves of her flowered housecoat with birdlike hands, blue in the veins, crooked fingers locked in an immutable grasp, "and I thank God you've got your mother's eyes and not ours."

Her own eyes can't be still but rove desperately around the room.

"I'm embarrassed for myself and Grover," she says. "I feel as though we've wronged you, although I'm thankful he feels nothing of it, the dear man, I don't believe he knows what's going on." All at once a nervous tic starts up in her left cheek and she straightens her spine, sitting up abruptly on the sofa.

"He showed me the river of the water of life, clear as crystal," she says, blinking.

There is just nothing to be said to this, for apparently she has left lucidity behind her, putting Maura in the position of an unwilling witness to a personal collapse. How can she get out, what can she do? There is nothing to do but sit there and make conversation during the rare lucid intervals.

"Seven stars and seven gold crowns, seven tapers, three trees, three thrones," says Ellie, shivering slightly. Then she shakes herself and tries to fix her eyes on Maura. "Grover wouldn't understand, would he?" she begs, and launches into the unforgettable.

"The house is full of gods," she begins, "all around us, gods and the dead. I saw my father yesterday, staring hatefully at the parquetry, and he told me that he didn't understand or like it, finding it bad taste and confusing to the eye. He told me not to marry and I wouldn't listen. I refused to listen though he told me from my cradle onward. I couldn't bear children though I wanted them so. I mustn't transmit my milky brains to them and yet I tried and tried because Grover wanted them so. They warned me against Grover, both of them. He'll never understand, they said, he'll never guess and you mustn't tell him. And yet our children might have been saved from it, if the doctors knew all they claimed, instead of letting my father go to his grave in the belief that he'd lost his mind.

"Naturally I meant to marry Edward. We were born in the same month to the same family, and outside the forbidden degrees of kindred by a hairsbreadth. He might have helped me and there'd be no question about the house. Because he was a physician, don't you see, and could have stopped me before I came this far. You'd have been my child and you are my child though you won't admit it." She glares almost directly at Maura, just missing her eyes.

"There he is," she says flatly, "sitting beside you, your father." And Maura vainly resists the motion of her head which assures her that the three-years'-dead man is not there at all.

"I see him. The house is full of him, twenty-eight years of him, poor Edward. He lived his soul into this house and there he is."

"He's dead," says Maura, speaking for the first time in minutes.

"Don't stare at me with those hard brown eyes. They don't belong to you. God knows I wanted children and where am I now? A sick old woman being kept a prisoner by a stranger who won't let me alone. I know. He's afraid, afraid." She spreads her palms over her cheeks and smoothes the twitches out. "Do you like the way we've changed the house?"

"I think it's all lovely, Ellie," says Maura, crossing the room and taking her by the arm, helping her to her feet. "I've been through it all with Grover. It's all lovely." She leads the other woman into the hallway.

"Are you leaving?"

"I think so. I told Mother I'd be home for lunch. Perhaps I can come over Sunday night."

"And then you go back to the city? You'll have children, Maura, I know it. You're going to be married, aren't you?"

207

At this prescience, Maura shudders. "I hope so," she admits, kissing a dry cheek, "and please take good care of yourself."

As she pushes the yielding shrubbery aside, as it whistles softly around her, she hears Ellie call, "It comes to Grover or to you, and soon, soon." And she resolves to herself that it can't possibly come to her.

"Oho!" says Mrs. Boston with delight of a kind. "Oho, oho! I told you, didn't I?"

"You told me something, but not all that," says Maura, utterly exhausted.

"She must have been having one of her bad days."

"All her days must be like that," reasons Maura tiredly. "She can't have any good days if she's as bad as that."

"It's partly assumed, you know."

"Oh, Mother, for goodness' sake! She's dying. She can't reason."

"The poor woman," says Mrs. Boston with real compassion, "and so she said that it would come to you or Grover."

"Yes."

"She must have meant the house."

"Oh, that and everything else."

"There's nothing else to inherit."

"You don't know. You don't know."

"There could be no two people more hardhearted, Maura, than you and Grover Haskell!"

"Why do you dislike him so much? You should be grateful to him."

"For heaven's sake, why?"

"Oh, I don't know," exclaims Maura, petulantly. "Perhaps because he got her out of the way. He's not a malicious person at all. I like him. I pity him."

"And well you may," says Mrs. Boston, "because he's caught; there's nothing he can do. He hoped for years to get his hands on our house and now he hasn't got it — it's got him. He caught a shark."

"I'll make a prediction," says Maura grimly, "and I want you to remember it. If Ellie dies and leaves the house to him, as I hope to God she does, you, Mother, will be over there three nights a week playing cards with him within six months."

Mrs. Boston springs to her feet and begins to pace up and down the narrow bed-sitting room which comprises the bulk of her small apartment. She doesn't resemble her daughter, at this strained point in their relationship, nearly as much as usual. She shows in her walk and in the defiant toss of her head how completely she knows that there can be no estrangement between them; she can trust Maura.

"My God, how right you are," she confesses with a full agitation, crushing a hand over her neat straw-coloured hair. "Of course I will be. Out of idle curiosity, you believe, and loneliness." She turns briskly to Maura. "I know mine is not a dignified position. I'm quite aware of what people say."

"People don't say anything, as far as I know."

"You live in Montreal."

"But I hear what goes on."

"Nonsense! You haven't been here in a year." As Maura protests, her mother puts up a grim hand for silence. "I'm not reproaching you. In your place I should do exactly the same. Stay away! Hunt some man down! You can do it!" She smiles at her daughter because they love one another. "I sound like a cheerleader."

"I've nearly done it," grins Maura sourly, "and Ellie knew all about it before I said a word."

"She has radar," says Mrs. Boston, "or second sight."

"You would adore your grandchildren if you had any."

Mrs. Boston winces. "My God, how right you are," she exclaims for the second time in three minutes. "Have some!" she begs. "Start the whole thing off again. I don't want you to be the last. We never meant you to be the only child."

"I've borne it," says Maura.

"So you see me over at Grover's house, playing double solitaire with him, the two of us mourning our barrenness, all alone and exactly like each other. Very well, I've admitted that I don't hate the man. He's not a wicked man, I suppose."

"It's simply that you're both caught."

"He's caught worse than I am, Maura. He's planned and worked to possess himself of that place. He used to come to us on vacations, and when we had him in to dinner he'd look around as if it were already his. You could see his mind at work, estimating the cost of new velour drapes for the dining room. I used to laugh."

"Not tactful, anyway."

"No, he's like an infant. He has no notion of tact. And then he asked us to move while your father was sickening with what killed him, though I will admit in justice that he couldn't have suspected it, and then he moved in and Ellie began to collapse, and now she's gone the way her parents did and at the end they were both suicidal."

"Her mother killed herself."

"So she did, so she did. He knows it and he can't get out; the house owns him." It is complete triumph for her. "When your father and I lived there, we owned the house, we had tenants in the smaller side and we mailed their rent to Ellie. But we had the house, it didn't have us. Now the only people he can find to live in the smaller side are the Hungarians, because everybody in town who can speak English is afraid to go near the place. So the house has him. Oh, I'll go and see him," she concludes.

But Maura is ahead of her, already at the door. "You and he can do the gardening together," she observes. "You can preserve Daddy's arbour. Grover loves the trees."

"You don't have to go down there tonight. You're under no obligation and you've got a train to catch."

"It's been a long weekend," says Maura, "but I told him I'd drop in."

"Well, don't *you* get caught!"

It was a promise fairly made, though one which she repents of as she walks along the shore toward the three tamaracks which guide her into the leafy paths. The river is flat calm, an end-of-autumn calm, with here and there faint smudges on the surface moved by the slight breeze. Maura pauses for a moment before she pushes through the hole in the fence to study the river and wish it altered. What we need here, she decides, are docks and cranes, smoke, drydocks, slipways, a hundred factories; the river has strangled Stoverville. Straining her eyes she looks across to the desolate New York banks behind which, she remembers from the motor trips of childhood, there is nothing. Daddy promised me bears on the New York side but there weren't any, not a bear. Oh God, she allows herself for one second to reflect, oh God, I want children. I want two children.

She pushes through the hole in the fence, remembering the afternoon she caught her party frock on a nail in this same board, sneaking home late from a birthday party by her secret route. She looks for the hole in her frock and the red splash of the rust but there isn't anything there at all, and up she goes along the path to where Grover stands in the twilight on the sagging steps, anxiously looking out for her, with his hands outstretched to help her through the leaves.

"The husband," he begins shakily as soon as he can see all of her, "is not really a blood relation of the wife, is he? That is, he isn't related to her. After all I come from another part of the province and I'm not a Phillips. Am I?" He insists on it. "I'm not a blood relation to my wife, am I? Because this place should be transmitted according to the blood strain and should naturally come to you, all to you. I tell you, Maura, and I'd tell your father, too, if I could, that I never wanted this place for myself. We have no children and you're part Phillips. You should get it, and I'm going to see that you do. Because I don't want it. I never did, not for myself. Never. For two whole days Ellie has been going over and over the matter, threatening to leave the place to me, but I told her that I'm not a blood relation. I'm related to her by marriage only."

"That's a closer relation."

"No it isn't," he shouts, leaping like a trout in a still pool. "This place belongs to you through your father and I've insisted to Ellie for thirty-six hours that she leave it to you. I've torn up her will. I'll make her write another before she gets worse." He shudders. "I'm afraid she's going to die soon." It has gone from twilight to dark through his speech.

"Where is she now?"

"She made me move her bed. She's lying down in your room at the top of the house. She's exhausted. I tell you, Maura, when she isn't herself she says things you wouldn't believe. I don't mean to complain or bear tales but I've never seen her like this and I can't bear it." His throat dries up and closes convulsively and then miraculously opens for his final words as they pace up and down hand in hand on the creaking porch.

"You'll take it, won't you? Look at me, Maura, please! It's so dark I can't see you." He turns to face her and throws his arms stiffly wide apart. "It's yours. It's yours! I don't want it. You will take it, won't you? Take it, take it, please!"

Her little bedroom is dark like a virginal cell in a cloister and Ellie lies on her bed with arms folded on her chest like an effigy on a tomb, her mind whirling with the effort to concentrate and control her thoughts. At regular intervals of maybe thirty seconds her body arches rigidly, projecting her torso and thighs forward and upward into the air, drawing her lower back up off the sheets, the cramped writhings of a woman in childbirth forcing her thighs apart and racking her abdomen, and all to no purpose. But her consciousness doesn't record these convulsions as the stream of her ideas grows fuller and stronger, swollen by many tributaries, sliding faster and faster. *Ppaaaarrrrpp* — I am going to starboard. *Mmeeeeuuuuhhhh* — I am going to port. S.S. *Renvoyle* upbound with package freight for Toronto. M.V. *Prins Willem Oranje* downbound for the locks and the Atlantic, half laden, looking for a full hull at Quebec City. The horns grow louder and merge with the full downward current of her thoughts. They were never like this before, never so loud, never right in my room like this. The ships are swimming over me and the river through me and the horns are inside my head muddling my ideas all together with the family downstairs in the living room with the captain from Oslo, seven stars and seven coronets and the three trees on the point for Christ and the two thieves hanging so straight and dark in the twilight on the darkening water. I am going to starboard under the stars on the current down the river down east past the Plains of Abraham, farther, to where the river yawns its mouth eleven miles wide, invisibly wide, bearing me away at last to the darkness, the sleety impassible impassable Gulf.

Hugh Hood (1928-) was born in Toronto and teaches at the University of Montreal. He has published several novels, including *You Can't Get There from Here* and *The Swing in the Garden*; a collection of essays, *The Governor's Bridge is Closed*; and three collections of stories: *Flying a Red Kite*, *Around the Mountain*, and *The Fruit Man, the Meat Man, and the Manager*.

Norman Levine
A Canadian Upbringing

When people ask me why did I leave Canada and go over to England, the answer I give depends on the kind of person who is doing the asking.

If it is someone of my own generation, at some party, I tell them it was because of the attractive English girl who sat beside me at college and took the same courses as I did, and who was going back when she graduated. If it is someone like my bank manager, I say it was because of the five-thousand-dollar fellowship I got for postgraduate study. The only condition being that I had to do it at some British university. And if the question comes from an editor, I tell him that at that time I had just written a first novel and my Canadian publisher (to be) having read the manuscript said that I would have to go to New York or London to get it published, then he would look after the Canadian market.

All of these have something of the truth about them. But what was behind them, and which I could not admit at the time, was the work of Alexander Marsden.

I had never heard of Marsden until I went to McGill. In my second year, Graham Pollack, one of the English professors — poor Graham, he's dead now. No one, apart from the handful of students who took his courses, gave him much credit for the range of his reading, nor understood the kind of humility he brought into the classroom. He lectured, in a weak voice, on Utopias throughout the ages; on Science Fiction; and on Comparative Literature. Wiping away with a large white handkerchief the sweat that broke out on his forehead.

His office, which he shared with an assistant professor, was swamped with his books. Not only were they around the walls, but in piles on the floor. And it was from one of these piles that he pulled out *A Canadian Upbringing* by Alexander Marsden.

"I think you might enjoy this," he said, blowing off the dust.

I began to read it late that night—in that large basement room on the corner of Guy and Sherbrooke that I rented from the Dean of Christ Church Cathedral. And when I finished the last page I was far too excited and disturbed to go to sleep.

It's a small book, 112 pages. It was published in England in 1939. The first half deals with Marsden's growing up in Montreal. The rest with a trip he made across country in the early thirties: by riding freight cars, by bus, hitch-hiking, and walking.

What first disturbed me was the shock that one gets when, without warning, you come across a new talent. But I was also disturbed by something else.

Although I was brought up in Ottawa—and Ottawa has, compared to Montreal, a small Jewish community—the kind of upbringing I had wasn't much different from the one Marsden describes in Montreal. He pinned down that warm, lively, ghetto atmosphere; the strong family and religious ties—as well as its prejudices and limitations. And when, at the end of the book, Marsden decides to leave Canada for England, not because he wants to deny his background but because he feels the need to accept a wider view of life, I knew that was the way I would go as well.

From Professor Pollack I found out what I could about Marsden, which was very little. Marsden had gone over to England in the late thirties, and as far as Pollack knew he had never come back.

I graduated that summer and set out for London. With my five-thousand-dollar fellowship; the English girl; the manuscript of my novel; and the well-marked copy of *A Canadian Upbringing*.

In London I soon discovered that I didn't care for the academic. And I dropped it. The attractive English girl went over to Paris and on the cross-Channel boat met an Englishman. And they married.

But I did get my novel accepted by an English publisher. And with this I decided to try and make, like Marsden, some kind of literary career over here.

I also tried to track down Marsden's whereabouts. But the publisher of *A Canadian Upbringing* was out of business. And it was only a chance remark by the librarian at Canada House that put me on his trail. She didn't know who he was, and had never heard of the book. But she remembered his name.

"I send him batches of Canadian papers," she said. And pulled out a card from a file that had Alexander Marsden on top. And below, a series of crossed-out addresses. The last one she had was: the Little Owls, Mousehole, near Penzance, Cornwall.

I copied it into my address book and there the matter rested.

Until this summer. One of my short stories was bought up for a film. And with the money from that I bought myself a small English car, rented a cottage in Mousehole, and took my wife and kids for our first holiday in Cornwall.

It was very pleasant. The weather was marvellous. The kids played along the rocks at low tide. And found rockpools with sea anemones in them. Towards evening we drove down to Land's End, stopping off at the coves, the small coastal villages, on the way. Or over to Penzance where my wife did some shopping and the kids played on the lawns of the Morrab Gardens.

On the sixth day I couldn't put it off any longer. I asked the postman where Marsden lived.

The small greystone cottage, without a front garden, was easy to find. Across the unpaved road water flowed in the ditch. A few chickens were wandering about further up the road, from a field. And a black dog was stretched out in the sun.

I knocked.

The man who opened the door was about five foot ten, a little on the plump side. He had a sardonic, very pale, face. And a short pointed blond beard. He reminded me of one of those engravings of Shakespeare.

"Mr. Marsden?"

"Yes," he said gently.

"I'm a Canadian, and since I was in Mousehole I thought I'd come over and tell you how much I've enjoyed *A Canadian Upbringing*."

The pale face looked very vulnerable.

"Come in," he said quietly. "How is Canada?"

"Fine," I said.

"When were you last there?"

"Eight years ago."

"What part?"

"Ottawa."

I then told him my name, that I left for much the same reason as he did. And that since my college days I had carried around his book, like a Bible.

"Would you like some tea?" he said in that gentle detached manner.

"Yes," I said. "Thank you."

"I'm sorry I haven't any spirits," he said, as he disappeared into the back.

It was a small tidy cottage, very simply furnished. An unvarnished wooden table in the middle. A couple of well-made wooden chairs. A fireplace with some coloured postcards on top.

Marsden returned with a tray that had a small tea-pot, two earthenware mugs, a loaf of bread, and a sliced lemon. Then he went back again.

"I've got a surprise," he said.

He came back with a large salami that had "Blooms" written across it, in white, several times.

"I get this sent to me once a month from a delicatessen in London. I tried to get some rye bread, but they won't send it."

214

He cut a thin slice of the salami and, spearing it with the knife, gave it to me.

"Delicious," I said.

He made me a salami sandwich and one for himself and we had tea and sandwiches sitting by the bare wooden table.

"That's what I miss most, the food," he said, and for the first time he sounded enthusiastic. "I tried to make *gefilte* fish. It turned out uneatable. I tried to make *putcha* and finally persuaded the local butcher to get me some calf's legs. But the thing looked like jellied dishwater, and I threw it away. Where are you staying?"

"In a cottage across from The Coastguards. We rented it for two weeks."

"Married?"

"Yes," I said. "I've got two kids."

"I never did," he said, and seemed to go off again on some private thought. But I wasn't going to let this meeting play itself out in small talk about food. I had rehearsed this occasion during too many sleepless nights. I wanted to talk about *A Canadian Upbringing*. And how he had made me aware of my background and why it was necessary to leave it.

"Go home," he said suddenly. "Go home while you are still young."

"But I thought you were critical of Canada?"

"Maybe. But I care less about England."

He cut some more salami, very carefully, and made another two neat sandwiches.

I decided to change the subject. "How is your work going?"

"Fine. I do that upstairs. Would you like to see my workroom?"

I said I would and felt somewhat flattered. Writers' workrooms are usually private things.

I followed him up the stairs — I noticed he wore brown leather slippers — to a largish airy room that had planks of wood on the floor, some packing cases, an electric saw, several planes, several chisels, tins of glue and paint.

He led me to the far side where, in what looked like former bookcases, were standing brightly painted toys.

"I make roundabouts," he said, picking one up for me.

They were the gayest roundabouts I have seen. Bright blues, crimsons, oranges, yellows, green — with a barber-shop pole in the middle around which farmyard animals went to the tinkle of a small silver bell.

"I make these for various toy shops in London, and they go all over —" Marsden said.

He saw me look at the Canadian newspapers on the floor.

"I get those sent from Canada House. They're handy for packing."

He had a large mirror on one wall with various postcards stuck along the inside of the frame. They showed Piccadilly with the Guinness clock and several red buses; the midnight sun over a lake at Landego, Norway; a snow scene in Obergurgl, Austria; a bull elephant from Kenya; and the Peace Tower and the lawns in Ottawa. On the backs of the cards was written much the same sort of message.

I think your roundabouts are
wonderful. They have given my
children much pleasure. Thank you.

I told Marsden that I thought the roundabouts were splendid.
"Do you make any other kind of toy?"
"No," he said, "just this one model."
Downstairs. The tea was cold. He had put away the salami and we had smoked all my cigarettes. I stood up and shook hands and said I would see him again before we left. He opened the door for me.
"I'm very glad you called," he said, in that gentle, unemotional way of his.

For the next few days I didn't go and see Marsden but thought of little else. I have not had many heroes lately and as I grow older they get less. But Marsden had meant something personal to me. And I felt I had been cheated. Of what exactly I didn't know. But the man who wrote *A Canadian Upbringing* no longer existed as far as I was concerned. And I was quite prepared to leave Cornwall without seeing him again.
But on the morning we were to leave, and as we were packing things to take back in the car, he turned up, looking very elegant in light cream trousers, brown sandals, yellow socks, and a maroon shirt.
"I hope you don't mind," he said. "I thought your children might like these." And he gave each of the kids a roundabout.
Their reaction was immediate. They kissed him. They jumped around him. They gave little squeals of delight. And Marsden was enjoying it as well.
For my wife he had an enormous bunch of anemones — and my wife is a sitting duck when it comes to flowers.
He played with the children while I and my wife finished bringing the packed things from the cottage into the car. I was trying to close the back when Marsden came up.
"Can I help?"
"Thanks," I said, shutting it. "It's all finished."
"It was good of you to come and see me," he said. "You're the first author who has." He was, I think, going to say something else, but the kids came running around. So we shook hands, and we all got into the car.
"I'll send you some rye bread," I said, starting the engine.
"I don't want to put you to all that trouble, but if you could send me a couple of loaves, just once —"

And he waved.

And we were waving as I drove away. Around the first bend he disappeared from sight. The road went by some large blue rocks and by the briny sea that lay flat to the horizon. It made everything, suddenly, seem awfully silent.

Norman Levine (1924-) was born in Ottawa and now lives in St. Ives, Cornwall, England. He has published a collection of poems, *The Tightrope Walker*; novels, including *From a Seaside Town*; and several collections of stories, including *One Way Ticket* and *I Don't Want to Know Anyone Too Well.*

Joyce Marshall
So Many Have Died

On that day, her last, Georgiana Dinsborough was three months into her ninety-first year. She was a marvel. Everyone told her so and, though the reiteration grew tiresome, Georgiana herself acknowledged that in many ways she was. Marvellously lucky, at least, for how much of her reasonably steady health and mental clearness she owed to nature, how much to the habit, so long part of her, of weeding out any hint of frailty or contradiction, she didn't know. (As if it were possible even to think of untangling what you'd brought to life — no doubt squawling from the weight of it in that big farm-bedroom in the Eastern Townships — from what life and you yourself had made of what you'd brought.) She'd continued in practice till she was eighty; her patients hadn't wanted her to retire and she had felt loyal to them, the grandchildren in many cases (even the male grandchildren) of those young women who had come timidly or in fierce feminist solidarity to the office she'd opened with her friend Mary Balsam in the living-room of this very flat. Loyal above all to her profession; anything so strenuously fought for acquired rights, couldn't be put aside the moment you began to feel a little tired. For ten years she'd taken no new patients and might have continued in that way, the attrition of death and dispersal slowly lightening the load, if she hadn't felt that quite new wish to have some time for herself, time to ask questions and find answers, evaluate her life. Wasn't that what you were supposed to do when you were very old? With the honesty she'd always required of herself, she'd wondered whether her decision wasn't a shade suspect, much like her Grandfather Dinsborough's announcement when he was eighty and cripped with arthritis, that deer were too beautiful to kill so he'd never hunt again. But if it was softness to want to go out proud, under her own steam, why not? She might even deserve it. So she booked passage for England and stayed away for six months, looked up old friends and family connections, learned about leisure in new places. When she returned, her office equipment had been sold, files stored in the basement, she was retired. It was as painless as such a thing could ever be.

She found that she rather liked this part of her life, as she'd liked all the other parts. (Liked it at least on her good days. Lying in bed, waiting for the telephone to ring, she was sure this would be one of the best. No aches, not even a twinge in her bad hip, broken in a fall three years ago. Sun washed through the room. Spring, that treacherous season, was coming in cool and bright — and very slow.) Despite urgings to move to a more compact apartment, she'd stayed on in the long duplex flat in Notre Dame de Grâce where her entire adult life had been lived — with Mary Balsam first, then briefly with her mother, for almost fifty years alone. She went to concerts, read, watched television, could count on at least one visit a week with some member of her large family connection. A varied lot, which provided stimulation and just enough irritation to keep her feeling alive. From time to time she considered her life (or, as it sometimes seemed, her life came back to consider her) though more as pure memory, she had to admit, than as material for questions she must answer. Perhaps once you've decided, as she had at eighteen, to be an agnostic, there were no questions, the notions of God and immortality having been packed away, to be taken out if ever only after you've ceased to breathe. She laughed at the thought of breathing her last, with relief if her final illness was painful (and she would fight, she knew that, even unconscious she'd fight) only to be roused at once by a voice — from where? — "Well now, Georgiana Lilian, about that deferred matter of My existence?" Her mind supplied the capital and she laughed again, for God had spoken in Grandfather Dinsborough's voice, coming clear and intimidating across seventy years.

She was still laughing when the phone gave its first warning ding. (Good. Now she'd be able to get up.) Who would it be today? Though she supposed they'd arranged some schedule, she'd never cracked it. Her lying alone all those hours with her hip broken had alarmed them — and God knows it had alarmed her — so she played along with their concern (and with their wariness of her that drove them to subterfuge) by pretending not to notice that, except on Tuesdays and Fridays when her charwoman came, there was always a call at just this time, when she was awake but not yet in her bath.

"Hi, Aunt George." The tiny voice identified herself as Phyllis, granddaughter of Raymond, her youngest brother, a skinny little creature who'd recently put on the trappings of rebellion — cascades of muffling hair, ragged trousers, a vocabulary her mother found distressing — and though this child wasn't one of the coterie of fussers, Georgiana said exactly what she'd planned when she picked up the phone, "Your great — no, *great* great grandfather just spoke to me out of a cloud like God."

"Aunt George, you're kidding." No humour. That was the real trouble with the young, the thing, at least, that worried her. It made conversation so patchy. The older lot, like Nora, her mother, could share the occasional joke, if you sneaked it in on them, though even they seemed to think your bones had become so brittle real laughter might break them. (Were we the last of the belly-laughers? It seems to me that we were always laughing and I miss it. How Charles and I could laugh. And after all these years, she wanted him. My God, it never ends, she thought, with astonishment, with delight.) "What did he say, Aunt George?" Phyllis was asking.

"Some rot about my soul. He was a sadly limited old man. Godlike. Ruling unto the third and fourth generation. With some success till he encountered me." Now why do I tell her this, she wondered, and said briskly, "Well, time's a-wasting. What can I do for you this fine May morning?"

"How's about lunch, Aunt George? I could pick you up, Mother says she'll let me have her car so if you like we can—"

"Out of the question, alas. Unless you want to eat here—no, that won't do either. Place will be a shambles. Got a man coming to take down double windows, put up screens."

"Oh," said Phyllis.

"Is it so urgent? Won't some other day do?"

"No, you see I'm going to Europe next week and Mother's laid on all sorts of dentists and—" ("Breathe, child," said Georgiana.) "Oh sorry, I—I'd like very much to see you, Aunt George, I'm proud of you. No one else in our group has a relative like you. Your generation made a lot of mistakes but *you* didn't chicken out, not about everything. Aunt George, I'm going *away*, I want to talk to you, you might even be able to tell me some things."

Touched by this longest, if rambling, speech she'd ever heard from the child, intrigued too, novelty wasn't all that abundant nowadays, "Well, come then," Georgiana said. "I'm charmed to hear I give you prestige with your group. Come at four. Fellow should be through and I'll be ready for a break."

"Oh thanks," said Phyllis. "I'll turn you over to Mother, she wants to—"

"But hasn't that been settled," said Georgiana, "that I'm still breathing and in one piece?" and hung up laughing.

Nora rang back at once. Georgiana had just started the slow vertebra-by-vertebra stretching that preceded the foot and ankle exercises that enabled her to walk so well. With a cane, of course, but well. (Steve, her doctor-nephew, had feared she'd never walk. "We'll see about that," she'd said.)

"Phyllis hung up." At fifty-five Nora still had almost the light, breathy voice of her youth. "I wanted to talk to you too, Aunt George."

"Then talk," said Georgiana, "while I get on with my exercises." When she'd lain in the dark in frightening pain, she'd sobbed for three people—her mother, Charles, and Nora. (Before she'd begun to inch that eternity down the hall to the point, just inside her bedroom door, where she could jiggle the phone from its stand. She'd learned then, she believed, what death would be like — an empty calling and help so far down the hall no inching could reach it.) The choice of names had startled her and she'd felt uneasy with her once-favourite niece since then. That was one of the risks in loving seldom. There was too much space in you, roots grew deep. For a few years she and Nora had seemed equal, almost contemporaries, and she, who confided seldom, had confided fully in Nora; even now the memory was humiliation. Rubbish, she thought, the girl probably doesn't remember. Though it might be amusing to try her out. You know, Nora, she could say, a moment ago I actually felt a stir of sexual longing for Charles.

"Aunt George," Nora was saying sternly, "Phyllis tells me you're going to be traipsing around after some man while he puts up screens."

"Did I say that? I'll only traipse if it seems necessary. Since Antoine died and I've had to rely on agencies — But tell me," she said, cutting off any impulse Nora might feel to come and supervise, as if even giving instructions was beyond you now. "This European jaunt of Phyllis's. Isn't it a bit sudden?"

"She just sprang it on us. She's going with one of her girl friends." And only eighteen, she wailed. And the way they dressed. Like fishermen. "I want her to look in on my English relatives. Use them as a base. She won't hear of it."

"Very wise," said Georgiana. "In your cousin Isabel's house, as I recall, there were plastic tulips and china dogs. And do you know? Each of those damn dogs had its snout pointing into the street."

Nora laughed. "Aunt George, you sure have a gift for putting people down. But when she comes... We tend to forget what it's like. How fragile they are. And you grew up in a tough school. She's gone a bit overboard about women's lib," and before Georgiana could say, "Well, good for her," "Don't try to influence her, Aunt George," said Nora firmly.

"I couldn't. I didn't succeed with you, did I?"

"Well, in a way you did." Nora paused, as if startled by her own words. "You may not believe this but there's always been something whispering in my ear. I may break out yet, Aunt George."

"No, not you, Nora," said Georgiana. "And look here. I believe I apologized at the time for any harm I might have done. I'll do so again if you insist."

"Aunt George, it's marvellous the way you never change." Why did she have to say that? What was so marvellous about continuing to be one's self? "I've often wondered. Have you ever had doubts in your life? About anything?"

"*Doubts?* Oh Nora."

At one time her life had been all doubt, she thought, after Nora had rung off and, with a final rotation of her ankles, she began to edge out of bed. (Whenever you became absorbed in a single thing, talking in this case, you forgot what a bag of recalcitrant bones you inhabited now. I have never felt more alive and yet it must take me thirty seconds to sit, then pull myself to my feet. Someone — Yeats? — put it well: *this caricature, decrepit age, that has been tied to me as to a dog's tail.* This *thing.* This hindrance. A tin can rattling behind. Never me.) Doubts, Nora? she repeated as she clumped down to the bathroom, the day's first steps so balky, feet like shovels, and set about preparing her bath. Doubt she'd be admitted to medicine at McGill, doubts she'd get through the course — discrimination could go to almost any length; you're damn right I grew up in a tough school — doubts she'd be allowed to intern, that patients would come. Doubt of herself. She might make some early disastrous error in diagnosis; she'd never be permitted another. But the War came — it would always be that to her, "the War," the word a gong, sounding only once. What a society, she thought with an old, undiminished rage — it had to murder its men before it could value its women. And a few years later she was appointed examining physician to some of the Protestant schools. One of those who read of her death next day remembered her from that time: a stumpy alarming figure who spoke disparagingly of her tonsils and gave her a note to take home, which "home," being somewhat harum scarum, ignored. She'd been puzzled at the doctor's being a lady, such a comically dressed lady — ankle-length skirt, frogged jacket hugging ample hips. Now she wondered whether the poor dear was impervious to her own appearance or couldn't afford to buy clothes. The suit in question, which gave Georgiana years of wear, had been a hand-me-down from her mother. And people seemed to like women doctors to be dowdy. Though Mary was always elegant, hard not to be with those delicate bones and perfect Grecian head.

Georgiana smiled, remembering the day during their second year when they'd marched down to St. James Street and sold their long hair to a wig-maker; the proceeds bought them a skeleton. (A screen lifted to show her the two of them running through a Montreal snowstorm, hats loose on their shorn heads.) What a furor that created, my little Phyllis. Sniggers from the male students, our mothers sobbing, Grandfather Dinsborough quoting St. Paul. (She eased onto the little stool in the tub, built by a handyman nephew at just the right, most comfortable height.) Imagine that little snip informing me coolly that we made mistakes. As if we had the time or the energy to be perfect. Still it was real rebellion and, if you don't understand, that's because we succeeded. Fun too; such vigour came from being an outsider. Though thank God for Mary, soft and boneless and tiny, but tough as the best steel. (Could she have managed alone? She'd often wondered.) One of the "mistakes," she supposed, was in not demanding sexual equality. But the child has no idea how vulnerable we were. Morally we had to be impeccable and only odd around the edges. In one of their "serious talks" — they'd had a great many in their little room at the residence; no chaperoned cocoa-parties or mountain sleigh-rides or dances for them (and don't think we didn't sometimes wish there were; it's part of being human to want everything)—she and Mary had renounced all thought of marriage, superfluously perhaps, since only the rarest of men, they knew, could take both their persons and their professions. And the two were indivisible, no question about that. (Laugh if you like, Phyllis. Call us pathetic, childish. It was so.)

Her graduation picture, when it turned up among her mother's things, had showed a round face, which she remembered as being rosy, good eyes and a cheerful mouth. Perhaps men's eyes had followed her and she hadn't known. Charles had said they must have, that she was one of the sexiest bits of goods he'd ever seen. Charles. Moving slowly, washing her old body, she could see him, though his face slid away in a dark smudge, leaving only his hands, rather small, always slightly cupped. She was forty-two, a useful and fairly happy woman but dry, she knew, a little too gruff and hearty. (They all read Huxley and Lawrence, knew the signs.) Two days, she thought—meeting at a medical convention, first kiss, first fondling, bedding down. Now, she'd told herself—belatedly, the harm done, looking with some amazement at her undergarments strewn about the hotel-room floor—she could risk this sort of thing. Discretion proved easy, privacy so much a matter of finances; she'd simply bought the building and moved her mother, who'd just come to live with her, into the upper flat. No one had guessed the connection that had continued so happily for twenty years.

Tamped down so long, she should have been impossible to rouse. But she'd known the ecstasies of any twenty-year-old. (How Charles would laugh at my trying to be poetic. It was wild and vigorous, heady as good wine.) The storms too, passions of jealous weeping when he stayed away too long, humiliation at what seemed to her servitude, less to Charles than to claims unleashed in her own body. This only for the first years till she realized that he was as bound to her as she to him. So that now she chiefly remembered their laughter. And when he died, suddenly of a stroke two days after they'd been together, it hadn't seemed to matter that her grief couldn't be public, that though there was a black-clad widow at the funeral, it wasn't she. (She'd had no wish to be present while Charles's body, washed by those lovely unmeaning words, was committed to the ground. Bad enough to have to see it done to parents, brothers, sister, friends. I am not resigned, she thought. I have never grown used to it. Death is the final obscenity, sooner or later taking almost every one of those I fought to keep. The first time a child she had delivered died under her care—only three years separating the birth-bellow, tiny gasp—she and Mary had got drunk in the kitchen. Or at least Georgiana had got drunk, for she had dim recollections of Mary helping her to bed. So only Mary had heard words she'd never repeated to anyone else, only Mary knew the despair that underlay her life. The battle is lost in advance yet I fight. I fight because it's lost.) She'd have shrieked and moaned at Charles's funeral; just as well she could grieve in her own way and in private. Her love hadn't been public either and perhaps the better and stronger for that.

This she'd tried to tell Nora, that it wasn't loss necessarily to be barred from dailiness; it could be gain. If you had enough in yourself, enough to bring and to go back to. And Nora hadn't. Perhaps everyone had a right to one mistake, Nora had certainly been hers. She'd felt so alone with Charles gone and Nora the only child of Raymond, her favourite brother, whom she'd watched for eighteen years as he coughed up lungs that had drunk mustard gas at Ypres. A rangy girl, not pretty but with something open and quirky about her, twenty-seven years old and still fighting to escape from her twittery Limey mother. Georgiana had helped set her up in a studio and, when Jérôme came along, encouraged that. Nora had been almost too apt a pupil; it was her nature to say yes. Georgiana hadn't realized she was saying yes, not to painting as a career (though she had talent), not to Jérôme as a lover (though she'd loved him) but to the admired (blind) aunt who talked to her and listened and made that absurd mistake of thinking she saw her ideas going forward in another. (She was the vanguard; Nora, the inheritor, would go farther, more freely.) And then tearfully, messily (at thirty-five) the girl tossed everything away for a "normal," very wealthy marriage with a man a little younger than herself, apologizing to Georgiana as if the last years had been a college course and she had failed. It had been the apology Georgiana had found hardest to forgive... "It's your life," she'd said. "You must live it. If you want to marry whoever-it-is, go ahead and marry him." And now there was Phyllis, cosseted child of Nora's middle years, who'd "gone a bit overboard" about women's lib (as well she might, given the example of her parents, Nora having assumed all her husband's opinions as swiftly as she'd once assumed Georgiana's) and wanted to see her mother's ancient aunt. When was the last time, Georgiana wondered, when anyone wanted to see me in that sense. People share with me now, give generously, kindly. No one takes.

Well, well, she thought, out of her bath and dressed. She'd trained herself to think along the edge of her mind so she wouldn't have to look too clearly at her body as she prepared it for the day. She'd been stocky, breasts and buttocks like rocks. (Built like a duck, they'd said at home.) Her breasts had emptied, everything else — hips, abdomen, thighs — slipped down till she became pear-shaped, then emptied in their turn. (*This caricature*, she thought. It isn't me but I'm *in* it.) Well, better think of something more cheerful such as what poor little Phyllis wanted. If the child was actually curious about the past — could she be? None of the young were — Georgiana would simply tell her about it. Trying not to sound like a character. She'd slipped rather on the phone. It was so easy; people trapped you with shrieks of "how marvellous," as if it were a miracle anyone so old could speak, let alone arrange words in sentences that ran coherently. So you performed. It was diverting at the time but shaming later. I didn't live so long just to become a stereotype peppery old lady. I'm very complex. I'm Georgiana.

At nine she was in the kitchen, eating the bowl of hot Roman Meal that had fuelled each of her days for fifty years. The man to do the windows was due at nine-thirty; she'd told the agency she wouldn't let him in if he arrived one minute before. She'd lit her first cigarette and poured coffee when Paul Thomas, her upstairs tenant, knocked and came in to leave his key. On family orders she'd consented to leave the door into the shared back vestibule unlocked; the day she broke her hip, Paul and her nephew Steve had had to smash it down. She'd been semi-delirious by then, the sounds and their faces above her had fitted into some black dream of rending and threatened attack. "Go away," she'd screamed. "I'm not ready for you yet." Since then, her tenants, a working couple in their forties, wandered in rather often, always with an excuse, to bring something, ask something. Of the two she preferred Paul. He had more life and, with her, sometimes dropped the over-heartiness she knew was a defence. Not today. He looked tired and agitated.

"Great morning, Dr. Din."

Georgiana agreed that it was, agreed that it would be fine to have the double windows off. She could leave his key on the table, he said, and if he got home before his wife, he'd pop in and get it.

"Is Cynthia quite up to par?" she asked. "I've wondered."

"Oh—well—she took a long time getting round after that London flu." Georgiana nodded. She'd had it too, had fought (successfully) against going to the hospital, had got even with Steve's insistence on a practical nurse by sharing the woman with Cynthia. "Needs some sun and rest," Paul said. "You know Cynthia. She won't ever give in, won't leave the floor without wax or a dish in the sink."

Georgiana was about to suggest he tell the girl to drop in—just the worried look (so known) on Paul's face. He seemed honestly to love that pinched, terribly house-proud little woman. "I forgot," she said, delighted. "Forgot I wasn't still a practising physician." She was going to add that she'd never felt more alive but to Paul, looking down at her froglike form and the face, firm and rosy once, now putty-coloured, creased and re-creased as if someone had gone at it too vigorously with a sewing-machine—no, that wouldn't do. No need to make a fool of yourself. So she merely laughed. "Been laughing like a maniac all morning. Losing my marbles, no doubt."

"Dr. Din, you're not losing a thing," Paul said. "Not only that. You're a living doll. If I were fifty years older, you'd be afraid to leave your door unlocked."

"God spare me from a ninety-five-year-old lover," she said, and they parted laughing. (He remembered this later with pleasure and pain, for he'd been fond of the old girl. "She was so gay this morning," he kept saying to Phyllis when he came in at five and found her coping so well for such a youngster.)

Georgiana had lit her second cigarette when the phone rang; she reached for it (phones in every room were another concession to the family)—Stella Farnham, not yet eighty but of all the people she knew now the closest in age. (One by one they toppled off the edge and left her the oldest.) Damn, she thought, outraged, barely hearing Stella as she twittered something about thinking of the old days (as if that fluttery idiot had been present in the real old days), sick suddenly, as happened every now and then, from the force of all those steady, single deaths. Her friends. her kind. The other early graduates in medicine, the pioneers with her in the women's suffrage movement (before they turned it over to the French where it belonged). How good and tolerant they'd been with each other, even those earnest souls who'd muddled prohibition of liquor with women's rights. Well, they'd all been odd in one way or another, but freed and strengthened by that. And every one of them had aged better than poor Stella, keeping enough of themselves to serve as reminders of how they'd once moved and looked. (She'd tell Phyllis this, so someone would know, what friends they'd been, how none of them had become senile; worked hard and widely, their minds had simply given out when the time came. Mary, dying of cancer at fifty-five, had been perfectly intact. Die, Mary, she'd thought, looking down at that bit of bone and waste. Stop fighting, Mary. But Mary couldn't and Georgiana had continued to help for as long as she must. And I still don't know why, why it has to be or what it means. This I was supposed to discover in my last years. This is one of the questions I put off asking.) Thank God, she needn't participate in another death—except one, but then the choice (at what point to withdraw and let the body die) would be Steve's. Thank God, she repeated, listening to Stella's voice, as she was forced to now that it was rising, lamenting that her son had done this and her daughter the other, or rather not done this and the other, for they were neglectful, wouldn't—

"Then tell them so," said Georgiana, who'd delivered both these children; the boy had been magnificent, lungs like bellows. "Aren't you a grown woman and their mother?"

"George, if I were only like you," Stella wailed.

"Well, why aren't you, for mercy's sake? Stella, I braced you during your pregnancies. I prevailed on you to nurse when you didn't want to. I tried to put starch into you. I'm an old woman now. I'm retired. You're on your own."

The doorbell rang. Georgiana excused herself, saying she'd call back. (A lie. She'd didn't intend to.) She reached for her cane, put her other hand palm-down on the table and pulled herself to her feet, then started the slow journey down the hall of this very stretched-out flat. (The hall she used to take at a run when the ring meant Charles; she could almost feel that other woman rising out of her bones and rushing forward. They're dead, she thought. Everyone who meant anything. There's no one who remembers what I remember. Damn. I didn't ask to be the survivor. It should have been someone stronger. Mary.)

"You were supposed to come to the back door," she told the young man from the agency. He muttered something, looking down. "Français?" He shook his head. "Too bad. I used to speak it pretty well, with a lousy accent. Like the Spanish cow, as the French say." He didn't answer. One of those battened-down young people clearly. Just what I need. About twenty-five, she judged, and with the green waxy look of malnutrition. Like so many of the young. Phyllis too. You'd swear Nora had never heard of vitamins. "Well, don't just stand there," she said, shooing him towards the kitchen.

"The strange thing about being old," she told his back as she stumped after him, "is that though your flesh goes, you don't get lighter. You get heavier. A paradox."

He was silent, just walked straight through to the kitchen and stood with his back against the farther door.

"See here," she said. "I won't have anyone in my house if I can't be human with him. You want your money, I suppose?"

"Yes," he said and did seem finally to look at her, at least move his eyes in her direction. He was pale in every respect, especially so about the mouth. Even his eyes and wispy hair were pale.

"Very well then," she said, "in future speak when you're spoken to," and told him in what part of the cellar he'd find the screens and the hose, how to line the screens against the fence while he washed them. "Sort them by rooms. My old valued handyman and friend pencilled it on in French. You can read French?" He said he could.

He was slow, she saw as she watched from the window, smoking another cigarette with some warmed-up coffee, trying to salvage this day that had started so well. Till the dead began to walk. (Be still, be still, she told them. I did what I could.) Look around you, Georgiana. Don't be a damned crybaby. The sky was that high, very dark blue of spring. Soon there'd be crocuses — Paul had moved the patch so she could see them from her window. Later they'd discuss colours and he'd fill the tiny yard with petunias. (Something's eating Paul. I must manage to learn what, must still serve. But I'm fussy and old; I snapped at foolish Stella. But Paul has life. Now watch it, Georgiana. Was it ever your right to decide who was worth your effort and who wasn't?) The young man was spraying the screens, making great pools of slop and walking through them. Naming his actions to himself as she had done during those humiliating months of learning to walk again.

Once headed in a particular direction, he continued in that way, no matter how muddy, made no free movements, never improvised. He finished, disconnected the hose and turned back to the house. She heard him scrape each foot on the stoop. Then he came in and stood silent in front of her.

"I'm a retired physician, not a member of the narcotics squad," she said. "Are you on drugs?"

He did actually smile then, just a swift tuck of the lips.

"You think that's the first thing we old people think of. Well, not this old person. Call me an interfering old party if you wish but I'm used to taking care of people, sometimes when they'd just as soon I didn't. It's hard to hide things from me. You look what my mother used to call mingy. Never did understand that word. A composite perhaps of miserable and mangy. Have you been ill?"

"No," he said, "I haven't," then, "Which floor'll I start on?" A shallow breather, the voice using only the upper segment of the lungs.

"Upstairs," she told him and handed him Paul's key, indicated the pail and cloths, told him where to stack the double windows when he scrubbed them. "Your lunch will be ready on the dot of twelve. Here on this table...Did you say something?"

"I go out to lunch."

"Not from this house you don't. You're going to eat properly for once. No French fries. No Coca Cola."

"I'd rather you didn't go to too much trouble." Curiously educated expression.

"I'll go to exactly as much trouble as it requires," she said, wanting to see that little smile again and thinking that, just briefly, she did so. "Ha — now I know why the lower part of your face is so white. You used to have a beard."

"What if I did?" He should have looked at her then but did not.

"Why are you so defensive? I suppose the agency made you shave it. Well, they're damned idiots. I'm accustomed to facial hair. My father and grandfather had beards — finer and bushier beards than you could grow."

Her mood lifted. She felt suddenly gay as a girl as she listened to his steps on the stairs and over her head, the pauses. In some ways old age was an adolescence, though a less painful one — hers had been hideous; no other part of her life had touched it for sheer darkness. The feeling of looseness, of belonging nowhere, not even with her own body. (That she might tell Phyllis too; from now on everything has to be better.) The gaieties of old age were like the rare gaieties of adolescence, same sense of spinning off towards some wonderful country that was waiting to receive you if you could only find the way. But now you knew there was no such country and no way, and treasured and drank the joy. There was a dark side too. Like the pubescent you were very conscious of your effect on others. Had to be, knowing they watched you for weakness, ready to take over. Still, life is wonderful, she told Phyllis, told the young man upstairs. If I could just prove it to you. (The dead would say so too. Every one of them, I assure you. There was a young man once who died of what we used to call blood poisoning. With his last bit of strength, he sat bolt upright, staring ahead. His mother thought he'd seen one of God's angels, perhaps the old man himself. But he was looking at me and in the instant before the light went out, there was rage in those eyes — rage and appeal. Having seen that even once, you *know*. It is precious just to be, in a body that will function, and to have senses — even though barely, and with tremendous struggle, as I have them. Don't ask why. It is.)

She'd have to start to fix the young man's lunch — he'd so quickly (though oddly) become an individual that she'd forgotten to ask his name — at half past eleven, was almost late because Nora called again.

"Aunt George, I felt I should warn you. I hope you won't mind. Phyllis has become awfully curious about your sex life."

"Don't be a solemn ninny, Nora. I'm flattered. It's such ages since anyone's thought I might have had one."

"She wonders if you were all lesbians. As a defence against chauvinist pigs." She sighed. "She's threatening to take that way herself. As a means of consciousness-raising or whatever they call it."

"Is she indeed? Seems a strange thing to discuss with one's mother. And don't say that you and she discuss everything. I don't believe it. . . As a matter of fact, several of my friends were — some by nature, others from fear. I think it was the latter with Mary."

"Aunt Mary Balsam? But she was so — womanly."

"Your father certainly thought so. I've always believed they'd have married, even though she was a good seven years older, if poor silly Raymond could have brought himself to let her continue in practice. But the War came and, as you know, he met your mother in England." She became aware of her gabbling voice and Nora's silence. "You didn't know this?"

"No. No, I never even — So that's why she was always so good to me. . . Aunt George, are you sure?"

"Oh yes. She told me herself." She'd gone in to get Mary to fit her for a diaphragm and Mary had made that wry joke about not needing that sort of thing herself. And I was shocked, though I should have seen it in the wind when Mother came to live with me after Father died and Mary moved in with Irene Sanders. But was she happy? How after all these years could it be of any importance or even interest to know whether Mary was happy? She said she was, though all I could think was that it must be sad to turn and find only a similar body, another self. And did I say the right things, so full of myself that day, myself and Charles? A scene in a doctor's examining room, two women talking — neither the room nor the furnishings nor the women (one now only a clumsy bag of bones, the other dust I may have washed from my hand or face) to be found anywhere now — yet I feel I could reach back, change the words. "What did you say, Nora?"

"That I'd rather you didn't tell Phyllis, Aunt George."

"Or about Charles? Or," she couldn't help adding, "Jérôme?" Silence, That had made the Westmount matron jump. "He still sends me cards at Christmas. Did you know? Always with a funny note. I do like a man with humour." Whoever-it-is had none.

"No, you never mentioned—it's not that I'm ashamed—but her own mother—"

"Really, Nora. I'm surprised at your thinking I'd give you away. But as for my life and my friends' lives, if the child asks, I'll tell her. No one knows, you see. I thought of writing a book, even made a great many notes. But I couldn't. It seemed so—with none of them here to—"

"Yes—I see." Abruptly, in a softened voice, she asked whether the man had come about the windows and was he doing a satisfactory—?

"Yes, he's a pretty good worker," Georgiana said. "And a bit of a challenge besides. . . Oh, why should I have to explain?" for Nora was trying to get her to do just that. "Really you're the world's most exasperating—a different sort of life. . . society. Have you any idea how unusual that is at my—"

"Aunt George, come and have dinner with us next week." ("Thank God," she kept saying later to Phyllis and Paul, "it was the last thing I said to her. She'd been baiting me, as she could, cruel almost, and then, I don't know, being *old*. Thank God I didn't lose my temper." They had a hard time silencing her. She kept thrusting Phyllis away, almost with hatred, and talking about people they didn't know.) "I'll call," she said now, "and make it more—I'm going to be miserably lonely without Phyllis, Aunt George."

Damn, Georgiana thought, rubbing angry tears from her eyes, trying to remember what it was she—Oh yes, casserole, put it in the oven. She'd slipped. With Nora of all people. Awkward having to sift each word. Out of character. Why shouldn't she be allowed to say that it was interesting, fun even, to have someone new about the house? Or mourn her friends? Without being found pitiable. Think of something else. So Phyllis was interested in her sexual habits. Well, well. Where had she put those notes? Several bulky folders. The child might like to see them. Georgiana, you old fool, don't go thinking you've found your inheritor so late in the day. Though wouldn't it be a wonderful revenge on whoever-it-is if Phyllis should turn out to be the woman Nora had only played at being? My heir straight from darling Raymond. The baby she'd held in her arms in the big farm kitchen, only hours after his birth. God, she was slow. Slower than a month ago? Washing and tearing greens for salad took so long, even putting bread and knife on the board and groping in the fridge for butter. She set a place and was about to fetch the tea-cart, which she'd ask the lad to wheel into the living-room, when impulsively she put a second set of cutlery on the table for herself.

At five past twelve he came downstairs—a spot of independence in this that she approved of—walked into the kitchen and stood with his back to her, washing his hands at the sink.

"Clean towel to your right," she told him. "I forgot to mention another rule of this house. I eat with the help."

He stiffened. She saw it in his back under the thin t-shirt. This was wrong. An intrusion. Unfortunately phrased too. But she'd have to go through with it now, could scarcely let him put her out of her own kitchen.

"I must ask you to humour me," she said. "I enjoy company."

"You're the boss." He dried his hands and came to sit in the chair she indicated, sat rather far back from the table, arms hanging at his sides. That nothing face, merely young, but with three tension-cracks across the forehead. Georgiana served him, hands slow but steady, planning what she would say.

"You a native Montrealer?" she asked finally.

"Yes." She waited, looking at him. "Yes, I am."

"I was born on a farm near Compton. In the Townships, as you may have noticed from my speech—if you're familiar with that twangy drawl we have. It was wholly English in those days. And now it's all—or almost all—French. Our farm and most of the neighbouring farms."

"Anything wrong with that?"

"Wrong? Of course not. Mercy, you *are* defensive." This was the way with the untalkative. Chatter on with seeming lack of aim while they listened or not, to give yourself space to make certain observations. "But it was a rather special society. Loyalists. In our case from Massachusetts. My grandfather's grandfather, who was what the French would call our first ancestor, had been a whaling captain sailing out of New Bedford. So, even landlocked, we were always within sight of the sea." She belched loudly. "Damn," she said and continued, "I wasn't impressed when I was young, all that leaning on the past. It was so hard to escape from, young ladies from such families just didn't become doctors. And now it's gone, something unique. Everything is unique though, wouldn't you agree? And every ending sad. I haven't been back since my father died. The younger of my brothers was to be the farmer but he was a casualty of the War, barely alive for eighteen years. So we sold the place. I've seen people change but I haven't wanted to see the house and the land changed, above all not the land. Is that strange, do you think?"

He didn't reply though she was sure he'd been listening, even that at one point—when?—she'd touched him. Her antenna still served. She felt exhilarated.

"Damned casserole needs salt," she said. "Here. It's sea-salt. I remember how mad I felt when I learned that even though I was the eldest I couldn't inherit the farm. I told my brother, the older of the two, a male chauvinist aged six, that I'd be a vet then, look after other people's stock. He said girls couldn't do that either so I said—I was eight years old and chewing a stalk of timothy, funny to remember that—'Very well, I'll be a people's doctor.' And so it all began. And you cannot imagine the furor—" But this the young didn't like to hear, that there was anything their imagination couldn't compass. "I am garrulous," she said.

He mumbled.

"What was that?"

He spoke for the first time clearly. "I said I wouldn't know. Not knowing you and how much you usually run on."

She laughed. "As a matter of fact, I don't as a rule. But you've hardly eaten." He took up a forkful and she waited for him to swallow, take up a second. "Why are you doing this kind of work? Don't say it's for the money— or bread as you undoubtedly call it. Surprised I know the term?"

She saw him trying to think of an answer, some sarcasm. He was in a mean mood but didn't know how to let it out. He shrugged finally as if the problem defeated him.

"You speak well," she said, "when you speak. Have good table manners. Are you educated?"

"Depends."

"On what I mean by educated? Good answer." She shot in a key question. "Are you married?"

"No." A lie, she suspected, the word spoken so much too swiftly, less tonelessly.

Ah, she thought, I can still do it, and asked him to fill the kettle for their tea.

"Unless you'd prefer coffee?"

"Tea's fine," he said and she told him where to find the canister, how much to measure into the pot.

"Can't help giving directions," she said. "Been doing it all my life."

"Guess I'm in no position to complain."

"I'd find you insolent," Georgiana said, "if I didn't know you were unhappy. And now you'll think that's none of my business." No answer, though she thought again that his back tightened. "Well, you may be right. Or so I'd have thought once, since you haven't come to me for help. But I haven't time any more for fine distinctions and niceties. And maybe you haven't either."

He took the cups and saucers from the counter and put them with the tea-pot beside her. He was sweating, she saw, just a few drops along his upper lip. "Got any honey?"

"Any—Oh, honey. For our tea. Excellent idea. Should be a jar towards the back of that second shelf. Good strong buckwheat honey with a bite to it, kind I grew up on."

He brought it to the table and she spooned some into their cups.

"Like it?"

"It's okay."

She provided another space by telling him of the wide fields of buckwheat, deep coral and scented—vigorous and coarse and beautiful as the strong things always are; perhaps she'd never had a taste for delicacy (Charles had not been a delicate lover)—and found that the memory and the link with Charles gave her immense pleasure. She longed to see buckwheat in flower again. In fact, must see it. She'd ask someone—Nora—no, one of the others, so the excursion wouldn't involve the presence of whoever-it-is.

"You have a strange effect on me," she told the young man. "Or I'm having it on myself. I keep going back. Like thinking about chewing timothy a moment ago. Be telling you next what I was wearing." And wondered whether she should just continue to go where her mind took her. He so clearly didn't want to open out to some ancient stranger. (Remember what he sees when he looks at you. Something held together with sticks.) No one had said she need do anything about him. Why not just go on rambling, silly old bag of bones, till the meal was over?

"Got a great-niece coming in later," she said. "Wants to quiz me about sex. How's that for irony, eh? What should I tell her?" He said nothing, gulped his tea, no doubt relieved that her attention had wandered. "Come, you must have some suggestions. Take this. Her mother's afraid she'll become a lesbian to—what was the phrase?—raise her consciousness. How could two young women bouncing about awkwardly in bed raise one another's consciousness? What does that mean even?" It was no use. She saw him trying to deal with this, face working, but, poor young devil, he was too barricaded within himself to come out and consider other people. (I owe him more than this. Owe it to him and to my life. This *will* be a good day. I'll make it so. I'll be useful. I'm not pitiable, damn you, Nora. I'm Georgiana. A very good doctor.) "Look here, let's be done with this," she said in the gruff offhand voice she'd always used for such matters. "You've come to the end of something, haven't you? That's where I reached you before. Endings. And it's chewing at your gut. Admit it. It's not shameful."

He breathed sawingly. "Suppose I have. Suppose it is. Isn't it my gut?"

"Not entirely," said Georgiana. "When you walked into my house and my life, I think it became partly my gut. Talk. It will be a release. You don't know me. I'll never confront you with it. And I'm not a psychiatrist, except of a rough and ready sort. There can be only one kind of ending at your age. Which of you broke it off? She? Or you?"

He gave that little tuck of the lip that with him might pass for a smile—or was perhaps only a tic, defensive.

"*She* did, eh?" she hazarded.

233

"What if she did?" Sweat formed again on his upper lip. "She had good reason to perhaps."

"She had good reason to perhaps. What sort of answer is that?"

"It's her life," he said, "and if she wants to—"

"Are you telling me you didn't fight? Not at all?" He looked at her, emptily but from somewhere very deep inside. "Obviously she means a lot to you or you wouldn't be walking around like a zombie without her. It's got into your muscles, every movement you make. Aren't you going to fight even now? It may not be too late. Women like strength. They always have and I don't fancy that just because they want to be more independent means they've changed all that—"

"I don't want to talk about it," he said. "I came here to do the windows. I'm the help. You said that. I don't have to—" Trembling, he laid his saucer on the plate, then the cup. They clattered.

"Oh leave those, for God's sake. I'll take care of them. Go on about your windows, you poor foolish—"

She snatched the dishes and started to the sink, so swiftly and impetuously that she forgot to hoist herself, forgot her cane, took an unassisted step or two. "Don't you know that nothing on God's green earth has been got without fighting? Do you imagine for an instant that I didn't fight? I fought all the way for every inch. I'm an old woman and I still know more about fighting—fighting for breath, fighting for strength—" (My God, here I go being a character again. As if life were ever that simple. This particular fighter feared death as few can have feared it. Fighting when you know you're going to lose, especially when, that's what I must tell them, Phyllis too. But is it enough? Enough to give from a long life?

She had started to speak again when something exploded in her head. She fell, heavily on all fours, as horses do. Good God, it's a stroke, she thought, so that's how, like a blow—"Thank God, you're here. My hand's cut from the—but don't worry about—just help me turn so I can—"

She had half turned on her own when her eyes looked into his. He was stooping over her with the cane. "You hit me," she said. "Oh you silly, silly. Well, just give me a hand and—"

"Let's see you fight now, old know-it-all. Just like her. Just like all of—" He struck again.

"No," she said. "No. You don't want to—you can't possibly—" She had averted her face but now, dangerous as she knew this was, she looked back, trying to catch his eye, hold him. "Your whole life—think of that—your whole life, you foolish, foolish—" The cane whistled down, found its mark, she couldn't move quickly enough. Blood spurted from her cheek. "But I'll be responsible." Did she say or only think these words? "And I'm not supposed to—not me—not destroy—"

"Why did you keep bugging me? Why did you? I didn't ask for your damn—" He was crying now, sobbing aloud. "Oh I didn't want to. You're not a bad old—Fuck you, I didn't want to."

The blows came down and down, rhythmically. Georgiana could no longer speak but even in her mind she did not call on any of the names of her life. She fought as she must, would continue to do till pain wiped out her world. Her nose was broken. She was blind. She had never felt more alive.

Joyce Marshall (1913-) was born in Montreal, and has lived for many years in Toronto. She is the author of two novels, *Presently Tomorrow* and *Lovers and Strangers,* and of a collection of short stories, *A Private Place.* She has translated seven books from French. Her most recent, *Enchanted Summer,* a translation of *Cet été qui chantait* by Gabrielle Roy, was awarded the Canada Council Translation Prize for 1976.

Mordecai Richler
Mortimer Griffin, Shalinsky and How They Settled the Jewish Question

I was, at the time, beginning my first scholastic year as a lecturer in English literature at Wellington College in Montreal. You've probably never heard of Wellington. It's a modest institution with a small student body. There's the Day College, composed, for the most part, of students who couldn't get into McGill, and the Evening College, made up of adults, most of them working at full-time jobs and trying to get a college education after hours. I was responsible for two Evening College courses, English 112 (Shakespeare) and English 129 (The Modern Novel). Shalinsky registered for both of them.

Until my fourth lecture I was only aware of Shalinsky as a ponderous presence in the third row. My fourth lecture dealt with Franz Kafka, and naturally I made several allusions to the distinctively Jewish roots of his work. Afterwards, as I was gathering my notes together, Shalinsky approached me for the first time.

"I want to tell you, Professor Griffin, how much intellectual nourishment I got out of your lecture tonight."

"I'm glad you enjoyed it."

I'm afraid I was in a hurry to get away that night. I was going to pick up Joyce at the Rosens'. But Shalinsky still stood before my desk.

His wisps of grey curly hair uncut and uncombed, Shalinsky was a small, round-shouldered man with horn-rimmed spectacles, baleful black eyes, and a hanging lower lip. His shiny, pin-striped grey suit was salted with dandruff round the shoulders. A hand-rolled cigarette drooped from his mouth, his eyes half-shut against the smoke and the ashes spilling unregarded to his vest.

"Why did you change your name?" he asked.

"I beg your pardon. Did you ask me why I changed my name?"

Shalinsky nodded.

"But I haven't. My name is Griffin. It always has been."

"You're a Jew."

"You're mistaken."

Shalinsky smiled faintly.

"Really," I began, "what made you think—"

"All right. I'm mistaken. I made a mistake. No harm done."

"Look here, if I were a Jew I wouldn't try to conceal it for a moment."

Still smiling, blinking his eyes, Shalinsky said: "There's no need to lose your temper, Professor *Griffin*. I made a mistake, that's all. If that's the way you want it."

"And I'm not a professor, either. *Mr.* Griffin will do."

"A man of your talents will be famous one day. Like. . . like I.M. Sinclair. A scholar renowned wherever the intelligentsia meet. Thanks once more for tonight's intellectual feast. Good night, Mr. Griffin."

In retrospect, on the bus ride out to Hy and Eva Rosen's house, I found the incident so outlandishly amusing that I laughed aloud twice.

Joyce had eaten with the Rosens, and Eva, remembering how much I liked chopped liver, had saved me an enormous helping. I told them about Shalinsky, concluding with ". . . and where he ever got the idea that I was Jewish I'll never know." I had anticipated plenty of laughter. A witty remark from Hy, perhaps. Instead, there was silence. Nervously, I added: "Look, I don't mean that I'd be ashamed. . . or that I was insulted that someone would think I was—Christ, you know what I mean, Hy."

"Yes," Hy said sharply. "Of course."

We left for home earlier than usual.

"Boy," Joyce said, "you certainly have a gift. I mean once you *have* put your foot in it you certainly know how to make matters worse."

"I thought they'd laugh. God, I've known Hy for years. He's one of my best friends. He—"

"*Was*," Joyce said.

"Look here," I said, "you don't seriously think that Hy thinks I'm an anti-semite?"

Joyce raised one eyebrow slightly—an annoying college-girl habit that has lingered.

"Don't be ridiculous," I said. "Tomorrow, the day after, the whole thing will be forgotten, or Hy will make a joke of it."

"*They* have an excellent sense of humour," Joyce said, "haven't they? There's Jack Benny and Phil Silvers and—"

"Oh, for Christ's sake!"

Two days later a copy of a magazine called *Jewish Thought* came in the mail. Attached was a printed note, WITH THE COMPLIMENTS OF THE EDITOR, and underneath, penned with a lavish hand, *Respectfully, J. Shalinsky*. It took me a moment or two to connect Shalinsky, the editor, with Shalinsky, my student. I began to flip through the pages of the little magazine.

The editorial, by J. Shalinsky, dealt at length with the dilemma of Jewish artists in a philistine community. The lead article, by Lionel Gould, B. COMM. (McGill), was titled "On Being a Jew in Montreal West." Another article, by I.M. Sinclair, M.D., was titled "The Anti-Semite as an Intellectual: A Study of the Novels of Graham Greene." There were numerous book reviews, two sentimental poems translated from the Yiddish, a rather maudlin Israeli short story, and, surprisingly, "Stefan Zweig and J. Shalinsky: A Previously Unpublished Correspondence."

That night, as soon as my Eng. 112 lecture was finished, Shalinsky loomed smiling over my desk. "You got the magazine?" he asked.

"I haven't had time to read it yet."

"If you don't like it, all you have to do is tell me why. No evasions, please. Don't beat around the bush." Shalinsky broke off and smiled. "I have something for you," he said.

I watched while he unwrapped a large, awkward parcel. The string he rolled into a ball and dropped into his pocket. The brown wrapping paper, already worn and wrinkled, he folded into eight and put into another pocket. Revealed was an extremely expensive edition of colour plates by Marc Chagall.

"It occurred to me," he said, "that a man so interested in Kafka might also find beauty in the art of Marc Chagall."

"I don't understand."

"Would you be willing," Shalinsky said, "to write me a review, a little appreciation, of this book for the next issue of *Jewish Thought?*"

I hesitated.

"We pay our contributors, of course. Not much, but—"

"That's not the point."

"And the book, it goes without saying, would be yours."

"All right, Mr. Shalinsky. I'll do it."

"There's something else. You have no lectures next Wednesday night. You are free, so to speak. Am I right?"

"Yes, but—"

"Next Wednesday night, Mr. Griffin, the Jewish Thought Literary Society will be meeting at my house. It is a custom, at these meetings, that we are addressed by a distinguished guest. I was hoping—"

"What would you like me to talk about?" I asked wearily.

"Kafka," he said. "Kafka and Cabbalism. Refreshments will be served."

The address Shalinsky had given me was on St. Urbain Street. His house smelled of home-baked bread and spices. The living-room, almost a hall once the double doors had been opened, was filled with folding chairs, all of them vindictively directed at the speaker's table. The walls were laden with enormous photographs of literary giants protected by glass and encased in

238

varnished wooden frames. Tolstoy, a bearded scarecrow on horseback, glared at the refreshments table. Dostoyevsky and Turgenev, their quarrels forgotten, stood side by side. Opposite, Marcel Proust smiled enigmatically.

At dinner I was introduced to Shalinsky's wife and daughter. Mrs. Shalinsky was a round rosy-cheeked figure with a double chin. The daughter—plump, plum-cheeked Gitel Shalinsky—wore a peasant blouse laced tightly over a tray of milky bosom, and a billowy green skirt. Her thick black hair she wore in an upsweep; glittering glass ear-rings dripped from her cup-shaped ears. A wooden clasp, GRETA, rode one breast, and a rose the other. Throughout dinner Gitel never said a word.

I handed Shalinsky my twelve-hundred-word article on Chagall, titled—rather brightly, I thought—*The Myopic Mystic*. My editor pondered the piece in silence, waving his hand impatiently whenever his wife interrupted him, a frequent occurrence, with remarks like, "Chew your meat, Jake," and, in an aside to me, "If I gave him absorbent cotton to eat, you think he'd know the difference?" and again, baring her teeth in a parody of mastication, "Chew, Jake. *Digest.*"

Shalinsky read my article unsmilingly and folded it neatly in four.

"Is there anything the matter?" I asked.

"As an intellectual exercise your article is A-I, but—"

"You don't have to print it if you don't want to."

"Did I say I wouldn't print it? No. But, if you'll let me finish, I had hoped it would be a little more from the soul. Take the title, for instance. *The Myopic Mystic,*" he said with distaste. "Clever. Clever, Mr. Griffin. But no heart. Still, this is a fine article. I wouldn't change a word. Not for the world."

The first of Shalinsky's guests arrived and he went into the living-room with him. Mrs. Shalinsky excused herself, too, and so I was left alone with Gitel. "Your father," I said, "is quite an extraordinary man. I mean at his age to take university courses and edit a magazine—"

"*The Ladies' Home Journal,*" Gitel said. "*There's* a magazine for you. But *Jewish Thought*. An eight-hundred-and-forty-two circulation, counting give-aways—that's no magazine."

"Your father tells me he's printed work by S.M. Geiger. He's a very promising poet, I think."

"Some poet. He comes up to here by me. Alan Ladd—there's another twerp. How long are you going to speak tonight?"

"I'm not sure."

"Make it short, Morty. The blabbers never get invited back."

Three-quarters of an hour after my lecture was supposed to have started, only twelve people, all middle-aged men, had turned up, though many more had been prepared for. "It's the rain," Shalinsky said. A half-hour later six more people had drifted into the living-room: eight, if you counted the woman with the baby in her arms. Her name was Mrs. Korber. She lived upstairs and, in passing, I overheard her say to Mrs. Shalinsky, "Tell Mr. Shalinsky it's no trouble. Harry and the boy will be here the minute *Dragnet* is finished."

At that moment my jacket was given a fierce tug from behind. Whirling around, I was confronted by a small, wizened man with rimless glasses. "I am I.M. Sinclair," he said.

Retreating, I said: "You're a doctor, I believe."

"Like Chekhov."

"Oh. Oh, I see."

"I'm the only poet in Canada. Go ahead, laugh." Then, as though he were composing on the spot, I.M. Sinclair said: "I am an old man... an old man in a dry month... waiting for rain."

"You ought to write that down," I said.

"I have burned better lines. We have a lot to talk about, Griffin. The moment in the draughty synagogue at smokefall...."

I broke away just in time to see Harry and the boy arrive. Shalinsky quickly called the meeting to order. There were three of us at the speaker's table—Shalinsky, myself, and a thin man with a fat ledger open before him. Shalinsky gave me a fulsome introduction, and Harry's boy—a fourteen-year-old with a running nose—poked two grimy fingers into his mouth and whistled. The others applauded politely. Then, as Mrs. Korber fed her baby with a bottle, I began.

"Louder," barked a voice from the back row.

So I spoke louder, elaborating on Kafka's difficulties with his father.

"What does he say?" somebody shouted. I waited while the man next to him translated what I had said into Yiddish. "Nonsense," his neighbour said. "A Jewish education never harmed anybody."

I rushed through the rest of my lecture, omitting half of it. A short question period was to follow. A Mr. Gordon was first.

"Mr. Griffin, my son is studying at McGill and he wishes to become a professor too. Now my question is as follows. How much can my Lionel expect to earn after five years?"

I had barely answered Mr. Gordon's question when a man in the back row began to wave his arm frantically.

"Yes," Shalinsky said. "What is it, Kaplan?"

Kaplan shot up from his seat. "I move a vote of thanks to Mr. Griffin for his excellent speech. I also move no more questions. It's nearly a quarter to eleven."

"Second both motions," cried a little man with thick glasses. "Segal. s,e,—no i—g,a,l. Get that in the minutes, Daniels."

A moment later Shalinsky and I were abandoned on one side of the room. Everyone else crowded round the refreshments table. I asked for my coat. At the door, Shalinsky thanked me profusely for coming.

"It's you I ought to thank," I said. "I enjoyed myself immensely."

"You see," Shalinsky said, "it's good to be with your own sometimes."

"Just what do you mean by that?"

Shalinsky smiled faintly.

"Look, will you please get it through your head that I'm not Jewish."

"All right, all right. I'm mistaken."

"Good night," I said, banging the door after me.

Joyce was waiting up for me in bed. "Well," she asked, "how did it go?"

"Skip it."

"What's wrong?"

"I don't want to talk about it, that's all."

"I don't see why you can't tell me about it."

I didn't answer.

"I mean you don't have to bite my head off just because I'm curious."

"There's nothing to tell."

"You've left a cigarette burning on the bureau."

"Oh, for Christ's sake. It would be so nice not to have all my filthy little habits pointed out to me for once. I know there's a cigarette burning on the bureau."

Retreating into the bathroom, I slammed the door after me. But even a bath failed to soothe my nerves. I lit a cigarette and lingered in the tub.

"What on earth are you doing in there?" Joyce shouted.

"Writing a book."

"Isn't he witty?"

"And next time you use my razor on your blessed armpits, kiddo, I'll thank you to wash it and replace the blade."

"Now who's pointing out whose filthy habits?"

I don't like mirrors. I make a point of never sitting opposite one in a restaurant. But tonight I had a special interest in studying my face.

"Mortimer!"

Mortimer, of course, could be a Jewish name.

"What are you doing in there?"

I'm a tall man with a long horse-face. But my nose is certainly not prominent. Turning. I considered my face in profile. When I finally came out of the bathroom, I asked Joyce. "Would you say I had a Jewish face?"

She laughed.

"I'm serious, Joyce."

"As far as I'm concerned," she said, "there's no such thing as a Jewish face."

I told her about the lecture.

"If you want my opinion," she said, "you wouldn't mind Shalinsky's notion in the least if you weren't a sublimated anti-semite."

"Thank you," I said, switching off the light.

An hour later, sensing that I was still awake, Joyce turned to me in bed. "I've been thinking, darling. Look, if—now please don't get angry. But *if* you were Jewish—"

"*What?*"

"I mean, if you have got Jewish blood I'd love you just as—"

"Of all the stupid nonsense. What do you mean, *if* I'm Jewish? You've met my parents, haven't you?"

"All I'm saying is that if—"

"All right. I confess. My father's real name is Granofsky. He's a goddam defrocked rabbi or something. Not only that, you know, but my mother's a coon. She—"

"Don't you dare use that word."

"Look, for the tenth time, if I had Jewish blood I would not try to conceal it. What ever made you think...?"

"Well," she said. "You know."

"Goddam it. I told you long ago that was done for hygienic reasons. My mother insisted on it. Since I was only about two weeks old at the time, I wasn't consulted."

"o.k.," she said. "o.k. I just wanted you to know where I would stand if—"

"Look, let's go to sleep. I've had enough for one day. Tomorrow first thing I'm going to settle this matter once and for all."

"What are you going to do?"

"I'm going to start a pogrom."

"Some of your jokes," Joyce said, "are in the worst possible taste."

"Yes. I know. I happen to be cursed with what Hy calls a Goyishe sense of humour."

The next morning I phoned Shalinsky.

"*Jewish Thought* here. Mr. Shalinsky is in Toronto. I'll have him get in touch with your office the minute he returns."

"Shalinsky, it's *you.*"

"Ah, it's you, Griffin. I'm sorry. I thought it was Levitt the printer. He usually phones at this hour on Thursday mornings."

"Look, Shalinsky, I'd like you to come over here at three this afternoon."

"Good."

Taken aback, I said: "What do you mean, *good?*"

"I was hoping you'd want to talk. Speaking frankly, I didn't expect it to happen so soon."

"Just be here at three," I said. "o.k.?" And I hung up.

By the time Shalinsky arrived I had amassed all manner of personal documents—my army discharge papers, passport, driving licence, McGill graduation certificate, marriage licence, a Rotary Club public speaking award, my unemployment insurance card, vaccination certificate, Bo-lo Champion (Jr. Division) Award of Merit, three library cards, a parking ticket, and my bank book. On all these documents was the name Mortimer Lucas Griffin. Seething with suppressed anger, I watched as Shalinsky fingered each document pensively.He looked up at last, pinching his lower lip between thumb and index finger. "Facts," he said. "Documents. So what?"

"So what? Are you serious? All this goes to prove that I was born a white Protestant male named Mortimer Lucas Griffin."

"To think that you would go to so much trouble."

"Are you mad, Shalinsky?"

"I'm not mad." Shalinsky smiled, blinking his eyes against the smoke of his cigarette. "Neither do I want to make problems for you."

"What do I have to do to prove to you that I'm not Jewish?"

Shalinsky sifted through the papers again. "And what about your father?" he asked. "Couldn't he have changed his name without you knowing it? I mean, this is within the realm of possibilities, is it not?"

"Or my grandfather, eh? Or my great-grandfather?"

"You're so excited."

"I'd take you to see my parents, but they're both dead."

"I'm sorry to hear that. Please accept my condolences."

"They died years ago," I said. "A car accident."

"Is that so?"

"I suppose you think I'm lying?"

"Mr. Griffin, please."

"You're ruining my life, Shalinsky."

"I hardly know you."

"Do me a favour, Shalinsky. Cut my courses. I'll be grateful to you for the rest of my life."

"But your lectures are marvellous, Mr. Griffin. A delight."

"Some delight."

"Why, some of your epigrams I have marked down in my notebook to cherish. To memorize, Mr. Griffin."

"I've got news for you, buster. They're not mine. I stole them from my professor at Cambridge."

"So what? Didn't Shakespeare, may he rest in peace, steal from Thomas Kyd? The oral tradition, Mr. Griffin, is —"

"Shalinsky, I beg of you. If you won't quit my courses, then at least don't come to classes. If you'll do that for me I promise to pass you first in the class."

"Absolutely no."

Emptied, undone, I collapsed on the sofa.

"You don't feel so hot?" Shalinsky asked.

"I feel terrible. Now will you please go."

Shalinsky rose from his chair with dignity. "One thing," he said. "Among all those papers, no birth certificate. Why? I ask myself."

"Will you please get the hell out of here, Shalinsky!"

My parents were very much alive. But I hadn't lied to Shalinsky because I was afraid. There were my mother's feelings to be considered, that's all. You see, I was born an indecent seven months after my parents' marriage. They never told me this themselves. They always pre-dated the ceremony by a year, but once I accidentally came across their marriage licence and discovered their deception. Not a very scandalous one, when you consider that they've been happily married for thirty-two years now. But the secret of my early birth belonged to my parents and, to their mind, had been carefully kept. There was something else. My father, a high-school teacher all these years, had been a poet of some promise as a young man, and I believe that he had been saving his money to go to Europe as soon as he graduated from McGill. He met my mother in his senior year, alas. I was conceived — suspiciously close to the Annual Arts Ball, I put it — and they were married. (A shock to their friends for, at the time, my mother was seeing an awful lot of Louis Cohen, a famous judge today.) Next year, instead of Europe, my father enrolled for a teacher's course. I have always been tormented by the idea that I may have ruined their lives. So I was certainly not going to open a belated inquiry into the matter for Shalinsky's sake. Let him think I was Jewish and that I was afraid to show him my birth certificate. I knew the truth, anyway.

But as far as Shalinsky was concerned, so did he.

Beginning with my next lecture he contrived to make life a misery for me.

"It seems to be your contention — correct me if I'm wrong — that Kafka's strict Jewish upbringing had a crippling effect on the man. Would you say, then, that this was also true of Hemingway, who had a strict Catholic upbringing?"

Another day.

"I may have misinterpreted you, of course, but it seems to me that you place Céline among the great writers of today. Do you think it possible, Mr. Griffin, that anti-semitism goes hand in hand with literary greatness. Answer me that."

Shalinsky filled all my dreams. He attacked me in alleys, he pursued me through mazes and, in a recurring nightmare, he dragged me screaming into the synagogue to be punished for nameless iniquities. Many an afternoon I passed brooding about him. I saw myself being led up the thirteen steps to the hangman's noose, the despised strangler of Shalinsky, with — because of my ambiguous state — neither minister nor rabbi to comfort me.

244

Because I was sleeping so badly, I began to lose weight, dark circles swelled under my eyes, and I was almost always in an unspeakable temper.

Fearful of Shalinsky, I cut *The Merchant of Venice* from Eng. 112.

"Ah, Mr. Griffin, a question please."

"Yes, Shalinsky."

"It seems to me that in our study of Shakespeare, may he rest in peace, we have so far failed to discuss one of the Bard's major plays, *The Merchant of Venice.* I wonder if you could tell me why."

"Look here, Shalinsky, I do not intend to put up with your insolence for another minute. There are other problems besides the Jewish problem. This is not the Jewish Thought Literary Society, but my class in English 112. I'll run it however I choose, and damn your perverse Jewish soul."

With that, and the sharper exchanges that were to come, my reputation as an anti-semite spread. Soon I found myself being openly slighted by other lecturers at Wellington. Several students asked to be released from my classes. It was rumoured that a petition demanding my expulsion was being circulated among the students with, I must say, huge success. Eventually, Joyce found out about it.

"Mortimer, this can't be true. I mean you didn't call Shalinsky a meddling Jew in class last week...?"

"Yes, I did."

"Is it also true, then, that you've stopped taking our newspapers from Mr. Goldberg because... you want to transfer our business to a Gentile store?"

"Absolutely."

"Mortimer, I think you ought to see an analyst."

"I'm crazy, eh?"

"No. But you've been overworking. I don't know what's come over you."

"Is this Hy's idea?"

She looked startled.

"Come off it. I know you've been seeing Hy and Eva secretly."

"Mortimer, how could you have written that article on Chagall for *Jewish Thought?*"

"What's wrong with it?"

"Did you have to call it 'A Jewish Answer to Picasso'? Hy's furious. He thinks that was so cheap of you. He—"

"I'll kill that Shalinsky. I'll murder him."

Joyce, holding her hands to her face, ran into the bedroom. Three days later, when I sat down to the tiresome job of correcting the Eng. 129 midterm essays, I was still in a rage with Shalinsky. But I swear that's not why I failed him. His essay on Kafka was ponderous, windy, and pretentious, and deserved no better than it got: F-minus. Unfortunately for me, Dean McNoughton didn't agree.

"Not only do I consider this failure unwarranted, Griffin, but frankly I'm shocked at your behaviour. For the past two weeks charges of the most alarming nature have been flooding my office. I've been in touch with your wife who tells me you've been overworking, and so I prefer not to discuss the charges for the present. However, I think you'd best take the second term off and rest. Hodges will take your courses. But before you go, I want you to mark this paper B-plus. I think Shalinsky's essay is worth at least that."

"I'm afraid that's impossible, sir."

Dean McNoughton leaned back in his chair and considered his pipe pensively. "Tell me," he said at last, "is it true you offered to mark Shalinsky first in your class if he only stopped attending your lectures?"

"Yes, sir."

"I'm afraid I have no choice but to mark this paper B-plus myself."

"In that case I must ask you to accept my resignation."

"Go home, man. Rest up. Think things over calmly. If after three weeks you still want to resign . . ."

I started impatiently for the door.

"I don't understand you, Griffin. We're not prejudiced here. If you're Jewish, why didn't you say so at first?"

Pushing Dean McNoughton aside roughly, I fled the office.

Joyce wasn't home when I got there. All her things were gone, too. But she had left me a note, the darling. It said, in effect, that she could no longer put up with me. Perhaps we had never been right for each other. Not that she wished me ill, etc., etc. But all her instincts rebelled against sharing her bed with a fascist — worse, a Jewish fascist.

I don't know how Shalinsky got into the house. I must have left the door open. But there he stood above me, smiling faintly, a hand-rolled cigarette in his mouth.

"My wife's left me," I said.

Shalinsky sat down, sighing.

"Joyce has left me. Do you understand what that means to me?"

Shalinsky nodded his head with ineffable sadness. "Mixed marriages," he said, "never work."

All this happened two years ago, and I have married again since then. I don't earn nearly as much money in my new job, and at times it's difficult to live with my father-in-law, but next spring, God willing, we hope to rent an apartment of our own (not that I don't appreciate all he's done for us).

I don't see any of my old friends any more, but my new life offers plenty of rewards. I.M. Sinclair, for instance, composed a special poem for our wedding and read it after the rabbi's speech.

Lay your sleeping head, my love,
human on my faithless arm...

When the last issue of *Jewish Thought* appeared, imagine my delight when I read on the title-page: EDITED BY J. SHALINSKY AND M. GRIFFIN. Our circulation, I'm pleased to say, is rising steadily. Next year we hope to sell 1,500 copies of each issue. Meanwhile it's a struggle for Gitel and me. For me especially, as I am not yet completely adjusted to my new life. There are nights when I wake at three a.m. yearning for a plate of bacon and eggs. I miss Christmas. My father won't have anything to do with me. He thinks I'm crazy. Hy's another matter. He's phoned a couple of times, but I no longer have much use for him. He's an assimilationist. Last week my application for a teaching job with Western High School was turned down flatly—in spite of my excellent qualifications.

It's hard to be a Jew, you see.

Mordecai Richler (1931-) was born in Montreal. He has published a number of novels, including *The Apprenticeship of Duddy Kravitz* and *St. Urbain's Horseman*, two collections of essays, and a collection of stories, *The Street*.

Clark Blaise
A Class of New Canadians

Norman Dyer hurried down Sherbrooke Street, collar turned against the snow. "Superb!" he muttered, passing a basement gallery next to a French bookstore. Bleached and tanned women in furs dashed from hotel lobbies into waiting cabs. Even the neon clutter of the sidestreets and the honks of slithering taxis seemed remote tonight through the peaceful snow. *Superb*, he thought again, waiting for a light and backing from a slushy curb: a word reserved for wines, cigars, and delicate sauces; he was feeling superb this evening. After eighteen months in Montreal, he still found himself freshly impressed by everything he saw. He was proud of himself for having steered his life north, even for jobs that were menial by standards he could have demanded. Great just being here no matter what they paid, looking at these buildings, these faces, and hearing all the languages. He was learning to be insulted by simple bad taste, wherever he encountered it.

Since leaving graduate school and coming to Montreal, he had sampled every ethnic restaurant downtown and in the old city, plus a few Levantine places out in Outremont. He had worked on conversational French and mastered much of the local dialect, done reviews for local papers, translated French-Canadian poets for Toronto quarterlies, and tweaked his colleagues for not sympathizing enough with Quebec separatism. He attended French performances of plays he had ignored in English, and kept a small but elegant apartment near a colony of *émigré* Russians just off Park Avenue. Since coming to Montreal he'd witnessed a hold-up, watched a murder, and seen several riots. When stopped on the street for directions, he would answer in French or accented English. To live this well and travel each long academic summer, he held two jobs. He had no intention of returning to the States. In fact, he had begun to think of himself as a semi-permanent, semi-political exile.

Now, stopped again a few blocks farther, he studied the window of Holt-

Renfrew's exclusive men's shop. Incredible, he thought, the authority of simple good taste. Double-breasted chalk-striped suits he would never dare to buy. Knitted sweaters, and fifty-dollar shoes. One tanned mannequin was decked out in a brash checkered sportscoat with a burgundy vest and dashing ascot. Not a price tag under three hundred dollars. Unlike food, drink, cinema, and literature, clothing had never really involved him. Someday, he now realized, it would. Dyer's clothes, thus far, had all been bought in a chain department store. He was a walking violation of American law, clad shoes to scarf in Egyptian cottons, Polish leathers, and woollens from the People's Republic of China.

He had no time for dinner tonight; this was Wednesday, a day of lectures at one university, and then an evening course in English as a Foreign Language at McGill, beginning at six. He would eat afterwards.

Besides the money, he had kept this second job because it flattered him. There was to Dyer something fiercely elemental, almost existential, about teaching both his language and his literature in a foreign country—like Joyce in Trieste, Isherwood and Nabokov in Berlin, Beckett in Paris. Also it was necessary for his students. It was the first time in his life that he had done something socially useful. What difference did it make that the job was beneath him, a recent Ph.D., while most of his colleagues in the evening school at McGill were idle housewives and bachelor civil servants? It didn't matter, even, that this job was a perversion of all the sentiments he held as a progressive young teacher. He was a god two evenings a week, sometimes suffering and fatigued, but nevertheless an omniscient, benevolent god. His students were silent, ignorant, and dedicated to learning English. No discussions, no demonstrations, no dialogue.

I love them, he thought. They need me.

He entered the room, pocketed his cap and ear muffs, and dropped his briefcase on the podium. Two girls smiled good evening.

They love me, he thought, taking off his boots and hanging up his coat; I'm not like their English-speaking bosses.

I love myself, he thought with amazement even while conducting a drill on word order. I love myself for tramping down Sherbrooke Street in zero weather just to help them with noun clauses. I love myself standing behind this podium and showing Gilles Carrier and Claude Veilleux the difference between the past continuous and the simple past; or the sultry Armenian girl with the bewitching half-glasses that "put on" is not the same as "take on"; or telling the dashing Mr. Miguel Mayor, late of Madrid, that simple futurity can be expressed in four different ways, at least.

This is what mastery is like, he thought. Being superb in one's chosen field, not merely in one's mother tongue. A respected performer in the lecture halls of the major universities, equipped by twenty years' research in the remotest libraries, and slowly giving it back to those who must have it.

Dishing it out suavely, even wittily. Being a legend. Being loved and a little feared.

"Yes, Mrs. David?"

A *sabra:* freckled, reddish hair, looking like a British model, speaks with a nifty British accent, and loves me.

"No," he smiled, *"I were* is not correct except in the present subjunctive, which you haven't studied yet."

The first hour's bell rang. The students closed their books for the intermission. Dyer put his away, then noticed a page of his Faulkner lecture from the afternoon class. *Absalom, Absalom!* — his favourite.

"Can anyone here tell me what *the impregnable citadel of his passive rectitude* means?"

"What, sir?" asked Mr. Vassilopoulos, ready to copy.

"What about *the presbyterian and lugubrious effluvium of his passive vindictiveness?"* A few girls giggled. "O.K.," said Dyer, "take your break."

In the halls of McGill they broke into the usual groups. French Canadians and South Americans into two large circles, then the Greeks, Germans, Spanish, and French into smaller groups. The patterns interested Dyer. Madrid Spaniards and Parisian French always spoke English with their New World co-linguals. The Middle Europeans spoke German together, not Russian, preferring one occupier to the other. Two Israeli men went off alone. Dyer decided to join them for the break.

Not *sabras,* Dyer concluded, not like Mrs. David. The shorter one, dark and wavy-haired, held his cigarette like a violin bow. The other, Mr. Weinrot, was tall and pot-bellied, with a ruddy face and thick stubby fingers. Something about him suggested truck-driving, perhaps of beer, maybe in Germany. Neither one, he decided, could supply the name of a good Israeli restaurant.

"This is really hard, you know?" said Weinrot.

"Why?"

"I think it's because I'm not speaking much of English at my job."

"French?" asked Dyer.

"French? Pah! All the time Hebrew, sometimes German, sometimes little Polish. Crazy thing, eh? How long you think they let me speak Hebrew if I'm working in America?"

"Depends on where you're working," he said.

"Hell, I'm working for the Canadian government, what you think? Plant I work in — I'm engineer, see — makes boilers for the turbines going up north. Look. When I'm leaving Israel I go first to Italy. Right away-bamm I'm working in Italy I'm speaking Italian like a native. Passing for a native."

"A native Jew," said his dark-haired friend.

"Listen to him. So in Rome they think I'm from Tyrol — that's still native,

250

eh? So I speak Russian and German and Italian like a Jew. My Hebrew is bad, I admit it, but it's a lousy language anyway. Nobody likes it. French I understand but English I'm talking like a bum. Arabic I know five dialects. Danish fluent. So what's the matter I can't learn English?"

"It'll come, don't worry," Dyer smiled. *Don't worry, my son;* he wanted to pat him on the arm. "Anyway, that's what makes Canada so appealing. Here they don't force you."

"What's this *appealing?* Means nice? Look, my friend, keep it, eh? Two years in a country I don't learn the language means it isn't a country."

"Come on," said Dyer. "Neither does forcing you."

"Let me tell you a story why I come to Canada. Then you tell me if I was wrong, O.K.?"

"Certainly," said Dyer, flattered.

In Italy, Weinrot told him, he had lost his job to a Communist union. He left Italy for Denmark and opened up an Israeli restaurant with five other friends. Then the six Israelis decided to rent a bigger apartment downtown near the restaurant. They found a perfect nine-room place for two thousand kroner a month, not bad shared six ways. Next day the landlord told them The deal was off. "You tell me why," Weinrot demanded.

No Jews? Dyer wondered. "He wanted more rent," he finally said.

"More—you kidding? More we expected. *Less* we didn't expect. A couple with eight kids is showing up after we're gone and the law in Denmark says a man has a right to a room for each kid plus a hundred kroner knocked off the rent for each kid. What you think of that? So a guy who comes in *after* us gets a nine-room place for a thousand kroner *less.* Law says no way a bachelor can get a place ahead of a family, and bachelors pay twice as much."

Dyer waited, then asked, "So?"

"So, I make up my mind the world is full of communismus, just like Israel. So I take out applications next day for Australia, South Africa, u.s.a., and Canada. Canada says come right away, so I go. Should have waited for South Africa."

"How could you?" Dyer cried. "What's wrong with you anyway? South Africa is fascist. Australia is racist."

The bell rang, and the Israelis, with Dyer, began walking to the room.

"What I was wondering, then," said Mr. Weinrot, ignoring Dyer's outburst, "was if my English is good enough to be working in the United States. You're American, aren't you?"

It was a question Dyer had often avoided in Europe, but had rarely been asked in Montreal. "Yes," he admitted, "your English is probably good enough for the States or South Africa, whichever one wants you first."

He hurried ahead to the room, feeling that he had let Montreal down. He wanted to turn and shout to Weinrot and to all the others that Montreal was the greatest city on the continent, if only they knew it as well as he did. If they'd just break out of their little ghettos.

At the door, the Armenian girl with the half-glasses caught his arm. She was standing with Mrs. David and Miss Parizeau, a jolly French-Canadian girl that Dyer had been thinking of asking out.

"Please, sir," she said, looking at him over the tops of her tiny glasses, "what I was asking earlier—*put on*—I heard on the television. A man said *You are putting me on* and everybody laughed. I think it was supposed to be funny but *put on* we learned means get dressed, no?"

"Ah—*don't put me on,*" Dyer laughed.

"I yaven't erd it neither," said Miss Parizeau.

"To put some*body* on means to make a fool of him. To put some*thing* on is to wear it. O.K.?" He gave examples.

"Ah, now I know," said Miss Parizeau. "Like bullshitting somebody. Is it the same?"

"Ah, yes," he said, smiling. French Canadians were like children learning the language. "Your example isn't considered polite. 'Put on' is very common now in the States."

"Then maybe," said Miss Parizeau, "we'll ave it ere in twenty years." The Armenian giggled.

"No—I've heard it here just as often," Dyer protested, but the girls had already entered the room.

He began the second hour with a smile which slowly soured as he thought of the Israelis. America's anti-communism was bad enough, but it was worse hearing it echoed by immigrants, by Jews, here in Montreal. Wasn't there a psychological type who chose Canada over South Africa? Or was it just a matter of visas and slow adjustment? Did Johannesburg lose its Greeks, and Melbourne its Italians, the way Dyer's students were always leaving Montreal?

And after class when Dyer was again feeling content and thinking of approaching one of the Israelis for a restaurant tip, there came the flood of small requests: should Mrs. Papadopoulos go into a more advanced course; could Mr. Perez miss a week for an interview in Toronto; could Mr. Giguère, who spoke English perfectly, have a harder book; Mr. Coté an easier one?

Then as he packed his briefcase in the empty room, Miguel Mayor, the vain and impeccable Spaniard, came forward from the hallway.

"Sir," he began, walking stiffly, ready to bow or salute. He wore a loud grey checkered sportscoat this evening, blue shirt, and matching ascot-handkerchief, slightly mauve. He must have shaved just before class, Dyer noticed, for two fresh daubs of antiseptic cream stood out on his jaw, just under his earlobe.

"I have been wanting to ask *you* something, as a matter of fact," said

252

Dyer. "Do you know any good Spanish restaurants I might try tonight?"

"There are not any good Spanish restaurants in Montreal," he said. He stepped closer. "Sir?"

"What's on your mind, then?"

"Please—have you the time to look on a letter for me?"

He laid the letter on the podium.

"Look *over* a letter," said Dyer. "What is it for?"

"I have applied," he began, stopping to emphasize the present perfect construction, "for a job in Cleveland, Ohio, and I want to know if my letter will be good. Will an American, I mean—"

"Why are you going there?"

"It is a good job."

"But Cleveland—"

"They have a blackman mayor, I have read. But the job is not in Cleveland."

"Let me see it."

Most honourable Sir: I humbly beg consideration for a position in your grand company...

"Who are you writing this to?"

"The president," said Miguel Mayor.

I am once a student of Dr. Ramiro Gutierrez of the Hydraulic Institute of Sevilla, Spain...

"Does the president know this Ramiro Gutierrez?"

"Oh, everybody is knowing him," Miguel Mayor assured, "he is the most famous expert in all Spain."

"Did he recommend this company to you?"

"No—I have said in my letter, if you look—"

An ancient student of Dr. Gutierrez, Salvador del Este, is actually a boiler expert who is being employed like supervisor is formerly a friend of mine...

"Is he still your friend?"

Whenever you say come to my city Miguel Mayor for talking I will be coming. I am working in Montreal since two years and am now wanting more money than I am getting here now...

"Well..." Dyer sighed.

"Sir—what I want from you is knowing in good English how to interview me by this man. The letters in Spanish are not the same to English ones, you know?"

I remain humbly at your orders...

"Why do you want to leave Montreal?"

"It's time for a change."

"Have you ever been to Cleveland?"

"I am one summer in California. Very beautiful there and hot like my

253

country. Montreal is big port like Barcelona. Everybody mixed together and having no money. It is just a place to land, no?"

"Montreal? Don't be silly."

"I thought I come here and learn good English but where I work I get by in Spanish and French. It's hard, you know?" he smiled. Then he took a few steps back and gave his cuffs a gentle tug, exposing a set of jade cufflinks.

Dyer looked at the letter again and calculated how long he would be correcting it, then up at his student. How old is he? My age? Thirty? Is he married? Where do the Spanish live in Montreal? He looks so prosperous, so confident, like a male model off a page of *Playboy*. For an instant Dyer felt that his student was mocking him, somehow pitting his astounding confidence and wardrobe, sharp chin and matador's bearing against Dyer's command of English and mastery of the side streets, bistros, and ethnic restaurants. Mayor's letter was painful, yet he remained somehow competent. He would pass his interview, if he got one. What would he care about America, and the odiousness he'd soon be supporting? It was as though a superstructure of exploitation had been revealed, and Dyer felt himself abused by the very people he wanted so much to help. It had to end someplace.

He scratched out the second "humbly" from the letter, then folded the sheet of foolscap. "Get it typed right away," he said. "Good luck."

"Thank you, sir," said his student, with a bow. Dyer watched the letter disappear in the inner pocket of the checkered sportscoat. Then the folding of the cashmere scarf, the draping of the camel's hair coat about the shoulders, the easing of the fur hat down to the rims of his ears. The meticulous filling of the pigskin gloves. Mayor's patent leather galoshes glistened.

"Good evening, sir," he said.

"*Buenas noches,*" Dyer replied.

He hurried now, back down Sherbrooke Street to his daytime office where he could deposit his books. Montreal on a winter night was still mysterious, still magical. Snow blurred the arc lights. The wind was dying. Every second car was now a taxi, crowned with an orange crescent. Slushy curbs had hardened. The window of Holt-Renfrew's was still attractive. The legless dummies invited a final stare. He stood longer than he had earlier, in front of the sporty mannequin with a burgundy waistcoat, the mauve and blue ensemble, the jade cufflinks.

Good evening, sir, he could almost hear. The ascot, the shirt, the complete outfit, had leaped off the back of Miguel Mayor. He pictured how he must have entered the store with three hundred dollars and a prepared speech, and walked out again with everything off the torso's back.

I want that.

What, sir?

That.

The coat, sir?

Yes.

Very well, sir.

And *that.*

Which, sir?

All that.

"Absurd man!" Dyer whispered. There had been a moment of fear, as though the naked body would leap from the window, and legless, chase him down Sherbrooke Street. But the moment was passing. Dyer realized now that it was comic, even touching. Miguel Mayor had simply tried too hard, too fast, and it would be good for him to stay in Montreal until he deserved those clothes, that touching vanity and confidence. With one last look at the window, he turned sharply, before the clothes could speak again.

Clark Blaise (1941-) was born in Fargo, North Dakota, of Canadian parents, and taught at Sir George Williams (later Concordia) University in Montreal for several years before moving to York University, Toronto. He has published two collections of short stories, *A North American Education* and *Tribal Justice,* and (with his wife, Bharati Mukherjee) *Days and Nights in Calcutta.*

Jacques Ferron
*Mélie and the Bull**

Mélie Caron had only thirteen children. She expected to have more, one a year until she died; but after the thirteenth, Jean-Baptiste Caron, her husband, said to her, "Stop, Mélie!"

So the poor woman stopped, not yet fifty years old. She remained unsatisfied, deprived of her due, all warm and trembling like an animal checked in full career. However, her trouble was not without remedy: did she not still have her thirteen children? Thirteen children is not much; but it is a family. Alas! the consolation was shortlived. One by one her children left her. She had fed them too well: full of ardour were the boys, ripe and tender the girls; once fully grown there was no holding them back. In the end Mélie lost them all. She remained alone with her old man.

He, like a prisoner whose sentence is served, now found his freedom. He was no longer to be found at home, but spent most of his time with the other freedmen of the village, old eccentrics of the same breed as himself, parleying and laying down the law, drinking whenever the opportunity arose, and then pissing, drop by drop, the burning fire of his repentance. Mélie would take advantage of this to offer herself: "Let me help you, old man."

The suggestion was enough to make the waters flow again. Forty years of married life had taught the old man much; he knew that at the slightest sign of weakness his wife would get him into her clutches and not let go till she had mollycoddled him into senility. He remained on his guard.

"Thank you, Mélie. I'm all right now."

Now it came to pass that the old lady, deprived of children and husband, her corpulence notwithstanding, began to feel confined, loath to be restricted to her own company. Humours began to rise to her brain. At first this made her head swim, then she felt unsteady. It was the end of August. Alone in her kitchen, with her fly-swatter in her hand, she listened: not a fly

*Translated by Betty Bednarski

in the house. This silence astounded her. In the absence of flies she was prepared for much worse: for the appearance of snakes, of preposterous frogs, of demons armed with scapularies, against which her fly-swatter would have been useless; prepared for an attack of raving madness. She was on the point of screaming when she heard a moo which saved her. Fleeing her monsters, she rushed out.

Outside, giving shade to the door, there rose a cherry tree, with flashes of sunlight and the redness of cherries moving among its leaves: beyond that there stretched a garden, then, as far as the river, a field. Mélie crossed the garden. The calf in the field saw her; with his tail in the air he came up towards her with faltering little leaps. The fence which separated the field from the garden brought them both to a stop. The old lady leant down; the calf raised a round, wet muzzle: they looked at each other. And suddenly Mélie Caron was moved by a feeling which was worthy of her heart. This muzzle, this trust had overwhelmed her; tears came to her eyes; had she been able to cry tears of milk she would have wept buckets to satisfy the appetite of the poor animal.

That evening when Jean-Baptiste Caron came home, she announced to him: "In future I shall look after the calf."

The soup was steaming on the table.

"Fine," said the old man, sitting down. Discussions have never been known to keep soup hot. Better polish it off now and talk later. When he had eaten his fill: "Why look after the calf, Mélie?" he asked.

She replied: "Because I want to."

"Have I by any chance not taken good care of him?"

"Good or bad, you'll not take care of him any more."

"Fine," said the old man, who in actual fact was not particularly concerned about the calf.

He was nevertheless surprised a few days later to see his old lady in the field, sitting under a huge, black umbrella, which protected her from the sun and whose light shade, far from hiding her from view, made her most conspicuous.

"What are you doing there, Mélie?"

"Knitting."

And so she was.

"Perhaps you'd be more comfortable knitting in the house."

"No, old man, I'm more comfortable here." And she added: "Besides, I can't leave him now."

He asked anxiously: "Leave who?"

"Come now, old man, the calf, of course!"

The animal was lying at Mélie's feet. The picture was not lacking in charm. But to Jean-Baptiste it gave not the slightest pleasure.

"Shall I tell you something, Mélie? Shall I?"

She made no objection.

"Well," he said, "you look like an escaped lunatic, and that's a fact."

"Old fool, yourself," she replied.

You cannot reason with a woman when she is in full possession of her faculties, much less when she loses them. Reason attacks front on; such bluntness is a drawback; with the weaker sex you have to use some stratagem, or simply take them from behind.

"If Mélie were twenty years younger," the old man said to himself, "a few little pats on the behind would bring her to her senses."

In fact he could have done with shedding a few years himself: he had long since lost the art of those little pats. So how was he to bring about a recovery? What could he do to stop the old lady's madness becoming the talk of the village?

"It'll be quite simple," thought Jean-Baptiste Caron. "Since she's mad over a calf, I'll sell the calf."

In this way he hoped to cure her. The remedy was simple indeed. He went off at once and made the necessary arrangements with the butcher. The next morning at daybreak along came his man, paunch bulging beneath a white apron. He had donned for the occasion a bowler hat. He took away the calf. Soon afterwards old Mélie, still heavy with sleep, came out of the house suspecting nothing. The cherry tree, branches held high, for it had not yet lowered its panoply, revealed a strangely slender trunk. The sun was coming up. Dazzled, the old lady stopped a moment to blink her eyes, and then set off along the garden path, calling: "Littl'un! Littl'un!"

She reached the fence; there was still no sign of the calf. Again she called him, but with no better luck. Then she made a thorough search: she searched high and she searched low, but, from the garden to the river, the field was empty.

"Ah, mercy me!" she cried.

And back she rushed, the sight of the water having convinced her that the animal had drowned. Is it Christian to put rivers at the bottom of fields? This arrangement of Nature's filled her with indignation. In her haste she bumped into the cherry tree, who, preoccupied himself, had not seen her coming, absorbed as he was in his foliage, distributing his fruit to the birds. The birds flew away, cherries fell to the ground, and the wicked servant was caught in the act at his very roots. Much to his surprise the old lady continued on her way. So he signalled to the birds to come back.

Mélie Caron went back into the house.

"Old man, old man, the most terrible thing has happened."

This most terrible thing roused no interest.

"Can you hear me, old man?"

He could not hear her, and for a very simple reason: he was not there.

The old lady ran to his room: she searched high and she searched low, but the bed of Jean-Baptiste Caron was empty.

"Ah, mercy me!"

But at the sight of the chamber-pot she was not alarmed. No old fellow who has trouble pissing is ever swept away by the flood. Besides, the pot was empty. However, this incapacity of her husband's for drowning did not altogether lessen the mystery of his disappearance. Mélie Caron remained as in a dream. At first her dream revealed nothing; on the contrary it masked her view; the veil was coloured, for she was dreaming with her eyes open. Suddenly the veil was drawn aside: she saw a knife, and behind the knife, holding it, his paunch bulging beneath a white apron, wearing for the occasion a bowler hat—the butcher.

"I'm dreaming," she said to herself.

With which statement the butcher agreed, closing the curtain. Then old Mother Mélie rushed into the wings, and off to the butcher's she trotted. On her way she passed the church.

"Mother Mélie," said the priest, "you're tripping along like a young girl."

"Yes, yes, Father, if you say so—like a young girl. But have you seen my old man?"

"I saw your old man and your calf, one joyful, the other pathetic."

"Oh, the poor dear! Oh, the ruffian! Pray for him, Father."

And the old lady continued on her way. She arrived at the butcher's. The butcher, who had not had time to remove his hat, was surprised to see her again so soon.

"Good day, butcher. Where is my calf?"

"Good day, ma'am. I don't know your calf."

"Oh, don't you now!"

She paused in the doorway just long enough to blink her eyes. The morning was behind her, radiant, making the room in front of her dark. However she was soon able to distinguish the carcasses hanging there.

"There are many calves here," said the butcher, showing her the carcasses. "Only they all look alike since we undressed them."

"I see one that seems to have kept its coat on."

"Where's that, Mistress Mélie?"

"Here."

And pointing her finger, she touched a very shame-faced Jean-Baptiste.

"That's your old man, Mistress Mélie."

"Cut me off a leg all the same."

"He's very skinny."

"Cut it off, I tell you!"

The butcher refused. The old lady took away his knife.

"Then I'll help myself to that leg."

259

Whereupon Jean-Baptiste Caron intervened. "Don't act so foolish, Mélie. Your calf's here."

He handed her a rope; the poor dear animal was on the end of it, his eyes startled, his muzzle round and wet.

"Littl'un!"

"We weren't going to hurt him," said Jean-Baptiste Caron: "only cut him."

"A calf develops better that way," volunteered the butcher.

"Quiet, you liars! My calf shall remain entire, as the Lord made him,"

Having made sure that he still had all his vital parts, including his little phallus, the old lady set off with him. The priest, who had not yet finished his breviary, was still in front of the church.

"Well, Mother Mélie, I see you've found your calf."

"Yes, Father, but I got there just in time: they were about to cut him, the poor dear animal. I stopped their cruelty. You see, Father, he still has all his vital parts, including his little pointed phallus."

"So I see, Mother Mélie, so I see."

The old lady continued on her way, pulling her calf behind her. Soon afterwards the old man, Jean-Baptiste, appeared on the scene, looking very dejected indeed.

"It appears," said the priest, "that you're jealous of a calf. Your old lady showed me what you were planning to deprive him of."

"She showed you! Forgive her — she's not herself any more."

"Forgive her for what? I don't take offence at that. Surely you wouldn't expect her to put drawers on her calf?"

The bell for Mass began to ring. The priest was obliged to leave the old man. One month later the latter called at the presbytery. He was looking even more dejected; he walked bent double. When he sat down the priest noticed his face: he thought he seemed worried.

"Worried, no. Let's just say I'm weak."

"Well now! You're getting older."

"That may be, but it's not just age; for the last month I've eaten nothing but mash and grass."

"No!"

"Yes, mash and grass."

"The same as a calf?"

"You said it, Father; the same as a calf. I like meat, beans and lean pork. This food doesn't suit me at all and Mélie won't listen to me. She says we're all one nation."

"What language do you speak at home?"

"We still speak like people, but only because we don't know how to moo."

The priest began to laugh. "It's just the same with French Canadians; they still speak like people, but only because they don't know how to speak English."

Jean-Baptiste Caron nodded his head. "It's quite possible that calf is English," said he; "he's taking my place."

"Your place! You mean you live in the stable?"

"No, Father, we don't live in the stable. But the calf is living in the house."

"You don't say," said the priest, "he must be an English calf."

"He must be: he's not at all religious."

The priest rose to his feet. "We must drive him out."

This was also the opinion of Jean-Baptiste Caron.

"But how?"

Jean-Baptiste Caron also wondered how. The priest put a finger to his forehead, and this was very effective.

"Return to your house," he said to the old man. "But first pull yourself together and look cheerful. Once home, eat your mash as though you enjoyed it and be loving to the poor dear little animal."

"I won't be able to."

"You will. After a week or two Mélie will think you share her feelings. At the same time, bring other animals into your house."

"You must be joking, Father!"

"Cats, dogs, mice, rabbits, even hens. I don't say you should bring in cows or pigs. Just domestic animals Mélie will grow attached to and so become less attached to the calf. Then it will be possible to use a stratagem."

Jean-Baptiste Caron: "A stratagem?"

The priest: "You will tell Mélie that you are worried about the calf's future."

"'I'll tell her the truth; in six months he'll be a bull. It seems to me that's something to worry about."

"Exactly, this is what we must prevent. After all he's an English calf: mating isn't for him."

"All the same, we're not going to send him to school!"

"No, not to school: to a seminary."

The priest added: "A professional in the family is no disgrace."

"You're right, Father; a professional in the family is no disgrace."

At times advice is worth heeding, especially when it comes from one's priest. Jean-Baptiste Caron decided to make use of that offered him. Under the circumstances there was little else for him to do. He therefore declared himself to be in favour of calves, which won him the confidence of the old lady. Then he brought up the subject of education.

"Well now, it's no joke; a professional in the family is a worthwhile and honourable thing."

Mélie Caron knew it was no joke. But completely wrapped up in her calf, she was not particularly concerned about honour or the family; she wondered which of the two, the bull or the professional, would suit her best. Her heart inclined to the one, her reason to the other, and the animal looked at her puzzled. She too was puzzled.

"What are we going to do with you, poor little fellow?" she asked him.

"Moo, moo," replied the calf.

This reply did not help her in the slightest. Then she reflected, not unreasonably, that once educated the animal would express himself more clearly. So she opted for the professional, telling herself that if by chance he did not like this condition he could always go back to being a bull. Without further delay she went to the priest and told him of her decision.

"A good idea, Mother Mélie! And since you want him to be educated, send him to the Quebec Seminary: that is where I studied."

The old lady looked at the priest. "You don't say!"

The priest was forced to climb down a little. "We mustn't exaggerate," he said. "But all the same I do think, with his intelligence, this little fellow could become a lawyer or even a doctor."

The old lady seemed disappointed.

"A doctor, that's no joke!"

The old lady knew it was no joke. She simply said "Pooh!"

"A lawyer then?"

She preferred the lawyer.

"Then the matter's settled, Mother Mélie; next week they'll come for your little one: a lawyer he shall be."

As had been arranged, one week later to the very day the Father Superior of the Quebec Seminary sent his representative, a great giant of a man, part beadle, part deputy, who arrived with much to-do in a carriage drawn by three horses. The carriage drew up in the courtyard of the presbytery. Immediately the postulant was brought forth.

"*Ali baba perfectus babam,*" cried the representative.

Which is to say that at first sight, without further inspection, he had judged the calf fit to become a lawyer. On hearing these words the animal moved his ears. The priest noticed this.

"Well, well, he understands Latin!"

Mélie Caron did not understand it. She said "Amen," however, with a heavy heart.

This amen had an effect she had not foreseen: the representative rose to his feet and standing up in the carriage, pointed his finger at her:

"Thou, Mélie, *repetatus.*"

"Amen," repeated the old lady.

Then the giant of a man leapt from the carriage; seized hold of the calf, and carried him off into the church barn.

"He's not as good as the Father Superior of the Quebec Seminary," said the priest, "only being his representative, but you'll see, Mother Mélie, he still knows all about giving an education."

Indeed, no sooner had he entered the barn with the calf, than he reappeared, alone, holding in his hands a long object, which he gave to the old lady.

"Thou, Mélie, *repetatus.*"

"Amen," said she.

And the terrible pedagogue went back into the barn.

"But it's my Littl'un's tail!" cried Mélie Caron.

"Yes," replied the priest, "it is your Littl'un's tail. Keep it. He no longer has any use for it."

At that same moment the door of the barn opened, and who should appear but the calf, stiff, in a long black frock-coat, walking like a little man.

"Littl'un!"

He stopped and slowly turned his head toward the old lady. This head did not fit, it was shaky and too high, its features motionless. And he stared at her with vacant eyes.

"Littl'un!" the old lady called again.

He did not even twitch his ears. The old lady did not know what to think. What had they done to her little one in the church barn that he should come out looking so distant? They had cut off his tail, to be sure; they had put clothes on him, true; he was walking on his hind legs like a prime minister, so much the better! In short they had educated him, but did that mean they had to make him blind and deaf? This being the case, education did make the farewell easier.

The seminarian calf, drawing a white handkerchief from his frock-coat, waved it, but distantly, oh so distantly: the fingers holding the handkerchief were already human. Mélie Caron made no attempt to hold him back. He climbed into the carriage beside the representative of the Father Superior of the Quebec Seminary, and there sat upright on his little behind, he who had never used it before. The carriage moved off and soon disappeared from sight.

"Well?" asked the priest.

Well, what? The old lady did not know, so she made no reply.

"Well, yes," the priest began again, "he is gifted, that little fellow! He's not even at the Seminary yet, and all there is left of the calf is its head. Education is for him. A lawyer he shall be, and what a lawyer!"

"What lawyer? asked the old lady.

"Why, Lawyer Bull! A famous lawyer. Come, come be proud: he'll be a credit to you."

Mother Mélie was holding the calf's tail in her hands, and it hung there pitifully. Proud? with her head down and her tail, so to speak, between her legs, she did not feel in the least like being proud. "I'm very happy," she said; and very sadly she went off. To see her leave like that worried the priest. The next day after Mass, without stopping to have lunch, he went to call on her, and found her in her garden, feeding the hens.

"I was afraid I might find you in bed, Mother Mélie."

"I very nearly did stay in bed, Father. When I woke up I had no desire to do anything, only to die. Surely at my age I'm entitled to a rest. Then I heard the clucking of the hens, the barking of the dog, the animals making their morning noise, and I thought of my poor rabbits twitching their noses without a sound. Who else would have looked after all these animals but me? So I got up."

The priest took off his hat while he recovered his breath. His plan had worked, the calf was out of the way, the old lady cured; what more could he ask, under the circumstances? He was satisfied; he remembered that he was hungry. Mélie Caron gave him a meal and he ate till he could eat no more. When he rose from the table she was still not satisfied: "Just one more little mouthful, Father?"

"So you're not cross with me, Mother Mélie?"

She was cross that he had eaten so little. Apart from that she had nothing against him, considering him to be a good Christian.

"But what about your calf, Mother Mélie?"

She saw no reason why she should be cross about that. Hadn't she parted with her calf so that he could become a lawyer? It had been for his own good; of what importance was the sacrifice she, poor woman, had made?

"Besides," said Mélie Caron, "I am used to these separations."

She was thinking of her thirteen children, well fed all of them, full of ardour the boys, ripe and tender the girls, who had left her one by one. And where had they gone? One to Maniwaki, another to the States, a third out West. As for the rest, she did not know. Besides, Maniwaki, Maniwaki... she had never been outside of Sainte-Clothilde de Bellechasse: what could Maniwaki mean to her? Or the States? or Abitibi? or the Far West? "I lost my children, Father; I can part with a calf. Besides, I still have my hens, some rabbits, a dog, a cat, and some mice, enough to keep me going for some time yet. My supply still hasn't run out."

"You'll die one day, all the same."

"The worms will console me."

"Come, come, Mother Mélie? And what about the good Lord?"

"After, once the worms have eaten their fill."

The priest thought of his position; there was nothing in the Scriptures to prevent Mélie Caron having her bones cleaned off by worms before going up to join the Almighty. "Very well," he said, taking his hat and preparing to leave. Whereupon Mélie Caron, still not satisfied, asked him if he thought that at the Seminary the little fellow would keep his head.

"His calf's head? Of course not."

"Then how shall I recognize him?"

The priest thought of his position and either because he had forgotten his theology or because the question had not been dealt with he could think of nothing very Catholic to say in reply. He hesitated, feeling somewhat ill at ease in his cassock.

"Mother Mélie," he said at last, "there exists something which, as a young bull, your little fellow would have worn in all innocence, but which as a lawyer he will have to conceal; it is by that incorruptible root—for education cannot touch it—that you will recognize him."

And doubtless judging he had gone too far, without explaining himself at greater length, he went off, leaving the old lady with her curiosity, naturally, unsatisfied. So when Jean-Baptiste Caron came home she eagerly asked him for an explanation. Jean-Baptiste Caron, who was not inhibited by theology, answered without hesitation: "It's the phallus, pointed in the case of a calf which has become a young bull."

"And in the case of Littl'un?"

"Likewise, since education cannot touch it. He'll keep his root even though he's a lawyer, and in this way will be easy to recognize."

And so, reassured, Mélie went back to her daily routine, and the months passed, the winter months, then spring, and the cherry tree bloomed; then came the summer months, June, July, and the ripe hay was harvested. In August the newspapers announced the famous fair to be held at Quebec in the early fall, and which Jean-Baptiste Caron had been wanting to see for a long time.

"Old girl," said he, "we really should see the Provincial Exhibition before we die."

The old lady burst out laughing. "Have you gone crazy, old man?"

In order that she might judge for herself he handed her a page of the newspaper. On it she found this professional announcement: "Maître Bull, lawyer."

"Anyway," she said, "it's not such a bad idea."

So to Quebec they went, their hearts heavy, their eyes wide. The city, the fair, amusement and pleasure soon lifted the weight from their hearts. Fatigue came more slowly; however, after two or three days, they could hardly keep their eyes open, and were beginning to miss the peace and quiet of Sainte-Clothilde.

"But," said the old lady, "before we go back, there's someone I have to see."

Jean-Baptiste Caron was not in the least surprised.

"Someone you have to see?" he asked.

"Yes, old man! Just because we've never had any fallings out, that's no reason why we shouldn't see a lawyer before we die."

Old Mélie was right: they should see a lawyer. It was unfortunate, however, that the lawyer had to be Maître Bull. Jean-Baptiste Caron could see no good coming of the encounter. It is one thing to recognize a young bull under a gown, but quite another to get the lawyer to agree to the test. At any rate, Mélie should go alone.

"I'm thirsty," said Jean-Baptiste Caron, "I'll wait for you at the Hôtel de la Traverse."

So Mélie went alone. To Maître Bull's office she came. "Come in," cried he in a beautiful deep voice. She went in and found, in a dusty little office, a young man dressed in black, handsome as an archangel, sad as an orphan, who, after the normal formalities, asked for her name, first name, and place of residence: Mélie Caron of Sainte-Clothilde. And the purpose of her visit: whom did she wish to bring action against?

"No one," the old lady answered.

Surprised, he looked at her; and said, with relief: "Thank you."

It was the old lady's turn to express surprise. He explained to her that the lawyer's profession served as an alibi.

"Who are you then?"

"A poet," he replied.

"Oh," said she.

"I keep it a secret; if men knew they would look upon me as some kind of animal."

Mélie Caron lowered her eyes at this modesty.

"Your name again?" the lawyer asked her.

"Mélie Caron."

"I do not know why," he said, "but that name brings to my mind the image of a field and the sound of a river."

At these words, no longer doubting that this was her Littl'un, the poor dear animal, old Mélie pulled from her bag the pitiful object which she had kept, and let it hang beside her. Meanwhile the archangel, the orphan, the young man in black, went on in his beautiful deep voice, saying that it was not the sound of a river, but that of the wind in the grass, the wind whose waters bleach it white in the sun.

"Earth's back is dark and stains the hand, but when the wind passes she forgets her sorrow and, moved, turns over, showing her white belly, where the grass is soft as down, where each blade is a nipple gorged with milk."

"Poor dear," thought the old lady, "he badly needs to graze!"

"Do you sometimes hear a voice," she asked him, "a voice calling you: Littl'un! Littl'un!"

"Yes, I hear it."

"It is mine," said Mélie Caron.

"I did not know," said the lawyer. "Besides, I cannot answer. I am imprisoned in a cage of bone. The bird in his cage of bone is death building his nest.* There was a time when I hoped to free myself by writing, but the poems I wrote then did not render my cry."

"Poor dear," thought the old lady, "he badly needs to moo."

"Are you married, Littl'un?"

The young man gave a horrified start; his archangel's wings trembled; he was deeply offended at being thought capable of something so low.

"Quite so, quite so," said the old lady, "I didn't mean to offend you. I only wanted to find out if you were free."

"I am free," he said, "subject only to the will of the ineffable."

She handed him the hairy member.

"Then take back your tail, Littl'un, and follow me."

She led him to the Hôtel de la Traverse where Jean-Baptiste Caron was waiting for them.

"Old man, it's Littl'un!"

Of this she seemed so sure that the old man lowered his eyes, embarrassed. Together they returned to Sainte-Clothilde. "Well, well!" called the priest, "it's back to the land, I see!" And back to the land it was! Though they had surpassed the prophesied return. Indeed, once he had grazed, it was not long before Maître Bull had recovered his coat. Meanwhile his gown was falling to shreds. Soon there was nothing left of the fine education he had received at the Quebec Seminary. One day, at last, he was able to utter his poet's cry, a bellow such as to drive all the cows in the county mad. Faithful to his root, he had found his destiny. From that day on, before the wondering eyes of old Mélie, he led an existence befitting his nature, and left behind him in Bellechasse, where they called him The Scholar, the memory of a famous bull.

Jacques Ferron (1921-) was born in Louiseville, Quebec, and now practises medicine in Montreal. He has published numerous plays and novels. Two of his novels, *Dr. Cotnoir* and *Saint Elias*, have appeared in English translations. His collection of stories, *Tales from the Uncertain Country*, won a Governor General's Award in its original French version.

*L'oiseau dans sa cage d'os
C'est la mort qui fait son nid
These lines are taken from Cage d'oiseau (Bird Cage) by the Quebec poet, Saint-Denys Garneau (1912-1943).

Anne Hébert
*A Grand Marriage**

Augustin Berthelot came out of the Basilica with Marie-Louise de Lachevrotière on his arm. The bridal procession followed in orderly fashion while the
deep tones of the organ rolled out into the church square, where a few
urchins clung to the iron gates to catch a glimpse of the bride and groom.

Augustin Berthelot waved a vague greeting towards the youthful heads
which decorated the spear-tips of the gates as though on skewers in two
dense and distinct rows. On his right were the sailor suits and silky ringlets of
the Upper Town; on his left, the tousled heads and dirty faces from the town
below.

The groom was tall and well-built, his face hard and fine. He accepted
his success calmly, as though it were owed to him by destiny; he scarcely felt
its weight upon his arm where the small hand in the white glove was resting.
It was more difficult for him to suppress his sense of freedom from family
and social ties: it went to his head like wine and intoxicated him. It was
perhaps the reason for a certain arrogance in his smile. No father, mother,
brothers, sisters, aunts, uncles, friends nor little cousins to betray him
among the rag-tag from the Lower Town who had come to admire so great a
wedding.

For Augustin Berthelot entered his new life free of all attachments, as free as
Lazarus resurrected. The long years spent in the Far North, his uncommon
success with the Hudson's Bay Company, his recent appointment with one of
the best furriers of la rue Buade all contributed to the kind of halo which
accompanies the prestige of a well-founded fortune.

For an instant, his eyes followed the band of puny children whom the
church warden had just dispersed. They fluttered off like a flock of sparrows

*Translated by Gwendolyn Moore

268

frightened by an intruder. "Let only one of them refuse to run away, and stay to flout the warden, he will be saved, and I shall bless him from the bottom of my heart," thought Augustin. But not one of the youngsters held his ground, and the sound of scampering footsteps disappeared. "Bad seed; a race of weaklings," the young husband muttered between his smiles as he greeted each guest with a fine discrimination as to their exact social standing. Through this marriage, Augustin Berthelot had come into the life of Mademoiselle de Lachevrotière as an equal partner and a guest of honour.

The hand on his arm was lifeless, and the profile as impenetrable as that of an anonymous angel behind the folds of the veil. Augustin looked upon his wife as a former dream, come to escort him for a while.

Marie-Louise, the fifth daughter of François-Xavier de Lachevrotière, according to age, had just joined her fate to his by the laws of God and the Church; but Augustin Berthelot could well believe that nothing had changed. He still saw himself—first as a child, and then as an adolsecent— half-hidden in the shadowed side-aisles of the church during vespers, watching the demoiselles de Lachevrotière. They were muffled in beaver in the winter, and in the summer wore *broderie anglaise*, with blue or pink ribbons at the waist. He had seen them disappear like that, in the proper order, led away by well-chosen husbands; the eldest, the second, then the third daughter, who suffered endlessly from a cold in the head. Then he had had ten years in Hudson Bay, in that tranquil possession of the earth which an ambitious and thoughtful heart can achieve when it puts itself forth fully, and is wholly convinced of its inalienable right. Upon his return to Québec, the fifth of the demoiselles de Lachevrotière was still unmarried, and Augustin had himself presented to François-Xavier by Canon Painchaud. Canon Painchaud had given Monsieur de Lachevrotière a precise account of Augustin's flourishing fortunes: an accredited representative of the Hudson's Bay Company to Holt Howard and Company, and a shareholder in the firm. The obscure origins of the young man, who was born on rue Sous-le-Cap in the Lower Town, were evoked only to emphasize his innate business sense and his unusual strength of character. Receiving confidence for confidence, Canon Painchaud had elicited from François-Xavier the fact that his manor at Saint-Joachim was heavily mortgaged and threatened with seizure. Augustin offered to take the matter in hand, and save François-Xavier's honour as though it were his own. Honour, therefore, held the same end for both men and the marriage of Marie-Louise was decided. Augustin (this was in April) dreamed of autumn at Saint-Joachim, with the wild geese passing overhead from Cap Tourmente, amidst the distant clamour of their massive migration.

The long days of hunting in the forest, the return to the manor at nightfall, the comfort of a log fire in the great hearth, not to mention the rents which had been left in sufferance by François-Xavier, and which he,

Augustin, would be able to extract from the peasants—the anticipation of all this put the young man in a pleasurable frame of mind and a pugnacious mood.

The young couple left the wedding reception, which was held at the home of Marie-Louise's parents on rue Saint-Denis, and proceeded directly to Saint-Joachim, as Augustin had decided beforehand.

Here and there, the violent autumn light set on fire the half-stripped, colourful trees, and the odour of damp soil and wet foliage filled the air. Augustin thrilled once more with the clarity of spirit he had felt in the North. His knowledge of the woods and of hunting, his experiences with the Indians and fur traders (whom he had learned to manipulate skilfully as the years of his apprenticeship flowed by, in a market that was more and more controlled by his own company), conferred upon him now a free and sure hand on the Saint-Joachim estate in the hunting of partridge, geese, and deer. As well as in the trapping of tardy rentals.

It was only when he returned from the woods in the evening, his body blissful and weary, or when he closed the door to François-Xavier's little unheated office, after having confronted the grievances and recrimination of the peasants while exercising his rights as the new *seigneur*, that Augustin Berthelot felt a slight hesitation, the shadow of a doubt, and a kind of unpleasant distrust of his most profound knowledge of the world.

He was obliged to join his wife in the drawing-room. She would be sitting by the hearth, lost within her skirts and shawls, taking refuge in the endless daydreams of a spoiled child.

Augustin would pretend to be checking his accounts, with the great ledger of the rentals open on his knees, while Marie-Louise hugged the fire closer, as though she wished to disappear into it, burn to a crisp, escape up the chimney in smoke, and fly over the rooftops, lighter than air and delivered forever from a young bride's body. But her barren and haughty soul had one great recourse in its present misfortune and distress. She offered Augustin no resistance except a most inward and perfect contempt.

Augustin would ask her, "What did you do all day?" And Marie-Louise would shrug and answer, "Nothing." How could she explain that she had stayed beside the fire all day long, watching the beautiful and destructive play of the flames, in the vain hope of absorbing some of their heat and courage through the pores of her skin? For she froze inevitably as evening approached, and the moment when the man who was her husband appeared in the doorway like a conquering warrior.

Marie-Louise tapped her foot nervously beneath her skirt, sometimes poking a log into an explosive shower of sparks. Augustin, watching the foot swinging, began his addition all over again for the third time, like a swimmer, out of breath, who grasps at the smallest twig for assistance.

"What did you do all day, Marie-Louise?" he asked once more in a voice that was barely audible.

Marie-Louise stood up abruptly, fluffing out her skirts and adjusting her bustle. She looked at her husband in a manner which she intended to be crushing, but she succeeded only in assuming the air of an offended little girl. Augustin smiled in his turn and went over to her. She kept repeating, "Nothing! Nothing! I have already told you! And what else would you have me do, I ask you?"

It was with pride that she uttered this "Nothing," as though this word were a kind of provocative banner, a reliable defence, and a declaration of irrefutable principles.

Marie-Louise went over to the window. Taking off her ring, she began deliberately to engrave her name in the glass with her solitaire, among the other feminine names which had been gradually appearing there over the generations. While she breathed on the window, repeating "Nothing," Augustin approached her from behind and put his hands on her shoulders.

He looked at the pane of glass, filled with the names of the women, written every-which-way as on an important document. They called to his mind a long chain of women without employment, the recluses of this manor whose use of their time had been this "Nothing," "Nothing," "Nothing," while a thousand flames were born and died in this same hearth, and the immense harsh river flowed by.

Augustin thought of his mother, crushed under the mountains of laundry to be washed, suffocating in the steam of the ironing. And he saw the strong, bony hands of Délia, the Métis woman who had shared his life for several years in the North. In the depths of his heart, he felt the injustice of the world, like an old wound which he had sworn to avenge.

Marie-Louise had turned around, with Augustin's hands still upon her childish shoulders. "Let me pass, if you please." Her breath was fast against his chest and she turned her head to avoid his gaze. She made a quick movement to get away from him, gathering her skirts in her hands. "Let me pass, please."

The skirts and the petticoats of Marie-Louise exalted Augustin. The whole landscape of his childhood: bleached and starched, passed through the blueing, embroidered, beribboned, pleated; drying in the kitchen in the winter, hanging on the clothes-lines in the wind in summer, in the days of the street named Sous-le-Cap. "Don't touch. Don't touch," his mother would repeat, a fine laundress, getting ready to climb the steep hill, her fragile packages under her arm. From the Grande Allée to the rue des Remparts, along the Esplanade and rue des Grisons, Augustin accompanied his mother, slim and wan, to help her deliver the laundry to the gentlewomen of the Upper Town. The boy would wonder how they could use so many petticoats and pantalettes. These outings both humiliated and fascinated him.

For a moment, Augustin had an impulse to turn Marie-Louise over on the carpet, and to lose himself boldly under a crazy mass of skirts and ruffles, The thought of the girl's terror, anger and fear of the possible arrival of a servant increased his desire. But he allowed her to pass, furious and blushing, without restraining her further. A domestic scandal could be harmful to Augustin Berthelot's relationship with François-Xavier de Lachevrotière, whom it was wiser to have as a stable ally in both business and social life.

And so it was that Augustin announced to his young wife, in a very calm voice, that the honeymoon was over and that they would return to Québec the following day. "All the rents have been collected except for a few of the most stubborn, which I shall discuss with your father," he stated sententiously, closing the ledger.

A maid, curly-haired and fat, announced in a high-pitched voice: "Dinner is served." Augustin stood aside to permit his wife to pass. He followed her with his eyes, and asked himself wearily how many children she would have to bear, before her thin body acquired maturity.

The tall house which Augustin Berthelot had just bought on la rue des Remparts overlooking the Louise Basin satisfied him entirely. "I am at the centre of the world," he thought, crossing the rich carpets and pulling aside the lace curtains to watch the movements of the ships below. Such an obstinate and introverted little city this Québec, defensive to its narrow heart since the English conquest. A society governed by unchanging rituals and genealogical trees so clear and precise that their branches could be traced down to the last insignificant couple, family trees sprung from the seed of the few old families remaining in the country after the Treaty of Paris. Within this structure one could easily get one's bearings and make the right connections, even by chance meetings, in the cities and country manors where at times one found noble and often poetic beings.

"My family tree," thought Augustin, "starts with me, and all the past is only stupidity and misery." Augustin's memories were closely guarded in an orderly corner of his lively heart, for he was preoccupied with the present and with his own power over reality.

"A town can be occupied and possessed like a house, from basement to attic." The coachman could vouch for the truth of his master's saying as he drove Augustin around every day, winter and summer. The steep hills of the town often winded the handsome team of horses.

The brokers of la rue Saint-Pierre, the tanners of the Saint-Roch quarter, the captains of the cargo ships, the English-speaking management of Holt Howard and Company, and the French of Révillon, the Hudson's Bay Company officials, the notaries and lawyers of the district, the higher and the lower clergy—almost all of them, for one reason or another, had business with Augustin Berthelot. Canon Painchaud, who had provided for Augustin's education with his own funds—in the hope of a priestly vocation—thought nostalgically what an energetic soul had been irretrievably lost to the church hierarchy.

But Marie-Louise remained thin and sterile. She suffered from dizziness and migraines, and arranged as much as possible to escape from her conjugal duties. Augustin accommodated himself very poorly to this. If the principle of refusing to entertain any reminiscence of the past had not been so firmly anchored within him, how happily he would have employed the vocabulary and manners of his father, which were stored there somewhere in his veins. A shoemaker, the man had spent his life bent over the worn shoes of the poor, and had slowly dried up like an old piece of leather. When he returned in the evening to the kitchen encumbered with laundry, one could imagine that he still chewed shoemakers' nails. But instead, there passed between his lips angry little phrases and pointed blasphemies, and he cuffed the children daily and often, in the same spirit.

Augustin never entered his wife's room without knocking. The acquisition of good manners and their perfection in such circumstances flattered him more than his masterly handling of business, and gave him more pleasure than any he might savour with Marie-Louise.

"My wife is both infuriating and boring!" Augustin put down his hat, cane, and gloves, forcing himself to remain impassive, while a clerk with a sly expression presented him with the latest mail, arrived just that morning from Hudson Bay.

Augustin settled into his leather armchair, looked around the smoky wainscoted office, waved the clerk to leave, but the man stopped.

"Pardon me, sir," he said very softly, closing his eyes, "Pardon me, but there was a lady who came several times to ask for you. . . ."

"A lady, Nicolas?"

"A lady. . . That is, a woman. Yes, sir, I should have said, a woman. . . ."

Augustin unfolded the sheet of yellow paper and ran his eyes over the list of accounts receivable. Suddenly the date at the top, on the right-hand side, caught his attention strangely, like the symbol of an important matter which was still secret and obscure, and which he would have to clarify in order to inscribe it victoriously on the credit side of the ledger, or else run a very grave risk.

"There's something very disturbing about this date. It's ridiculous how it affects me," he fretted. "The twenty-fifth of May. . . What is so extraordinary about that?. . . Up there, it is the beginning of summer. The sudden, brief and feverish summer of the North, with its thousand unleashed streams, its soft mosses, its overwhelming luminosity, and its endless armies of mosquitoes. And its own, distinctive odours."

The clerk continued:

"A woman, sir. That is, I would say, an Indian, I think, sir. . . Yes, an Indian woman. . . ."

Augustin looked at the clerk calmly, as though he would pin him to the wall like a little black butterfly, already crumpled.

"An Indian woman, Nicolas? No doubt she has come from Lorette to sell moccasins. You should have referred her to Peterson, you know."

"She was asking for you, sir. She seemed to understand nothing, and kept repeating, like a chant, 'I must see Monsieur Augustin Berthelot. I must see Monsieur Augustin Berthelot...'"

Augustin read his mail, signed a few letters, and had his coach called to the door. It took all his self-command to appear sure of himself, controlled, unchallengeable, even more so than usual, as though on this summer's day of 1890 the entire equilibrium of his life depended upon the perfect steadiness of his nerves.

Within him, something was starting to break down, and he did not know how or why. By a strict inner discipline, he had accustomed himself for a very long time to attach no importance to the images and sensations arising from his imagination. He gave no recognition to this evasive, incoherent, useless and deleterious inner world which lay dormant within him. "Let memories and souvenirs be damned," he had often told himself. A beautiful, clear, and strong thought had always been, for him, a thing to focus and direct towards a definite objective, to be accomplished by efficient and conscious action.

And so, on that morning, nothing in his outer behaviour would have given rise to the least suspicion. Although images of the North passed before his eyes, tenacious and alive, preventing him from thinking clearly about other matters, he was certainly not in a state of reverie. On the contrary, the insistence of these images irritated him. To shake off the annoyance to which these menacing thoughts gave rise, he decided to have a drink at the *Chien d'Or*, and thus committed his first blunder. For this first drink was to open him to an invasion by the other life which was hidden, bitter-sweet, within him.

As the coachman, who was both agile and simple-minded — a rare combination of characteristics in a human being — had already leapt down from the carriage, in order to go and buy his master's cigars as usual, Augustin called him back, and told him that he would go himself, "to loosen up his legs."

Incapable of any reaction even resembling astonishment, the servant leapt back into the driver's seat in a single bound, where, fatigued by his own agility, he promptly fell asleep, his chin on his chest, his thin neck exposed, like that of a plucked chicken, to the passers-by.

Well ensconced in the red plush seats of the *Chien d'Or*, Augustin had had several glasses of beer, when the owner whispered in his ear that an Indian woman had been asking for him early that morning. Augustin lit a cigar, engaged the man in a casual conversation, and slipped in the thought, between puffs, that the Indians of Lorette were always bothering the Holt Howard representatives with bundles of beaded moccasins. "The market is completely saturated with them. But try and make them understand that—or anything else!" The manager nodded and replied: "The Indians are more obstinate than the devil himself, or God, or both together—if you will pardon my expression, Monsieur Berthelot."

Augustin left the *Chien d'Or* damning the stubbornness of the Indians at large, which had somehow become mingled in a tangible way with the aftertaste of beer that clung to his breath.

When he arrived at Pelletier & Pelletier, rue de la Fabrique, Augustin, rocked by the slow trot of the horses, had had time to succumb to a curious feeling of uneasiness, as though an avalanche of moccasins, like lost bullets, threatened him from all sides whenever he closed his eyes.

Mademoiselle Fréchette, cashier for thirty-five years, trembled when she informed Augustin that "an Indian woman has been asking brazenly for Monsieur Berthelot at the cash desk, in a loud voice—just like that!"

Augustin, appearing calm and sure of himself, had his usual conference with the Pelletiers, father and son, and admired for the nth time the hereditary genius of this family; since the time of the Conquest they had been able to maintain and expand their business and even deal with the English as equals.

Augustin climbed back into his carriage, damned the absurd obstinacy of this woman who was looking for him all over the city, and began to experience a feeling of profound anguish. A specific face which he had tried since morning to keep at the bottom of his memories rose to the surface, and imposed itself like the announcement of a scandal on its way towards him.

It was useless for the young man to repeat to himself, "I have only to find this woman who is asking for me with such fanfare, and confront her." The image of Délia was now awakened, and bathed in a clear light. "If this woman is not Délia, the whole thing is of no importance. But if it is she, that mule of a Métis, no power of mediation on this earth, civil, religious, legal, or illegal will prevail against her obstinacy."

At this point, Augustin was tempted again by the fresh taste of beer, as though the mere fact of drinking a glass in the promiscuity of a crowded room could bring an immediate and certain solution to his problem. And also, in a tavern, he was sure of not finding himself nose to nose with that damned Indian woman who had been looking for him since morning, nor with her furious counterpart, left on account at Hudson Bay.

"I am running away, the better to plan my attack," he told himself. But the idiocy of such an excuse turned him away from any preoccupation other than satisfying his sharp thirst.

Augustin ordered his coachman to take la Côte de la Montagne. "I am going down into the lower world," he thought, tasting the voluptuous feeling

275

of remorse, withdrawing into himself to an unknown region of defeat, flight and surrender. "Let the devil take me when he will, provided I do not have to decide anything or face anything, nor prove, nor explain, nor justify anything, nor win or lose."

The hill was steep and badly paved. Augustin was testy over the cautious pace of the horses, but his coachman, clearly taking sides with the horses, "against Monsieur," took pains to brake the vehicle as much as possible the whole length of the descent.

Revived by his overstimulated nerves, sure of the strength of his fists and the endurance of his body, Augustin undertook a tour of the taverns of the Lower Town. Without abandoning his haughty and carefree attitude, he outstared the hostile glances of the greasy lumbermen and bearded sailors, and even while sipping his beer or gin, he could scarcely resist the impulse to throw off his jacket and start a fight, man to man, for no other reason than the stirring within his blood, and the reassurance of his physical force.

But this innocent pastime was no longer permitted him. When he threw aside his jacket, Augustin would also cast away both his position and his fortune. One is never freed of a scandal, and when he returned to his carriage, the foreboding of imminent scandal gripped his heart like a vise. "Let another damned Irishman make fun of me and I shall lose control."

However, at La Traverse, he went down to the bar and had a glass with the captain of the ferry, an acquaintance. The ritual small-talk took place; the captain commented on beer which is bottled without aging, and of his preference for rum, and informed Augustin that an Indian woman had been around the docks looking for him since that morning.

Augustin smiled vaguely at the ferry captain, and offered him a cigar. He left the bar precipitately and went back to his carriage, signalling his coachman to follow the road along the river.

There was a sharp wind, and the road was soaked and deeply rutted. Augustin had taken off his hat. Twice the fine horses galloped along the edge of the river, once from La Traverse to Les Foulons, and from Les Foulons back to La Traverse. "The fresh air will clear my head, and then I shall go home," Augustin kept telling himself, as though saying a prayer. But the sight of the angry river and the waves dashing against the shore and along the wooden quays, instead of calming him, plunged him into a vague melancholy to which he gradually yielded. "I am losing ground," he thought, "delivered over without my consent to this overwhelming nostalgia. It is frightening."

At the entrance of the Café Louis XIV, a tall fellow was staggering onto the street. Augustin would have liked to hug him as a brother and tell him that his own worthless soul was still miraculously intact beneath the fine clothes and good manners, which were only an imposture and a masquerade. When the carriage entered the little street of Sous-le-Cap for the second time, Augustin was carried away by an infinite tenderness, as though a painful vein had burst, giving free passage to his whole injured childhood. "My damned childhood is coming up in my throat," he muttered angrily to himself.

Washing was hanging out everywhere on clotheslines stretched across the narrow street. Women in aprons were chatting on the door-steps, and dirty children watched as the carriage passed. One of them picked up a stone and threw it at the team with all his strength but it missed, and ricocheted off the fender of the carriage. When Augustin turned around, the mother was slapping the child vigorously.

The shop of the shoemaker Jean-Baptiste Berthelot was no longer there, nor was the tiny back-shop that his mother had transformed into a laundry. But nothing could stop the acrid odour of old shoes and wet laundry from encroaching upon the elegant young man in the light carriage.

"Don't touch!" A fine refrain. A fine childhood, between these two beings riveted to their ill-paying jobs and the worries over their livelihood. The child between them was only an annoying distraction that took away their precious time, already so devoured by the few hours required for sleep and the brief, insufficient, and silent time taken for meals. He had suffocated then, with neither living-space nor love. The awl, the wax-end, the boot-trees, the needles; the iron, the fine linens, the coarse linens, the soap. Why couldn't one make a game of it? Or a song? Couldn't one laugh a little? Just to see? "Don't touch! Don't touch! Don't touch, or your face will sting!"

As Augustin went by, the old quarter stirred, became sensitive like the needle of a compass. It was within him that it lived, moved, and suffered and bent beneath the affront. La rue Sous-le-Cap found its North through him as though the heart of the child had become this living point, this epicentre of tears and powerless rage. No, he could not stand it. "Let this boy throw stones at my carriage. Too bad for him. Let them slap him, and then let him wipe his nose. Let him get out of it himself. What can I do about it? Each one in his turn has to choose life or death."

Augustin urged the coachman to go faster, as though a mob of avenging children were threatening to jump into the carriage, to crush it beneath their weight, and drag Augustin with them, back to la rue Sous-le-Cap, delivering him utterly confused, unmasked, to misery and shame.

"Faster, Hormisdas! Every man for himself. I will have nothing to do with that child throwing stones at us. I will have nothing to do with that woman hanging around my neck. Love is a trap! And so is pity!"

When they had gone some distance, the horses slowed down. The shore was deserted, the river foamed in the distance. Augustin now felt the same joyous sense of liberation he used to have as a boy, when he imagined magnificent voyages towards some unknown country, there to be master and king.

But the dreams of the child Augustin had been divided; willingly, he would leave the good, strong smells of oil, tar, water, and wood for carriage rides along the Terrasse and the Place de la Basilique, where the Upper and Lower Towns provided a mutual spectacle for each other on Sundays and holidays.

He had made his first choice when he was twelve years old. Canon Painchaud had thought he discerned a religious vocation for the child, who was of a studious disposition and who seemed to revel in the sumptuousness of the Basilica; but Augustin had not felt the slightest attraction to this vocation. The Canon had offered to finance the higher studies of the son of Jean-Baptiste Berthelot at both the Petit and the Grand Séminaire. The boy had looked the canon in the eye, and to the great surprise of the latter had asked to think about it until the next day before giving his answer. But in the child's mind, the following irrepressible answer had arisen immediately: "Anything to escape from la rue Sous-le-Cap, from the shoeleather and the washing. Anything, to study and master the unjust laws of the world, even to appropriating them in their injustice in order to live. Anything, rather than die here among the defeated." The following morning, Augustin replied to Canon Painchaud that "he would like very much to study for the clergy."

Wearing a peaked cap, a long tunic, and a large, green belt drawn around his waist, like a bishop, Augustin began his classical studies. His curiosity, power of concentration, and working capacity were tremendous. He paid particular attention to the study of the English language, which his comrades, who were devoted to the gratuitous beauty of Greek and Latin, treated with disdain. "If the dead languages lead towards the humanities and to God, I prefer the English language, which is alive. And if I am clever, I shall be able to deal effectively in English, which is, above all other tongues, the mistress of the goods of this world."

The shoemaker had died first, and then, a few months later, the laundress mother. Augustin was called to the notary, who informed him that the shoe-repair shop and the kitchen-laundry had reverted to him upon the death of his parents. But in order to dispose of these miserable possessions, he would have to await his majority.

The young man was then nineteen years of age and had finished his first year in philosophy at the Petit Séminaire. He looked forward with dread to the grand ceremonies at the end of the term, especially the selection of the ribbons, by which each student officially proclaimed his choice of a liberal profession or a religious vocation.

For Augustin, the dice seemed to be loaded. All freedom of choice was reduced to a single alternative: secular orders or monastic orders. Canon Painchaud's decision. But Augustin's own mute and guarded resolve was nonetheless made and had been for a long time, during all those years of austere and monotonous study. When the ribbons were chosen, he announced in a voice filled with defiance that he had decided to study law.

A fine scandal in the old hall, and in the heart of the Canon Augustin was called an "ingrate, a hypocrite." The offended and embittered benefactor withdrew his gracious favour and refused to defray the costs of legal studies.

Augustin left the Seminary the next day. He sold his books and, his belongings in a bundle on his shoulders, went to the notary, Cyrille Desnoyers. Mastering his uncertainty with difficulty, for he feared not to be taken seriously, the young man ordered the notary to sell the house on la rue Sous-le-Cap and to place the money as advantageously as he could. The notary, as much amused at such juvenile audacity as he was overcome by the unquenchable self-confidence on the strong and serious face of the adolescent, remarked to himself that looking after the affairs of Augustin Berthelot certainly did not resemble any other routine trusteeship. Augustin felt that he had just won a point. He retrieved a child-like smile, well aware of its seductive effect. Then, in a voice husky with apprehension and pride, he requested an advance of five dollars on his parental inheritance, to which Cyrille Desnoyers acquiesced at once.

The next day, Augustin was washing down the decks of the schooner Sancta-Maria, on his way to Hudson Bay. Already they had reached Cap-à-l'Aigle, and the wild, dark shores, flanked with black spruce and fir, appeared through the rain and mist like a wall cast there by an evil spell. Oh, the country was well-guarded! But Augustin swore to conquer it and to carry out his destiny. What did he care for the limitless wilderness? He dreamed of conquering a little town perched on a cliff. "In ten years I will return to Québec and I will be its master!"

The coach had stopped and the driver, in consternation, was wiping the sweat-soaked necks of the horses. "Too much galloping is bad. Too much galloping is bad. It's crazy to force such beautiful animals to run like that!"

The little park of Notre-Dame-des-Victoires was deserted. Augustin called out to him to water the team at the watering-trough. Gusts of wind swept over the dead leaves and bits of paper. The horses' drinking made a strange, arhythmic counterpoint in the silence. Augustin stretched his legs. He passed his hand over his forehead, as though to dismiss a nightmare, and was surprised to find himself without a hat. "I've had enough of this running around. Let us go home. I am tired, mired, and expired." But the great pleasure he took in the sound of these words gave way immediately to a drunken sadness. He repeated, but now without pleasure, "Tired, mired, expired. . . This damned drinking is addling my brains. Bah! Alcohol passes off without leaving a trace. Like the taste we might have for a certain woman. Love is a sickness, when it is finished, it is completely finished!" Augustin looked at the grey river, fringed with foam. "The best thing to do would be to leave. But I am bound now to this town of my childhood, voluntarily bound to it; and I will dig my burrow here with my teeth if necessary...I am finished with the North, the endless grey waters, the ungracious earth frozen like the moon; fur clothing as greasy on the inside as sardines, savage dogs with blue eyes, and the singular summer with the soft moss underfoot, the rocky landscape, the May days blinding with light, and the woman with the strong odour, who gives herself, and will not take herself back..."

"What do we do now, sir? What do we do now?" The strained voice of the coachman whined, as though he were on the verge of tears.

"We are going home, nitwit! Home!"

The clock of Notre-Dame-des-Victoires struck six. The notion of time returned to him, slowly: it embittered him, and he felt irritated with himself. "A whole afternoon lost!" Augustin tasted the acrid flavour of a bad conscience. But his head on the block, he would have insisted that his only regret was that he had wasted an afternoon in alcoholic dreams. "Bah! a couple of pills and some black coffee, and it will all be over, including the headache," he tried to persuade himself. But the image of the Indian woman clung to him tightly and repeated to his face: "You promised. You swore to it, in the name of Christ and the Church. You swore by the medal."

Augustin reasoned with himself, enumerating his goods and holdings, his hold on real life, in self-defence against this insidious woman's voice within him: rue des Remparts, the Holt Howard Company, the Hudson's Bay Company, François-Xavier de Lachevrotière, the Saint-Joachim manor. His life was in good order. Woe unto the dreamer who crosses the forbidden zone of the past.

"Home, Hormisdas! and don't forget to stop at the pharmacy for some tablets."

The team turned around. Augustin closed his eyes, and a kind of game began in his weary head, a game in which the horses and carriage rolled along an imaginary narrow road from which all cross-roads were being carefully eliminated.

Irritated by the harsh, grating sound of an ill-greased axle, Augustin opened his eyes. On the steps of the church was a human form huddled in a blanket, stone-still. But now it suddenly rose up. Augustin stopped the carriage, leapt down and went straight to the mass of clothing from which emerged a head as smooth as that of a bird.

"Might as well know what's going on and be ready for anything." With these words, Augustin found again the simple heart of the young, ambitious fighter, washed clean of self-reproach and free from all obstacles, ready to engage in a new adventure and emerge the victor, come what may.

The woman was as still as death. She looked at him without seeing, her large eyes set in a compact face the colour of old brick. The hard line of the cheekbone, the well-defined upper lip, the slightly violet colour of the clenched mouth, all expressed nothing—nothing but a long-drawn, stubborn, and intolerable fatigue. Augustin took her arm. She neither flinched nor fended him off, unfeeling and hard in the gusts of wind. He could feel the bone of her forearm through the fabric. For a moment he thought she would topple over, without moving a joint, with the dull sound of a dead tree.

"But how did you manage to get here?" he asked.

She stiffened with all her strength, as though all the evil impulse of her irrational voyage were newly alerted and massed with overwhelming violence for a renewed assault. Then she shivered from head to foot. But she did not reply. No doubt she would never speak of the several thousand miles she had journeyed, in spite of and through all obstacles: in solitude or according to the good will of such travelling companions as a missionary, a trapper or sailor, over land and by water, by the most diverse and rudimentary means of transportation, often on foot, hounded by the fear of losing her way on the plains, or in the forest, devoured by insects; confronting cold, frost, and wind, the great sun, prey to wild animals and to chance encounters with other human beings, suffering hunger, thirst, filth, with the patience and the fanatic strength of one who is craving for life.

The cruelty of this adventure and the fierce energy that had driven her were so evident, so stamped upon her features, that for a moment Augustin was lost in admiration of the wild flame which had thus burned his former mistress to the bone.

Délia would have collapsed on the steps of the church if Augustin had not taken her in his arms, recovering his self-possession and summoning the coachman to bring up the carriage.

At the Hôtel-Dieu, Augustin obtained a small room in an out-of-the way corner of the hospital for Délia. For two weeks, the Métis hovered between life and death. She seemed to be struggling between a heavy silence which suffocated her and a wild impulse to scream which she could scarcely restrain. Sister Claire, whose mission it was to watch over her and to take down her least words, was astonished at the feverish silence to which the young woman continued to cling.

Augustin himself did not go to see her. He delegated Canon Painchaud, after explaining the whole story to him. That is, that he had lived with this woman for ten years, that he no doubt had loved her, but that what now complicated the whole matter was the senseless promise he had made to marry her. He had evoked the tradition of the Catholic Church which permits a man and a woman to live together in isolated regions where there is no priest, on condition that they unite according to the laws of the Church and of God when circumstances permit. Délia was a Christian, and she had not yielded to Augustin until they both had sworn to marry in proper form. Canon Painchaud stormed at Augustin's rashness and against the weaknesses of the flesh which had led him to such a poor bargain, one which promised such poor returns. Was not scandal one of the greatest of evils, and did not Augustin now risk spreading it like the fires of evil joy to the four corners of the town? It was absolutely necessary that the Métis return whence she came, and as swiftly as possible, without having the opportunity to speak to anyone in the town.

Neither the Canon's dignified manner nor the silver cross he held out to her, which she kissed with respect and veneration, made any impression on Délia.

When the Canon began to explain softly, covering his cruel words with the most pious sweetness, Délia closed her eyes and turned her head towards the wall, while the honeyed voice whispered horrible things to her: that Augustin was married, according to the laws of God and the Church, to a young woman in high society; that they were an ideal Christian couple, distinguished, dignified, and above reproach; that no one and nothing could separate those whom God had thus united by the sacred bonds of marriage. As for Délia, she could only forget her regrettable past, and return to her own part of the country like a good Christian, submitting to the inscrutable decrees of God and respectful of them. Who knows but that one day a good Christian half-breed, touched by charity, might be disposed to overlook this unfortunate adventure at Hudson Bay and marry Délia, quite simply? Nothing is lost when one has faith in God.

But the young woman's stubborn silence filled the whole room with the immense weight of refusal and distrust. The Canon breathed heavily. He felt too warm, and kept wiping his forehead. Embarrassed and exasperated, he got up and left the room precipitately. He had obtained neither a word nor a glance from Délia.

The Canon sought to find peace, pacing the vaulted corridors of the Hôtel-Dieu, reassuring himself methodically, as though reciting a sermon to himself. Scandal had at last fallen upon them; this he felt with a biting certainty. But so far, only one half-breed woman had been struck by the shock, and if it could deflect God's wrath, the town might yet be spared. But shame took such a firm hold on the Canon's heart that he began to fear a resurgence of all his own past weaknesses. "I wash my hands of it. Let Augustin get out of it himself. Let him play his own game, my stakes have already been too high."

When Augustin entered the little white room and closed the heavy oak door behind him, he was unable to take another step and stood motionless, leaning against the door. Pity welled up in his heart for an instant, like a threat. Délia arose. She stood there, holding close to her chest the flowered dressing-gown which had been given her, and which was too large for her. Augustin spoke in brief phrases, clear and distinct, like a lesson he had learned. His speech was broken by heavy silences.

Délia was crying softly, the great cry of delusion so long restrained, now melting into a torrent of infantile tears. She kept repeating: "You promised. You swore to me in the name of Christ and the Church. Remember — you swore on the medal."

Augustin found again, with Délia's tears, the great force of his own will, as though a dark god in his heart were fortifying its complete insensitivity.

Augustin's attitude, the unassailable fact of his marriage to Mademoiselle de Lachevrotière, and Délia's own almost superstitious respect for any pledge sanctioned by the Church left her with no other defence than the despairing resolve not to lose sight of Augustin, and to live henceforth in this city of Québec so that she might catch sight of him sometimes, even if only from a street-corner. She would find work, and no one could stop her from living where she wanted, within the orbit of this man who had possessed and destroyed her.

Neither the Canon nor Augustin could pierce Délia's resolve. And the Upper Town continued to function at its own rhythm of work and idleness, while here and there boredom sowed its evil seed — quickly to be stifled. No one could have said just how it happened, but one day Délia, the Métis from the Far North, entered into the service of Madame Augustin Berthelot, who for several months had been much annoyed by the unreliability of her servants.

At this news, the Canon attempted, without much conviction, to play the game, in the hope of bestowing a more noble interpretation on this turn of events. Doubtful and ironic, he congratulated Augustin on his charitable spirit in providing his former mistress with bed, board, and work.

Weeks passed, and during this time Délia learned her duties under Madame Berthelot's high-handed guidance. Then there happened what had to happen: one Sunday, when Marie-Louise was visiting her parents, Augustin knocked at Délia's room, at the far end of a tiny hallway, far from the servants' quarters, that section of the attic reserved as a storage room for garlands of fine onions, pyramids of orange pumpkin, and barrels of sour apples.

Délia greeted Augustin without apparent joy; her pride and faith were still too shaken; but already in her heart she was overwhelmed, suffocated by the irrepressible gift of herself which she could not refrain from offering, again and again, to this man whom she now loved with the bitter taste of tears. Calmly undressing, she pulled off the silver chain with the medal of Our Lady, which she had never before removed.

Délia never again wore the chain with the medal, thus abandoning all prayer and recourse to God's help, entering at once into a life of shameful love. No power of Heaven or Earth could ever restore her lost pride.

As for Augustin, he found his taste for Délia as whole and quick as when he had first taken her as a tall and sinewy girl of sixteen. During the time she had been at the Hôtel-Dieu, and since then at the Berthelots', the young woman had recovered, she had filled out like certain plants after a storm. The scent of her hair and her firm, brown body inflamed Augustin, and he could not leave off caressing her. The young man told himself that one could always make arrangements, provided one were willing to pay the price. Happy that love had been restored to him, he could nevertheless think of the contract he had prepared so meticulously, with which he expected to trip up Holt Howard and Company's most astute customer the following day.

It was about this time that peace seemed to settle upon the Berthelot household on la rue des Remparts. Marie-Louise had just borne a son, who was baptised with great pomp at the Basilica, with the name of Augustin-de-Lachevrotière Berthelot. The young father had just established himself in business on his own account in an elegant shop on la rue Fabrique.

Did Marie-Louise know about her husband's nocturnal visits to the garret? The question never arose between them. But on the evening of the baptism, after the guests had gone and the last traces of the reception had been carefully removed by Délia, with the help of the chambermaid and the handy-boy, Marie-Louise and Augustin made a pact: now that an heir had been born to them, they agreed that any further conjugal relations between them were pointless and indecent. The young wife made her conditions in such a threatening tone that Augustin was convinced that she was aware of the whole situation, and was much relieved to pass on certain duties to her servant.

Years passed. When Marie-Louise accompanied her husband on social occasions, she radiated grace and serene joy. Her migraines had disappeared forever. Everyone remarked that she had bloomed in marriage, and that a couple so well-matched were a credit to any gathering in which they chose to take part. Augustin, always calm and sure of himself, was also greatly admired, as much for his superb deportment as for his abstinence from alcohol.

Canon Painchaud did not take well to old age; he became stiffer and stiffer. He had caught a bad conscience from his interview with Délia, and the disease was incurable. And if by chance the good manners that prevailed in the town were praised (for there was nothing that could give rise to the slightest reproach, so well did the public behaviour of the wealthy prevent the truth from coming to light) the Canon would think, in impotent anger: "What a hoax, this business of self-knowledge and the understanding of others. What is the use of knowing that I am a rotter and that others are, too? It changes nothing within any of us. And such a cold realization is dearly bought with my lost peace of mind."

This sharp thorn clinging to the old heart of the Canon pained him most at Christmas and at Easter, when the Basilica, perfumed with incense, glowing with light, and resounding to the chords of the great organ and the strong voices of the church choir, emptied its swarms of the faithful into the aisles leading to the Holy Table.

The entire Berthelot household kneeled for communion in the proper order: first the masters, father, mother, and child, then the domestics according to seniority—Clémée, the cook, who had a moustache and had used up two husbands; Hormisdas, the coachman, who managed to refrain from using his elbows to make progress more rapidly; Louisette, the chambermaid, who held mankind—particularly men—in abhorrence; and Jos, the handyman, who took pleasure in the cracking of his shoes on the deserted aisle.

Only Délia, the Métis, remained in her pew, kneeling on the prayer-stool, her head in her hands. Neither the threats nor the pleas of Augustin, nor his exasperated anger, could sway her. Her sole demand, to which she stuck, with all her strength, as though it were all that remained of her honour, was a refusal to take communion for fear of committing an imposture towards the God who had abandoned her.

Anne Hébert (1916-) was born at Sainte-Catherine de Fossambault, Quebec, and now lives in France. She has published several collections of poems, and has won Governor General's Awards for *Poemes* (1960) and for her recent novel *Les Enfants du sabbat*. Her best-known novel is *Kamouraska*; two collections of her short stories, *The Torrent* and *The Silent Rooms,* have been published in English.

Alistair MacLeod
The Boat

There are times even now, when I awake at four o'clock in the morning with
the terrible fear that I have overslept; when I imagine that my father is
waiting for me in the room below the darkened stairs or that the shorebound
men are tossing pebbles against my window while blowing their hands and
stomping their feet impatiently on the frozen steadfast earth. There are
times when I am half out of bed and fumbling for socks and mumbling for
words before I realize that I am foolishly alone, that no one waits at the base
of the stairs and no boat rides restlessly in the waters by the pier.

At such times only the grey corpses on the overflowing ashtray beside my
bed bear witness to the extinction of the latest spark and silently await the
crushing out of the most recent of their fellows. And then because I am
afraid to be alone with death, I dress rapidly, make a great to-do about
clearing my throat, turn on both faucets in the sink and proceed to make
loud splashing ineffectual noises. Later I go out and walk the mile to the all-
night restaurant.

In the winter it is a very cold walk and there are often tears in my eyes
when I arrive. The waitress usually gives a sympathetic shiver and says,
"Boy, it must be really cold out there; you got tears in your eyes."

"Yes," I say, "it sure is; it really is."

And then the three or four of us who are always in such places at such
times make uninteresting little protective chit-chat until the dawn reluctantly arrives. Then I swallow the coffee which is always bitter and leave with a
great busy rush because by that time I have to worry about being late and
whether I have a clean shirt and whether my car will start and about all the
other countless things one must worry about when he teaches at a great Mid-
western university. And I know then that that day will go by as have all the
days of the past ten years, for the call and the voices and the shapes and the
boat were not really there in the early morning's darkness and I have all

kinds of comforting reality to prove it. They are only shadows and echoes, the animals a child's hands make on the wall by lamplight, and the voices from the rain barrel; the cuttings from an old movie made in the black and white of long ago.

I first became conscious of the boat in the same way and at almost the same time that I became aware of the people it supported. My earliest recollection of my father is a view from the floor of gigantic rubber boots and then of being suddenly elevated and having my face pressed against the stubble of his cheek, and of how it tasted of salt and of how he smelled of salt from his red-soled rubber boots to the shaggy whiteness of his hair.

When I was very small, he took me for my first ride in the boat. I rode the half-mile from our house to the wharf on his shoulders and I remember the sound of his rubber boots galumphing along the gravel beach, the tune of the indecent little song he used to sing, and the odour of the salt.

The floor of the boat was permeated with the same odour and in its constancy I was not aware of change. In the harbour we made our little circle and returned. He tied the boat by its painter, fastened the stern to its permanent anchor and lifted me high over his head to the solidity of the wharf. Then he climbed up the little iron ladder that led to the wharf's cap, placed me once more upon his shoulders, and galumphed off again.

When we returned to the house everyone made a great fuss over my precocious excursion and asked, "How did you like the boat?" "Were you afraid in the boat?" "Did you cry in the boat?" They repeated "the boat" at the end of all their questions and I knew it must be very important to everyone.

My earliest recollection of my mother is of being alone with her in the mornings while my father was away in the boat. She seemed to be always repairing clothes that were "torn by the boat," preparing food "to be eaten in the boat" or looking for "the boat" through our kitchen window which faced upon the sea. When my father returned about noon, she would ask, "Well, how did things go in the boat today?" It was the first question I remember asking, "Well, how did things go in the boat today?" "Well, how did things go in the boat today?"

The boat in our lives was registered at Port Hawkesbury. She was what Nova Scotians called a Cape Island boat and was designed for the small inshore fishermen who sought the lobsters of the spring and the mackerel of the summer and later the cod and haddock and hake. She was thirty-two feet long and nine wide, and was powered by an engine from a Chevrolet truck. She had a marine clutch and a high-speed reverse gear and was painted light green with the name *Jenny Lynn* stencilled in black letters on her bow and painted on an oblong plate across her stern. Jenny Lynn had been my mother's maiden name and the boat was called after her as another link in the chain of tradition. Most of the boats that berthed at the wharf bore the names of some female member of their owner's household.

I say this now as if I knew it all then. All at once, all about boat dimensions and engines, and as if on the day of my first childish voyage I noticed the difference between a stencilled name and a painted name. But of course it was not that way at all, for I learned it all very slowly and there was not time enough.

I learned first about our house which was one of about fifty which marched around the horseshoe of our harbour and the wharf which was its heart. Some of them were so close to the water that during a storm the sea spray splashed against their windows while others were built farther along the beach as was the case with ours. The houses and their people, like those of the neighbouring towns and villages, were the result of Ireland's discontent and Scotland's Highland Clearances and America's War of Independence. Impulsive emotional Catholic Celts who could not bear to live with England and shrewd determined Protestant Puritans who, in the years after 1776, could not bear to live without.

The most important room in our house was one of those oblong old-fashioned kitchens heated by a wood- and coal-burning stove. Behind the stove was a box of kindlings and beside it a coal scuttle. A heavy wooden table with leaves that expanded or reduced its dimensions stood in the middle of the floor. There were five wooden homemade chairs which had been chipped and hacked by a variety of knives. Against the east wall, opposite the stove, there was a couch which sagged in the middle and had a cushion for a pillow, and above it a shelf which contained matches, tobacco, pencils, odd fish hooks, bits of twine, and a tin can filled with bills and receipts. The south wall was dominated by a window which faced the sea and on the north there was a five-foot board which bore a variety of clothes hooks and the burdens of each. Beneath the board there was a jumble of odd footwear, mostly of rubber. There was also, on this wall, a barometer, a map of the marine area, and a shelf which held a tiny radio. The kitchen was shared by all of us and was a buffer zone between the immaculate order of ten other rooms and the disruptive chaos of the single room that was my father's.

My mother ran her house as her brothers ran their boats. Everything was clean and spotless and in order. She was tall and dark and powerfully energetic. In later years she reminded me of the women of Thomas Hardy, particularly Eustacia Vye, in a physical way. She fed and clothed a family of seven children, making all of the meals and most of the clothes. She grew miraculous gardens and magnificent flowers and raised broods of hens and ducks. She would walk miles on berry-picking expeditions and hoist her skirts to dig for clams when the tide was low. She was fourteen years younger than my father, whom she had married when she was twenty-six, and had been a local beauty for a period of ten years. My mother was of the sea as were all of her people, and her horizons were the very literal one she scanned with her dark and fearless eyes.

Between the kitchen clothes rack and barometer a door opened into my father's bedroom. It was a room of disorder and disarray. It was as if the wind which so often clamoured about the house succeeded in entering this single room and after whipping it into turmoil stole quietly away to renew its knowing laughter from without.

My father's bed was against the south wall. It always looked rumpled and unmade because he lay on top of it more than he slept within any folds it might have had. Beside it, there was a little brown table. An archaic goose-necked reading light, a battered table radio, a mound of wooden matches, one or two packages of tobacco, a deck of cigarette papers, and an overflowing ashtray cluttered its surface. The brown larvae of tobacco shreds and the grey flecks of ash covered both the table and the floor beneath it. The once-varnished surface of the table was disfigured by numerous black scars and gashes inflicted by the neglected burning cigarettes of many years. They had tumbled from the ashtray unnoticed and branded their statements permanently and quietly into the wood until the odour of their burning caused the snuffing-out of their lives. At the bed's foot there was a single window which looked upon the sea.

Against the adjacent wall there was a battered bureau and beside it there was a closet which held his single ill-fitting serge suit, the two or three white shirts that strangled him and the square black shoes that pinched. When he took off his more friendly clothes, the heavy woollen sweaters, mitts, and socks which my mother knitted for him and the woollen and doeskin shirts, he dumped them unceremoniously on a single chair. If a visitor entered the room while he was lying on the bed, he would be told to throw the clothes on the floor and take their place upon the chair.

Magazines and books covered the bureau and competed with the clothes for domination of the chair. They further overburdened the heroic little table and lay on top of the radio. They filled a baffling and unknowable cave beneath the bed, and in the corner by the bureau they spilled from the walls and grew up from the floor.

The magazines were the most conventional: *Time, Newsweek, Life, Maclean's, The Family Herald, The Reader's Digest.* They were the result of various cut-rate subscriptions or of the gift subscriptions associated with Christmas, "the two whole years for only $3.50."

The books were more varied. There were a few hard-cover magnificents and bygone Book of the Month wonders and some were Christmas or birthday gifts. The majority of them, however, were used paperbacks which came from those second-hand bookstores which advertise in the backs of magazines: "Miscellaneous Used Paperbacks 10¢ Each." At first he sent for them himself, although my mother resented the expense, but in later years they came more and more often from my sisters who had moved to the cities. Especially at first they were very weird and varied. Mickey Spillane and

Ernest Haycox vied with Dostoyevsky and Faulkner, and the Penguin Poets edition of Gerard Manley Hopkins arrived in the same box as a little book on sex technique called *Getting the Most Out of Love*. The former had been assiduously annotated by a very fine hand using a very blue-inked fountain pen, while the latter had been studied by someone with very large thumbs, the prints of which were still visible in the margins. At the slightest provocation it would open almost automatically to particularly graphic and well-smudged pages.

When he was not in the boat, my father spent most of his time lying on the bed in his socks, the top two buttons of his trousers undone, his discarded shirt on the everready chair and the sleeves of the woollen Stanfield underwear, which he wore both summer and winter, drawn halfway up to his elbows. The pillows propped up the whiteness of his head and the goose-necked lamp illuminated the pages in his hands. The cigarettes smoked and smouldered on the ashtray and on the table and the radio played constantly, sometimes low and sometimes loud. At midnight and at one, two, three and four, one could sometimes hear the radio, his occasional cough, the rustling thud of a completed book being tossed to the corner heap, or the movement necessitated by his sitting on the edge of the bed to roll the thousandth cigarette. He seemed never to sleep, only to doze, and the light shone constantly from his window to the sea.

My mother despised the room and all it stood for and she had stopped sleeping in it after I was born. She despised disorder in rooms and in houses and in hours and in lives, and she had not read a book since high school. There she had read *Ivanhoe* and considered it a colossal waste of time. Still the room remained, like a solid rock of opposition in the sparkling waters of a clear deep harbour, opening off the kitchen where we really lived our lives, with its door always open and its contents visible to all.

The daughters of the room and of the house were very beautiful. They were tall and willowy like my mother and had her fine facial features set off by the reddish copper-coloured hair that had apparently once been my father's before it turned to white. All of them were very clever in school and helped my mother a great deal about the house. When they were young they sang and were very happy and very nice to me because I was the youngest and the family's only boy.

My father never approved of their playing about the wharf like the other children, and they went there only when my mother sent them on an errand. At such times they almost always overstayed, playing screaming games of tag or hide-and-seek in and about the fishing shanties, the piled traps and tubs of trawl, shouting down to the perch that swam languidly about the wharf's algae-covered piles, or jumping in and out of the boats that tugged gently at their lines. My mother was never uneasy about them at such times, and when her husband criticized her she would say, "Nothing will happen to them there," or "They could be doing worse things in worse places."

By about the ninth or tenth grade my sisters one by one discovered my father's bedroom and then the change would begin. Each would go into the room one morning when he was out. She would go with the ideal hope of imposing order or with the more practical objective of emptying the ashtray, and later she would be found spellbound by the volume in her hand. My mother's reaction was always abrupt, bordering on the angry. "Take your nose out of that trash and come and do your work," she would say, and once I saw her slap my youngest sister so hard that the print of her hand was scarletly emblazoned upon her daughter's cheek while the broken-spined paperback fluttered uselessly to the floor.

Thereafter my mother would launch a campaign against what she had discovered but could not understand. At times, although she was not overly religious, she would bring in God to bolster her arguments saying, "In the next world God will see to those who waste their lives reading useless books when they should be about their work." Or without theological aid, "I would like to know how books help anyone to live a life." If my father were in, she would repeat the remarks louder than necessary, and her voice would carry into his room where he lay upon his bed. His usual reaction was to turn up the volume of the radio, although that action in itself betrayed the success of the initial thrust.

Shortly after my sisters began to read the books, they grew restless and lost interest in darning socks and baking bread, and all of them eventually went to work as summer waitresses in the Sea Food Restaurant. The restaurant was run by a big American concern from Boston and catered to the tourists that flooded the area during July and August. My mother despised the whole operation. She said the restaurant was not run by "our people," and "our people" did not eat there, and that it was run by outsiders for outsiders.

"Who are these people anyway?" she would ask, tossing back her dark hair, "and what do they, though they go about with their cameras for a hundred years, know about the way it is here, and what do they care about me and mine, and why should I care about them?"

She was angry that my sisters should even conceive of working in such a place and more angry when my father made no move to prevent it, and she was worried about herself and about her family and about her life. Sometimes she would say softly to her sisters, "I don't know what's the matter with my girls. It seems none of them are interested in any of the right things." And sometimes there would be bitter savage arguments. One afternoon I was coming in with three mackerel I'd been given at the wharf when I heard her say, "Well I hope you'll be satisfied when they come home knocked up and you'll have had your way."

It was the most savage thing I'd ever heard my mother say. Not just the words but the way she said them, and I stood there in the porch afraid to breathe for what seemed like the years from ten to fifteen, feeling the damp moist mackerel with their silver glassy eyes growing clammy against my leg.

Through the angle in the screen door I saw my father, who had been walking into his room, wheel around on one of his rubber-booted heels and look at her with his blue eyes flashing like clearest ice beneath the snow that was his hair. His usually ruddy face was drawn and grey, reflecting the exhaustion of a man of sixty-five who had been working in those rubber boots for eleven hours on an August day, and for a fleeting moment I wondered what I would do if he killed my mother while I stood there in the porch with those three foolish mackerel in my hand. Then he turned and went into his room and the radio blared forth the next day's weather forecast and I retreated under the noise and returned again, stamping my feet and slamming the door too loudly to signal my approach. My mother was busy at the stove when I came in, and did not raise her head when I threw the mackerel in a pan. As I looked into my father's room, I said, "Well, how did things go in the boat today?" and he replied, "Oh, not too badly, all things considered." He was lying on his back and lighting the first cigarette and the radio was talking about the Virginia coast.

All of my sisters made good money on tips. They bought my father an electric razor which he tried to use for a while, and they took out even more magazine subscriptions. They bought my mother a great many clothes of the type she was very fond of, the wide-brimmed hats and the brocaded dresses, but she locked them all in trunks and refused to wear any of them.

On one August day my sisters prevailed upon my father to take some of their restaurant customers for an afternoon ride in the boat. The tourists with their expensive clothes and cameras and sun glasses awkwardly backed down the iron ladder at the wharf's side to where my father waited below, holding the rocking *Jenny Lynn* in snug against the wharf with one hand on the iron ladder and steadying his descending passengers with the other. They tried to look both prim and wind-blown like the girls in the Pepsi-Cola ads and did the best they could, sitting on the thwarts where the newspapers were spread to cover the splattered blood and fish entrails, crowding to one side so that they were in danger of capsizing the boat, taking the inevitable pictures or merely trailing their fingers through the water of their dreams.

All of them liked my father very much and, after he'd brought them back from their circles in the harbour, they invited him to their rented cabins which were located high on a hill overlooking the village to which they were so alien. He proceeded to get very drunk up there with the beautiful view and the strange company and the abundant liquor, and late in the afternoon he began to sing.

I was just approaching the wharf to deliver my mother's summons when he began, and the familiar yet unfamiliar voice that rolled down from the cabins made me feel as I never felt before in my young life or perhaps as I had always felt without really knowing it, and I was ashamed yet proud, young yet old and saved yet forever lost, and there was nothing I could do to control my legs which trembled nor my eyes which wept for what they could not tell.

The tourists were equipped with tape recorders and my father sang for more than three hours. His voice boomed down the hill and bounced off the surface of the harbour, which was an unearthly blue on that hot August day, and was then reflected to the wharf and the fishing shanties where it was absorbed amidst the men who were baiting their lines for the next day's haul.

He sang all the old sea chanties which had come across from the old world and by which men like him had pulled ropes for generations, and he sang the East Coast sea songs which celebrated the sealing vessels of Northumberland Strait and the long liners of the Grand Banks, and of Anticosti, Sable Island, Grand Manan, Boston Harbor, Nantucket, and Block Island. Gradually he shifted to the seemingly unending Gaelic drinking songs with their twenty or more verses and inevitable refrains, and the men in the shanties smiled at the coarseness of some of the verses and at the thought the the singer's immediate audience did not know what they were applauding nor recording to take back to staid old Boston. Later as the sun was setting he switched to the laments and the wild and haunting Gaelic war songs of those spattered Highland ancestors he had never seen, and when his voice ceased, the savage melancholy of three hundred years seemed to hang over the peaceful harbour and the quiet boats and the men leaning in the doorways of their shanties with their cigarettes glowing in the dusk and the women looking to the sea from their open windows with their children in their arms.

When he came home he threw the money he had earned on the kitchen table as he did with all his earnings but my mother refused to touch it and the next day he went with the rest of the men to bait his trawl in the shanties. The tourists came to the door that evening and my mother met them there and told them that her husband was not in although he was lying on the bed only a few feet away with the radio playing and the cigarette upon his lips. She stood in the doorway until they reluctantly went away.

In the winter they sent him a picture which had been taken on the day of the singing. On the back it said, "To Our Ernest Hemingway" and the "Our" was underlined. There was also an accompanying letter telling how much they had enjoyed themselves, how popular the tape was proving, and explaining who Ernest Hemingway was. In a way it almost did look like one of those unshaven, taken in Cuba pictures of Hemingway. He looked both massive and incongruous in the setting. His bulky fisherman's clothes were too big for the green and white lawn chair in which he sat, and his rubber boots seemed to take up all of the well-clipped grass square. The beach umbrella jarred with his sunburned face and because he had already been singing for some time, his lips which chapped in the winds of spring and burned in the water glare of summer had already cracked in several places producing tiny flecks of blood at their corners and on the whiteness of his teeth. The bracelets of brass chain which he wore to protect his wrists from chafing seemed abnormally large and his broad leather belt had been slackened and his heavy shirt and underwear were open at the throat revealing an uncultivated wilderness of white chest hair bordering on the semi-controlled stubble of his neck and chin. His blue eyes had looked directly into the camera and his hair was whiter than the two tiny clouds which hung over his left shoulder. The sea was behind him and its immense blue flatness stretched out to touch the arching blueness of the sky. It seemed very far away from him or else he was so much in the foreground that he seemed too big for it.

Each year another of my sisters would read the books and work in the restaurant. Sometimes they would stay out quite late on the hot summer nights and when they came up the stairs my mother would ask them many long and involved questions which they resented and tried to avoid. Before ascending the stairs they would go into my father's room and those of us who waited above could hear them throwing his clothes off the chair before sitting on it or the squeak of the bed as they sat on its edge. Sometimes they would talk to him a long time, the murmur of their voices blending with the music of the radio into a mysterious vapour-like sound which floated softly up the stairs.

I say this again as if it all happened at once and as if all of my sisters were of identical ages and like so many lemmings going into another sea and, again, it was of course not that way at all. Yet go they did, to Boston, to Montreal, to New York with the young men they met during the summers and later married in those far away cities. The young men were very articulate and handsome and wore fine clothes and drove expensive cars and my sisters, as I said, were very tall and beautiful with their copper-coloured hair and were tired of darning socks and baking bread.

One by one they went. My mother had each of her daughters for fifteen years, then lost them for two and finally forever. None married a fisherman. My mother never accepted any of the young men, for in her eyes they seemed always a combination of the lazy, the effeminate, the dishonest, and the unknown. They never seemed to do any physical work and she could not comprehend their luxurious vacations and she did not know from whence they came nor who they were. And in the end she did not really care, for they were not of her people and they were not of her sea.

I say this now with a sense of wonder at my own stupidity in thinking I was somehow free and would go on doing well in school and playing and helping in the boat and passing into my early teens while streaks of grey began to appear in my mother's dark hair and my father's rubber boots dragged sometimes on the pebbles of the beach as he trudged home from the wharf. And there were but three of us in the house that had at one time been so loud.

Then during the winter that I was fifteen he seemed to grow old and ill at once. Most of January he lay upon the bed, smoking and reading and listening to the radio while the wind howled about the house and the needle-like snow blistered off the ice-covered harbour and the doors flew out of people's hands if they did not cling to them like death.

In February when the men began overhauling their lobster traps he still did not move, and my mother and I began to knit lobster-trap headings in the evenings. The twine was as always very sharp and harsh, and blisters formed upon our thumbs and little paths of blood snaked quietly down between our fingers while the seals that had drifted down from distant Labrador wept and moaned like human children on the ice-floes of the Gulf.

In the daytime my mother's brother, who had been my father's partner as long as I could remember, also came to work upon the gear. He was a year older than my mother and was tall and dark and the father of twelve children.

By March we were very far behind and although I began to work very hard in the evenings I knew it was not hard enough and that there were but eight weeks left before the opening of the season on May first. And I knew that my mother worried and my uncle was uneasy and that all of our very lives depended on the boat being ready with her gear and two men, by the date of May the first. And I knew then that *David Copperfield* and *The Tempest* and all of those friends I had dearly come to love must really go forever. So I bade them all good-bye.

The night after my first full day at home and after my mother had gone upstairs he called me into his room where I sat upon the chair beside his bed. "You will go back tomorrow," he said simply.

I refused then, saying I had made my decision and was satisfied.

"That is no way to make a decision," he said, "and if you are satisfied I am not. It is best that you go back." I was almost angry then and told him as all children do that I wished he would leave me alone and stop telling me what to do.

He looked at me a long time then, lying there on the same bed on which he had fathered me those sixteen years before, fathered me his only son, out of who knew what emotions, when he was already fifty-six and his hair had turned to snow. Then he swung his legs over the edge of the squeaking bed and sat facing me and looked into my own dark eyes with his of crystal blue and placed his hand upon my knee. "I am not telling you to do anything," he said softly, "only asking you."

The next morning I returned to school. As I left, my mother followed me to the porch and said, "I never thought a son of mine would choose useless books over the parents that gave him life."

In the weeks that followed he got up rather miraculously and the gear was ready and the *Jenny Lynn* was freshly painted by the last two weeks of April when the ice began to break up and the lonely screaming gulls returned to haunt the silver herring as they flashed within the sea.

On the first day of May the boats raced out as they had always done, laden down almost to the gunwales with their heavy cargoes of traps. They were almost like living things as they plunged through the waters of the spring and manoeuvred between the still floating icebergs of crystal-white and emerald green on their way to the traditional grounds that they sought out every May. And those of us who sat that day in the High School on the hill, discussing the water imagery of Tennyson, watched them as they passed back and forth beneath us until by afternoon the piles of traps which had been stacked upon the wharf were no longer visible but were spread about the bottoms of the sea. And the *Jenny Lynn* went too, all day, with my uncle, tall and dark, like a latter-day Tashtego standing at the tiller with his legs wide apart and guiding her deftly between the floating pans of ice and my father in the stern standing in the same way with his hand upon the ropes that lashed the cargo to the deck. And at night my mother asked, "Well, how did things go in the boat today?"

And the spring wore on and the summer came and school ended in the third week of June and the lobster season on July first and I wished that the two things I loved so dearly did not exclude each other in a manner that was so blunt and too clear.

At the conclusion of the lobster season my uncle said he had been offered a berth on a deep sea dragger and had decided to accept. We all knew that he was leaving the *Jenny Lynn* forever and that before the next lobster season he would buy a boat of his own. He was expecting another child and would be supporting fifteen people by the next spring and could not chance my father against the family that he loved.

I joined my father then for the trawling season, and he made no protest and my mother was quite happy. Through the summer we baited the tubs of trawl in the afternoon and set them at sunset and revisited them in the darkness of the early morning. The men would come tramping by our house at 4:00 a.m. and we would join them and walk with them to the wharf and be on our way before the sun rose out of the ocean where it seemed to spend the night. If I was not up they would toss pebbles to my window and I would be very embarrassed and tumble downstairs to where my father lay fully clothed atop his bed, reading his book and listening to his radio and smoking his cigarette. When I appeared he would swing off his bed and put on his boots and be instantly ready and then we would take the lunches my mother had prepared the night before and walk off towards the sea. He would make no attempt to wake me himself.

It was in many ways a good summer. There were few storms and we were out almost every day and we lost a minimum of gear and seemed to land a maximum of fish and I tanned dark and brown after the manner of my uncles.

My father did not tan — he never tanned — because of his reddish complexion, and the salt water irritated his skin as it had for sixty years. He burned and reburned over and over again and his lips still cracked so that they bled when he smiled, and his arms, especially the left, still broke out into the oozing salt-water boils as they had ever since as a child I had first watched him soaking and bathing them in a variety of ineffectual solutions. The chafe-preventing bracelets of brass linked chain that all the men wore about their wrists in early spring were his the full season, and he shaved but painfully and only once a week.

And I saw then, that summer, many things that I had seen all my life as if for the first time and I thought that perhaps my father had never been intended for a fisherman either physically or mentally. At least not in the manner of my uncles; he had never really loved it. And I remembered that, one evening in his room when we were talking about *David Copperfield*, he had said that he had always wanted to go to the university and I had dismissed it then in the way one dismisses his father's saying he would like to be a tight-rope walker, and we had gone on to talk about the Peggotys and how they loved the sea.

And I thought then to myself that there were many things wrong with all of us and all our lives and I wondered why my father, who was himself an only son, had not married before he was forty and then I wondered why he had. I even thought that perhaps he had had to marry my mother and checked the dates on the flyleaf of the Bible where I learned that my oldest sister had been born a prosaic eleven months after the marriage, and I felt myself then very dirty and debased for my lack of faith and for what I had thought and done.

And then there came into my heart a very great love for my father and I thought it was very much braver to spend a life doing what you really do not want rather than selfishly following forever your own dreams and inclinations. And I knew then that I could never leave him alone to suffer the iron-tipped harpoons which my mother would forever hurl into his soul because he was a failure as a husband and a father who had retained none of his own. And I felt that I had been very small in a little secret place within me and that even the completion of high school was for me a silly shallow selfish dream.

So I told him one night very resolutely and very powerfully that I would remain with him as long as he lived and we would fish the sea together. And he made no protest but only smiled through the cigarette smoke that wreathed his bed and replied, "I hope you will remember what you've said."

The room was now so filled with books as to be almost Dickensian, but he would not allow my mother to move or change them and he continued to read them, sometimes two or three a night. They came with great regularity now, and there were more hard covers, sent by my sisters who had gone so long ago and now seemed so distant and so prosperous, and sent also pictures of small red-haired grandchildren with baseball bats and dolls which he placed upon his bureau and which my mother gazed at wistfully when she thought no one would see. Red-haired grandchildren with baseball bats and dolls who would never know the sea in hatred or in love.

And so we fished through the heat of August and into the cooler days of September when the water was so clear we could almost see the bottom and the white mists rose like delicate ghosts in the early morning dawn. And one day my mother said to me, "You have given added years to his life."

And we fished on into October when it began to roughen and we could no longer risk night sets but took our gear out each morning and returned at the first sign of the squalls; and on into November when we lost three tubs of trawl and the clear blue water turned to a sullen grey and the trochoidal waves rolled rough and high and washed across our bows and decks as we ran within their troughs. We wore heavy sweaters now and the awkward rubber slickers and the heavy woollen mitts which soaked and froze into masses of ice that hung from our wrists like the limbs of gigantic monsters until we thawed them against the exhaust pipe's heat. And almost every day we would leave for home before noon, driven by the blasts of the northwest wind, coating our eyebrows with ice and freezing our eyelids closed as we leaned into a visibility that was hardly there, charting our course from the compass and the sea, running with the waves and between them but never confronting their towering might.

And I stood at the tiller now, on these homeward lunges, stood in the place and in the manner of my uncle, turning to look at my father, and to shout over the roar of the engine and the slop of the sea to where he stood in the stern, drenched and dripping with the snow and the salt and the spray and his bushy eyebrows caked in ice. But on November twenty-first, when it seemed we might be making the final run of the season, I turned and he was not there and I knew even in that instant that he would never be again.

On November twenty-first the waves of the grey Atlantic are very very high and the waters are very cold and there are no signposts on the surface of the sea. You cannot tell where you have been five minutes before and in the squalls of snow you cannot see. And it takes longer than you would believe to check a boat that has been running before a gale and turn her ever so carefully in a wide and stupid circle, with timbers creaking and straining, back into the face of storm. And you know that it is useless and that your voice does not carry the length of the boat and that even if you knew the original spot, the relentless waves would carry such a burden perhaps a mile or so by the time you could return. And you know also, the final irony, that your father, like your uncles and all the men that form your past, cannot swim a stroke.

The lobster beds off the Cape Breton coast are still very rich and now, from May to July, their offerings are packed in crates of ice, and thundered by the gigantic transport trucks, day and night, through New Glasgow, Amherst, Saint John and Bangor and Portland and into Boston where they are tossed still living into boiling pots of water, their final home.

And though the prices are higher and the competition tighter, the grounds to which the *Jenny Lynn* once went remain untouched and unfished as they have for the last ten years. For if there are no signposts on the sea in storm there are certain ones in calm and the lobster bottoms were distributed in calm before any of us can remember and the grounds my father fished were those his father fished before him and there were others before and before and before. Twice the big boats have come from forty and fifty miles, lured by the promise of the grounds, and strewn the bottom with their traps, and twice they have returned to find their buoys cut adrift and their gear lost and destroyed. Twice the Fisheries Officer and the Mounted Police have come and asked many long and involved questions and twice they have received no answers from the men leaning in the doors of their shanties and the women standing at their windows with their children in their arms. Twice they have gone away saying: "There are no legal boundaries in the Marine area"; "No one can own the sea"; "Those grounds don't wait for anyone."

But the men and the women, with my mother dark among them, do not care for what they say, for to them the grounds are sacred and they think they wait for me.

It is not an easy thing to know that your mother lives alone on an inadequate insurance policy and that she is too proud to accept any other aid. And that she looks through her lonely window onto the ice of winter and the hot flat calm of summer and the rolling waves of fall. And that she lies awake in the early morning's darkness when the rubber boots of the men scrunch upon the gravel as they pass beside her house on their way down to the wharf. And she knows that the footsteps never stop, because no man goes from her house, and she alone of all the Lynns has neither son nor son-in-law that walks toward the boat that will take him to the sea. And it is not an easy thing to know that your mother looks upon the sea with love and on you with bitterness because the one has been so constant and the other so untrue.

But neither is it easy to know that your father was found on November twenty-eighth, ten miles to the north and wedged between two boulders at the base of the rock-strewn cliffs where he had been hurled and slammed so many many times. His hands were shredded ribbons as were his feet which had lost their boots to the suction of the sea, and his shoulders came apart in our hands when we tried to move him from the rocks. And the fish had eaten his testicles and the gulls had pecked out his eyes and the white-green stubble of his whiskers had continued to grow in death, like the grass on graves, upon the purple, bloated mass that was his face. There was not much left of my father, physically, as he lay there with the brass chains on his wrists and the seaweed in his hair.

Alistair MacLeod was born in Inverness County, Nova Scotia. He teaches English and Creative Writing at the University of Windsor, Ontario. His work has appeared in various journals in Canada and the United States. A collection of his fiction, *The Lost Salt Gift of Blood*, was published in 1976.

W.D. Valgardson
Bloodflowers

Danny Thorson saw Mrs. Poorwilly before he stepped off the freight boat onto Black Island. He couldn't have missed her. She was fat and had thick, heavy arms and legs. She stood at the front of the crowd with her hands on her hips.

"You the new teacher?" Mrs. Poorwilly said.

"Yes, I'm—"

Mrs. Poorwilly cut him off by waving her arm at him and saying, "Put your things on the wheelbarrow. Mr. Poorwilly will take them up to the house. Board and room is fifty a month. We're the only ones that give it. That's Mr. Poorwilly."

Mrs. Poorwilly waved her hand again, indicating a small man who was standing behind an orange wheelbarrow. He had a round, red face, and his hair was so thin and blond that from ten feet away he looked bald.

Danny piled his suitcases and boxes onto the wheelbarrow. He was tired and sore from the trip to the island. The bunk had been too short. The weather had been bad. For the first three days of the trip, he hadn't been able to hold anything down except coffee.

When the wheelbarrow was full, Mr. Poorwilly took his hands out of his pockets. They were twisted into two rigid pink hooks. He slipped them through two metal loops that had been nailed to the handles of the wheelbarrow, then lifted the barrow on his wrists.

At the top of the first rise, Mr. Poorwilly stopped. As if to reassure Danny, he said, "Mrs. Poorwilly's a good cook. We've got fresh eggs all winter, too."

Danny glanced back. Mrs. Poorwilly was swinging cases of tinned goods onto the dock. Her grey hair blew wildly about her face..

They started off again. As there were no paths on the bare granite, Danny followed Mr. Poorwilly. They walked along a ridge, dropped into a hollow. The slope they had to climb was steep, so Danny bent down, caught the front of the wheelbarrow, and pulled as Mr. Poorwilly pushed. They had just reached the top when they met an elderly, wasted man who was leaning heavily on the shoulder of a young girl as he shuffled along.

Danny was so surprised by the incongruity of the pair that he stared. The girl's black hair fell to her shoulders, making a frame for her face. She looked tired, but her face was tanned and her mouth was a warm red. Her cheeks were pink from the wind. She stopped when she saw Danny.

The man with her made no attempt to greet them. His breath came in ragged gasps. His dark yellow skin was pulled so tightly over his face that the bone seemed to be pushing through. His eyes protruded and the whites had turned yellow. He gave the girl's shoulder a tug. They started up again.

When they had passed, Danny said, "Who was that? The girl is beautiful."

"Sick Jack and his daughter. It's his liver. Mrs. Poorwilly helps Adel look after him. She says he won't see the spring. He'll be the second. How are you feeling after the trip? You look green."

"I feel green. It was nine days in hell. The boat never quit rolling."

"Good thing you're not going back with them, then." Mr. Poorwilly twisted his head toward the dock to indicate who he meant. "Sunrise was red this morning. There'll be a storm before dawn tomorrow."

Mr. Poorwilly slipped his hands back into the metal loops. "Sorry to be so slow, but the arthritis causes me trouble. Used to be able to use my hands but not anymore. It's a good thing I've got a pension from the war. Getting shot was the best thing has ever happened to me."

Danny noticed a small, red flower growing from a crack in the rock. When he bent down to get a better look, he saw that the crack was filled with brown stems. He picked the flower and held it up. "What is it?"

"Bloodflower," Mr. Poorwilly replied. "Only thing that grows on the island except lichen. Shouldn't pick it. They say it brings bad luck. If you cut your finger or make your nose bleed, it'll be OK."

Danny laughed. "You don't believe that, do you?"

"Mrs. Poorwilly says it. She knows quite a bit about these things."

When they reached the house, Danny unloaded his belongings and put them into his bedroom. Mr. Poorwilly left him and went back to the dock for the supplies Mrs. Poorwilly had been unloading.

While the Poorwillys spent the day sorting and putting away their winter's supplies, Danny walked around the island. What Mr. Poorwilly said was true. Nothing grew on the island except lichen and bloodflowers. Despite the cold, patches of red filled the cracks that were sheltered from the wind.

The granite of the island had been weathered smooth, but there was nowhere it was truly flat. Three-quarters of the island's shoreline fell steeply into the sea. Only in scattered places did the shoreline slope gently enough to let Danny walk down to the water. To the west the thin blue line of the coast of Labrador was just barely visible. Two fishing boats were bobbing on the ocean. There were no birds except for some large grey gulls that rose as he approached and hovered in the air until he was well past them. He would have liked to have them come down beside him so he could have touched them, but they rose on the updrafts. He reached toward them and shouted for them to come down, then laughed at himself and continued his exploring.

Except for the houses and the fish sheds, the only other buildings were the school and the chicken roost behind the Poorwillys. All the buildings were made from wood siding. Because of the rock, there were no basements. Rock foundations had been put down so the floors would be level.

Most of the houses showed little more than traces of paint. The Poorwillys' and Mary Johnson's were the only ones that had been painted recently. Danny knew the other house belonged to Mary Johnson because it had a sign with her name on it. Below her name it said, "General store. Post office. Two-way radio."

Danny explored until it started to get dark, then went back to the Poorwillys.

"Heard you've been looking around," Mrs. Poorwilly said. "If you hadn't come back in another five minutes, I would have sent Mr. Poorwilly to bring you back."

"There's no danger of getting lost." Danny was amused at her concern.

"No," Mrs. Poorwilly agreed, "but you wouldn't want to slip and fall in the dark. You're not in a city now with a doctor down the street. You break a leg or crack your skull and you might have to wait two, three weeks for the weather to clear enough for a plane to come. You don't want to be one of the three."

Danny felt chastised, but Mrs. Poorwilly dropped the subject. She and Mr. Poorwilly spent all during supper asking him about the mainland. As they talked, Mrs. Poorwilly fed her husband from her plate. He sat with his hands in his lap. There were no directions given or taken about the feeding. Both Mr. and Mrs. Poorwilly were anxious to hear everything he had to tell them about the mainland.

When he got a chance, Danny said, "What'd you mean, 'one of the three'?"

"Trouble always comes in threes. Maybe you didn't notice it on the mainland because things are so complicated. On the island you can see it because it's small and you know everybody. There's just thirty-five houses. Somebody gets hurt, everybody knows about it. They can keep track. Three, six, nine, but it never ends unless it's on something made up of threes.

"You'll see before the winter is out. Last month the radio said Emily died in the sanatorium. TB. Now Sick Jack's been failing badly. He's got to be a hard yellow and he's lost all his flesh. He dies, then there'll be one more thing to end it. After that, everything will be OK."

Mrs. Poorwilly made her pronouncement with all the assuredness of an oracle. Danny started on his dessert.

"Mr. Poorwilly says you think Adel's a nice bit of fluff."

Danny had started thinking about the book on mythology he'd been reading at summer school. The statement caught him off guard. He had to collect his thoughts, then he said, "The girl with the long dark hair? I only caught a glimpse of her, but she seemed to be very pretty."

"When her father goes, she'll be on her own," Mrs. Poorwilly said. "She's a good girl. She works hard."

"Does she have any education?"

"Wives with too much education can cause a lot of trouble," Mrs. Poorwilly said. "They're never satisfied. The young fellows around here and on the coast have enough trouble without that."

Danny tried not to show his embarrassment. "I was thinking in terms of her getting a job on the mainland. If her spelling is good and she learned to type, she could get a government job."

"Might be that she'll go right after her father. No use making plans until we see what the winter brings." Mr. Poorwilly turned to his wife for confirmation. "It's happened before."

Mrs. Poorwilly nodded as she scraped the last of the pudding from the dish and fed it to her husband.

"What you want is what those people had that I was reading about. They used to ward off evil by choosing a villager to be king for a year. Then so the bad luck of the old year would be done with, they killed him in the spring."

"They weren't Christians," Mr. Poorwilly said.

"No," Danny replied. "They gave their king anything he wanted. A woman, food, gifts, everything, since it was only for a year. Then when the first flowers bloomed, they killed him."

"Must have been them Chinese," Mr. Poorwilly said.

"No. Europeans. But it was a long time ago."

"Have you ever ridden on a train?" Mrs. Poorwilly asked. "Mr. Poorwilly and I rode on a train for our honeymoon. I remember it just like yesterday."

Mr. and Mrs. Poorwilly told him about their train ride until it was time to go to bed. After Danny was in bed, Mr. Poorwilly stuck his head through the curtain that covered the doorway. In a low voice, he said, "Don't go shouting at the sea gulls when you're out walking. Most of the people here haven't been anywhere and they'll think you're sort of funny."

"OK," Danny said. Mr. Poorwilly's head disappeared.

The next day Mrs. Poorwilly had everyone in the village over to meet Danny. As fast as Danny met the women and children, he forgot their names. The men were still away fishing or working on the mainland. Mr. Poorwilly and Danny were the only men until Adel brought Sick Jack.

Sick Jack looked even thinner than he had the day before. The yellow of his skin seemed to have deepened. As soon as he had shaken Danny's hand, he sat down. After a few minutes, he fell into a doze and his daughter covered him with a blanket she had brought.

Mrs. Poorwilly waited until Sick Jack was covered, then brought Adel over to see Danny.

"This is Adel. She'll come for coffee soon, and you can tell her about the trains and the cities. She's never been off the island."

Adel blushed and looked at the floor. "Certainly," Danny said. "I've a whole set of slides I'm going to show Mr. and Mrs. Poorwilly. If you wanted, you could come and see them."

Adel mumbled her thanks and went to the side of the room. She stayed beside her father the rest of the evening, but Danny glanced at her whenever he felt no one was looking at him.

She was wearing blue jeans and a heavy blue sweater that had been mended at the elbows and cuffs with green wool. It was too large for her so Danny assumed that it had belonged to her father or one of the other men. From what Mrs. Poorwilly had said, Danny had learned that Adel and her father were given gifts of fish and second-hand clothing. When the men went fishing, they always ran an extra line for Sick Jack.

In spite of her clothing, Adel was attractive. Her hair was as black as he had remembered it and it and it hung in loose, natural waves. Her eyes were a dark blue. Underneath the too-large sweater, her breasts made soft, noticeable mounds.

She left before Danny had a chance to speak to her again, but he didn't mind as he knew he'd see her during the winter.

For the next two weeks, busy as he was, Danny couldn't help but notice the change in the village. The men returned at all hours, in all kinds of weather. Mostly they came two and three at a time, but now and again a man would come by himself, his open boat a lonely black dot on the horizon.

Most of the men brought little news that was cheerful. The fishing had been bad. Many of them were coming home with the absolute minimum of money that would carry them until spring. No one said much, but they all knew that winter fishing would be necessary to keep some of the families from going hungry. In a good year, the winter fishing provided a change in diet for people sick of canned food. This year the fishing wouldn't be so casual.

By the end of September the weather had turned bitterly cold. The wind blew for days at a time. The houses rocked in the wind. Danny walked the smallest children to their homes. The few days the fishermen were able to leave the island, there were no fish. Some of the men tried to fish in spite of the weather, but most of the time they were able to do little more than clear the harbour before having to turn around.

The evening Sick Jack died, Danny had gone to bed early. The banging on the door woke him. Mr. Poorwilly got up and answered the door. Danny heard the muttered talk, then Mr. Poorwilly yelled the news to Mrs. Poorwilly. They both dressed and left right away. Danny would have offered to go with them, but he knew that he would just be in the way so he said nothing.

Mrs. Poorwilly was back for breakfast. As she stirred the porridge, she said, "She's alone now. We washed him and dressed him and laid him out on his bed. She's a good girl. She got all his clothes out and would have helped us dress him, but I wouldn't let her. Mr. Poorwilly is staying with her until some of the women come to sit by the body. If the weather holds, we'll have the funeral tomorrow."

"Why not have the funeral while the weather stays good? It could change tomorrow."

"Respect," Mrs. Poorwilly said. "But it's more than that, too. I wouldn't say it to her, but it helps make sure he's dead. Once just around when I married, Mrs. Milligan died. She was seventy. Maybe older. They rushed because the weather was turning. They were just pushing her over the side when she groaned. The cold did it. She died for good the next week, but since then we like to make sure."

Danny went to the funeral. The body was laid out on the bed with a shroud pulled to its shoulders. Mary Johnson sang "The Old Rugged Cross." Mrs. Poorwilly held the Bible so Mr. Poorwilly could read from it. Adel sat on a kitchen chair at the foot of the bed. She was pale and her eyes were red, but she didn't cry.

When the service was over, one of the fishermen pulled the shroud over Sick Jack's head and tied it with a string. They lifted the body onto a stretcher they had made from a tarpaulin and a pair of oars. The villagers followed them to the harbour.

They laid the body on the bottom of the boat. Three men got in. As the boat swung through the spray at the harbour's mouth, Danny saw one of the men bend and tie and anchor to the shrouded figure.

Mrs. Poorwilly had coffee ready for everyone after the service. Adel sat in the middle of the kitchen. She still had a frozen look about her face, but she was willing to talk.

Sick Jack's death brought added tension to the village. One day in class while they were reading a story about a robin that had died, Mary Johnson's littlest boy said, "My mother says somebody else is going to die. Maybe Miss Adel now that her father's gone."

Danny had been sharp with him. "Be quiet. This is a Grade Three

306

lesson. You're not even supposed to be listening. Have you done your alphabet yet?"

His older sister burst out, "That's what my mother said. She said—"

Danny cut her off. "That's enough. We're studying literature, not mythology. Things like that are nothing but superstition."

That night Danny asked about Adel. Mrs. Poorwilly said, "She's got a settlement coming from the mine where he used to work. It's not much. Maybe five or six hundred dollars. Everybody'll help all they can, but she's going to have to get a man to look after her."

During November, Danny managed to see Adel twice. The first time, she came for coffee. The second time, she came to see Danny's slides of the mainland. Danny walked her home the first time. The second time, Mrs. Poorwilly said, "That's all right, Mr. Thorson. I'll walk with her. There's something I want to get from Mary Johnson's."

Danny was annoyed. Mrs. Poorwilly had been pushing him in Adel's direction from the first day he had come. Then, when he made an effort to be alone with her, she had stepped between them.

Mrs. Poorwilly was back in half an hour with a package of powdered milk.

Danny said, "I would have got that for you, Mrs. Poorwilly."

"A man shouldn't squeeze fruit unless he's planning on buying," she replied.

Adel walked by the school a number of times when he was there. He got to talk to her, but she was skittish. He wished that she was with him in the city. There, at least, there were dark corners, alleyways, parks, even doorsteps. On the island, you couldn't do anything without being seen.

At Christmas the villagers held a party at the school. Danny showed his slides. Afterwards they all danced while Wee Jimmy played his fiddle. Danny got to dance with Adel a good part of the night.

He knew that Mrs. Poorwilly was displeased and that everyone in the village would talk about his dancing for the rest of the year, but he didn't care. Adel had her hair tied back with a red ribbon. The curve of her neck was white and smooth. Her blouse clung to her breasts and was cut low enough for him to see where the soft curves began. Each time he danced with one of the other women, Danny found himself turning to see what Adel was doing. When the party was over, he walked Adel home and kissed her goodnight. He wanted her to stay with him in the doorway, but she pulled away and went inside.

Two days before New Year's, Mrs. Poorwilly's prediction came true. The fishing had remained poor, but Michael Fairweather had gone fishing in a heavy sea because he was one of those who had come back with little money. Two hundred yards from the island his boat capsized.

Danny had gone to school on the pretext of doing some work, but what he wanted was some privacy. He had been sitting at the window staring out to sea when the accident happened. He had seen the squall coming up. A violent wind whipped across the waves and behind it a white, ragged line on the water raced toward the island. Michael Fairweather was only able to turn his boat halfway round before the wind and sleet struck.

Danny saw the boat rise to the crest of a wave, then disappear, and Michael was hanging onto the keel. Danny bolted from the room, but by the time he reached the dock, Michael had disappeared.

The squall had disappeared as quickly as it had come. Within half an hour the sea was back to its normal rolling. The fishermen rowed out of the harbour and dropped metal bars lined with hooks. While one man rowed, another held the line at the back of the boat. As Danny watched, the boats crossed back and forth until it was nearly dark.

They came in without the body. Danny couldn't sleep that night. In the morning, when a group of men came to the Poorwillys', Danny answered the door before Mr. Poorwilly had time to get out of his bedroom. The men had come for the loan of the Poorwillys' rooster.

Mrs. Poorwilly nestled the rooster in her jacket on the way to the dock, then tied it to Mr. Poorwilly's wrist with a leather thong. Mr. Poorwilly stepped into the front of the skiff. The rooster hopped onto the bow. With that the other men climbed into their boats and followed Mr. Poorwilly and the rooster out of the harbour.

"What are they doing?" Danny asked.

Mrs. Poorwilly kept her eyes on the lead boat, but she said, "When they cross the body, the rooster will crow."

Danny turned and stared at the line of boats. In spite of the wind, the sun was warm. The rooster's feathers gleamed in the sun. Mr. Poorwilly stood as still as a wooden figurehead. The dark green and grey boats rose and fell on the waves. Except for the hissing of the foam, there was no sound.

Danny looked away and searched the crowd for Adel. He had looked for a third time, when Mrs. Poorwilly, without turning, said, "She won't come for fear the current will have brought her father close to shore. They might bring him up."

All morning and into the afternoon the boats crossed and recrossed the area in front of the harbour in a ragged line. No one left the dock. The women with small babies didn't come down from their houses, but Danny could see them in their doorways.

As the day wore on, Danny became caught up in the crossing and recrossing of the boats. None of the men dragged their hooks. The only time the men in the rear of the boats moved was to change positions with the men at the oars.

When the cock crew, the sound caught Danny by surprise. The constant, unchanging motion and the hissing of the spray had drawn him into a quiet trance. It had been as if the boats and he had been there forever.

The sound was so sharp that some of the women cried out. The men with the iron bars covered with hooks threw them into the sea, and shoved the coils of rope after them. They didn't want to pass the spot where the cock crew until the hooks were on the bottom. The bars disappeared with little spurts of white foam. Danny could hear the rope rubbing against the side of the boat as it was pulled hand over hand.

"It's him," Mrs. Poorwilly said. "God have mercy, they've got him."

Danny turned back. It was true. Instead of a white shroud, the men were pulling a black bundle into the boat.

The funeral was bad. Marj Fairweather cried constantly and tried to keep the men from taking the body. As they started to leave, she ran to the dresser for a heavy sweater, then sat in the middle of the floor, crying and saying, "He'll be so cold. He'll be so cold."

In spite of Marj, the tension in the community eased after the funeral was over. People began to visit more often, and when they came they talked more and stayed longer.

Adel came frequently to the Poorwillys'. When she came, she talked to the Poorwillys, but she watched Danny. She wasn't open about it, but when Danny looked at her, she let her eyes linger on him for a second before turning away. She had her colour back and looked even better than before. Most of the time, Danny managed to walk her home. Kissing her was not satisfactory because of the cold and the bulky clothes between them, but she would not invite him in and there was no privacy at the Poorwillys'. In spite of the walks and goodnight kisses, she remained shy when anyone else was around.

The villagers had expected the weather and the fishing to improve. If anything, the weather became worse. Ice coated the boats. The wind blew night and day. Often, it only stopped in the hour before dawn.

Then, without warning, Marj Fairweather sent her children to the Poorwillys, emptied a gas lamp on herself and the kitchen floor, and lit a match.

This time there was no funeral. The entire village moved in a state of shock. While one of the sheds was fixed up for the children, Marj's remains were hurried to sea and dumped in the same area as her husband's.

The village drew into itself. The villagers stayed in their own houses. When they came to the door, they only stayed long enough to finish their business. The men quit going to the dock. Most of them pulled their boats onto the island and turned them over.

A week after the fire, Danny arrived to find his room stripped of his belongings. Mrs. Poorwilly waited until he had come into the kitchen. "Mr. Poorwilly and I decided to take two of the Fairweather children. We'll take the two youngest. A fourteen-year-old can't take care of six kids."

Danny was too stunned to say anything. Mrs. Poorwilly continued.

"Some of us talked about it. We hope you don't mind, but there's nothing else to do. Besides, there's going to be no money from the mine. Adel needs your board and room worse than we do. We'll keep the Fairweather children for nothing."

When Danny didn't reply, Mrs. Poorwilly added, "We got help moving your things. We gave Adel the rest of this month's money."

Danny hesitated for a moment, but there was nothing to say. He went outside.

He knocked at Adel's door. She let him in. "Mrs. Poorwilly says you're to stay with me now."

"Yes, she told me," Danny said.

Adel showed him to his bedroom. All his clothes had been hung up and his books had been neatly piled in one corner. He sat on the edge of the bed and tried to decide what to do. He finally decided he couldn't sit in the bedroom for the next five months and went back into the kitchen.

The supper was good, but Danny was too interested in Adel to pay much attention. In the light from the oil lamp, her eyes looked darker than ever. She was wearing a sweater with a V-neck. He could see the soft hollow of her throat and the smooth skin below her breastbone. Throughout supper he told her about the mainland and tried to keep his eyes above her neck.

The next morning when he went to school, he expected to see a difference in the children's attitudes. Twice he turned around quickly. Each time the children had all been busy writing in their notebooks. There was no smirking or winking behind their hands. At noon, he said, "In case any of you need to ask me something, there's no use your going to the Poorwillys'. I'm staying at Miss Adel's now."

The children solemnly nodded their heads. He dismissed them and went home for lunch.

Adel was at home. She blushed and said, "The women at the sheds said I should come home early now that I've got you to look after. Since the men aren't fishing there isn't much to do."

"That's very good of them," Danny replied.

Danny and Adel were left completely alone. He had expected that some of the villagers would drop by, but no one came to visit. Danny and Adel settled into a routine that was disturbed only by Danny's irritation at being close to Adel. Adel shied away from him when he brushed against her. At the end of the second week, she accepted his offer to help with the dishes. They stood side by side as they worked. Danny was so distracted by Adel's warmth and the constant movement of her body that the dishes were only half dried.

Danny put his hand on Adel's shoulder and turned her toward him. She let him pull her close. There was no place to sit or lie in the kitchen so he picked her up and carried her to the bedroom. She didn't resist when he undressed her. After he made love to her, he fell asleep. When he woke up, Adel had gone to her own bed.

Danny took Adel to bed with him every evening after that, but during the night she always slipped away to her own bedroom. At the beginning of the next week, they had their first visitor. Mrs. Poorwilly stopped by to see how they were doing. They had been eating supper when she arrived. Normally, they would have been finished eating, but Adel had been late in coming from the fish sheds. The weather had improved enough for the men to go fishing. Mrs. Poorwilly accepted a cup of coffee and sat and talked to them for an hour.

It was as if her coming had been a signal. After that, villagers dropped by in the evenings to talk for a little while. They nearly always brought something with them and left it on the table. Danny had wanted to protest, but he didn't know what to say that wouldn't embarrass their visitors so he said nothing.

Adel stopped going back to her own bed. Danny thought about getting married but dismissed the idea. He was comfortable with things the way they were.

The day Danny started to get sick he should have known something was wrong. He had yelled at the children for no particular reason. When Adel had come home, he had been grouchy with her. The next day his throat had been sore, but he had ignored it. By the end of the day, he was running a temperature and his knees felt like water.

Adel had been worried, but he told her not to call Mrs. Poorwilly. Their things had become so mixed together that it was obvious they were using the same bedroom.

For the next few days he was too sick to protest about anything. Mrs. Poorwilly came frequently to take his temperature and to see that Adel kept forcing whisky and warm broth into him. All during his sickness Danny was convinced that he was going to die. During one afternoon he was sure that he was dead and that the sheets were a shroud.

The crisis passed and he started to cough up phlegm, but he was so weak that it was an effort for him to lift his head. The day he was strong enough to sit up and eat in the kitchen, Mrs. Poorwilly brought him a package of hand-rolled cigarettes.

"Nearly everyone is coming to see you tomorrow. They'll all bring something in the way of a present. It's a custom. Don't say they shouldn't or they'll think you feel their presents aren't good enough."

Danny said that he understood.

The school children came first with hand-carved pieces of driftwood. He admired the generally shapeless carvings, and after the first abortive attempt carefully avoided guessing at what they were supposed to be.

After the children left, the McFarlans came. Mr. McFarlan had made a shadow box from shingle. He had scraped the shingle with broken glass until the grain stood out. Inside the box he had made a floor of lichen and pebbles. Seagulls made from clam shells sat on the lichen.

His wife stretched a piece of black cloth over the end of a fish box. On it she had glued boiled fish bones to form a picture of a boat and man.

Someone brought a tin of pears, another brought a chocolate bar. One of the men brought half a bottle of whisky.

Each visitor stayed just long enough to inquire how Danny felt, wish him well, and leave a present on the table. When the last visitor had gone, Danny was exhausted. Adel helped him to bed.

He felt much better by the end of the week, but when he tried to return to work, Mrs. Poorwilly said, "Mary Johnson's doing a fine job. Not as good as you, of course, but the kids aren't suffering. If you rush back before you're ready, everybody will take it that you think she's doing a poor job. If you get sick again, she won't take over."

Adel returned to work at the sheds, but the women sent her home. The weather had held and there was lots of fish, but they said she should be at home looking after Danny.

At first it was ideal. They had little to do except sit and talk or make love. Danny caught up on his reading. They both were happy, but by the end of March their confinement had made them both restless.

To get out of the house, Danny walked to Mrs. Poorwilly's. While they were having coffee, Danny said, "I guess everyone must have got the flu."

"No," Mrs. Poorwilly replied, "just some colds among the children. Adel and you making out all right?"

"Yes," Danny said.

"Her mother was a beauty, you know. I hope you didn't mind moving, but these things happen."

"No, I didn't mind moving."

They sat for five minutes before Danny said, "Could I ask you something? I wouldn't want anyone else to know."

Mrs. Poorwilly nodded her assent.

"Mary Johnson is doing such a good job that I thought I might ask her to radio for a plane. Maybe it would be a good idea for me to take Adel to the mainland for a week."

"Any particular reason?"

"Yes. If she wants, I'll marry her."

"Haven't you asked her?"

Danny shook his head. It had never occurred to him that she might say no.

"Wait until you ask her. The superintendent will want a reason. You'll have to tell him over the radio and everyone will know. You wouldn't want to tell him and then have her turn you down."

Adel was standing at the window when he returned. He put his arms around her. "You know, I think we should get married."

Adel didn't answer.

"Don't you want to marry me?" he asked.

"Yes. I do. But I've never been off the island. You won't want to stay here always."

"We can stay for a couple of years. We'll go a little at a time. We can start with a week on the mainland for a honeymoon. We'll go somewhere on a train."

That evening he went to Mary Johnson's. Mary tried to raise the mainland operator, but the static was so bad that no contact could be made. Danny kept Mary at the radio for half an hour. He left when she promised to send one of the children with a message if the radio cleared.

Danny returned the next night, but the static was just as bad. Mary promised to send for him as soon as the call went through.

A week went by. The weather continued to improve. Danny checked the thermometer. The temperature was going up a degree every two days.

At the end of the week he returned to Mary's. The radio wasn't working at all. One of the tubes needed to be replaced. He left. Halfway home he decided to go back and leave a message for the plane. The radio might work just long enough for a message, but not long enough for him to be called to the set. When he came up to the house, he was sure that he heard the radio. He banged on the front door. Mary took her time coming. When she opened the door, he said, "I heard the radio. Can you send a message right away?"

Mary replied that he must have just heard the children talking.

Danny insisted on her trying to make the call. She was annoyed, but she tried to get through. When she had tried for five minutes, Danny excused himself and left.

He walked part-way home, then turned and crept back over the rock.

The windows were dark. He lay in the hollow of rock behind the house until the cold forced him to leave.

In the morning, he went to the dock to talk to the fishermen. He offered to pay any one of them triple the normal fare to take him down the coast. They laughed and said they would bring him some fresh fish for supper.

When he had continued insisting that he wanted to leave, they said that a trip at this time of year was impossible. Even planes found it difficult to land along the coast. A boat could be crushed in the pack ice that was shifting up and down the shore.

Danny told Adel about the radio and the boats. She sympathized with him, but agreed with the men that it was hopeless to try and make the trip in an open boat.

"Besides," she said, "the freight boats will be coming in a month or so."

True to their word, the fishermen sent a fresh fish. Danny tried to pay the boy who brought it, but he said that he had been told not to accept anything. Danny had put the money into the boy's hand. The boy had gone, but a few minutes later he returned and put the money in front of the door.

Late that afternoon, Danny walked to the dock. After looking around to see that no one was watching, he bent down and looked at the rope that held one of the boats. He untied it, then tied it again.

He returned to the house and started gathering his heavy clothing. When Adel came into the room, she said, "What are you going to do?"

"I'm leaving."

"Is the plane coming?"

"I'm taking myself. I've had enough. I'm not allowed to work. You're not allowed to work. Everyone showers us with things they won't let us pay for. I try to use the radio, but it never works." He turned to face her. "It always worked before."

"Sometimes it hasn't worked for weeks," Adel replied. "Once it was six weeks. It's the change in temperature."

"But it works. The other night I heard it working. Then when I asked Mary Johnson to call, she said it was just the children talking."

"Mary told me," Adel said. "You made her very upset. She thinks you're still not feeling well."

"I'm feeling fine. Just fine. And I'm leaving. I don't know what's going on here, but I'm getting out. I'm going to get a plane and then I'm coming back for you."

"You said we could leave a little at a time."

"That was before this happened. What if something goes wrong? Three people have died. One of them died right before my eyes and I couldn't do anything about it. What if we needed a doctor? Or a policeman? What if someone took some crazy notion into his head?"

Danny took Sick Jack's nor'westers off a peg. He laid out the clothes he wanted and packed two boxes with food. He lay awake until three o'clock, then slipped outside and down to the boats.

The boats were in their usual places. He reached for the rope of the first boat. His hand closed on a heavy chain. Danny couldn't believe it. He jumped onto the boat and ran his hand around the chain. He climbed out and ran from boat to boat. Every boat was the same. He tried to break the chains loose. When they wouldn't break, he sat on the dock and beat his hands on the chains. When he had exhausted himself, he sat with his face pressed into his hands.

In the morning, Mary sent one of the boys to tell Danny that the radio had worked long enough for her to send a message. It hadn't been confirmed, but she thought it might have been heard. For the rest of the day, Danny was elated, but as the days passed and the plane did not appear, he became more and more depressed. Adel kept saying that the plane would come, but Danny doubted that it would ever come.

The weather became quite mild. Danny walked to the dock every day. The chains were still on the boats. He had spent an hour on the dock staring at the thin blue line that was the mainland and was walking back to Adel's when he noticed that the snow had melted away from some of the cracks in the granite. The cracks were crammed with closely packed leaves.

He paused to pick a leaf. *April the first*, he thought, *April the first will come and we'll be able to go*. Then, as he stared at the small green leaf in his hand, he realized that he was wrong. It was weeks later that the first freight boat came.

The rest of the day he tried to make plans for Adel and himself, but he could not concentrate. The image of thousands and thousands of blood-flowers kept spilling into his mind.

W.D. Valgardson (1939-) was born in Winnipeg and now teaches at Cottey College, Nevada. He has published two collections of stories, *Bloodflowers* and *God is Not a Fish Inspector*.

Acknowledgements

Thanks are due to the copyright-holders indicated for permission to reprint the stories in this book.

"Aquarius" by Audrey Thomas from *Ladies and Escorts:* Oberon Press

"Material" by Alice Munro from *Something I've Been Meaning to Tell You:* McGraw-Hill Ryerson

"The Window" by Ethel Wilson from *Mrs. Golightly and Other Stories:* Macmillan of Canada

"The Broken Globe" by Henry Kreisel: the author

"Polarities" by Margaret Atwood from *Dancing Girls and Other Stories:* McClelland and Stewart

"One's a Heifer" by Sinclair Ross from *The Lamp at Noon and Other Stories:* McClelland and Stewart

"Tudor King" by Rudy Wiebe from *Where Is the Voice Coming From?:* McClelland and Stewart

"That Yellow Prairie Sky" by Robert Kroetsch: the author

"A Tramp at the Door" by Gabrielle Roy from *Garden in the Wind* translated by Alan Brown: McClelland and Stewart

"A Gourdful of Glory" by Margaret Laurence from *The Tomorrow-Tamer:* McClelland and Stewart

"On the River" by Dave Godfrey from *Death Goes Better with Coca-Cola:* Press Porcépic

"The Lady and the Travelling Salesman" by Leo Simpson from *The Lady and the Travelling Salesman:* the author

"House of the Whale" by Gwendolyn MacEwen from *Noman:* Oberon Press

"A Wedding-Dress" by Morley Callaghan from *Morley Callaghan's Short Stories:* Macmillan of Canada

317

"Ada" by Margaret Gibson from *The Butterfly Ward:* Oberon Press

"Three Halves of a House" by Hugh Hood from *Flying a Red Kite:* Oberon Press

"A Canadian Upbringing" by Norman Levine from *I Don't Want to Know Anyone Too Well:* the author

"So Many Have Died" by Joyce Marshall: the author

"Mortimer Griffin, Shalinsky, and How They Settled the Jewish Question" by Mordecai Richler: the author

"A Class of New Canadians" by Clark Blaise from *A North American Education:* Doubleday Canada

"Mélie and the Bull" by Jacques Ferron from *Tales from the Uncertain Country* translated by Betty Bednarski: House of Anansi Press

"A Grand Marriage" by Anne Hébert from *The Torrent* translated by Gwendolyn Moore: Harvest House

"The Boat" by Alistair MacLeod from *The Lost Salt Gift of Blood:* the author

"Bloodflowers" by W.D. Valgardson from *Bloodflowers:* Oberon Press

Design / David Shaw & Associates Ltd.
Composition / ATTIC Typesetting
Manufacturing / T.H. Best Printing Co. Ltd.